STAR TREK™
CHRONOLOGY
The History of the Future

MICHAEL OKUDA

DENISE OKUDA

POCKET BOOKS

New York   London   Toronto   Sydney   Tokyo   Singapore

For Gene

An *Original* Publication of POCKET BOOKS

 POCKET BOOKS, a division of Simon & Schuster Inc.
1230 Avenue of the Americas, New York, NY 10020

This book is published by Pocket Books, a division of
Simon & Schuster Inc., under exclusive license from
Paramount Pictures.

ISBN: 0-671-79611-9

First Pocket Books trade paperback printing April 1993

10 9 8 7 6 5 4 3 2 1

POCKET and colophon are registered trademarks of
Simon & Schuster Inc.

Printed in the U.S.A.

CONTENTS

Introduction   iv

Acknowledgments   vii

Chapter 1.0: The Distant Past   1

Chapter 2.0: The Twentieth Century   12

Chapter 3.0: The Twenty-first Century   18

Chapter 4.0: The Twenty-second Century   22

Chapter 5.0: The Twenty-third Century   27

      5.1 *Star Trek:* Original Series, Year 1 (2266-7)   41
      5.2 *Star Trek:* Original Series, Year 2 (2267-8)   52
      5.3 *Star Trek:* Original Series, Year 3 (2268-9)   60
      5.4 *Star Trek:* Motion Pictures I - VI (2271-93)   70

Chapter 6.0: The Twenty-fourth Century   79
      6.1 *Star Trek: The Next Generation,* Year 1 (2364)   95
      6.2 *Star Trek: The Next Generation,* Year 2 (2365)   105
      6.3 *Star Trek: The Next Generation,* Year 3 (2366)   113
      6.4 *Star Trek: The Next Generation,* Year 4 (2367)   125
      6.5 *Star Trek: The Next Generation,* Year 5 (2368)   137

Chapter 7.0: The Far Future   150

Appendix A: Undatable events and other uncertainties   151
Appendix B: Alternate timelines   158
Appendix C: Timeline chart   160
Appendix D: Regarding stardates   162
Appendix E: Writing credits   163

Index   166

About the Authors   184

INTRODUCTION

Do you remember when you first watched *Star Trek?* Even though it was a lot of fun, it was probably a little confusing at first. You had to figure out what was special about the guy with pointed ears, who were the Klingons, how did transporters work, what was the Federation, and a host of other background details. This learning process became part of the fun of watching *Star Trek:* Watching the show carefully to learn more about the elaborate background developed for the series. What was especially delightful was that there was so much material being constantly revealed, a whole future society, complete with a history spanning the time between our present day and *Star Trek*'s future. Even better, the details of this future scenario seemed to have a pretty good degree of internal consistency from episode to episode. (Sure, when you watched *very* closely, you began to notice that some things didn't *quite* add up, but by that time you were hooked. Or at least, we were.)

This project started when Michael wanted to do a simple timeline to show the relationship of the two *Star Trek* series for use by the writers of *Star Trek: The Next Generation.* Mike was well aware of the inconsistencies and contradictions that can creep into a complex show like *Star Trek,* and he was afraid of going into too much detail for fear of running into too many such errors. Several hours and many pages of notes later, he discovered, to his surprise, that the *Star Trek* timeline held together pretty well. Former *Star Trek* research consultant Richard Arnold proved to be a tremendous help at this stage, providing for us (as he had for some of *Star Trek: The Next Generation*'s writers) many of the basic assumptions that form the framework on which this chronology is built.

At about the same time, *Star Trek* creator Gene Roddenberry coincidentally expressed his concern with the difficulties involved in keeping *Star Trek* books and other projects consistent with the show itself. He was especially concerned because it was so difficult for an outside writer to be aware of all the intricate back story for *Star Trek* that has accumulated over the years. Gene admitted that this was even a problem for *Star Trek* staff writers and for himself, simply because there were so many *Star Trek* episodes and movies to keep track of. (Of course, the more successful the show becomes, the worse the problem gets.) At a meeting called to discuss the issue, Gene realized that the solution was to compile a chronology to serve as a reference to writers. Gene suggested that *Star Trek* designer Mike Okuda might be interested in undertaking such a project, not knowing that Mike had already started preliminary work on this document! Encouraged by Gene's confidence, Mike and Denise compiled the book you now hold in your hands.

We choose, in this volume, to treat *Star Trek*'s invented universe as if it were both complete and internally consistent. In effect, we are pretending that the *Star Trek* saga has unfolded according to a master plan, and that there is a logical, consistent timeline in those episodes, even though we (and you) know very well that this is not entirely true. In fact, the producers of both *Star Trek* television series as well as the feature films made things up as they went along. The truth is that it is virtually impossible to invent everything for a show like *Star Trek* in advance. Producers usually want to leave many things somewhat vague so as much room as possible is left for writers to explore and "discover" nifty new things, and quite frankly, time pressures work very strongly against too much preplanning. This is not to demean their impressive efforts to maintain consistency despite the extraordinary schedules of television and film production.

Indeed, this book celebrates the fact that they were amazingly successful in this endeavor, and we hope this volume will be of use to future *Star Trek* writers who wish to continue in this tradition. Nevertheless, one of the challenges in compiling this chronology was to deal with the inevitable gaps and inconsistencies that have cropped up over *Star Trek*'s quarter-century of existence. Where things added up in a logical manner, we have documented it here. But where things didn't quite make sense, we noted the apparent errors. In some such cases, we have often offered what we think are plausible-sounding explanations, but we leave it up to the reader to accept or reject the rationalization. In our eyes, the fact that the show's writers and producers were quite capable of mistakes in no way diminishes their extraordinary achievements under the often-brutal pressures of weekly television production.

Research for this volume turned out to be quite a project. At this writing, there are some 80 hours of the original *Star Trek* series, six feature films, over 120 episodes of *Star Trek: The Next Generation,* and *Star Trek: Deep Space Nine* just getting off the ground, all of which had to be gone over in excruciating detail. Denise was responsible for this massive endeavor, with a *lot* of help from Debbie Mirek. It's fun to watch *Star Trek,* but they soon discovered that watching the episodes while taking detailed notes was quite a painstaking task. We eventually ended up developing a detailed three-page form to fill out while watching the shows. This form made it easler to make sure we wrote down everything we needed, although it seemed there was *always* something else we had to go back and check. Most fans can recall an amazing number of historical data points from the show, but even the most observant viewer is unlikely to recall the many off-handed references in dialog that implied past events. Frankly, we were surprised that there was so much material, and we were delighted to discover that much of the historical background for the show hung together remarkably well. (Writer Dorothy Fontana tells us that from the very beginning of the original series, they made a real effort to keep track of things as much as possible.)

Some specific notes: Following are some of the guidelines we used in compiling this chronology.

Basic assumptions: This chronology is built on a number of basic assumptions. The first is that the original *Star Trek* series was set 300 years in the future of the first airings of the episodes, meaning that the first season was set in 2266-67. Although a few references exist suggesting the producers of that show vacillated between 200 to 800 years, the 300-year figure seems to be the most internally consistent. (This assumption has also been used by writers of the *Star Trek* feature films and *The Next Generation* when determining dates referring back to the original series.) The second basic assumption is that the first season of *Star Trek: The Next Generation* was set in 2364, as established in "The Neutral Zone." These dates have been used by the producers of *Star Trek: The Next Generation* and some of the writers of the *Star Trek* features, so many ages and dates mentioned in the show have been consistent with these assumptions. Most of the dates set forth in this chronology were derived from these two basic assumptions.

Conjectural dates: In some cases, an event may not have a specific date established, but other contextual information may limit the "window" in which the event could have occurred. In cases where this window is fairly narrow, we have sometimes arbitrarily picked a date for these events. An example is the date for Spock's promotion to captain. The exact date for this event was never established, but it clearly had to be between *Star Trek: The Motion Picture* (2271) and *Star Trek II: The Wrath of Khan* (2285). We arbitrarily picked 2284. This is not to say that the promotion could not have occurred in 2283 (it certainly could have), but there was a sufficiently small range of possible dates that this bit of conjecture seemed reasonable. We tried to be careful about which dates we conjectured, trying to remain faithful to the source material. In cases where we have arbitrarily chosen a date, we have noted that the dating is conjectural, and we have included some indication as to the basis for the conjecture. The reader is, of course, free to agree or disagree with our interpretations.

Undated events: The above notwithstanding, there were many events for which there were insufficient data to even guess at a date. In such cases, we have generally omitted the reference from the main chronology, even though some of these are of significant importance to the *Star Trek* scenario. In other words, just because a particular event isn't listed in this document doesn't mean it didn't happen or that it's not considered to be important. It means only that we didn't feel we could derive a reasonably credible date for that event. Many of these undated events are listed in Appendix A.

Scripts: We tried to use only data from aired versions of episodes and the finished versions of movies. Although we cross-checked the spellings of names with scripts, for virtually all other information we regarded the aired version as authoritative. It was our goal to create as authentic a reference as possible, derived almost totally from the show itself.

Filling in the blanks: Certain events, such as Earth's first contact with extraterrestrial life, or the fates of original series characters, are obviously very important to the *Star Trek* universe, but have not (yet) been depicted in any episode or film. In the vast majority of cases, we resisted the temptation to fill in these blanks because we did not want to step on the toes of future *Star Trek* writers. We wanted to document where the show has been, but not to limit the places where future writers might want to go. Again, see Appendix A.

Chronological order of episodes: *Star Trek* episodes (especially those of the original series and early in *The Next Generation*) were usually produced so that they could be viewed in almost any order without significant continuity problems. This may have been a conscious financial decision designed to make it easier to syndicate the show on independent television stations. Nevertheless, we have arbitrarily chosen to assume that the events in the episodes happened pretty much in the order in which the episodes were produced. Specific exceptions were made in cases like "Unification, Parts I and II," which were filmed in reverse order (because of Leonard Nimoy's schedule), or "Symbiosis," in which Denise Crosby plays Tasha Yar, but which was filmed after "Skin of Evil" (in which that character is killed.)

Dating conventions: Most past events in *Star Trek* history are described not in terms of specific dates, but in relative terms. For example, it is common for something to be described as having happened "four months ago" or "two centuries in the past." In such cases, there are often significant ambiguities as to the exact time of such events. We found, however, that by applying some simple general rules, we were able to derive a significant number of usable data points. Using such rules enables us to paint a far more detailed picture of *Star Trek* history, but it is important to remember that these dating conventions introduce a certain margin for error.

Years: When a particular event is described as having taken place "about a century" before a given episode, we are in most cases arbitrarily assuming that it was exactly one hundred years ago. We realize that most people tend to round such expressions off in everyday speech, but we wanted a general rule. When we assumed that a given event happened exactly one hundred years ago, we generally find it would not really have made a significant difference if it had been 97 years or 103 years. In a similar fashion, we arbitrarily assumed that all references to numbers of years have been converted to Earth-standard years. In other words, when Worf says something happened to him ten years ago, we are assuming he is speaking of Earth years rather than Klingon years. We realize that this assumption is probably unrealistic, but we felt that it was no more so than the *Star Trek* convention of having so many aliens breathe oxygen and speak English.

Episode time spans: We are generally assuming that episodes span an average of approximately two weeks. If an event is described as having occurred two months before a given episode, we will typically put the event as having happened about four episodes earlier. There are certainly many specific cases where a given episode clearly takes only a day or two, but we are assuming in such cases that there are twelve or so days that we didn't see on television before the next episode. There are also episodes, like "The Paradise Syndrome," from the original series, which take more than two weeks.

Early draft scripts: In our research, we reviewed many early drafts of *Star Trek* scripts. Many of these scripts contained fascinating background information that never made it to film. Even revised final draft scripts often contain lines of dialog and other tidbits that were not shot or somehow ended up on the cutting room floor. Unfortunately, one problem with using material from early drafts is that many times such drafts will contain information that is inconsistent with other drafts or the aired version. Choosing which version is "authoritative" would be difficult. Our solution was to stick fairly strictly with the actual episodes and films as produced and aired. (One of the very few exceptions to this was some material from an early draft of "Journey to Babel," which made it possible to conjecture the year in which Spock was born. We broke our rule here because Spock's birth is of such importance to the *Star Trek* universe.)

The animated *Star Trek*: This show, produced several years after the network run of the first series, is considered controversial in that there is significant question as to whether these episodes are part of the "official" *Star Trek* saga. Convincing arguments can be made for both sides of this issue, especially since Gene Roddenberry and Dorothy Fontana were both very actively involved with its planning and production. On the other hand, in later years Gene would express regret at some elements of the show and instructed Paramount not to consider this series as part of the "official" *Star Trek* universe. For this reason, we have not included material from the animated series despite our fondness for many of these stories. The only exception to this is some events in Spock's childhood as depicted in "Yesteryear," written by Dorothy Fontana.

Star Trek V and VI: Gene indicated that he considered some of the events in *Star Trek V: The Final Frontier* and *Star Trek VI: The Undiscovered Country* to be apocryphal. Among these events was the birth of Spock's long-lost half-brother, Sybok. We did not want simply to pretend that the films did not exist, but also wanted to respect Gene's feelings. Our compromise was to mention Gene's discomfort with the material, leaving it up to the reader to judge its "authenticity."

Star Trek novels: Many fine and imaginative novels, comic books, and other stories based on *Star Trek* have been published over the years. Some of these are adaptations of episodes and movies, while others are original works of fiction. We considered including key elements of some of these works in this chronology, since many such stories detail fascinating events not depicted in the episodes or movies. We finally chose not to do so, not out of dislike for these stories, but because it became too difficult to choose which books and events to include. We instead fell back on our original purpose, to provide a reference to the show itself. We hope this way, the chronology will be of use both to fans, as well as to Trek writers of both scripts and novels.

Eugenics Wars and other present-day events: Some late 20th-century events suggested in the first *Star Trek* series probably seemed comfortably far in the future to the producers of that show. Little did they know that their creation would survive long enough to see a number of their "predictions" proven wrong. Such events include the launch of an orbital nuclear platform in 1968 ("Assignment Earth") and the rise of Khan Noonien Singh to power in the early 1990s ("Space Seed"). While we are grateful these events have not come to pass, we are including them in this chronology because of our desire to make this a complete record of the *Star Trek* universe as established to date.

Finally: We hope this document will make it easier for *Star Trek* writers to remain consistent with what's been established to date and for fans to keep track of *Star Trek*'s elaborate back story. We do not, however, want this to intimidate our writer friends or inhibit the imaginations of fans who may have differing interpretations of the *Star Trek* timeline. As such, we encourage both fans and writers to take this material with a grain of salt and to enjoy it in the spirit intended, as a fun way to explore the *Star Trek* universe.

ACKNOWLEDGMENTS

This book was an enormous project and we could not have completed it without the help and support of our friends, family, and colleagues.

We want to thank Debbie Mirek for hundreds of hours of sitting through episodes and helping to catalog literally volumes of minutae that were distilled into this *Chronology*, and for compiling the index. If it were not for Debbie, this book would have taken another year to research and produce. This, despite the fact that Debbie also works as a registered nurse, serves as president of her condominium association, and somehow still finds time to take care of her husband and their three children. Debbie is living proof of the old adage that if you *really* want something done, find a busy person to do it.

We are immensely grateful to Dorothy Fontana for reviewing this manuscript in great detail and for offering many fascinating insights into both the original series and *The Next Generation*. Dorothy's comments were especially valuable because of her pivotal role in helping to establish and maintain such an extraordinary degree of continuity in the first *Star Trek* series, and because of her role in helping the second series get started on the right foot. Her notes helped us steer clear of many misconceptions that have crept into Trek lore.

We also want to thank Bob Justman, associate producer on the first *Star Trek* series and supervising producer on *Star Trek: The Next Generation,* for reviewing this text and for offering his veteran's perspective into the making of both shows.

We want to acknowledge Richard Arnold for serving as a valuable resource in helping us pin down dozens of obscure references which served as the framework for this chronology. Richard also lent a significant hand with research and proofreading. His encyclopedic knowledge of *Star Trek* did much to help keep this book on track.

Our appreciation to *Star Trek: The Next Generation* producer Ronald D. Moore, for giving us a lot of nifty behind-the-scenes insights into the show. Ron is also very knowledgeable about both *Star Trek* series, and his comments helped us catch quite a number of errors.

We are indebted to Leslie Blitman for doing an excellent job editing the index to this book, a daunting task, indeed. Much assistance with research and proofreading was provided by Mike Rosen, Kurt Hanson, Guy Vardaman, Nancy Ohlson, Richard Barnett, Carole Lyne Ross, Tim DeHaas, Diane Lee Baron, Greg and Mary Varley, Jeff and Kiku Annon, Shelly Perron, and John Tuttle. Thank you, all.

Greg Jein built several original spacecraft models used in some of the photographs in this volume. We're very pleased and grateful to have had his talent and energy on this project. Those familiar with Trek history might recognize Greg's model of the never-before-seen *Daedalus* class starship, which is based on an early concept for the U.S.S. *Enterprise*, designed in 1964 by original series art director Matt Jefferies. Greg also built an old Romulan ship based on descriptions in an early draft of "Balance of Terror," as well as conjectural designs for Zefram Cochrane's first warp-powered spaceship and for the S.S. *Valiant* (mentioned but not seen in "Where No Man Has Gone Before.") Greg's models were photographed by Doug Drexler (who also lent a hand with retouching the photos in the book.) Thanks to Greg and Doug, all these ships are seen for the first time in photographs included in this book.

At Paramount Pictures, we want to recognize the assistance, support and enthusiasm of Rick Berman, Michael Piller, Ralph Winter, Jeri Taylor, David Livingston, Peter Lauritson, Merri Howard, Brad Yacobian, Bobby della Santina, Brannon Braga, Ira Steven Behr, Peter Allan Fields, Wendy Neuss, Gary Hutzel, Heidi Julian, Steve Frank, Susan Sackett, Denny Martin Flinn, and Ralph Johnson. Our colleagues and friends at the *Star Trek* art departments: Tom Betts, Nathan Crowley, Ricardo Delgado, Wendy Drapanas, Doug Drexler, Bill Hawkins, Joseph Hodges, Richard James, Alan Kobayashi, Jim Magdaleno, Randy McIlvain, Jim Martin, Andy Neskoromny, Louise Nielsen, Andrew Probert, Gary Speckman, Rick Sternbach, and Herman Zimmerman. At Paramount's Merchandising and Licensing department: Paula Block, Brooks Branch, Suzie Domnick, Bonnie Foley, Andrea Hein, Terri Helton, Carla Mason, Christin Miller, Tammy Moore, Helene Nielsen, Neil Newman, Pamela Newton, Debbi Petrasek, David Rosenbaum, and Valerie Shavers.

At Pocket Books, we want to thank Dave Stern, Kevin Ryan, and Scott Shannon. We are also grateful to our agent, Sherry Robb, who was unflagging in her support of this book.

This book was written on Apple Macintosh computers (especially Mike's PowerBook) using Microsoft Word *software. Page layout was done with the Aldus* PageMaker *program. Photographs were digitized using a Computer Eyes board and a Microtek scanner. Photo retouching was done with Adobe* Photoshop*, and graphics were done with Adobe* Illustrator*. These tools enabled us to write, design, revise, and deliver a finished book in an amazingly short time, despite the fact that we were also working full-time on two weekly* Star Trek *series while doing this project. Ain't science wonderful?*

We want in particular to recognize the pioneering work of Bjo Trimble, whose *Star Trek Concordance* was a valuable resource in compiling this chronology, as it has been in the production of all *Star Trek* films and episodes since the original series. Bjo's concordance is even more amazing when you consider that it was originally written in the days before videocassette recorders. (Bjo, in turn, has acknowledged the work of Dorothy Jones Heydt, whose research was the basis of the original fan version of the concordance.)

We also want to acknowledge the *Star Trek* enthusiasts who have shared us with their own versions of the *Star Trek* timeline. Their considerable ingenuity and detailed research served as helpful references for this volume. Alex Rozensweig, Erik Pflueger, Gary Wallace, David B. Dornburg, Terry Jones, Melvin H. Schuetz, and Ronald M. Roden, Jr., all came up with differing but credible alternate versions of this history. Thanks also to Bjo Trimble for providing us with timeline material that she's compiled. The fact that some of our key dates differ from those in some of these fan-developed histories is not a reflection on their work and doesn't necessarily mean they're wrong; it merely shows that we used some different basic assumptions. We hope they'll like what we've come up with.

Special thanks to Keith Birdsong, Charlie and Beverly Kurts, Diane Saunders, Naren Shanker, Marc Okrand, David Gerrold, Jackie Edwards, Carmen Carter, Jeanne Dillard, George Kalogridis, Bob Greenberger, Larry Yaeger, Peter Kavanagh, Carl Done, Bobby Richardson, Diane Castro, Jim and Barbara Van Over, Scott Leyes, Ira C. Neuss, Anthony Fredrickson, Donna Drexler, "Microbe" York, Tom Servo (space hero), Liz Radley, Terry Erdmann (did we get the spelling right this time?), Dennis Bailey, Michael J. Lim, Gerald Kawaoka, Wayne Momii, Mary van de Ven, Bob Abraham, Glee and Tom Stormont, Lillian Holt, Ed Miarecki, Larry Nemecek, Roy Cameron, Steve Horch, K. M. "Killer" Fish, Ken and Trish Yoshida, Dr. Chris Hill, M.D., Tom Mirek, Kathy Leprich, Pat Repalone, James Arakaki, Craig Nagoshi, Judy Saul, Tamara Haack, Todd Tathwell, Craig Okuda, Annette Yokoyama, and finally to Caitie Mirek for research and for letting her mother monopolize the videotape machine.

Photo credits: Many photographs in this volume were directly taken from film and video frames of the actual episodes and movies. As a result, the directors of photography of the shows should be credited: Jerry Finnerman and Al Francis (original *Star Trek* series), Richard H. Kline *(Star Trek: The Motion Picture)*, Gayne Rescher *(Star Trek II: The Wrath of Khan)*, Charles Correll *(Star Trek III: The Search for Spock)*, Don Peterman *(Star Trek IV: The Voyage Home)*, Andrew Laszlo *(Star Trek V: The Final Frontier)*, Hiro Narita *(Star Trek VI: The Undiscovered Country)*, Ed Brown, Jr. *(Star Trek: The Next Generation*, years 1 and 2), and Marvin Rush *(Star Trek: The Next Generation,* years 3-5). Production stills by: Mel Traxel *(Star Trek I)*, Bruce Birmelin *(Star Trek II, IV, and V)*, John Shannon *(Star Trek III)*, and Gregory Schwartz *(Star Trek VI)*. *Star Trek: The Next Generation* still photographers have included Kim Walker, Julie Dennis, Robbie Robinson, Fred Sabine, and Michael Paris. (We apologize in advance because we know this is not a complete list of unit still photographers.) ILM effects stills by Terry Chostner and Kerry Nordquist.

Additional photographic source material was provided by Greg Jein, Doug Drexler, the National Aeronautics and Space Administration, Mary Henderson (Smithsonian National Air and Space Museum), Bill George (Industrial Light and Magic), Brian Young, and Richard Barnett. Many thanks to Paula Block for help with Paramount's archives and photo clearances. Thanks also to Majel Barrett Roddenberry for permission to use her husband's photograph. Eighth-dimension images courtesy of John Whorfin, Yoyodyne Propulsion Systems. All *Star Trek* photos are copyrighted by, and courtesy of, Paramount Pictures, who reserves all rights.

Debbie Mirek, whose vital assistance to this project is acknowledged on the previous page, has a few thanks of her own: To Jane Hully, R.N., and Midge Gerhardt, R.N., for continuing to work with a person who mutters all night about stardates and for calling long-distance to both their fathers to ask them my stupid questions. To Robert Hully, M.D., and Thomas Gerhardt, USN (ret.) for answering my stupid questions. To Bob and Jean Mirek for buying me a new VCR when I wore the old one out. To Roxanne Bunn and especially to my mom, Pat Packard, for baby-sitting above and beyond the call of duty!

We want to thank our parents, Hiromi and Patsy Okuda, and Jack and Carolyn Tathwell. Without their support, encouragement, and love, we wouldn't be where we are, and this book wouldn't be in your hands.

Finally, our love and thanks to Gene Roddenberry, who brought so many people together to produce a television show that has brought so much enjoyment to audiences for the past quarter-century. This book is a celebration of his work.

— Michael Okuda

— Denise Okuda

1.0 THE DISTANT PAST

*God-machine Vaal
of planet Gamma Trianguli VI,
approximately 10,000 years ago*

The indicated dates or ages of the items in this section are mostly conjectural. It is entirely possible that many individual events took place in a sequence considerably different from that shown here, but these estimates should convey a sense of the overall flow of history.

Dates in this section are reckoned backward from the original Star Trek television series (c. 2266), meaning that something described as happening 500 years ago is approximately 200 years prior to our present day. We have included a few non-Trek data points in this and the following section in order to lend some perspective as to what was happening in "real" history.

15 BILLION YEARS AGO

The universe was formed in a massive explosion known as the Big Bang. In the aftermath of the explosion, matter and energy gradually condensed into the universe we know today.

Scientific theory.

6 BILLION YEARS AGO

The Guardian of Forever

The Guardian of Forever was a time portal created billions of years ago. It remains functional until at least the 23rd century, and it may be the last surviving artifact of an incredibly ancient civilization, although its origin and purpose are still a total mystery.

"The City on the Edge of Forever." The Guardian said it had been awaiting a question "since before your sun burned hot in space and before your race was born," suggesting it was at least five billion years old. Interestingly, the ruins surrounding the Guardian registered on Spock's tricorder as being on

the order of 10,000 years old. One might speculate that the Guardian was not an artifact of that civilization, or that the civilization in question spanned billions of years, perhaps with the help of the Guardian itself.

5 BILLION YEARS AGO

The star that would one day be known as Sol began to condense out of nebular material, forming the sun and our solar system.

Scientific theory.

The formation of a solar system

2 BILLION YEARS AGO

The civilization on planet Tagus III flourished two billion years ago. By the 24th century, much still remains a mystery about this ancient race, at least partially because the ruins on the planet have been sealed off since Earth's 23rd century. Nevertheless, Tagus remains a subject of interest to many archaeologists and enthusiasts, including Captain Jean-Luc Picard.

"Qpid." Q told Picard that the folks on Tagus "really knew how to have fun" two billion years ago.

First single-celled organisms evolved on Earth.

Scientific theory.

MILLIONS OF YEARS AGO

The inhabitants of planet Organia underwent a transformation from humanoid bodies to beings of pure energy.

"Errand of Mercy." Ayelborne said that his people had evolved beyond the need for physical bodies millions of years ago.

Organians in their form of pure energy

ONE MILLION YEARS AGO

The Tkon Empire became extinct about 600,000 years ago when their sun went supernova during a period of time known to the Tkons as the Age of Makto. According to legend, the Tkons were once enormously powerful, even capable of moving stars. Prior to the Age of Makto, other Tkon eras included the Ages of Fendor, Ozari, Xora, Cimi, and Bastu. The population of the Tkon had numbered in the trillions.

"The Last Outpost." Data described the history of the Tkon Empire from computer records.

Portal of the Tkon Empire

Sargon's people, a technologically advanced civilization, explored the galaxy aboard space vessels and planted colonies on many planets. Spock speculated that Sargon's account of such colonization might explain certain elements of Vulcan prehistory, suggesting that Spock's people may have originally been from Sargon's planet.

"Return to Tomorrow." Sargon told Kirk that his people had established colonies 600,000 years ago.

500,000 YEARS AGO

Civilization flourished on the planet Bajor many millennia ago. The culture boasted architects, artists, builders, and philosophers. By Earth's 24th century, the Bajoran culture was all but destroyed by the Cardassians, who forced the Bajorans to resettle on neighboring planets.

"Ensign Ro." Picard noted he'd studied ancient Bajoran civilization in the fifth grade, and that the ancient Bajorans had flourished "when humans were not yet standing erect," suggesting a time frame of about 500,000 years ago. This corresponds to the emergence of Homo Erectus, generally accepted by anthropologists as the first humans.

Android Ruk

The star Exo, which had at one time been bright enough to support life on its planet Exo III, began to fade about 500,000 years ago, eventually rendering the planet's surface uninhabitable, with temperatures of 100 degrees below zero. Dr. Roger Korby's research discovered that as the sun dimmed, the civilization moved underground for survival, becoming more mechanized and less human. The android Ruk had been built by the ancient civilization that he called "the Old Ones." At the time of Korby's arrival on Exo III, Ruk had been tending the Old Ones' machinery for many centuries. Androids had apparently been commonplace in the now-vanished culture, but at some point the Old Ones began to fear their creations, and tried to deactivate them. The androids eventually learned to defend themselves, resulting in the deaths of the Old Ones.

"What Are Little Girls Made Of?" Spock noted that the star had been fading for a half million years.

Survival canisters stored beneath the surface of Sargon's planet

A terrible cataclysm on Sargon's planet totally ripped the atmosphere away about 500,000 years ago. The planet was left almost totally dead, the only survivors suspended in special protected canisters stored deep below the surface. Millennia later, Sargon would describe the cataclysm as being the result of a crisis faced when a civilization becomes so powerful that its inhabitants dare think of themselves as "gods." Prior to this disaster, Sargon's people roamed the galaxy aboard starships.

"Return to Tomorrow." Spock noted the planet's atmosphere had been destroyed about a half million years ago.

The technologically advanced inhabitants of planet Talos IV were nearly wiped out by a terrible war thousands of centuries ago. The war made the surface of the planet uninhabitable, and the few remaining Talosians survived by living underground. They found this life limiting, so they devoted themselves to developing their mental powers, while their technical skills atrophied. They developed a practice of telepathically sharing illusory experiences with specimens in their menagerie of alien life-forms, gathered prior to the war, when the Talosians were a spacefaring race. The Talosians eventually found such illusions to be a dangerous narcotic that very nearly destroyed what was left of their civilization.

Talosian

"The Menagerie"/"The Cage." Vina told Pike about the war "thousands of centuries ago" and its consequences. This would seem to imply that the Talosian war had happened somewhere between 100,000 to 900,000 years ago.

200,000 YEARS AGO

The civilization of the planet Iconia flourished many millennia ago, becoming a strong influence on many ancient cultures, as evidenced by linguistic similarities between Iconian, Dewan, Iccobar, and Dinasian. Ancient texts described the Iconians as "demons of air and darkness," suggesting the Iconians could travel to other planets without the use of spaceships, possibly with the use of an interdimensional transport system. The Iconian civilization was evidently destroyed some 200,000 years ago when all major cities on Iconia were heavily damaged by large-scale orbital bombardment.

"Contagion." Some 200,000 years ago, per Captain Donald Varley's interpretation of archaeological evidence from Denius III.

The surface of planet Iconia, nearly all signs of civilization eradicated by orbital bombardment

50,000 YEARS AGO

The Horta of planet Janus VI began their most recent cycle of rebirth about 50,000 years ago. At that time, their entire race died, except for one individual who guarded their Vault of Tomorrow which contained the eggs for the next generation of Horta. This individual became the "mother" of her race.

"The Devil in the Dark." Spock learned the history of the Horta during his mind meld.

Lokai of the planet Cheron attempted to lead a revolution against that planet's government, fighting against what he saw as racial injustice and oppression of his people. Although the Cheron government claimed to have been making reforms, these were deemed inadequate by Lokai and his followers. Lokai was convicted of treason, but managed to flee from the planet. He was followed by Commissioner Bele on a pursuit that would last some 50,000 years, ending only after racial hatred had destroyed their entire civilization.

Mother Horta tends her children in the Vault of Tomorrow

"Let That Be Your Last Battlefield." Bele explained that he'd been chasing Lokai across the galaxy for 50,000 years.

Two unknown adversaries outside of our galaxy fought a terrible war, culminating in the use of a "doomsday machine." Intended as a bluff, the device was so powerful, it would destroy both sides. Unfortunately, the planet-killing weapon apparently did exactly that, and subsequently wandered through intergalactic space for unknown millennia before attacking at least six solar systems near L-374 in our own galaxy.

"The Doomsday Machine." Date for the ancient war is unknown, but it would likely have been many millennia ago during which the weapon apparently crossed an intergalactic distance prior to the episode.

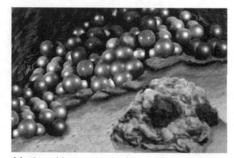

The planet-killer

25,000 YEARS AGO

The first of at least 947 archaeological expeditions was conducted at the ancient ruins on planet Tagus III, about 22,000 years ago. Among these studies were a number of Vulcan expeditions that concentrated on the northeastern part of the city.

"Qpid." Picard described the history of Tagus archaeological research in his speech to the Archaeology Council's annual symposium.

The Trill began living as a "joined species," a pairing of intelligent but helpless creatures who live in humanoid host bodies. So complete is the symbiotic relationship that most outside observers deal with the joined Trill as single entities.

"The Host." Odan noted his people have survived in this fashion for "millennia."

10,000 YEARS AGO

Machine-god Vaal

The machine-god Vaal on planet Gamma Trianguli VI was built at least 10,000 years ago in order to protect the inhabitants of that planet by providing food and climate control.

"The Apple." Spock described Vaal as being *"very ancient, very high order of workmanship."* McCoy noted that the people had apparently had *"no change or progress in at least ten thousand years,"* suggesting that Vaal was constructed at least that long ago.

A race of intelligent spacefaring organisms became nearly extinct some millennia ago. These organisms formed symbiotic relationships with humanoid life-forms that lived within their bodies, providing life support, and effectively becoming "living spaceships" to their humanoid companions. The last surviving specimen, an individual that called itself Gomtuu (and would eventually be known as Tin Man to the Federation), suffered injury when radiation from an explosion penetrated its outer layers, killing its crew. Gomtuu wandered alone through space for millennia, looking unsuccessfully for others of its kind, eventually becoming despondent because it was dependent on its humanoid crew for emotional sustenance.

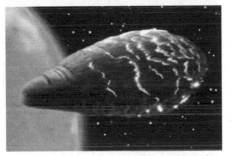

Gomtuu, a spaceborne organism

"Tin Man." Tam Elbrun noted that Tin Man had been wandering in space for millennia.

The sun of the Fabrini system went nova about 10,000 years ago, destroying the planets in that system. Before this happened, the inhabitants of the planet Fabrina created a giant space ark to insure the survival of their species. The ark, fashioned from a 200-mile-diameter asteroid, was known as *Yonada* to its inhabitants, and was designed to simulate perfectly the surface of their home world for a ten-millennium voyage to a planet near Darin V.

"For the World Is Hollow and I Have Touched the Sky." Spock noted *Yonada* had been in transit for 10,000 years.

The Kalandans constructed a small planet, about the size of Earth's moon, for colonization. Despite the planet's small size, it had a Class-M environment and supported a Kalandan outpost until a deadly disease organism, accidentally created in the planet's formation, killed all the inhabitants. This left the automated defense systems to protect the now-vacant outpost.

"That Which Survives." The Kalandan planetoid was described as being just a few thousand years old.

6,000 YEARS AGO

Landru of Beta III

The great leader Landru of planet Beta III in star system C-111 chose to provide for his people's future after his death by creating a powerful computer system that would run the planet's society. Prior to Landru's rise to power, the planet had been wracked by war. Landru changed his society, returning to a simple time of peace and tranquility. The computer, which was made operational about 6,000 years ago, was programmed with the sum of Landru's knowledge and was given the prime directive of always acting for the good of the people. The knowledge that Landru had been replaced after his death with a computer was kept from the people.

"Return of the Archons." Reger described a high-tech lighting panel as being very old, before the time of Landru, then added that some had speculated that this made the artifact as old as 6,000 years. Spock noted that Landru had built and programmed the machine 6,000 years ago.

Unknown aliens took several humans from Earth to be raised on a distant planet some 6,000 years ago. The descendants of these humans were trained for generations so that they could secretly be returned to Earth as part of an effort to prevent Earth from destroying itself before it could mature into a peaceful society.

Gary Seven, a descendant of humans raised by unknown aliens

"Assignment: Earth." Gary Seven described his mission to the Beta Five computer.

An ice age began on planet Sigma Draconis VI, triggering a remarkable regression in the civilization there. Once technologically advanced beyond the Federation's 23rd-century level, the society regressed to a virtual Stone Age. Although some elements of their past technological achievements remained, the inhabitants no longer possessed any understanding of the technology in the 23rd century.

"Spock's Brain." Spock described the planet's history.

Surface conditions on planet Sigma Draconis VI

5,000 YEARS AGO

Planet Earth was visited by a group of aliens who settled the Mediterranean area some five thousand years ago. The aliens, who possessed powerful psychokinetic abilities, were worshiped by the ancient Greeks as gods and were apparently the origin of many Greek myths. The humans eventually outgrew the cultural need for these gods, who departed Earth for planet Pollux IV. Many years later, the last alien — who was once known as the god Apollo — attempted to persuade members of the *Enterprise* crew to worship him as did the ancient Greeks.

Greek god Apollo

"Who Mourns for Adonais." Apollo described the history of his people, mentioning their visit with the ancient Greeks 5,000 years ago.

Planet Sarpeidon experienced an ice age some 5,000 years ago. A woman from Sarpeidon's present, Zarabeth, was exiled into this past by the tyrant Zor Khan, after two of Zarabeth's kinsmen conspired to kill the dictator. Zarabeth lived completely alone in this past, except for a brief visit from Spock and McCoy, who accidentally traveled into the past thorough Sarpeidon's Atavachron time portal.

Zarabeth

"All Our Yesterdays." Spock and McCoy went 5,000 years into Sarpedon's past.

4,000-3,000 B.C. First large-scale human civilizations developed in Sumer region of the Nile river valley on Earth. The Sumerians were responsible for the earliest known form of writing, known as cuneiform. The civilization also had the first known records of the use of wheeled vehicles. The first epic tales of Gilgamesh began in this period.

Historical accounts.

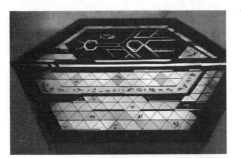

Control console of the Custodian

Flint

The Progenitors of planet Aldea in the Epsilon Mynos star system install a powerful cloaking shield around their entire planet, controlled by a sophisticated computer called the Custodian. The Aldeans, who sought anonymity to avoid marauders and other hostile passersby, eventually faded into mythology until the cloaking shield began to cause major environmental damage on Aldea, forcing the Aldeans to seek outside help in 2364.

"When the Bough Breaks." Rashella noted that their shield "has confused outsiders for millennia." Duana noted that their main computer, the Custodian, had been built by the Progenitors many centuries ago.

3834 B.C. The (nearly) immortal Flint was born in Mesopotamia on Earth. Flint described his early self as a bully who didn't die, despite serious injuries in an ancient war. Flint lived under a variety of assumed names, including Merlin, Leonardo da Vinci, and Johannes Brahms, finally settling on a small planet he purchased under the name of Mr. Brack.

"Requiem for Methuselah." Flint described his history.

The star known as Sahndara went nova, presumably destroying the planets in that system over 2,500 years ago. At least a few of the natives of one of the planets were able to escape. They spent some time on planet Earth, circa 400 B.C., where their leader, Parmen, became a great admirer of the philosopher Plato. After leaving Earth, circa 200 B.C., they settled on a planet that they named Platonius, and attempted to pattern their world after Plato's Republic. About six months after their arrival on this planet, the Platonians began to develop powerful telekinetic abilities, the result of having absorbed trace quantities of kironide from the planet's environment.

"Plato's Stepchildren." Parman noted his people had arrived on their planet some 2,500 years ago. Philiana, Parmen's wife, said she was 2,300 years old, but may have been lying about her age.

500–600 B.C. First records of parts of the Old Testament. Birth of Confucianism and Buddhism. Height of the Greek age of philosophy and the influence of the Greek oracle at Delphi.

Historical accounts.

Spock's ancestors adopted a ceremonial ground that remains in their family at least until the 23rd century. These ceremonial grounds, used for the mating rituals, embody the Vulcan heart and soul, reflecting Vulcan culture from the "time of the beginning."

"Amok Time." Spock noted the grounds had been held by his family for over 2,000 years. T'Pau's comments about the ceremonies suggest that these grounds predate the Vulcan reformation.

4 B.C. Jesus Christ was born. Christ's teachings would become the basis of Earth's Christian religion.

Historical accounts.

A.D. 1ST–10TH CENTURIES

The inhabitants of planet Vulcan were engaged in terrible and destructive wars, a result of the passions and emotions that governed the Vulcan people. Spock described this period as savage, even by Earth standards. The great philosopher Surak led the Vulcan people on the path toward logic and

Spock's family ceremonial grounds

peace, demonstrating enormous courage working for peace in the face of war. This may also have been the event that triggered the departure of Vulcan dissidents who left their home planet to found what eventually became the Romulan Star Empire.

Surak, father of Vulcan philosophy

"The Savage Curtain." Spock described Surak as the father of Vulcan civilization. *"Balance of Terror," "The* Enterprise *Incident,"* and *"Unification, Parts I and II"* allude to the common Vulcan-Romulan ancestry. Date is not specifically established, but *"Amok Time"* (see previous item) would seem to imply that the reformation was about 2,000 years ago. In *"All Our Yesterdays,"* McCoy notes that the primitive Spock has reverted to what Vulcans were like some 5,000 years before he was born, implying that the reformation was less than 5,000 years ago.

Editors' Note: Although the date for the Vulcan-Romulan schism is also not clearly established, this would seem to suggest that the Vulcans had significant interstellar spaceflight capabilities perhaps two millennia before Earth did.

The society on planet 892-IV, evolving on a path similar to that of Earth, developed a culture similar to Earth's ancient Rome, a remarkable example of Hodgkin's Law of parallel planet development.

"Bread and Circuses." Kirk noted the planet was ruled by leaders who could trace their line back 2,000 years.

A terrible war broke out on planet Solais V some 1,500 years ago. The conflict lasts into the 24th century, at which time the historic enemies are on the verge of extinction.

An inhabitant of planet Solais V

"Loud as a Whisper." The Solais war had lasted for fifteen centuries prior to the episode.

The people of planet Kaelon II adopted the custom of the Resolution, a ceremony in which individuals commit suicide at the age of 60 to avoid being a burden to their society. This practice, still observed in the 24th century, is considered to be a celebration of life, allowing it to end in dignity.

"Half a Life." Timicin said the Resolution was instituted *"fifteen or twenty centuries ago."*

An individual of the Metron civilization was born about 1,500 years ago. In the year 2266, this individual was responsible for his race incapacitating the Starship *Enterprise* and a Gorn space vehicle, attempting to end a conflict between the two by allowing the commanders of the two spacecraft to engage in physical combat. Little else is known of the Metrons, as they have chosen to remain undetectable to Federation science.

A Metron

"Arena." The Metron said he was about 1,500 years old.

11TH–18TH CENTURIES

The technologically advanced civilization on planet Ventax II was suffering from overcrowding, environmental pollution, and terrible wars a thousand years ago. The Ventaxians, according to historical record, entered into a pact with a supernatural being called Ardra. The agreement called for Ardra to grant the planet a millennium of peace and prosperity. At the end of this span, Ardra would be entitled to claim the planet and its inhabitants.

"Devil's Due." Ventaxian leader Jared described their agreement with Ardra, noting it had been signed ten centuries ago.

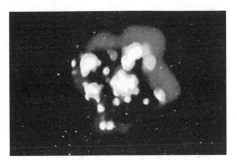

The lights of Zetar

Nearly all life on the planet Zetar was destroyed about a thousand years ago by some terrible cataclysm. Only a hundred individuals from that planet survived in the form of energy patterns representing their thoughts and their will. These individuals searched for a millennium to find a suitable physical body through which they could live.

"The Lights of Zetar." The Zetarians described their plight to Kirk.

Promellians and Menthars fought a devastating war near planet Orelious IX at least 1,000 years ago. The war was so fierce that it resulted in the destruction of the planet as well as both cultures. Space near the former Orelious IX is now occupied by an asteroid field, the remains of the planet.

"Booby Trap." The war was at least a millennium ago.

The planet Kataan in the Silarian sector experienced a severe drought, found by the planet's inhabitants to be due to a gradual increase in solar radiation. Over a number of years the increase culminated in the star going nova, destroying all life in the system. Prior to the explosion, the Kataans were successful in launching a small space probe containing a memory record of life on that planet. The probe travels for a thousand years before encountering the Starship *Enterprise* commanded by Captain Picard.

"The Inner Light." Data noted the star had exploded a thousand years prior to the episode, set in the year 2368.

The inhabitants of the planet Thasus once had corporeal bodies of solid matter, but have long since evolved into forms of pure energy.

An interpretive "chorus" serves as a medium of communication to the rulers of the Ramatis system.

"Charlie X." The Thasian, in communicating with Kirk, said he was reverting to his form of "centuries ago," implying that his people had corporeal bodies that long ago.

The ruling family of the Ramatis star system was discovered centuries ago to lack the gene required for the sense of hearing. A system was developed whereby a "chorus" of interpreters both hear and speak for members of the ruling family. This ingenious arrangement continued for centuries, with each succeeding generation of chorus family members continuing to provide services to the ruling family members.

"Loud as a Whisper." Riva's chorus noted that the arrangement had lasted for centuries.

The cloud city Stratos above Ardana

The people of planet Ardana built a magnificent city in the clouds. The city, named Stratos, was built centuries ago and was described as the finest example of sustained antigravity elevation in the galaxy. The leaders of the cloud city promised the people of Ardana that all would be able to live in Stratos, but after construction was completed, the members of the working class were not allowed to live there.

"The Cloud Minders." Vana described Stratos as having been built "centuries" ago.

A.D. 625. Mohammed began writing the Koran. This work would become the cornerstone of the Muslim religion.

Historical accounts.

A civil war began centuries ago on planet Daled IV. The planet, which rotates only once per year, has one hemisphere in perpetual light and the other in eternal darkness. As a result, two disparate civilizations had evolved on the world, so different that they fought each other for many centuries. A young woman, whose parents each came from a different side, is later raised on a neutral planet in the hope she can bring peace to her world.

"The Dauphin." Data described the planet's history, noting the war had lasted for centuries.

A.D. 1609. Galileo Galilei constructed Earth's first astronomical telescope. Galileo would later become known as the father of modern science for his work supporting the Copernican view of the universe.

Historical accounts.

18TH CENTURY

A group of alien interstellar anthropologists called the Preservers visited planet Earth at least several hundred years ago. They judged Earth's American Indians to be in danger of extinction, and transplanted a small group of Delaware, Navajo, and Mohicans to a distant Class-M planet, where they were encouraged to live in a manner that preserved their culture. Since this planet was near a potentially dangerous asteroid belt, the Preservers provided a powerful deflector beam mechanism to protect the settlement from asteroid impacts. The transplanted Indians refer to their alien benefactors as The Wise Ones.

Asteroid deflector mechanism provided by the Preservers

"The Paradise Syndrome." Judging from the Indian culture seen in the episode, the colony would probably have been established at least 500 years prior to the episode, about 200 years in our past.

Neural parasite creature

Archaeological research cited by Spock indicates the Beta Portolan system was overcome by mass insanity in the distant past. This was apparently the same affliction that struck planet Deneva in 2267, killing many colonists, including Kirk's brother and sister-in-law. Spock suggested that Beta Portolan was the original source of the insanity that also affected planets Lavinius V in 2067 and Ingraham B in 2265.

"Operation: Annihilate!" Date is pure conjecture, Spock's research suggested their knowledge of Beta Portolan was based on archaeological data, suggesting the mass insanity was centuries old.

The two inhabited planets of the Eminiar star system began a bitter war. The planets, known as Eminiar VII and Vendikar, were in danger of destroying each other, when an agreement was reached in which the war would be conducted by computer simulations, with the computers determining casualties on each side. Once casualties were calculated, the appropriate individuals would report to disintegration chambers so that their deaths could be recorded. Representatives of Eminiar VII defended the arrangement as one that permitted both societies to survive despite a devastating war. The computer war lasted some 500 years, until the intervention of Captain Kirk in 2267 broke the radio link between the two planets.

Computer war room on planet Eminiar VII

"A Taste of Armageddon." Anan Seven noted that the war had lasted for 500 years.

Colonists from planet Peliar Zel migrated to that world's two moons. Relations between the two offworld colonies were strained at best, and Peliar Zel

Governor Leka would later describe them as "two squabbling children." Hostilities extend into the 24th century, when the services of Trill Ambassador Odan are instrumental in maintaining peace in the system.

"The Host." Governor Leka described the planets' history, noting that the two moons had been settled five centuries ago.

Hundreds of condemned criminals from a star system called Ux-Mal were imprisoned on a moon of the planet Mab-Bu VI. The criminals were somehow separated from their bodies and their life entities were left to drift in the electromagnetic storms in the moon's atmosphere.

"Power Play." The entity occupying Troi's body said they'd been imprisoned for five centuries.

19TH CENTURY

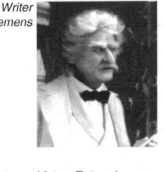

Writer Samuel Clemens

1893. Lieutenant Commander Data is accidentally thrown back into the past while investigating evidence that aliens from the future may have attempted to interfere with Earth's history. While in 19th-century San Francisco, Data encountered writer Samuel Clemens, who became suspicious of Data's activities. Data also met Guinan in the past, learning that the future *Enterprise* bartender had visited Earth some 472 years prior to her service aboard the starship.

"Time's Arrow." Date established in newspaper headline. (The date is about 500 years prior to Star Trek: The Next Generation.*)*

Data and future Enterprise *crew member Guinan*

2.0 THE TWENTIETH CENTURY

"We came in peace for all mankind."

1905

Albert Einstein publishes his special theory of relativity. Einstein is later honored with the Nobel Prize for his work.

Contemporary accounts.

1930

Dr. Leonard McCoy in Earth's past, having gone through the Guardian of Forever while under influence of accidental overdose of cordrazine, causes major damage to the flow of history by preventing the death of social worker Edith Keeler. Kirk and Spock, on a mission to prevent this occurrence, are able to reverse the damage by permitting the death to occur. It is reported that failure to permit Keeler's death would have triggered a chain of events in which Nazi Germany was able to develop atomic weapons, resulting in Hitler's winning of World War II.

"The City on the Edge of Forever." Edith Keeler told McCoy the year.

*Social worker
Edith Keeler*

1932

Seven women are knifed to death in Shanghai, China, on planet Earth. The murders remain unsolved until 2267, when new information suggests they had been committed by an energy being that thrives on fear.

"Wolf in the Fold." Computer research revealed the account.

1934

Dixon Hill enthusiast Jean-Luc Picard

The first short story featuring fictional detective Dixon Hill is published in *Amazing Detective Stories Magazine.* Many years later, *Enterprise* captain Jean-Luc Picard becomes an avid fan of the Dixon Hill mysteries.

"The Big Goodbye." Data reads bibliography of Dixon Hill stories from ship's computer records.

Editors' Note: The computer readout screen that Data reads when studying Dixon Hill stories lists episode writer Tracy Tormé as the author of those stories!

1936

Another Dixon Hill detective story, "The Long Dark Tunnel" is published in *Amazing Detective Stories Magazine.*

"The Big Goodbye." Date from Data's computer research.

1945

Sputnik I

The United Nations is chartered on planet Earth in the city of San Francisco. The organization represents a significant effort in the quest for planetary peace.

Contemporary accounts.

1957

Sputnik I, Earth's first artificial satellite, is launched, marking the dawn of Earth's space age.

Contemporary accounts.

1959

Yuri Gagarin, aboard space vehicle *Vostok I,* becomes first human to travel in space.

Contemporary accounts.

1960

Cosmonaut Yuri Gagarin

Earth-based radio telescopes are used to listen for evidence of radio signals from Tau Ceti and Epsilon Eridani as part of Project Ozma, one of Earth's first attempts to search for extraterrestrial life.

Contemporary accounts.

1963

Nuclear Test Ban Treaty is adopted on planet Earth. The agreement represents a significant early step toward the control of nuclear weapons.

Contemporary accounts.

1966

Scientists on Miri's planet begin a "life prolongation project," creating a virus intended to halt the aging process. The project is a terrible disaster and results in the deaths of all the adults on the planet. The planet's children survive, aging at a greatly reduced rate, although the virus causes their death upon the onset of puberty.

"Miri." Spock indicated the project began 300 years prior to the episode (2266).

1968

The U.S.S. *Enterprise*, on a historical research mission into the past, encounters Gary Seven, a human trained by unknown aliens, being returned to Earth to help that planet survive its critical nuclear age. Kirk accidentally interferes with this mission, but is able to restore events before a nuclear missile can cause a disastrous explosion.

"Assignment: Earth." Year established by Kirk in captain's log. Note that from Kirk's perspective, these events occurred after *the 1969 events from "Tomorrow Is Yesterday."*

Editors' Note: This episode was actually a pilot for a proposed television series, Assignment: Earth. *The show would have chronicled the adventures of Gary Seven and his assistant, Roberta Lincoln, defending the Earth against malevolent extraterrestrials. The pilot did not sell, and the series was never produced.*

Gary Seven

1969

The U.S.S. Enterprise *in Earth's upper atmosphere*

The U.S.S. *Enterprise*, accidentally sent into the past by near collision with a black hole, is detected as an unidentified flying object in Earth's atmosphere. In attempting to prevent further detection, Kirk accidentally captures U.S. Air Force Captain John Christopher. Christopher is returned during the light-speed breakaway factor maneuver which also returns the *Enterprise* to its own time.

"Tomorrow Is Yesterday." Radio broadcast intercepted by Uhura said that first moon landing mission would be launched "next Wednesday," which puts the episode within a week before Wednesday, July 16, 1969, when Apollo 11 was launched.

Editors' Note: One of Star Trek's *least-recognized prognostications about the future is the fact that writer Dorothy Fontana accurately predicted that the first moon landing mission would be launched on a Wednesday!*

July 20, 1969. Neil Armstrong becomes first human to walk on Earth's moon. Dedication on landing ship *Eagle* proclaims: "We came in peace for all mankind."

Contemporary accounts.

First human footprint on the moon

1974

Five women are brutally knifed to death in Kiev, USSR, on planet Earth. It is later discovered that these murders were probably committed by the same

The surface of Mars as seen by Viking

energy entity responsible for similar killings on planet Argelius II in 2267.

"Wolf in the Fold." According to computer records.

1976

Viking I space probe lands on planet Mars, Earth's first major attempt to employ space exploration in the search for extraterrestrial life.

Contemporary accounts.

1977

First spaceship *Enterprise* (Space Shuttle OV-101) undergoes flight testing.

Contemporary accounts.

Editors' Note: NASA's shuttle was, of course, named after Star Trek's starship. The naming was ordered by President Gerald Ford after an outpouring of support by Star Trek fans. It's only fitting, therefore, that the Starship Endeavour, a Nebula class vessel mentioned (but not seen) in "Redemption, Part II," was named after the NASA space shuttle orbiter.

Space shuttle Enterprise

1981

Shuttle *Columbia*, Earth's first reusable spaceship, makes first orbital flight.

Contemporary accounts.

1983

Pioneer 10 spacecraft becomes first human-launched space probe to leave Earth's solar system. The craft drifts in deep space until it is destroyed in 2287 by a Klingon Bird-of-Prey. *Pioneer 10* had been launched from Earth on March 2, 1972.

Contemporary accounts. Pioneer 10 was destroyed in Star Trek V: The Final Frontier.

Pioneer 10 *space probe*

1986

Seven astronauts killed when spaceship *Challenger* explodes 73 seconds after liftoff.

Contemporary accounts.

Saving the whales

Klingon Bird-of-Prey piloted by Kirk and his crew land in old San Francisco to take two humpback whales back to the future. Using the ship's cloaking device, the vessel remains undetected by terrestrial authorities, although Commander Pavel Chekov is temporarily incarcerated by military authorities while working to repair the spacecraft. Cetacean biologist Gillian Taylor leaves this time period and travels to 23rd century with Kirk.

Dr. Nichols, a scientist and plant manager at Plexicorp in San Francisco, begins to develop the molecular matrix for transparent aluminum on his Macintosh computer.

Star Trek IV: The Voyage Home.   *Date is conjecture, based on studio publicity suggesting our heroes had gone back to 1986.*

1992

The book *Chicago Mobs of the Twenties* is published in New York. A copy of this book is carried aboard the Federation starship U.S.S. *Horizon* in 2168, and is accidentally left on planet Sigma Iotia II in that year.

The Book

"A Piece of the Action." Spock reads publication date from the Book, no doubt due in print soon from Pocket Books, albeit a bit behind schedule.

Khan Noonien Singh rises to power, assuming dictatorial control over one quarter of the planet Earth, from South Asia to the Middle East. Khan is the product of genetic engineering and eugenics experiments.

Khan Noonien Singh

"Space Seed." Spock reveals date and description of the Eugenics Wars from historical research.

Editors' Note: If we assume Khan was in his thirties at this point, we are left with the interesting conclusion that he would probably have been born before the original airing of the episode in 1967. Fortunately, none of this seems to have come to pass, at least the last time we checked with CNN and our local newspapers.

1993

A group of eugenically bred "superior" humans seize power simultaneously in some forty of Earth's nations. Terrible wars ensue, in part because the genetic "supermen" take to fighting among themselves. Entire populations are bombed out of existence during these Eugenics Wars, and Earth is believed to be on the verge of a new dark age.

"Space Seed." More from Spock's historical research.

1994

Claire Raymond, a woman living on Earth, dies of an embolism. Her husband, Donald Raymond, has her cryogenically frozen and sent into space for possible revival at some future date. The satellite containing her body is eventually discovered in 2364 by the starship *Enterprise*.

"The Neutral Zone." Dr. Crusher said Raymond had died some 370 years prior to the episode.

1996

S.S. Botany Bay *departs Earth orbit.*

Eugenics Wars over, Khan Noonien Singh is overthrown and escapes from Earth on the DY-100 class sleeper ship S.S. *Botany Bay* along with 96 of his fellow genetic "supermen."

"Space Seed" and Star Trek II: The Wrath of Khan. *Khan mentions the year.*

Editors' Note: It is unfortunate that neither NASA nor any other terrestrial space agency seems likely to have any spacecraft as advanced as the Botany Bay *by 1996. This is one place where* Star Trek's *technological predictions have missed by a significant margin. On the other hand, we should probably be grateful that the show was also wrong about predicting the rise to power of genetic tyrants.*

Poet Tarbolde writes "Nightingale Woman," a love sonnet considered to be among the most passionate for the next two centuries.

"Where No Man Has Gone Before." Gary Mitchell mentions date after quoting a passage from the work. Mitchell mentions that Tarbolde is from the Canopius Planet, presumably implying that this was written prior to human contact with this alien world, and that Tarbolde's work was later translated into English.

Editors' Note: The words to "Nightingale Woman" were actually written by Gene Roddenberry as a love poem from a pilot to his airplane!

1999

Voyager 6 *near Io*

The machine planet

Voyager 6 spacecraft launched from Earth. This probe eventually fell into a black hole, emerging on the other side of the galaxy, where it encountered a planet of living machines that enhanced the craft and returned it to Earth in 2271.

Date is conjecture from Star Trek: The Motion Picture. *This probe was probably launched before construction of the more advanced* Nomad *probe in the early 2000s ("The Changeling"). In actual fact, as of this writing NASA has launched only two spacecraft in the* Voyager *series, and additional probes seem unlikely due to severe cutbacks in planetary sciences programs. This is especially unfortunate since the* Voyager *program has been an important part of what some have termed the greatest exploratory era in human history (so far, at least).*

Editors' Note: Following production of the episode "Q Who?" for Star Trek: The Next Generation, *Gene Roddenberry half jokingly speculated that the planet encountered by* Voyager *might have been the Borg homeworld.*

3.0 THE TWENTY-FIRST CENTURY

Breaking the warp barrier

2002

Space probe *Nomad* launched from Earth, the first interstellar probe intended to seek out new life-forms. The probe was designed by scientist Jackson Roykirk. *Nomad* is later believed destroyed in a meteoroid collision.

"The Changeling." Exact date is conjecture, but Kirk noted that Nomad had been launched in the early 2000s. (The script for the episode gives the launch date as 2002, but we are not accepting this as authoritative since it was not mentioned in the final air version of "The Changeling.")

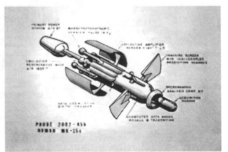

Engineering drawings of original Nomad *space probe*

2009

Captain Shaun Geoffrey Christopher commands the first successful Earth-Saturn space-probe mission.

Conjecture from "Tomorrow Is Yesterday." Assumes 40 years from the episode (1969) during which Shaun is born and raised.

Editors' Note: Episode writer Dorothy Fontana named Shaun Geoffrey Christopher for fellow Star Trek writer John D. F. Black's three sons, Shaun, Geoffrey, and Christopher.

DY-750 class sleeper ship

2018

Advances in sublight propulsion technologies make "sleeper ships" obsolete.

"Space Seed." Marla McGivers says that sleeper ships were necessary prior to this date. She was apparently not referring to the invention of warp drive, since this is before Cochrane's birth.

2025

Reunification of Ireland. Speaking about the Ansata separatists of planet Rutia IV, Data cites this event as an example of how terrorist activity can sometimes result in political change.

"The High Ground." Data mentioned the date to Picard.

2026

Joe DiMaggio's hitting record broken by a shortstop from the London Kings.

"The Big Goodbye." Data mentioned date to news vendor in the holodeck program.

Zefram Cochrane

2030

Zefram Cochrane, inventor of warp drive, is born. His work makes such an enormous contribution to space exploration that great universities and even entire planets are one day named after him.

"Metamorphosis." Cochrane disappeared 150 years before the episode (2267), and was 87 years old at that time.

Editors' Note: Cochrane is described in "Metamorphosis" as "Zefram Cochrane of Alpha Centauri." Because interstellar travel would have taken many, many years prior to the invention of warp drive, we are assuming that Cochrane was born on Earth, and that he later moved to Alpha Centauri, presumably after the invention of warp drive.

James Kirk and Edith Keeler look toward left star in Orion's belt.

A "famous novelist" writes a classic on the theme "Let me help." He recommends these words even over "I love you."

"The City on the Edge of Forever." Kirk, back in 1930, tells Edith Keeler that this will be written a hundred years in her future by an author living on a planet orbiting the far left star in Orion's belt.

2033

Fifty-second state is admitted to the United States of America.

"The Royale." Riker notes that a United States' flag with 52 stars would indicate a date between 2033 and 2079. This would suggest that the United States survives as a political entity until at least the latter date.

Editors' Note: Star Trek: The Next Generation executive producer Rick Berman insisted that the U.S. flag seen on the Charybdis's wreckage be painted to have 52 stars, for the benefit of those watching the episode with VCRs. (On the other hand, by amazing coincidence, the mission patch on Richey's spacesuit looks a whole lot like the Apollo 17 emblem.)

American flag, circa 2033

2036

New United Nations rules that Earth citizens may not be held responsible for crimes committed by ancestors.

"Encounter at Farpoint." Picard cites date to Q during trial.

2037

NASA launches spacecraft *Charybdis* on July 23, commanded by Colonel Steven Richey. It is the third attempt to explore beyond Earth's solar system. The ship is declared missing after telemetry is lost.

"The Royale." Data describes mission.

2040

Television no longer survives as a significant form of entertainment. *Star Trek* is no doubt an exception.

"The Neutral Zone." Data mentions date to L. Q. Sonny Clemonds.

Emblem of the National Aeronautics and Space Administration

2044

Space vehicle *Charybdis*, launched from Earth in 2037, arrives at the eighth planet in the Theta 116 system. An unknown alien intelligence on the planet discovers a book *(Hotel Royale)* in the possession of mission commander Richey and creates an environment based on the book in an effort to sustain Richey's life.

"The Royale." Data describes mission.

Editors' Note: It is probably reasonable to assume that this unknown alien intelligence was also responsible for transporting the Charybdis *across interstellar distances, since Earth science had not yet developed the warp drive at the time the ship was launched. (Warp drive inventor Zefram Cochrane would have been only six years old at the time the* Charybdis *was launched. Cochrane was undoubtedly smart, but not* that *smart.)*

2061

First successful demonstration of light-speed propulsion by Zefram Cochrane. This became the basis for early warp drive technology.

Date is conjecture from Cochrane's career as described in "Metamorphosis," further assuming that early warp drive had to be invented before the S.S. Valiant *embarked on its expedition, circa 2065, since that ship clearly crossed significant interstellar distances.*

Zefram Cochrane's first warp-powered spacecraft

2065

S.S. *Valiant* embarks on deep space exploration mission. Expedition is lost and is eventually swept out of the galaxy. The ship is nearly destroyed while trying to return across the energy barrier at the edge of the galaxy. Six crew members are killed, but a seventh experiences a mutation that dramatically enhances latent ESP powers, making that person a threat to the ship and its crew. The *Valiant*'s captain later orders the ship destroyed to prevent the mutated crew member from escaping.

"Where No Man Has Gone Before." Valiant *expedition was 200 years prior to the episode (2265).*

S.S. Valiant *approaches the barrier at the edge of the galaxy*

2067

British astronomer John Burke of the Royal Academy maps the area of space including Sherman's Planet. This region is later the subject of a territorial dispute between the Federation and the Klingon empire.

"The Trouble with Tribbles." Spock and Chekov's discussion established date as about 200 years prior to episode (2267).

Planet Lavinius V is infested by the same parasite creatures that later attacked planet Deneva.

"Operation: Annihilate." Two hundred years prior to episode (2267).

An unknown planet launches a sublight freighter vessel carrying large quantities of unstable nuclear waste products. The ship drifts through space, unattended, for about 300 years before settling into orbit around planet Gamelan V, where radiation leakage threatens life on the planet.

"Final Mission." Data noted the freighter's reactor core elements appeared to have been inactive for about 300 years prior to the episode (2367).

Neural parasite creature

The people of planet Argelius II undergo a "great awakening," a significant cultural milestone in their hedonistic society devoted to love and pleasure.

"Wolf in the Fold." Prefect Jarvis noted the "great awakening" had taken place 200 years prior to the episode (2267).

2079

An official of a postholocaust court

Earth recovers from a nuclear war. In this postatomic horror, the legal system is based on the principle of "guilty until proven innocent." Lawyers have fallen into disfavor as Shakespeare's suggestion to "Kill all the lawyers" has been taken quite seriously.

"Encounter at Farpoint." Q says that this is the year that his re-created courtroom is based on. It is unclear exactly when the nuclear conflict occurred, although Picard referred to a terrible "nuclear winter" having occurred during the middle of this century in "A Matter of Time." This conflict is presumably the "third world war" Dr. McCoy referred to in "Bread and Circuses," in which 37 million people were killed.

2082

Colonel Steven Richey, commander of the space vehicle *Charybdis*, dies in captivity on the eighth planet in the Theta 118 system.

"The Royale." Richey died 283 years prior to the episode (2365).

2086

The Lornack clan of the planet Acamar III begins a bitter blood feud with their rival clan, the Tralestas. The feud lasts until the year 2286, when the Lornacks massacre all but five of the Tralestas.

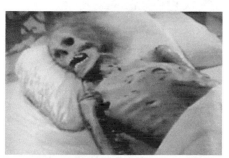

Remains of Colonel Steven Richey

"The Vengeance Factor." The massacre was described as having taken place 80 years prior to the episode (2366), and the feud had run for 200 years prior to that.

4.0 THE TWENTY-SECOND CENTURY

*The Great Seal of the
United Federation of Planets,
incorporated in 2161*

2105

Eight women brutally knifed to death by an unknown assailant in the Martian
Colonies. This is later found to be the same entity that committed several
murders on planet Argelius II in 2267.

*"Wolf in the Fold." Date given by library computer during Scotty's trial on
board the* Enterprise.

2117

Zefram Cochrane, now residing in the Alpha Centauri system, departs at the age
of 87 for parts unknown. He is believed to have died, but his body is never
found.

*Zefram
Cochrane*

"Metamorphosis." Cochrane left 150 years prior to episode (2267).

*Editors' Note: Cochrane, of course, made it to a planetoid in the Gamma
Canaris system, where he was cared for by an entity known as the
Companion, who loved him. This account, as well as the Companion's
merging with Commissioner Nancy Hedford, should theoretically not be
part of this chronology because of Kirk's promise to Cochrane not to reveal
that information.*

2123

Spaceship *Mariposa* is launched for colonization of Ficus sector on November
27. The craft settles colonists on planet Bringloid V. It later crashes on
planet Mariposa while attempting to settle a second group of colonists.

There are only five survivors of the crash, who attempt to keep their colony viable using cloning technology.

"Up the Long Ladder."

2156

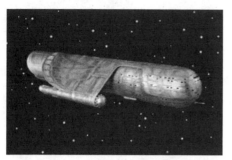

Early Romulan spacecraft

Romulan Wars begin between Earth forces and the Romulan Star Empire. The war is fought with primitive atomic weapons, and the Romulan fleet is not even equipped with warp drive. Among the human casualties are several members of the Stiles family.

Date is conjecture from "Balance of Terror." War ended about 100 years prior to episode; this date was four years prior to that. The conflict was described as being between Earth and the Romulans, suggesting that the United Federation of Planets did not exist at this point.

Two women knifed to death at Heliopolis City on planet Alpha Eridani II. The murders remain unsolved until 2267 when it is learned that the same entity had committed several similar murders on planet Argelius II.

"Wolf in the Fold." Date mentioned in Scotty's trial.

2160

Romulan Wars ended by the Battle of Cheron. The Romulans suffer a humiliating military defeat at the hands of Earth forces.

"The Defector." Admiral Jarok (as Setal) mentioned the battle but not the date, although this was presumably just before the peace treaty is signed, since he associated the battle with the establishment of the Neutral Zone. (See next entry.)

Editors' Note: The Battle of Cheron may refer to the planet seen in "Let That Be Your Last Battlefield," although Spock, in that episode (set in 2268), indicated an unfamiliarity with the inhabitants of Cheron. It is also possible that the Battle of Cheron may refer to Captain Garth's defeat of a Romulan ship (mentioned in "Whom Gods Destroy").

Romulan Neutral Zone and Earth outposts

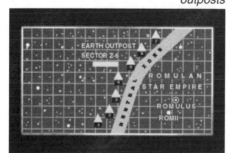

City of Paris, location of the Federation Council President's office

Romulan peace treaty signed, establishing the Romulan Neutral Zone as a buffer between the planets Romulus and Remus and the rest of the galaxy, violation of which is considered to be an act of war. All negotiations were conducted by subspace radio, without face-to-face contact between the parties. The pact is known as the Treaty of Algeron.

"Balance of Terror." About one hundred years prior to episode. "The Defector" established the formal name of the agreement in Picard's log when he decided to cross the Neutral Zone "in direct violation of the Treaty of Algeron."

Editors' Note: The names of Romulan homeworlds were given as Romulus and Remus in "Balance of Terror," although Spock's star map in that episode listed them as Romulus and Romii.

2161

United Federation of Planets incorporated. Starfleet established with a charter "to boldly go where no man has gone before." The Federation is governed by a Council, located in the city of San Francisco on Earth, and the Federation council president's office is located in the city of Paris. The Constitution of the Federation includes important protections of individual rights including the Seventh Guarantee, protecting citizens against self-incrimination.

The Great Seal of the United Federation of Planets

"The Outcast." Troi mentions that the Federation was founded in 2161. The Starfleet Academy emblem in "The First Duty" also gives this as the year in which the Academy was established. The Federation Council chambers were established as being in San Francisco in Star Trek IV: The Voyage Home. *The Federation president's office is seen in* Star Trek VI: The Undiscovered Country. *The view out the window shows the Eiffel Tower and the city of Paris. The Seventh Guarantee established in "The Drumhead."*

Editors' Note: The Romulan Wars ("Balance of Terror") were described as being between Earth and the Romulans, suggesting that the Federation was not established until at least that point. Starfleet was apparently responsible for the Starship Archon *and* Horizon *missions a few years later (2167 and 2168), thereby suggesting that both Starfleet and the Federation were in existence by then. The U.S.S.* Essex, *also lost in 2167, was clearly a part of the Federation Starfleet. (An early draft of this document, which speculated that 2161 might be the date for the Federation's founding, was used for reference when supervising producer Jeri Taylor needed information for "The Outcast," thus making 2161 "official"!)*

Starfleet Headquarters, located in the city of San Francisco

The term "United Federation of Planets" was not used until the 23rd episode of the original Star Trek *series, "A Taste of Armageddon." "Starfleet" did not come into use until the 15th episode, "Court Martial." During the first few episodes, the operating authority for the* Enterprise *was variously referred to as Space Command ("Court Martial"), Space Central ("Miri"), the Star Service ("Conscience of the King") and the United Earth Space Probe Agency ("Tomorrow Is Yesterday"). The latter name was once even abbreviated as UESPA, pronounced "you-spah" in "Charlie X." Nevertheless, later episodes imply Starfleet to have existed prior to "Court Martial," so we are assuming that it did. Writer Dorothy Fontana tells us that the term UESPA was suggested by story editor John D. F. Black. Fontana said that some of the other names listed above were mistakes, but she also notes that the present-day U.S. Navy personnel use at least as many terms when they refer to the Navy, CINCPAC, the "Silent Service," and the Pentagon.*

2164

The drug felicium is used to halt a plague on planet Onara. It is not realized at the time, but felicium, a product of the planet Brekka, has powerfully addictive properties, making the Onarans dependent on the substance long after the plague has been controlled.

"Symbiosis." Two hundred years prior to episode (2364).

2165

Sarek of Vulcan

Sarek of Vulcan is born, the child of Skon and Solkar. He becomes one of the Federation's most distinguished diplomats.

"Journey to Babel." Sarek gives his age as 102.437 in the episode. He names his parents during the fal-tor-pan *ceremony in* Star Trek III: The Search for Spock.

Guinan

Editors' Note: It has been pointed out to us that Sarek's ancestors mentioned in Star Trek III may not be his father and mother. It is conceivable that Skon was his father, and that Solkar was his grandfather. This would be more in keeping with the notion that Vulcan females tend to have names beginning with the letter T.

Guinan has her last encounter with Q prior to 2365. The two are not particularly fond of each other.

"Q Who?" She said her last meeting was 200 years prior to episode.

The planet Deneva is colonized by the Federation to provide a freighting line base. The planet is held to be one of the most beautiful in the galaxy.

"Operation: Annihilate!" Kirk noted the planet had been colonized over a century prior to the episode (2267).

Colony on planet Deneva

2167

The Starship *Archon* visits planet Beta III in star system C-111. The planet's master computer, known as Landru, destroys the ship by pulling it out of orbit. Many *Archon* crew members are killed, but many more are "absorbed" into Beta III's computer-controlled society, becoming known as "the Archons" to the planet's inhabitants.

"Return of the Archons." One hundred years prior to episode (2267).

The U.S.S. *Essex,* (registry number NCC-173) a *Daedalus* class starship under the command of Captain Bryce Shumar and First Officer Steven Mullen, is caught in an electromagnetic storm and destroyed above the Class M moon of planet Mab-Bu VI. There are no survivors of the crew of 229. The fate of this ship remains a mystery until 2368. Shumar's immediate superior in the sector had been Admiral Uttan Narsu of Starbase 12.

"Power Play." Exact date is conjecture, but the ship had crashed over 200 years prior to the episode (2368).

Editors' Note: Since the Essex *was operating at about the same time as the* Horizon *(from "A Piece of the Action") and the* Archon *("Return of the Archons"), we conjecture that those two other vessels were also* Daedalus *class starships.*

U.S.S. Essex

2168

The Starship *Horizon* visits planet Sigma Iotia II, about one hundred light years beyond Federation space. The crew reports the humanoid population of the planet to be on the verge of industrialization.

The Book

At this point, Starfleet has not yet instituted the Prime Directive of non-interference, and a member of the *Horizon* crew leaves behind a copy of a book entitled *Chicago Mobs of the Twenties*. The disastrous though unintended result is that the people of Iotia adopt the book as a model for their society.

Shortly after the contact at Sigma Iotia II, the U.S.S. *Horizon* is lost along with all crew members. Because of this, Starfleet remains unaware of the contact and the cultural contamination until radio signals from the *Horizon* are received a hundred years later.

"A Piece of the Action." Kirk noted the contact was one hundred years prior to episode (2268).

Editors' Note: Kirk mentioned that subspace radio had not yet been invented at this point.

Settlers from Earth establish a colony on planet Moab IV. They create a sealed, well-planned, genetically balanced biosphere in which they hope to forge a perfect society.

"Masterpiece Society." Benbeck noted his people had been working for two centuries to create their paradise.

Sealed biosphere colony on planet Moab IV

2170

Last detonation of Kavis Alpha neutron star prior to 2366, when Dr. Stubbs used that star's burst as part of his astrophysical research.

"Evolution." Stubbs noted that the phenomenon occurs regularly, every 196 years, the stellar equivalent of Earth's Old Faithful.

2196

Starfleet withdraws the last *Daedalus* class starship from service.

"Power Play." Data explained those ships had not been in service for 172 years prior to the episode (2368).

Daedalus *class starship*

5.0 THE TWENTY-THIRD CENTURY

The Klingon battle cruiser, a feared symbol of military power in the twenty-third century

2215

Planet Selcundi Drema begins disintegration, forming an asteroid belt in that solar system.

"Pen Pals." One hundred fifty years prior to episode (2365).

2217

The U.S.S. *Valiant* contacts planet Eminiar VII in star cluster NGC 321. The ship and its crew becomes casualties of the ongoing war between Eminiar and Vendikar.

"A Taste of Armageddon." Fifty years prior to the episode (2267).

Editors' Note: This was presumably another Starship Valiant, *since an earlier ship of the same name was launched in 2065 and never returned ("Where No Man Has Gone Before").*

2218

First city of the Klingon Empire

First contact with the Klingon Empire. As a result of this disastrous initial contact with the Klingons, Starfleet thereafter adopts a policy of covert surveillance of newly discovered civilizations before first contact is attempted.

"Day of the Dove." McCoy noted that Klingons and humans had been adversaries for 50 years prior to the episode, set in 2268.

Editors' Note: "First Contact" also described this as having happened "centuries ago," but it is only 144 years before that episode (2367).

2219

Richard Daystrom

Richard Daystrom is born. He becomes a brilliant computer scientist, the inventor of duotronic systems, and winner of the Nobel and Zee-Magnees prizes.

"The Ultimate Computer." Daystrom invented duotronics 25 years prior to the episode, and Kirk noted Daystrom was 24 years old at the time (2268).

2222

Montgomery Scott

Montgomery Scott is born. He becomes chief engineer of original U.S.S. *Enterprise* under the command of Captain Kirk.

Date is conjecture, assumes Scotty was 44 years old during the first season of the original Star Trek *series. This was coincidentally the age of actor James Doohan at that point.*

2223

Sybok

Relations with the Klingon Empire degenerate, giving rise to some 70 years of unremitting hostility between the Klingons and the Federation until the Khitomer Conference of 2293.

Star Trek VI: The Undiscovered Country. *Spock said that there had been hostility between the two powers for 70 years prior to that film, set in 2293.*

2224

Sybok is born, son of Sarek and a Vulcan princess. The princess, Sarek's first wife, dies shortly after Sybok's birth. Sybok is Spock's elder half-brother.

Date is conjecture from Star Trek V: The Final Frontier *and "Journey to Babel." This is seven years prior to conjectural date for Spock's birth, based on the Vulcan seven-year mating cycle.*

Editors' Note: Gene Roddenberry considered some events in Star Trek V *to be apocryphal; however, they are included in this chronology because of our desire to be as complete as possible.*

2227

Leonard H. McCoy

Leonard H. McCoy is born. He becomes chief medical officer of the original U.S.S. *Enterprise*. His father is David McCoy.

Data gave McCoy's age as 137 during "Encounter at Farpoint." His middle initial and his father's name were established in Star Trek III.

2229

Sarek and Amanda

Sarek of Vulcan and Amanda Grayson of Earth are married. Sarek would later describe his decision to marry the human Amanda as a "logical thing to do."

Date is conjecture from "Journey to Babel." A line in an early draft of the script suggested they were married 38 years prior to the episode (2267).

Editors' Note: In virtually all cases, we did not consider material from early

script drafts to be "official," preferring to accept only information from aired episodes. There were, however, a very few items from scripts that we chose to include because of their importance within the Star Trek *universe. The marriage of Sarek and Amanda is one such event.*

2230

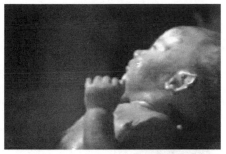

The infant Spock

Spock is born, son of Sarek and Amanda. Spock, a Vulcan-human hybrid, becomes science officer on the *Enterprise* under the command of Captain Christopher Pike and Captain James Kirk. He later plays a crucial role in negotiating peace between the Federation and the Klingon Empire, and in the effort for Vulcan/Romulan reunification.

Date is conjecture: A year after conjectural date for Sarek and Amanda's marriage. (See previous entry.) Dorothy Fontana, writer of "Journey to Babel," notes that this birth date would make Spock the same age as actor Leonard Nimoy at the time the episode was first aired.

T'Pring is born. When she and Spock are seven years old, they are telepathically joined by parental arrangement so that they will be married when they reach adulthood.

"Amok Time." Spock said both he and T'Pring were seven at the time of their mind-joining, suggesting they were born in the same year.

2233

James Tiberius Kirk

James T. Kirk is born in Iowa on Earth on March 22. He has at least one older brother, George Samuel Kirk.

Kirk's age is given as 34 in "The Deadly Years." In Star Trek IV: The Voyage Home, *he told Gillian he was born in Iowa. Kirk's brother described in "What Are Little Girls Made Of?" Sam Kirk's age is not given, but in "Operation: Annihilate!" Sam is seen briefly and appears to be significantly older than his brother. Reliable sources from the town of Riverside, Iowa, inform us that their city will be the birthplace of the* Enterprise *captain. We have no reason to doubt their veracity, although the Riverside birthplace is not derived from any episode or film.*

2236

Columbia *crew member Vina, disfigured in the crash of her ship*

S.S. *Columbia* crashes on planet Talos IV, crew member Vina is the only survivor. She is listed as an adult on the ship's manifest, although she appears as a youthful woman to Captain Pike some eighteen years later. The severely injured Vina is cared for by the Talosians, although their ability to repair her body is limited by the fact that they had never seen a human before.

"The Cage." Eighteen years prior to episode (2254).

2237

Spock, age 7, causes his parents considerable concern by disappearing overnight into the Llangon mountains near his home city of ShirKahr in an effort to test himself with the traditional *kahs-wan* survival ordeal. His pet sehlat, I-Chaya, is seriously injured by a wild animal, and Spock chooses to have his pet euthanized by a healer rather than die a lingering, painful death.

"Yesteryear," "Unification, Part I," and "Journey to Babel." Spock's age, the name of his hometown, and the death of his pet are established in the animated episode "Yesteryear." Sarek, in "Unification, Part I" confirms that Spock often disappeared into the mountains, apparently in reference to the "Yesteryear" back story. Spock's pet sehlat was established in "Journey to Babel."

Editors' Note: As indicated in the preface, we are not using material from the animated Star Trek *series. This information from "Yesteryear," written by Dorothy Fontana, is the sole exception, partly because it is reinforced by material in "Unification, Part I" and "Journey to Babel," but also because of Fontana's pivotal role in developing the background for the Spock character in the original* Star Trek *series. Note that we are using only the back story elements of Spock's childhood from "Yesteryear," and that we are not including the framing story, which had the adult Spock journey back in time to visit his younger self.*

Young Spock is telepathically joined to T'Pring in a ritual Vulcan ceremony arranged by their parents. Less than a marriage but more than a betrothal, the mind-touch insures the two will be drawn together at the proper time once they are grown.

Spock at age 7

"Amok Time." Spock said the joining had taken place when he was 7 years old. We are arbitrarily putting this after the events in "Yesteryear," since that episode represented a rite of passage.

Hikaru Sulu is born in San Francisco on planet Earth. He serves a distinguished career in Starfleet, first as staff physicist and helm officer on the U.S.S. *Enterprise*, and later as captain of the U.S.S. *Excelsior*.

Date is conjecture. Assumes Sulu was 29 during the first season of Star Trek. *Sulu's birthplace is established to be San Francisco in* Star Trek IV: The Voyage Home. *He served as* Enterprise *physicist in "Where No Man Has Gone Before," prior to his duty at the helm. Sulu commanded the Excelsior (and got a first name) in* Star Trek VI: The Undiscovered Country.

Sulu

2239

Uhura is born in the United States of Africa on planet Earth. She becomes communications officer aboard the U.S.S. *Enterprise*, and later serves at Starfleet Command in San Francisco.

Date is conjecture. Assumes Uhura was 27 years old during the first season of Star Trek, *based on Nichelle Nichols's age. Her birthplace is also conjectural, and was suggested in the* Star Trek *writers' guide. Uhura's stint at Starfleet was shown in* Star Trek III: The Search for Spock.

A reclusive individual known as Mr. Brack purchases the planet Holberg 917-G, a Class-M world in the Omega system. Brack is later discovered to be a pseudonym for the (nearly) immortal Flint.

Uhura

"Requiem for Methuselah." Spock's research revealed that Brack had purchased the planet thirty years prior to the episode (2269).

2242

The battle of Donatu V is fought near Sherman's Planet, in a region disputed by the Klingon Empire and the United Federation of Planets.

"The Trouble with Tribbles." Spock noted the battle was fought 23 solar years prior to the episode (2267).

2243

Dr. Richard Daystrom

Dr. Richard Daystrom invents duotronic computer technology and is awarded the Nobel and Zee-Magnees prizes. His revolutionary systems become the basis for the main computers used aboard the Starship *Enterprise*. Daystrom, still a relatively young man at this point, spends much of his later years trying to live up to this achievement, but is largely unsuccessful. Many years later he is recognized when the Daystrom Technological Institute is named in his honor.

"The Ultimate Computer." Spock noted that the duotronic breakthrough had taken place twenty-five years prior to the episode (2268). Existence of Daystrom Institute established in "Measure of a Man," "The Offspring," "Captain's Holiday," and "Data's Day."

2245

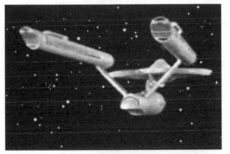

Starship Enterprise, *NCC-1701*

First Starship *Enterprise*, NCC-1701, is launched from the San Francisco Yards facility in orbit around Earth. Captain Robert April assumes command of the *Constitution* class ship and begins a five-year mission of exploration. One of the ship's designers is a young engineer named Lawrence Marvick.

Assumption based on Gene Roddenberry's suggestion that the Enterprise *was twenty years old at the time of "Where No Man Has Gone Before." Marvick established in "Is There in Truth No Beauty?"*

Captain Robert April, first commander of the Starship Enterprise

Editors' Note: Gene Roddenberry said he wanted the Enterprise, *as seen in the original* Star Trek *television series, to be a ship with "some history." Given a date of 2265 for "Where No Man Has Gone Before," a 20-year-old ship would put the* Enterprise's *launch in 2245. This is inconsistent with Admiral Morrow's line in* Star Trek III: The Search for Spock, *where he says the ship was 20 years old at that point (2285), which would put the* Enterprise *launch in 2265. The problem with Morrow's date is that it would mean that the ship was launched just prior to the first season of the original series. This would contradict "The Menagerie," which suggests that Spock served aboard the* Enterprise *with Captain Pike for over 11 years, since 2252. For this reason, we are using Gene's date of 2245 for the* Enterprise's *launch.*

Captain Robert April is not based on any direct evidence from any episode or film, but is included at Roddenberry's suggestion. The character name is from Gene's first proposal for the Star Trek *series, back in 1964, which listed April as* Enterprise *captain and series lead. April was depicted in the animated* Star Trek *episode "The Counter Clock Incident," written by Fred Bronson, using the pseudonym John Culver. (An intermediate draft of the script for "The Cage" also gave the character the name of Captain James Winter, no doubt a descendant of* Star Trek *feature film producer Ralph Winter.)*

Pavel Chekov

Pavel A. Chekov born. He is an only child. Chekov later becomes navigator and tactical officer on the *Enterprise* under the command of James Kirk, and also serves as first officer aboard the *Reliant* under Captain Clark Terrell.

"Who Mourns for Adonais." Chekov noted he was 22 years old at the time of the episode (2267). The fact that Chekov is an only child was established by Sulu in "Day of the Dove." Chekov's Reliant *stint seen in* Star Trek II.

Leonard McCoy enters college, pursuing a medical degree.

Conjecture. Assumes McCoy was 18 years old at the time of admission. See note on questions regarding McCoy's past in Appendix A.

2246

Kodos the Executioner seizes power, declares martial law, and orders 4,000 people killed on planet Tarsus IV when a food shortage caused by an exotic fungus becomes critical. Emergency supplies arrive too late to prevent killings. Future *Enterprise* crew members James Kirk and Kevin Riley are among the nine eyewitnesses who survive the incident. Riley loses his parents in the massacre. Another surviving eyewitness is Kirk's friend Thomas Leighton. Later, a burned body is discovered and identified as Kodos. This was the last known record of Kodos prior to 2266, when it is learned the identification of the body is mistaken.

*Anton
Karidian*

"The Conscience of the King." Twenty years prior to episode (2266), according to the computer record.

Editors' Note: Kirk would have been about 13 years old at this point, and Kevin Riley would have been several years younger.

2247

Lenore Karidian is born. Her birth is also the first known record of actor Anton Karidian, later discovered to be the same person who was known as Kodos the Executioner.

"Conscience of the King." Lenore is 19 years old at the time of the episode (2266).

*Lenore
Karidian*

2249

Spock chooses to enter Starfleet instead of the Vulcan Science Academy, thereby alienating his father, Sarek, until the Babel conference of 2267.

*Charles Evans
at age 17*

"Journey to Babel." Amanda said Spock and Sarek had not spoken as father and son for eighteen years prior to episode (2267). Note that this date is inconsistent with Garth's speech in "Whom Gods Destroy," which suggests that Spock may have joined Starfleet after the Axanar peace mission. (See next page.)

Charles Evans is born. His parents are part of an unsuccessful colonization project that ends with a disastrous crash on planet Thasus.

"Charlie X." He's 17 at the time of the episode (2266).

2250

James Kirk enrolls in Starfleet Academy. Mallory, father of a future *Enterprise* crew member, helps Kirk get into the academy. One of his most influential professors is historian John Gill. Kirk's personal hero is Fleet Captain Garth, considered to be the prototypical starship captain, whose exploits are still required reading at the Academy. Spock also studies under Gill, although Kirk and Spock were apparently not in that class together.

*Starfleet Academy campus in
San Francisco*

Date is conjecture: Assumes Kirk was seventeen years old at the time of his admission, as suggested by the Star Trek [original series] writers' guide. This is reasonably consistent with references in "Where No Man Has Gone Before," which establish that Kirk had been in the Academy some fifteen years prior to that episode, although Kirk seems to have been of a prior graduating class than Mitchell. (See later entry on Mitchell.) Mallory established in "The Apple." Gill established in "Patterns of Force," and Garth is from "Whom Gods Destroy."

Ben Finney

James Kirk, a midshipman at Starfleet Academy, befriends Ben Finney, an instructor. The two become so close that Ben later names his daughter, Jamie, after Kirk.

"Court Martial." Date is conjecture, but Kirk is described as being a midshipman at the Academy when they met.

Ensign James Kirk serves on U.S.S. *Republic*, NCC-1371. He reports an error made by his friend, Ben Finney, causing Finney to be passed over for promotion. According to Kirk's report, Kirk had relieved Finney on watch and had discovered the circuits to the atomic matter piles improperly left open, endangering the safety of the ship. Years later Finney holds this against Kirk, believing the report to be the sole reason why Finney never attained the command of a starship.

"Court Martial." Date is conjecture. Kirk's Farragut tour of duty ("Obsession," in which Kirk is a lieutenant) was described as his "first assignment," suggesting the Republic incident may have occurred while he was still at Starfleet Academy. This is reinforced by the fact that Kirk was an ensign at the time, suggesting Kirk's service on the Republic occurred before Kirk met Mitchell, who was at some point, a student of Kirk's at the Academy.

Editors' Note: The apparent fact that Kirk would have been an ensign (and later a lieutenant) while still at the Academy will probably raise some eyebrows among those familiar with protocol at present-day military schools, but we are told that at such institutions it is possible (though very uncommon) for a student to be accorded a rank such as ensign prior to graduation. Additionally, it's probably reasonable to assume that Starfleet, while steeped in tradition, has also changed a few things from the way its 20th-century predecessors did them.

Captain Garth

James Kirk, apparently still on the *Republic*, visits the planet Axanar on a peace mission. The operation is a major achievement for Captain Garth, in overall charge of the mission. Starfleet awards Kirk the Palm Leaf of Axanar for his role in the assignment.

Date is conjecture. "Court Martial" establishes that Kirk got the award, although the back story is established in "Whom Gods Destroy," when Kirk notes he visited Axanar as a "new fledged cadet," implying he was still with the Academy at the time. The episode seems to suggest that Kirk was not under Garth's command during the Axanar mission. Kirk's assignment to the Republic at this point is conjecture, based on the theory that Academy cadets spend part of their training on an actual starship. This would be consistent with practices at present-day Navy and Coast Guard academies, which require cadets to perform at-sea duty.

Gary Mitchell

Kirk meets Gary Mitchell at the Academy. They become best friends, although Mitchell, attending classes taught by Kirk, would later describe Kirk as an instructor who forced you to "think or sink." Kirk later asks for Mitchell to serve under him on his first command. Another acquaintance of Kirk's is

Finnegan, an upperclassman whom Kirk would later recall as having a penchant for practical jokes.

"Where No Man Has Gone Before." Fifteen years prior to the episode. Mitchell described Kirk as a lieutenant, so perhaps Kirk was an instructor or a teaching assistant after his assignment to the Republic ("Court Martial"), in which Kirk was an ensign. On the other hand, it might be possible that Kirk was serving as an instructor at the Academy after his graduation in 2254. This would be consistent with the fact that Kirk was described as a lieutenant when he served aboard the Farragut, his first assignment after the Academy, but it would be inconsistent with the reference to Kirk having met Mitchell fifteen years ago. Unfortunately, of all the major Star Trek characters, Kirk's back story seems to have the greatest number of internal contradictions. Finnegan established in "Shore Leave."

Starship Enterprise

Starship *Enterprise*, under the command of Captain Robert April, returns from five-year voyage and begins refitting for the next mission. Christopher Pike assumes position of *Enterprise* captain.

Conjecture.

Captain Christopher Pike

2251

Starship *Enterprise*, under command of Captain Christopher Pike, sets out on the ship's second five-year mission to explore the unknown.

Conjecture, see reference to Spock's beginning of service on the Enterprise in 2252.

2252

Spock, still an Academy cadet, begins serving aboard the U.S.S. *Enterprise* under the command of Captain Pike.

Spock

"The Menagerie." Spock said he had served with Pike for 11 years, 4 months. Pike apparently served as Enterprise captain until 2263. This date might also be interpreted as evidence that Pike had commanded two five-year missions of the Enterprise. The notion that Spock might have served aboard the Enterprise while still a cadet is consistent with the implication that Kirk was also apparently a cadet while aboard the Republic ("Court Martial.") It is also possible that part of Spock's service with Pike was aboard some other ship, although this is not consistent with our speculation that Pike had commanded two five-year missions.

Charles Evans, aged 3, is sole survivor of a spaceship crash on planet Thasus. He is cared for by the mysterious, noncorporeal Thasians, which give him extraordinary mental powers in order to insure his survival.

Ruth

"Charlie X." Fourteen years prior to episode (2266).

Kirk is romantically involved with Ruth. Kirk also becomes acquainted with R. M. Merrick, a student who is eventually dropped from the Academy when he fails a psycho-simulator test.

"Shore Leave." Fifteen years prior to episode (2267). (No last name was given for Ruth.) Merrick is from "Bread and Circuses." Date is speculation as these could have happened at any point when Kirk was at the Academy. (See Editors' Note under "Bread and Circuses" regarding Merrick.)

2253

Spock graduates from Starfleet Academy.

Dr. Leonard H.
McCoy

> *Conjecture. Assumes Spock entered the Academy in 2249 (as per "Journey to Babel") and that he completed the standard four-year curriculum. Of course, Spock is a pretty smart guy and may well have graduated in fewer than four years, although no direct evidence exists to suggest this.*

Dr. Leonard McCoy graduates from medical school.

> *Conjecture. Assumes McCoy began college in 2245 and that he completed an eight-year medical program. (See note in Appendix A regarding significant uncertainties in McCoy's back story.)*

2254

James Kirk graduates from Starfleet Academy. He is the only cadet ever to beat the "no-win scenario" of the *Kobayashi Maru* simulation. Kirk is awarded a commendation for original thinking for reprogramming the simulation to make it possible to win.

> *Date is conjecture, assumes Kirk was seventeen when he entered the Academy. "The Drumhead," "Datalore," and "The First Duty" establish Starfleet Academy to be a four-year curriculum. Kobayashi Maru simulation established in Star Trek II: The Wrath of Khan.*

James T.
Kirk

Lieutenant Kirk is assigned duty aboard the Starship *Farragut* under the command of Captain Garrovick.

> *"Obsession." The episode establishes that the Farragut was Kirk's first assignment after his graduation from the Academy. Kirk noted that Garrovick was "my commanding officer from the day I left the Academy."*

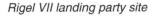

Rigel VII landing party site

U.S.S. *Enterprise*, under the command of Captain Pike, is involved in a violent conflict on planet Rigel VII. Three crew members, including the captain's yeoman, are killed, and seven are injured. Pike later blames the incident on his own carelessness in not anticipating hostilities by the Rigelians.

> *"The Cage." Two weeks prior to the incident on Talos IV.*

"The Cage." (No stardate given in episode.) U.S.S. *Enterprise*, en route to the Vega colony, detects distress call from spaceship S.S. *Columbia*, which records indicate had disappeared near the Talos Star Group some 18 years ago. Investigation leads to discovery of the *Columbia*'s crash site on planet Talos IV, and contact with the planet's indigenous inhabitants. The Talosians attempt to capture Pike in an effort to insure survival of their race, but Pike and the *Enterprise* escape by convincing the Talosians of human unsuitability for captivity.

Captain Christopher Pike faces his
Talosian captors.

> *Thirteen years prior to "The Menagerie," according to Spock's testimony at the court-martial.*

> *Editors' Note: José Tyler tells Dr. Haskins that space travel has become much faster in the eighteen years since the Columbia's crash because "the time barrier has been broken." This might be interpreted as a reference to the development of warp drive, but this would be inconsistent with other dating information that suggests that Zefram Cochrane invented the space*

warp around 2061. (Warp drive clearly had to exist prior to the Columbia's crash because the Columbia and other craft were already operating across considerable interstellar ranges.) We therefore choose to interpret Tyler's line as referring to some significant but unspecified improvement in warp drive technology.

Captain Pike's greeting to the illusory survivors on Talos IV gives his ship's name as the "United Space Ship Enterprise," establishing what "U.S.S." stands for.

Captain Pike and Mr. Spock on the bridge of the U.S.S. Enterprise

Lieutenant Kirk, commanding his first planet survey, befriends Tyree, an inhabitant of a technologically unsophisticated Class-M planet. Years later, Kirk returns to Tyree's planet when the Klingons intervene in a local dispute.

"A Private Little War." Thirteen years prior to episode.

Editors' Note: The episode never establishes the name of Tyree's planet, although a draft of the script suggests that the planet's name may be Neural. Although the episode does not make this clear, Kirk would seem to have been serving aboard the Starship Farragut at this point.

Tyree

2255

Last contact between the reclusive Sheliak Corporate and the United Federation of Planets prior to 2366. The two parties agree to the Treaty of Armens in which the Federation cedes planet Tau Cygna V to the Sheliak. The treaty contains 500,000 words and took 372 Federation legal experts to draft.

"Ensigns of Command." Riker says the Federation and the Sheliak hadn't communicated for 111 years prior to the episode (2366).

2256

U.S.S. Enterprise, still under the command of Captain Christopher Pike, completes Pike's first five-year mission of exploration (the second for the ship, counting Captain April's earlier mission) and begins a year of refit work in spacedock.

Conjecture.

Leonard McCoy ends a romantic relationship with the future Mrs. Nancy Crater.

"The Man Trap." McCoy says, "We walked out of each other's lives ten years ago." (Episode was set in 2266.)

The future Mrs. Nancy Crater

2257

Lieutenant Kirk, still serving aboard the U.S.S. Farragut, (his first assignment after leaving Starfleet Academy) encounters a dangerous "vampire cloud" near planet Tycho IV. When facing the creature, Kirk hesitates for a moment before firing ship's phasers, and afterward feels responsible when the creature causes the death of 200 people, including Farragut captain Garrovick. Years later Garrovick's son serves aboard the Enterprise with Kirk in command.

"Obsession." Eleven years prior to episode (2268).

U.S.S. *Enterprise* embarks on Captain Pike's second five-year mission of exploration (the third for the ship).

Conjecture. The fact that Spock said he'd served with Pike for eleven years (as established in "The Menagerie") seems to support the notion that Pike commanded two five-year missions, with a year's hiatus between them for refit.

Karidian company of actors begins a tour of official installations under sponsorship of the Galactic Cultural Exchange Program. They are recognized for their performances of classic Shakespearean plays.

"Conscience of the King." Nine years prior to episode (2266), according to Enterprise *historical computer banks.*

2261

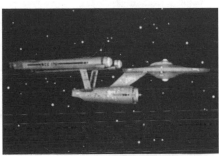

Starship Enterprise

U.S.S. *Enterprise*, under the command of Captain Christopher Pike, completes its second five-year mission of exploration. The ship enters spacedock for a major refit. During this refit, the ship's crew capacity is boosted from 203 to 430.

Conjecture. Reference to increase in crew complement is based on Pike's comment in "The Cage" that suggested the ship's capacity is 203 at that point. During the first season of the original series, Kirk indicated that the ship's crew is about 430.

Exploratory vessel S.S. *Beagle,* a small Class-IV stardrive vessel, crashes on planet 892-IV after having sustained meteor damage. The ship had been performing the first survey of the sector. The crew are captured by the planet's inhabitants and forced to fight as Roman gladiators. The ship's commander, Merrick, survives by becoming a strongman in local politics until 2267, when the U.S.S. *Enterprise* makes contact with the planet.

Beagle *captain*
R.M. Merrick

"Bread and Circuses." Kirk said the Beagle *was missing for six years prior to episode (2267).*

David Marcus born to Carol Marcus and James Kirk. Carol Marcus asks Kirk not to be involved with the boy's upbringing. Kirk does not see his son again until 2285.

Star Trek II: The Wrath of Khan. *Date is conjecture. Assumes David was about 24 years old at the time of* Star Trek II.

*Dr. David Marcus
at age 24*

Robert and Nancy Crater arrive at planet M-113 for archaeological research of the ancient ruins there. Nancy Crater is later killed by the last surviving native of the planet.

"The Man Trap." Spock noted the Craters had arrived five years prior to the episode (2266).

The last message is received from Dr. Roger Korby's archaeological expedition on planet Exo III. Korby's signal describes the discovery of underground caverns. Neither Korby nor his expedition are heard from again, and two subsequent expeditions are unsuccessful in locating them on the planet. Korby, who is known as the Pasteur of archaeological medicine, is recognized for his translation of medical records from the Orion ruins, resulting in a revolution in immunization techniques.

"What Are Little Girls Made Of?" Kirk noted it had been five years since Korby's last message. (Episode set in 2266.)

James Kirk is romantically involved with the future Janet Wallace. The relationship does not work out because of differences in career goals. Janet eventually marries a scientist, Theodore Wallace, a man 26 years her senior.

"The Deadly Years." Janet reminded Kirk it had been "six years, four months, and an odd number of days" since they'd last seen each other.

The future
Janet Wallace

Spock meets botanist Leila Kalomi on Earth. Kalomi is romantically attracted to Spock, but Spock indicates he cannot return the feeling due to his Vulcan heritage.

"This Side of Paradise." Leila reminded Spock that she'd told him of her love six years prior to the episode (2267).

Leila
Kalomi

2263

Spock visits his parents on Vulcan for the last time before the Babel conference on the Coridan admission. The visit is strained because of Sarek's disapproval of Spock's career choice.

"Journey to Babel." Amanda chided Spock for not having visited them for four years prior to the episode (2267).

James Kirk sees Areel Shaw for the last time before Kirk's trial at Starbase 11. The two had been romantically involved.

"Court Martial." Areel said they hadn't seen each other for "four years, seven months, and an odd number of days" prior to the episode (2267).

James Kirk is promoted to captain of the Starship *Enterprise* and meets Christopher Pike, who is promoted to fleet captain.

Conjecture. In "The Menagerie," Kirk said he met Pike once prior to that episode, when the latter was promoted to fleet captain.

Areel
Shaw

Miners Childress, Gossett, and Benton begin work at the lithium mining operation on planet Rigel XII.

"Mudd's Women." Ruth noted the three miners had been there for almost three years. (Episode set in 2266.)

A group of 150 colonists under the leadership of Elias Sandoval leave Earth to settle on planet Omicron Ceti III.

"This Side of Paradise." Kirk noted the Sandoval expedition had settled on the planet three years prior to the episode, and that the trip had taken a year, suggesting they had departed four years prior to the episode (2267).

Starship *Enterprise*

2264

Captain James Kirk, in command of the U.S.S. *Enterprise*, embarks on a historic five-year mission of exploration.

Date is conjecture: Assumes "Where No Man Has Gone Before" took place 13 months and 12 days into the mission, per one conjectural theory for stardates. (The episode was set on stardate 1312.) This system of determining stardates was not adhered to in later episodes, but is at least useful for pegging the start of Kirk's mission in relation to that episode.

Harcourt Fenton Mudd is convicted of purchasing a space vessel with counterfeit currency. He is sentenced to psychiatric treatment and his master's license is revoked, effective stardate 1116.4. Mudd had previously been convicted of smuggling, although that sentence had been suspended.

Harcourt Fenton Mudd

"Mudd's Women." Date is conjecture, but it is apparently prior to "Where No Man Has Gone Before" because the stardate of his license suspension is lower than the stardate in "Where No Man."

The real Nancy Crater is killed by planet M-113's last surviving native. The creature later assumes Nancy's form and lives with Professor Robert Crater, an archaeologist studying M-113.

"The Man Trap." Exact date is conjecture, but Professor Crater noted that Nancy had been killed a year or two prior to the episode (2266).

The Sandoval expedition arrives at planet Omicron Ceti III for colonization. Unfortunately, the planet is later found to have high levels of deadly Berthold rays, threatening the lives of the colonists.

"This Side of Paradise." Kirk noted the colonists had been there for three years prior to the episode (2267).

Elizabeth Dehner

2265

Dr. Elizabeth Dehner, a psychiatrist studying crew reactions in emergency situations, joins the *Enterprise* crew when the ship is at the Aldebaron colony.

Shortly before "Where No Man has Gone Before."

The Enterprise *approaches the barrier.*

"Where No Man Has Gone Before." Stardate 1312.4. The *Enterprise* encounters recorder buoy of the S.S. *Valiant*, which had disappeared near the galaxy's edge two centuries ago. Evidence from the buoy's record tapes suggest the ship was destroyed by her captain. Kirk orders the *Enterprise* to explore beyond the galaxy's rim, where the ship encounters a strange energy barrier, resulting in the deaths of nine personnel. Gary Mitchell, Kirk's friend from his Academy days, is somehow mutated by the barrier, and gains tremendous psychokinetic powers. It is later learned that psychiatrist Elizabeth Dehner had been similarly mutated as well. An attempt to quarantine Mitchell at the Delta Vega mining facility is unsuccessful, and Kirk is forced to kill him to protect the ship. Dehner is also killed in the incident.

Delta Vega lithium cracking station

Date is conjecture: Assumes the episode was six months to a year prior to Star Trek's first season. This is to allow sufficient time to account for the costume and set changes between this pilot episode and the costumes and sets seen in the series.

Editors' Note: The tombstone created by Gary Mitchell for Kirk gives the captain's name as "James R. Kirk." The captain's name would later be changed to "James T. Kirk." Dorothy Fontana notes that Kirk's middle initial changed because Gene Roddenberry simply forgot that this episode had established it as "R," but noted that Gene was also fond of giving his characters the middle name "Tiberius." (Gary Lockwood's character in Roddenberry's series The Lieutenant *was named William Tiberius Rice.)*

This episode (and "Mudd's Women") establishes that the Enterprise *uses "lithium crystals" in its engines, although later episodes changed this to "dilithium crystals." According to Fontana, RAND Corporation physicist (and* Star Trek *technical adviser) Harvey Lynn suggested the change. The reason was that lithium is real, but dilithium is not, thus giving Star Trek's writers more freedom to tell stories without being scientifically wrong. Fontana further suggests that the change might have been a technological upgrade to the ship's engines.*

The Borg destroy Guinan's home planet. A small number of Guinan's people manage to survive by spreading themselves across the galaxy.

"Q Who?" One hundred years prior to the episode (2365).

Guinan

Planet Ingraham B is attacked by the same parasite creatures that later decimated the population of planet Deneva.

"Operation: Annihilate!" Two years prior to the episode (2267).

2266

Dr. Leonard H. McCoy assigned to duty aboard the U.S.S. *Enterprise* as ship's surgeon. He replaces Dr. Mark Piper.

McCoy

Date is conjecture: He was apparently assigned after "Where No Man Has Gone Before," in which Dr. Piper was ship's surgeon, but before "The Corbomite Maneuver," which marked McCoy's first appearance.

Dr. Simon Van Gelder is assigned as associate director of the Tantalus V penal colony. He serves on the staff of colony director Tristan Adams.

"Dagger of the Mind." Spock's computer research indicated Van Gelder had been assigned six months prior to the episode

Lieutenant Hikaru Sulu accepts a transfer from staff physicist to helm officer aboard the U.S.S. *Enterprise.*

Sulu

Date is conjecture: He was apparently transferred after "Where No Man Has Gone Before," but before "The Corbomite Maneuver."

The Starship *Enterprise* begins routine star mapping mission.

Three days prior to "The Corbomite Maneuver."

5.1 STAR TREK: THE ORIGINAL SERIES — YEAR 1

"...to boldly go where no man has gone before."

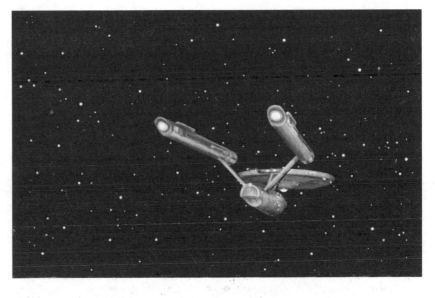

Assumes the original Star Trek *television series was set 300 years after the first air date of the show (September, 1966).*

Balok's false image

"The Corbomite Maneuver." Stardate 1512.2. The U.S.S. *Enterprise*, on a routine star-mapping mission, makes first contact with the spaceship *Fesarius* of the First Federation. Although *Fesarius* commander Balok is initially wary of the *Enterprise*, presenting a false image, he eventually accepts the assurances of good intentions by *Enterprise* personnel after Kirk offers assistance when Balok's ship appears to be disabled. Kirk assigns Lieutenant Bailey to cultural exchange duty aboard the *Fesarius*.

A number of women on planet Rigel IV are brutally murdered by an unknown assailant, popularly known as *Kesla*. The killer is later discovered to be the same energy entity responsible for similar murders a year later on planet Argelius II. The entity is believed to have traveled in the body of Hengist, a native of Rigel IV, hired by the Argelian government as an administrator.

"Wolf in the Fold." Computer records indicated the killings had taken place one year prior to the episode (2267).

Harcourt Fenton Mudd

"Mudd's Women." Stardate 1329.8. The *Enterprise* attempts to rescue a small Class-J cargo ship that has strayed too close to an asteroid belt. The attempt fails, although the crew of the vessel is successfully beamed aboard the *Enterprise* before the smaller ship is destroyed. In the rescue attempt, however, the *Enterprise* lithium crystal circuits are damaged, nearly crippling the ship. The captain of the transport, Harcourt Fenton Mudd, is later coerced into assisting Kirk in dealing with lithium miners on Rigel XII to provide crystals to save the *Enterprise* from a decaying orbit.

Three women traveling with Mudd, who had apparently been recruited by Mudd as wives for settlers on planet Ophiucus III, elect instead to remain with the lithium miners on Rigel XII.

Harcourt Fenton Mudd is turned over to Federation authorities for illegal operation of transport vessel.

Just after "Mudd's Women."

"The Enemy Within." Stardate 1672.1. The U.S.S. *Enterprise* on routine geological survey to planet Alfa 177. Magnetic ore contamination from landing party site causes a transporter malfunction, resulting in a partial replication of Captain Kirk. The duplication is nearly perfect, but each copy has only part of the personality traits of the original, thereby threatening the survival of both copies. Science Officer Spock and Engineer Scott successfully modify the transporter to recombine Kirk to his original form.

Incompletely duplicated replica of Captain Kirk, embodying aggressive personality traits

Remaining members of the *Enterprise* landing party are trapped on the surface of Alfa 177 until the repair of the transporter, resulting in severe frostbite and exposure to those personnel. Upon return to the *Enterprise* all landing party members are treated by medical personnel and are given excellent prognoses for a full recovery.

Editors' Note: This episode marks the invention of the Vulcan nerve pinch, used to neatly (and nonviolently) render the "evil" Kirk unconscious. Star Trek production staffers (and several scripts) would later refer to the trick as FSNP, the "Famous Spock Nerve Pinch." To the question of why Spock couldn't have sent a shuttlecraft down to the planet surface after the transporter broke, the answer is that at this relatively early point in the series the show didn't yet have a shuttlecraft.

"The Man Trap." Stardate 1513.1. The U.S.S. *Enterprise* is assigned to perform routine health examinations of archaeological personnel at planet M-113. An investigation is conducted when three members of the *Enterprise* crew are discovered dead on the planet, killed under unknown circumstances. It is learned that the killer is the last specimen of a species indigenous to M-113. The creature, which is later found to possess an unusual hypnotic ability to cause its prey to see it as someone else, is also discovered to live on sodium chloride that it extracts from its victims' bodies. Two additional casualties are discovered on board the *Enterprise*, including archaeologist Robert Crater, before the creature is killed while it is attempting to attack Captain Kirk.

The last M-113 creature

Editors' Note: Spock tells Uhura that his home planet of Vulcan has no moon, although we see several moons around that planet in Star Trek: The Motion Picture. *Curiously, none of these satellites were seen when the Starships* Enterprise *visited that planet in "Amok Time" or "Sarek." (It has been suggested that the "moons" seen in* Trek I *may have been other planets whose orbits pass very near to Vulcan.) "The Man Trap" is also the source of the fannish blessing, "May the Great Bird of the Galaxy bless your planet," spoken by Sulu, which was itself derived from* Star Trek *associate producer Bob Justman's gag reference to producer Gene Roddenberry.*

Discovery of frozen members of the Psi 2000 science team

Dr. McCoy spills a small amount of acid on a table in his medical laboratory, scarring the table. A year later he notices an identical scar on the same table on the alternate universe version of the *Enterprise*.

"Mirror, Mirror." McCoy noted that he'd spilled acid there a year ago.

"The Naked Time." Stardate 1704.2. U.S.S. *Enterprise* assigned to pick up science team from planet Psi 2000. Landing party discovers all researchers to be dead under unusual circumstances, later determined to have been

Sulu under influence of Psi 2000 virus

caused by an alien virus. The landing party accidentally brings back the virus to the ship, infecting most of the crew, and threatening the *Enterprise* when the virus causes personnel to lose emotional control. Among those most seriously affected is Lieutenant Kevin Riley, who commandeers the ship's engine room. McCoy develops a serum that enables personnel to regain emotional stability. An emergency restart of ship's engines using a theoretical intermix formula results in the accidental regression of the *Enterprise* and all ship's personnel through some 71 hours into the past.

Editors' Note: This episode was originally planned to be the first part of a two-part story. According to Dorothy Fontana, episode writer John D. F. Black left the series without doing the second part, so Fontana eventually did that story as a separate episode, "Tomorrow Is Yesterday." "The Naked Time" does not clearly describe the nature of the Psi 2000 infection, but it is established to be a virus when the same malady strikes the crew of the Tsiolkovsky *and the* Enterprise-D *in "The Naked Now." This episode establishes the* Enterprise *warp drive to be powered by antimatter reactions. Prior to this point, the motive power of the ship's engines was not specifically described.*

Charles Evans is rescued from the planet Thasus by the crew of the science probe vessel *Antares*, under the command of Captain Ramart. Evans, a 17-year-old human boy, is the only survivor of a spaceship crash on Thasus some 14 years ago.

Prior to "Charlie X."

Charles Evans

"Charlie X." Stardate 1533.6. First contact with mythical Thasians. U.S.S. *Enterprise* assigned to rendezvous with the spaceship *Antares* to transport the orphaned Charles Evans to his nearest living relatives on Colony 5. Evans is found to exhibit unusual telekinetic powers, evidence of the existence of the Thasians, previously believed to be purely mythical. Evans eventually returns to Thasus, where his powers, given to him to aid his survival, would not be a threat as they would be in normal human society. Evans is believed to have been responsible for the destruction of the science vessel *Antares* shortly after its rendezvous with the *Enterprise*.

Editors' Note: The term "Starfleet Command" had not yet been decided on when this episode was filmed. In these early episodes, various terms were used to describe the operating authority for the Enterprise, *including "United Earth Space Probe Agency." In this episode Kirk refers to this as UESPA Headquarters, which he pronounces as "you-spah."*

Romulan Bird-of-Prey spacecraft

"Balance of Terror." Stardate 1709.2. Neutral Zone outposts 2 through 4 are reported destroyed in apparent Romulan attack. The *Enterprise* responds, determining the Romulan action to be a measure of Federation resolve, untested by the Romulans since the establishment of the Neutral Zone a century ago. The Romulan spacecraft, while capable of sublight speeds only, is discovered to be equipped with a cloaking device that can render a ship nearly invisible to sensors, as well as a powerful new plasma energy weapon used to destroy the Neutral Zone outposts. The *Enterprise*, acting in direct violation of Starfleet orders, enters the Neutral Zone under the authority of Captain Kirk and successfully destroys the Romulan ship, thereby repelling a potential Romulan incursion.

The sole casualty aboard the *Enterprise* is phaser specialist Robert Tomlinson. He is survived by his fiancée, Angela. Their wedding ceremony had been in progress when interrupted by news of the Romulan attack.

Romulan commander

An accident aboard an old Class-J starship causes the death of several Starfleet cadets. The toll would have been higher if not for Fleet Captain Christopher Pike, who dragged several cadets to safety. Pike is seriously injured in the incident and is later confined to a wheelchair due to severe delta-ray exposure.

Captain Pike, wheelchair-bound following the accident

"The Menagerie, Part I." Exact date is conjecture, but Commodore Mendez describes the accident as having happened "months" before the episode.

"What Are Little Girls Made Of?" Stardate 2712.4. U.S.S. *Enterprise* at planet Exo III on a search mission for missing scientist Dr. Roger Korby, fiancé of *Enterprise* nurse Christine Chapel. Korby is discovered alive, but it is learned he had imprinted his personality into an android body, using ancient alien technology he had discovered on the planet. Also transferred to an android body is Korby's assistant, Dr. Brown. Korby ultimately discovers that the process somehow diminishes his human emotions, and he destroys himself.

Dr. Roger Korby

Nurse Christine Chapel elects to remain on board the *Enterprise*. Chapel had given up a promising career in bioresearch to sign aboard a starship in the hopes of someday finding her lost fiancé.

Editors' Note: This episode marks the first appearance of Christine Chapel, played by Majel Barrett, the future Mrs. Gene Roddenberry. Barrett had previously portrayed the mysterious "Number One," second in command of the Enterprise *in the pilot episode, "The Cage." Barrett also lent her voice to the* Enterprise *computer in both the original* Star Trek *series as well as in* Star Trek: The Next Generation, *and also played Lwaxana Troi.*

"Dagger of the Mind." Stardate 2715.1. The *Enterprise,* on a resupply mission to Tantalus V penal colony, accidentally takes on an inmate attempting to escape. The inmate is later discovered to be Dr. Simon Van Gelder, associate director of the rehab colony. Investigation by Kirk and psychiatrist Helen Noel reveals Van Gelder to be suffering from adverse effects of an experimental neural neutralizer device developed by colony director Dr. Tristan Adams. The device, intended for treatment of violent patients, had induced temporary mental disorders in Van Gelder. The device is destroyed, and Van Gelder is apparently promoted to colony director. Dr. Adams is reported to have died as a result of overexposure to the neural neutralizer.

Spock uses Vulcan mind-meld to obtain information from Dr. Van Gelder.

Editors' Note: This episode is the first time we've seen Spock perform the Vulcan mind-meld.

The U.S.S. *Enterprise*, on a star-charting mission, reports finding seven planets in star system L-370.

"The Doomsday Machine." Exact date is conjecture, but Spock said they'd charted seven planets in the system a year prior to the episode.

"Miri." Stardate 2713.5. The *Enterprise* responds to a distress call, discovered to be from a Class-M planet virtually identical to Earth. Indigenous humanoid inhabitants determined to be nearly all dead, found to be victims of a disastrous research project whose goal, ironically, was to prolong life. Investigation reveals the only survivors are a group of children, who are discovered to be aging at a rate equivalent to one month for every century of real time. A native child, a young woman named Miri, provides information from which *Enterprise* personnel determine that these children die upon reaching puberty. The *Enterprise* landing party, infected with the same disease, is quarantined on planet surface until a viable antitoxin can

Miri

be developed by Dr. Leonard McCoy.

Federation authorities dispatch a sociological team to help the children on Miri's planet.

Just after "Miri."

Klingon operatives attempt to influence local politics on Tyree's planet by providing firearms to the technologically unsophisticated inhabitants.

"A Private Little War." Exact date is conjecture, but Tyree noted that the "firesticks" had appeared nearly a year before the episode.

Enterprise summoned by scientist Dr. Thomas Leighton to Planet Q to investigate reports of a new synthetic food process. Because of the hope that this development will end the threat of famine at the Earth colony on planet Cygnia Minor, Kirk orders the *Enterprise* to divert three light-years off course to meet with Leighton.

Just prior to "The Conscience of the King."

*Lenore and Anton Karidian
face Captain James Kirk.*

"The Conscience of the King." Stardate 2817.6. Kirk learns that Dr. Thomas Leighton's report was an effort to inform Kirk covertly of a suspicion that actor Anton Karidian, currently performing on Planet Q, is in fact the infamous Kodos the Executioner. These allegations are eventually borne out, but not before Karidian's daughter is found to be responsible for a series of murders, an attempt to eliminate all remaining witnesses of Karidian's crimes 20 years ago. Among Lenore Karidian's victims is Dr. Thomas Leighton, killed shortly after he revealed his suspicions to Kirk. Attempts are also made against James Kirk and Kevin Riley, the last surviving eyewitnesses to Kodos's killings.

The people of planet Acamar III, having endured generations of clan wars, finally establish peace for nearly all concerned. A significant exception is the outcast nomadic Gatherers, who continue to be a source of violence for a century, raiding many nearby planets and star systems.

"The Vengeance Factor." Sovereign Marouk said her people have had peace for a century prior to the episode (2366).

A space vessel carrying visitors from planet Ingraham B to planet Deneva carries a deadly parasitic life-form that has already caused mass insanity on Ingraham B over a year ago.

"Operation: Annihilate!" Aurelan Kirk noted the parasites had arrived eight months prior to the episode.

A serious plague threatens the inhabitants of the New Paris colonies. The U.S.S. *Enterprise* is assigned to transport emergency medical supplies to planet Makus III for transfer to New Paris under the direction of Galactic High Commissioner Ferris.

Shuttlecraft Galileo

Prior to "The Galileo Seven."

2267

"The Galileo Seven." Stardate 2821.5. The *Enterprise* is on an emergency medical supply mission to Makus III. Mission is delayed when shuttlecraft

Galileo is lost investigating Murasaki 312, a quasar-like phenomenon. *Galileo*, under command of Science Officer Spock, is later discovered to have crash-landed on planet Taurus II, but attains a suborbital trajectory sufficient for detection by *Enterprise* sensors before criticality of New Paris mission forces ship to leave the system. *Galileo* crew members Latimer and Gaetano are reported killed by indigenous life-forms on Taurus II.

The U.S.S. *Enterprise* proceeds at warp speed to Makus III to deliver emergency medical supplies for the New Paris colonies.

Just after "The Galileo Seven."

Stardate 2945.7. The Starship *Enterprise* encounters ion storm, Records Officer Benjamin Finney is reported killed when sensor pod is ejected.

Just prior to "Court Martial."

"Court Martial." Stardate 2947.3. The *Enterprise* makes an unscheduled layover at Starbase 11 for repairs from ion storm. Kirk is accused of negligent homicide in the death of Ben Finney, but court-martial investigation reveals Finney to be still alive. Kirk, who becomes the first starship captain to stand trial, is exonerated of all charges when it is revealed that Finney had tampered with *Enterprise* computer records. Kirk's case is prosecuted by Areel Shaw, with Samuel T. Cogley serving for the defense and Commodore Stone presiding. The *Enterprise* departs Starbase 11.

Editors' Note: The term "Starfleet Command" is used for the first time in "Court Martial," during the computer records of Kirk, Spock, and McCoy. Kirk refers to his former assignment, the U.S.S. Republic, as being a "United Star Ship," offering a second possible meaning to the letters "U.S.S." Kirk repeats the term United Star Ship in "Squire of Gothos," as well. (Captain Pike, in "The Cage," said the Enterprise *was a United Space Ship.)*

Spock receives a promotion from lieutenant commander to the rank of full commander.

His rank is given as lieutenant commander in "Court Martial," but he's a full commander in "The Menagerie."

U.S.S. *Enterprise* First Officer Spock reports orders for the ship to return to Starbase 11, although no computer record is found of the message.

Just prior to "The Menagerie, Part I."

"The Menagerie, Part I." Stardate 3012.4. The *Enterprise* arrives at Starbase 11, but investigation by Commodore Mendez fails to reveal source of orders to return to starbase. Further investigation shows the orders to have been falsified by Commander Spock, who kidnaps Fleet Captain Pike, then commandeers the *Enterprise* to planet Talos IV in violation of General Order 7, which prohibits such contact. Pike had been seriously injured several months prior in an accident aboard a training vessel. Kirk and Mendez, who had been left behind at Starbase 11 when the *Enterprise* departed, are successful in pursuing the ship aboard a shuttlecraft. Once Kirk and Mendez are aboard the *Enterprise*, Spock submits himself for arrest, and Mendez orders a general court-martial convened against Spock.

"The Menagerie, Part II." Stardate 3013.1. The *Enterprise*, en route to Talos IV, is site of court-martial proceedings against Commander Spock on charges of commandeering the *Enterprise*, sabotage, abduction of Captain Pike, and attempted violation of General Order 7. All charges are dropped

Starbase 11

Spock

Spock uses computer voice synthesis to falsify orders for the *Enterprise*.

Court-martial of Spock

when it is determined that Spock had been acting on behalf of the Talosians in the best interest of Captain Pike. Captain Kirk, under special authority from Starfleet Command, permits Captain Pike to accept an offer from the Talosians to live the remainder of his life on their planet, where he need not suffer the infirmities of his injured body.

A fictional character created by the amusement park planet

"Shore Leave." Stardate 3025.3. The U.S.S. *Enterprise* surveys a newly discovered planet in the Omicron Delta region for possible shore leave. Initial studies suggest a near-idyllic environment, but later reports indicate some highly unusual phenomena. The ship is briefly incapacitated due to crew unfamiliarity with the planet's technology, which is determined to have been built as a vast amusement park.

Enterprise crew personnel (except for Spock) enjoy R&R on the "amusement park planet."

Just after "Shore Leave."

U.S.S. *Enterprise* on resupply mission to colony on planet Beta VI.

Just prior to "The Squire of Gothos."

Trelane, the Squire of Gothos

"The Squire of Gothos." Stardate 2124.5. U.S.S. *Enterprise* bridge personnel are abducted by an unknown alien agency to Gothos, a newly discovered "rogue planet" in a star desert. Investigation reveals the alien to be an entity named Trelane, who is learned to be a child member of an extremely advanced and powerful race who possess the ability to create and manipulate planets.

Editors' Note: Trelane indicates that he has observed Earth history of nine centuries ago, but describes events in the early nineteenth century. If Trelane is correct, then this episode (and Star Trek's first season) would be set in the early twenty-eighth century. Since this is inconsistent with the preponderance of other dating information, we assume that it is an error, perhaps another example of Trelane's fallibility and youth.

A Federation outpost on planet Cestus III is destroyed by a Gorn spacecraft. The Gorn ship reportedly approached at sublight speeds along standard Federation approach lanes before knocking out the outpost's phaser batteries with their first salvo.

One day prior to "Arena." This was apparently the first contact between the Gorns and the Federation.

Commodore Travers of Cestus III base apparently invites Captain Kirk and senior *Enterprise* staff to dinner. It is not discovered until later that the message had been falsified by the Gorns, and that the Cestus III outpost had already been destroyed at the time the messages were sent.

Just prior to "Arena."

Gorn

"Arena" Stardate 3045.6. The U.S.S. *Enterprise* arrives at planet Cestus III, discovering the base destroyed by an apparently unprovoked Gorn attack. The *Enterprise* pursues the attacking vessel, but chase is interrupted by intervention and first contact with the Metrons. The Enterprise crew learns that Gorn hostilities may have been due to Federation ignorance of boundaries of Gorn space. Ultimately, the Metrons decline to establish diplomatic relations with the Federation.

Editors' Note: This episode establishes for the first time that warp factor six

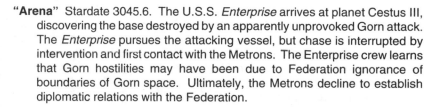

is the normal maximum cruising speed of the Enterprise, *and that things get really hairy when you reach warp eight. This is also the first time it is shown that the transporter can't work when shields are in place.*

The Starship *Enterprise* returns to Cestus III.

After "Arena."

Federation miners on planet Janus VI open a new underground level in search of mineral pergium deposits.

"The Devil in the Dark." Vanderberg noted that their troubles began about three months before the episode, when the new level was opened.

"The Alternative Factor." Stardate 3087.6. The U.S.S. *Enterprise* detects a violent time/space discontinuity while surveying an uncharted planet. Investigation suggests the time/space phenomenon was triggered by Lazarus, a being from our universe, and his mentally unstable counterpart from a parallel continuum composed of antimatter. Their conflict threatens the existence of both universes, but the Lazarus from the alternate universe succeeds in sealing himself and his counterpart in an isolated time pocket.

Lazarus

The U.S.S. *Enterprise* puts in for general repair and maintenance at Cygnet XIV. The technicians at Cygnet XIV, a society dominated by women, reportedly felt the *Enterprise* computer lacked character, and gave it a stereotypically female personality.

"Tomorrow Is Yesterday." Date is conjecture, but Kirk explained to Captain Christopher about the repair stopover at Cygnet XIV. We speculate that it was after "The Alternative Factor" because the giggling computer didn't seem to be a problem in that episode. Dorothy Fontana insists the computer wasn't so much giggling as it was sexually teasing the good captain.

U.S.S. *Enterprise* heads toward Starbase 9, but suffers near collision with a black hole. Full reverse warp power is successful in pulling the ship away, but the resulting whiplash effect propels the *Enterprise* across space and backward in time.

Just prior to "Tomorrow Is Yesterday."

The Enterprise *in Earth's upper atmosphere*

"Tomorrow Is Yesterday." Stardate 3113.2. The *Enterprise* is accidentally thrown back in time to 1969 after near collision with black hole, where the starship's appearance results in potential disruption of Earth history. This potential disruption is in the form of U.S. Air Force Captain John Christopher, accidentally taken aboard the *Enterprise* when the ship is sighted as a UFO in Earth's atmosphere. Research suggests Christopher's inadvertent abduction would prevent him from fathering a child who, according to records, will lead the first successful Earth-Saturn probe. Kirk leads a landing party to Earth's surface to avoid altering history before the *Enterprise* can employ the light-speed breakaway factor to return to present day.

Editors' Note: When Air Force Captain Fellini threatens to lock Kirk up "for two hundred years," Kirk wryly responds, "That ought to be just about right." If taken literally, this conflicts with the basic assumption that the original Star Trek series is set 300 years in the future. One might, on the other hand, grant Kirk a bit of poetic licence in what seemed to be a pretty tough situation. (See also the Editors' Note after "Space Seed.")

Kirk's line to Captain Christopher establishes that there were only twelve

U.S. Air Force
Captain John
Christopher

Constitution *class starships in the Starfleet at this point. Despite the fact that the term "Starfleet Command" had been established several episodes earlier, the operating authority for the* Enterprise *is described in this episode as being either Starfleet Control (heard in a Starfleet comm voice over the radio) or the United Earth Space Probe Agency (mentioned by Kirk to Christopher). See also the Editors' Note following "The Naked Time."*

Lawgivers enforce the will of Landru

"Return of the Archons." Stardate 3156.2. The U.S.S. *Enterprise* investigates the loss of the starship *Archon*, which disappeared near planet Beta III in 2167. Landing party discovers the *Archon* had been destroyed by a sophisticated computer that acts to protect and provide for the planet's inhabitants. The self-aware computer system, known as "Landru" to the planet's inhabitants, self-destructs when it realizes it has become harmful to the society it was designed to protect.

Enterprise sociologist Lindstrom and a team of experts remain on planet Beta III to help the native inhabitants, now free of Landru's control, guide their culture back to a more normal form.

After "Return of the Archons."

The *Enterprise* heads for star cluster NGC 321 under orders from Federation Ambassador Robert Fox. Thousands of Federation lives have been lost in the region over the past twenty years, and it is hoped that a treaty port can be established at planet Eminiar VII to help avoid future loss of life.

Just prior to "A Taste of Armageddon."

Capital city on Eminiar VII

Eminiar official Anan Seven

"A Taste of Armageddon." Stardate 3192.1. The U.S.S. *Enterprise* is warned to remain away from planet Eminiar VII, where the Starship *Valiant* had disappeared in 2217. Despite a Code 710 forbidding contact, Ambassador Fox orders the *Enterprise* to make contact with the local planetary government. The ship's crew is declared a casualty in a computerized war with neighboring planet Vendikar, according to Eminiar official Anan Seven. Kirk, acting to protect his ship, causes the war agreement to be abrogated, resulting in both sides suing for peace rather than facing actual armed combat.

"Space Seed." Stardate 3141.9. The Starship *Enterprise* detects a distress signal from old DY-100 interplanetary space vehicle, adrift near the Mutara sector. Investigation determines the craft to be the S.S. *Botany Bay*, a sleeper ship carrying refugees from Earth's Eugenics Wars.

Khan Noonien Singh

One surviving passenger on the ship is identified as Khan Noonien Singh, former dictator of one-quarter of planet Earth. Captain Kirk renders an administrative ruling permitting Khan and his shipmates to settle on planet Ceti Alpha V. Also choosing to settle on Ceti Alpha V is *Enterprise* historian Marla McGivers, charged with acting improperly in rendering aid to Khan during an unsuccessful bid to take control of the ship.

Editors' Note: There is a possible inconsistency in Kirk's mention to Khan that the Botany Bay *had been in transit for about two centuries. Given a 1996 launch, this would put the episode at about 2196, instead of 2266. One might rationalize that Kirk was not giving an exact figure, or that he was making a deliberate effort to avoid giving Khan accurate information. It is likely that the producers of the original* Star Trek *series had not yet tied down a specific date for the* Enterprise*'s adventures at this relatively early point in the show's production. Another point: If the first season of the original* Star Trek *series was indeed two hundred years in the future, it would mean that the S.S.* Valiant *(from "Where No Man Has Gone Before"),* *which was lost 200 years prior to the episode, would have been launched around 1965. The notion that the* Botany Bay *was found near the Mutara Sector is, of course, purely based on circumstantial evidence from* Star Trek II: The Wrath of Khan.

An inconsistency is the fact that the character of Chekov was not yet part of the Star Trek *cast when "Space Seed" was filmed, although Khan claimed to remember him in* Star Trek II. *Writer Ron Moore speculates that Kirk may have been breaking the rules in releasing Khan, and that he therefore never told Starfleet about the settlement on Ceti Alpha V. This could explain why the* Reliant*'s crew knew nothing about Khan.*

"This Side of Paradise." Stardate 3417.3. The U.S.S. *Enterprise* investigates the Omicron Ceti III colony, believed to be seriously endangered by prolonged exposure to lethal Berthold rays. Medical tests show all colonists to be in perfect health, a phenomenon later found to be due to the effects of a symbiotic alien spore which also protected the colonists from the Berthold rays. The spores also had unusual psychological effects upon their hosts. *Enterprise* personnel are also affected by these spores, but exposure to intense subsonic energy is found to nullify their effects.

Colony leader Elias Sandoval

Fifty mining personnel on planet Janus VI are killed by a mysterious subterranean entity. The U.S.S. *Enterprise* is summoned by colony administrator Vanderberg to help investigate the deaths.

Prior to "The Devil in the Dark."

"The Devil in the Dark." Stardate 3196.1. The U.S.S. *Enterprise* arrives at Janus VI pergium mining colony to probe mysterious deaths. Investigation determines the deaths to have been caused by a silicon-based indigenous life-form known as a Horta. Further investigation reveals the Horta to be intelligent and the killings to have occurred in self-defense after miners inadvertently damaged the Horta's underground egg chamber when opening a new level three months ago. Peaceful relations are established with the newly discovered life-form.

Janus VI pergium processing facility

Negotiations with the Klingon Empire over disputed areas of space are reported in danger of breaking down. Starfleet Command anticipates a possible surprise attack by the Klingons, who have just issued an ultimatum to withdraw from disputed areas. Starfleet learns the Klingons have invaded the planet Organia, and orders the *Enterprise* to intervene.

Prior to "Errand of Mercy," according to Kirk.

Editors' Note: This back story was also alluded to in Star Trek VI: The Undiscovered Country, *which suggested that hostilities with the Klingons had extended back as far as 2223, 70 years prior to that film and in "Day of the Dove" which together suggest that first contact with the Klingons had taken place in 2218.*

"Errand of Mercy." Stardate 3198.4. The Starship *Enterprise* is assigned to prevent an anticipated Klingon incursion at Organia, a planet believed to be inhabited by an agrarian humanoid culture of relatively low technical sophistication. This incursion becomes the focal point of the long-simmering dispute between the Federation and the Klingon Empire, threatening to erupt into interstellar war.

Klingon Commander Kor, military governor of planet Organia

Local planetary government declines offer of Starfleet assistance, at which time the true noncorporeal form of the Organians is discovered. The immensely powerful Organians announce the imposition the Organian

Peace Treaty on both the Klingons and the Federation, predicting that the two adversaries would become friends.

Editors' Note: This episode marks the first appearance of the Klingons in Star Trek. It is interesting to note how the Klingons evolved over the years from being relatively simplistic villains into a complex, aggressive, yet highly honorable and tradition-bound society. Similarly, it is interesting to note how the look of the Klingons continually evolved as makeup and costuming techniques (and budgets) improved over the years. Dorothy Fontana tells us that the Klingons were used more often than the Romulans in the original series because their makeup was simpler, and therefore less expensive. Fontana notes that she felt the Romulans offered more interesting elements as adversaries, but that the tightly budgeted show just couldn't afford all those pointed ears!

The Guardian of Forever

Kirk and social worker Edith Keeler

"The City on the Edge of Forever." (No stardate given in episode.) The U.S.S. *Enterprise* investigates a time/space distortion phenomena, later discovered to be a time portal, an artifact of an ancient dead civilization. While treating helmsman Sulu for injuries suffered during a shipboard mishap, ship's surgeon Leonard McCoy is accidentally injected with an overdose of cordrazine. Suffering from the resulting paranoid delusions, McCoy flees through the time portal, effecting disastrous changes in Earth's history. Kirk and Spock follow in an attempt to undo the damage. While searching for McCoy in the past, Kirk falls in love with a social worker named Edith Keeler. Although Kirk and Spock are ultimately successful in restoring the time continuum, the mission is made infinitely more difficult when Kirk learns that to repair the damage, he must permit the death of Keeler.

"Operation: Annihilate!" Stardate 3287.2. The Starship *Enterprise* makes an unsuccessful attempt to save the pilot of a small spacecraft on a course directly into the sun of the planet Deneva. Further investigation reveals that the entire population of the Deneva colony (approximately 1,000,000 individuals) had been infected by a parasite that dominates its host through control of the nervous system.

Neural parasite creature undergoing analysis in Enterprise *science lab*

Among the victims are Kirk's brother, George Samuel Kirk, and his sister-in-law, Aurelan Kirk. They are survived by their son Peter Kirk.

This same parasite, which was apparently of extragalactic origin, was also believed responsible for planetwide infestations in the Beta Portalan system, on planet Lavinius V, and on Ingraham B. McCoy develops a means of eradicating the parasites by exposing them to high levels of ultraviolet radiation. Planetwide treatment of Deneva is effected through the use of 210 ultraviolet satellites placed into orbit around the planet.

Editors' Note: In "What Are Little Girls Made Of?" James Kirk says his brother Sam has three sons. This seems to suggest that Sam has two other surviving sons besides Peter. That episode also indicated that Sam had wanted to transfer to the Earth Colony Two research station. Since Sam was apparently older than James, these other two sons may have been old enough to have been away at college, or pursuing careers of their own. The reason why Sam Kirk's body bears such a family resemblance to his brother is that the part was "played" by William Shatner!

5.2 STAR TREK: THE ORIGINAL SERIES — YEAR 2

Diplomatic reception preceeding the Babel conference of 2267

"Catspaw." Stardate 3018.2. The U.S.S. *Enterprise* explores planet Pyris VII, making first contact with entities of unknown origin. These aliens are found to possess technology permitting transmutation of matter.

The *Enterprise* is assigned to treat Assistant Federation Commissioner Nancy Hedford for Sakuro's disease. An *Enterprise* shuttlecraft is dispatched to pick up Commissioner Hedford from Epsilon Canaris III for transport to the ship. Hedford had been assigned to Epsilon Canaris III to prevent a war.

Just prior to "Metamorphosis."

"Metamorphosis." Stardate 3219.8. The Shuttlecraft *Galileo*, carrying Kirk, Spock, McCoy, and Commissioner Hedford, loses control and makes an emergency landing on a planetoid in the Gamma Canaris region. The shuttlecraft is successfully recovered, along with the missing *Enterprise* personnel, but the terminally ill Commissioner Hedford chooses to remain behind and is presumed to have died.

Editors' Note: In the episode Kirk and company meet Zefram Cochrane and his mysterious friend, the Companion, but later promise not to reveal Cochrane's whereabouts. We therefore assume that historical records based on Kirk's logs would not include any mention of Cochrane, Hedford's recovery, or the Companion on the planetoid.

"Friday's Child." Stardate 3497.2. The U.S.S. *Enterprise* is assigned to negotiate a mining treaty with inhabitants of planet Capella IV. Also bidding for rights is a Klingon agent. Negotiations are complicated by local power struggle, resulting in selection of a new leader, whose regent agrees to a treaty with the Federation. The new leader, an infant chosen according to Capellan law, is named Leonard James Akaar, in recognition of the assistance of Leonard McCoy and James Kirk in maintaining Capellan independence.

Unknown alien creatures discovered on planet Pyris VII

Commissioner Nancy Hedford

Apollo

"Who Mourns for Adonais?" Stardate 3468.1. The *Enterprise*, collecting data on planets in the Beta Geminorum system, discovers a previously unknown life-form near planet Pollux IV. This life-form, identifying itself as Apollo, was apparently the last of a group of entities that resided on ancient Earth, and claimed to be the basis of the Greeks' myths of the gods.

Spock, under the influence of *pon farr,* the Vulcan mating drive, ceases eating and becomes severely withdrawn. Dr. McCoy later examines Spock and expresses the opinion that Spock must return to his home world within a week or die.

Three days prior to "Amok Time."

Spock with traditional Vulcan Lirpa weapon

"Amok Time." Stardate 3372.7. The U.S.S. *Enterprise* is on a diplomatic mission to planet Altair VI. Kirk, acting against Starfleet orders, diverts the ship instead to planet Vulcan so that Science Officer Spock may return to his native world to fulfill the normal Vulcan seven-year mating cycle.

On Vulcan, T'Pring, Spock's betrothed, demands a *Koon-ut-kal-if-fee* challenge for the right of marriage. T'Pring later chooses instead to marry Stonn, thus freeing Spock.

Commodore Matt Decker

The U.S.S. *Enterprise* proceeds to planet Altair VI on its diplomatic mission, albeit a bit late. The mission entails participation in a presidential inauguration ceremony, expected to stabilize the entire Altair system after a long interplanetary conflict.

Just after "Amok Time."

Stardate 4202.1. The Starship *Constellation*, under the command of Commodore Matt Decker, encounters several destroyed solar systems, presumably including system L-370. Science officer Masada reports the fourth planet of system L-374 seems to be breaking up, but heavy subspace interference prevents notification of Starfleet Command.

Prior to "The Doomsday Machine."

The Starship *Constellation* is nearly destroyed by an automated weapon of unknown origin. In an effort to save his crew, Commodore Matt Decker transports the ship's company to the third planet of system L-374, but all are subsequently killed when the robot weapon destroys that world as well.

Derelict U.S.S. Constellation

Just prior to "The Doomsday Machine."

"The Doomsday Machine." (No stardate given.) The U.S.S. *Enterprise*, responding to a distress call from Starship *Constellation*, discovers widespread destruction in solar systems L-370, L-374, and other systems in the sector. The *Constellation* is discovered to be derelict, apparently attacked by an immensely powerful force. Commodore Matt Decker, in command of the *Constellation*, is found to be the sole surviving crew member. Decker reports his findings on the nature of the automated planet killer, theorizing that it is of ancient extragalactic origin. Tactical projections suggest that if unchecked, this device will pass through the most densely populated portion of the galaxy near the Rigel colonies. In an effort to prevent this, Decker pilots a shuttlecraft on a suicide mission into the "doomsday machine." Decker is unsuccessful, but data from his attempt are used to conduct a second effort, using the more powerful reactors from the derelict *Constellation*. The second attempt is successful, resulting in the destruction of the *Constellation* and the deactivation of the planet-killer.

Spock, Sulu, and Decker struggle to maintain control while under attack by the planet-killer.

Engineering officer Montgomery Scott is injured in an explosion aboard the U.S.S. *Enterprise.*

Prior to "Wolf in the Fold."

Scott confronted with evidence of murder on planet Argelius II

"Wolf in the Fold." Stardate 3614.9. Engineering officer Scott, on therapeutic shore leave on planet Argelius II, is accused of the brutal murder of a native woman. Inquiry by local authorities supports the accusation, and diplomatic relations between Argelius and the Federation are strained by two additional murders for which Scott is also accused. Further investigation reveals the presence of a previously undiscovered energy entity which feeds on the emotion fear in humanoids. It is further discovered that this life-form was the actual cause of the murders, as well as numerous other previously unsolved crimes.

The four planets of the Malurian system are attacked by an unknown agency. More than four billion people are wiped out, including members of a Federation science team headed by Dr. Manway.

Prior to "The Changeling."

"The Changeling." Stardate 3451.9. The U.S.S. *Enterprise* investigates the recent unexplained attack on the Malurian system, and discovers the cause of the destruction to be an ancient space probe. The probe, known as *Nomad*, had been launched from Earth in the early 21st century on a mission to search for extraterrestrial life. It is determined that a freak accident involving an alien space probe called *Tan Ru* caused *Nomad* to execute a mission of "sterilizing" all life-forms. It is believed that *Tan Ru* had been programmed to sterilize soil samples, possibly as a prelude to colonization, and that the control programs of the two probes had somehow merged in the collision. Kirk succeeds in destroying the errant *Nomad* with a minimum of further destruction.

Space probe Nomad

Planet Ceti Alpha VI explodes, disrupting the orbit of Ceti Alpha V. The resulting climatic changes are devastating to the colony there, headed by Khan Noonien Singh. Starfleet remains unaware of the explosion and of its consequences until 2285, when the Starship *Reliant* investigates the planet as a possible site for Project Genesis testing.

Star Trek II: The Wrath of Khan. *Exact date is conjecture, but Khan said Ceti Alpha VI had exploded six months after the events in "Space Seed."*

Kirk, Spock, and McCoy on survey mission to planet Gamma Trianguli VI

"The Apple." Stardate 3715.3. The *Enterprise* conducts a routine survey of planet Gamma Trianguli VI. Survey party reports discovery of a primitive humanoid culture, but further investigation yields evidence of an immensely powerful and ancient computer system that controls the planet's climate. It is determined that the computer, known to the planet's inhabitants as Vaal, has become the central object of the planet's religion, as the native civilization apparently exists primarily to provide fuel for the computer system. Upon detection of *Enterprise* personnel on the planet, Vaal attempts to discourage the investigation by causing the death of two *Enterprise* crew members and attempting to destroy the starship in orbit. Arguing that Vaal has served to stagnate the planet's culture, Kirk orders ship's phasers to destroy the computer, thus permitting the inhabitants of Gamma Trianguli VI to return to a normal course of cultural development.

Alternate-universe Spock

"Mirror, Mirror." (No stardate given.) The *Enterprise* is on a diplomatic mission to the Halkan system to secure dilithium mining rights. The assignment is impeded by a severe ion storm that nearly results in the loss of the *Enterprise* landing party due to the storm's disruption of transporter

McCoy and mirror Spock

functions. It is later learned that transport disruption resulted in exchange of landing party members with corresponding individuals from a parallel dimension, and both parties are returned to their original universes.

Upon their return, landing party members report the alternate universe to be remarkably similar to their own, but much more violent, controlled by a repressive empire. They also report that the alternate Spock, understanding the inevitability of change and the accompanying potential for loss of life, may be willing to help guide his society in a more humane direction.

Starfleet loses contact with Federation cultural observer John Gill, stationed on planet Ekos.

About six months prior to "Patterns of Force."

U.S.S. *Enterprise* assigned to transport Commodore Stocker to Starbase 10.

Just before "The Deadly Years."

Dr. McCoy, afflicted with hyperaccelcrated aging disease

"The Deadly Years." Stardate 3478.2. U.S.S. *Enterprise* on resupply mission to Gamma Hydra IV research colony. Landing party reports all colonists dead or dying, victims of an unusual hyperaccelerated aging disease. Shortly thereafter, nearly all landing party personnel are discovered to have similar symptoms. Commodore Stocker orders the *Enterprise* on a direct course to Starbase 10 so that the starbase's medical facilities can be employed to help cure the hyper aging disease. The course takes the *Enterprise* across the Romulan Neutral Zone, resulting in a confrontation with a Romulan spacecraft. Medical Officer McCoy develops a cure for the disease, based on old adrenaline-based therapies for radiation exposure.

Crew member Norman, recently assigned to duty aboard the U.S.S. *Enterprise*, evades several attempts by Dr. McCoy to schedule a routine physical examination.

Three days prior to "I, Mudd."

Deep Space Station K-7

"I, Mudd." Stardate 4513.3. The U.S.S. *Enterprise* is hijacked by an android masquerading as *Enterprise* crew member Norman, who takes the ship to a previously unknown Class-K planetoid. The perpetrator of the hijacking is discovered to be known criminal Harcort Fenton Mudd. The android population of the planet, which attempts to assume control of both Mudd and the *Enterprise*, is disabled by Kirk and his staff. It is learned that the androids were originally from the Andromeda galaxy and had been stranded when their home sun went nova. Mudd is released into custody of the android population.

The U.S.S. *Enterprise* is summoned to Deep Space Station K-7 by a Priority-1 distress call, indicating near or total disaster. Accordingly, the entire quadrant is placed on defense alert.

Just prior to "The Trouble with Tribbles."

Kirk discovers the tribbles in the quadrotriticale.

"The Trouble with Tribbles." Stardate 4523.3. The *Enterprise,* at Deep Space Station K-7, determines Priority 1 distress call was initiated to protect agricultural supplies of quadrotriticale, a special hybrid wheat deemed strategically essential to the development of Sherman's Planet. The planet had been claimed by both the Federation and the Klingon Empire. The concern for security is proven justified when a Klingon operative attempts to sabotage the Federation development claim by poisoning supplies of quadrotriticale. The sabotage is accidentally discovered when some pet tribbles are learned to have been poisoned by the tainted grain.

A magazine published on planet 892-IV

"Bread and Circuses." Stardate 4040.7. The *Enterprise* discovers wreckage of space vehicle *Beagle* on planet 892-IV, reported missing in the area some six years ago. *Enterprise* landing party, investigating the wreckage, is captured by planet's inhabitants. Engineering Officer Scott is successful in rescuing the landing party without violating Prime Directive protection of indigenous life-forms by causing a brief failure of local power utilities.

Postmission analysis suggests a variation of Earth's Christian religion may be evolving on planet 892-IV, potentially reforming the planet's Roman culture into a more humane form.

Editors' Note: Kirk said he had known Beagle *captain R. M. Merrick at Starfleet Academy, noting that Merrick had been dropped in his fifth year after failing a psycho-simulator test. This would seem to contradict other references which establish Starfleet Academy to be a four-year institution. On the other hand, "The First Duty" establishes that Wesley Crusher will have to repeat his sophomore year (meaning it will take him five years to graduate) and perhaps something similar happened to Merrick.*

The Starship *Enterprise* picks up 114 Federation dignitaries, including 32 ambassadors, for transport to a conference on the neutral planetoid Babel.

About two weeks prior to "Journey to Babel." McCoy complained that the dignitaries had been on the ship for that long.

Ambassador Sarek of Vulcan suffers a mild heart attack, his second. Benjasidrine medication is prescribed for the condition.

Shortly prior to "Journey to Babel."

"Journey to Babel." Stardate 3842.3. The U.S.S. *Enterprise* is en route to planetoid Babel, providing transport of dignitaries for talks to consider the question of planet Coridan's admission to the Federation. The conference is disrupted by apparent Andorian terrorism, later discovered to be the work of the Orion government, which opposes Coridan's admission.

Ambassador Sarek's party arrives on board the Enterprise.

Ambassador Sarek suffers another heart attack, and is treated by Dr. Leonard McCoy, using blood donated by Commander Spock. The operation is a success, although Sarek's wife, Amanda, opposes the procedure on the grounds of risk to both patients. This is McCoy's first actual surgical experience with a Vulcan patient.

Editors' Note: Although Spock's parents had been referred to in previous episodes, "Journey to Babel" is the first time they were seen and referred to by name. Sarek and Amanda became recurring characters in the Star Trek *features, and Sarek even made two appearances in* Star Trek: The Next Generation.

Coridan is admitted to the Federation.

Tellarite ambassador Gav

After "Journey to Babel." The episode "Sarek" establishes that the issue was decided in favor of admission.

"A Private Little War." Stardate 4211.4. An *Enterprise* landing party conducts botanical study of a technologically unsophisticated Class-M planet, but becomes embroiled in a local dispute. Spock is seriously injured in this dispute, exposing evidence that the indigenous population has been provided access to relatively advanced weaponry. Further investigation

Dr. M'Benga

reveals Klingon operatives to be responsible for this cultural contamination. Captain Kirk, who had surveyed the planet some 13 years ago, determines measured provision of similar weaponry to all local groups to be the only means of maintaining survival of all.

Editors' Note: Dr. M'Benga, who cared for Spock after his injury on the planet's surface, is established as having interned in a Vulcan ward. M'Benga appeared again in "That Which Survives."

The U.S.S. *Enterprise* is assigned to perform a routine check of the automated communications and astrogation facilities on planetoid Gamma II.

Just prior to "The Gamesters of Triskelion."

The Romulan, Klingon, and Federation governments, in a joint venture, establish a colony on planet Nimbus III, dubbing it the Planet of Galactic Peace. The experiment is a failure, although the colony survives for at least 20 years.

Star Trek V: The Final Frontier. Romulan ambassador Caithlin Dar said the settlement had been established 20 years prior to the film (2287).

2268

Kirk confronts the gamesters of Triskelion.

"The Gamesters of Triskelion." Stardate 3211.7. The U.S.S. *Enterprise* at planet Gamma II for routine inspection of automatic communications and astrogation equipment. During beam-down, landing party personnel are abducted by a previously unknown, technically advanced civilization of planet Triskelion in the M24 Alpha system. Captain Kirk learns the inhabitants of Triskelion practice a form of slavery, using captured beings known as "thralls" as expendable participants in athletic competition. Faced with an untenable situation, Kirk successfully gambles and wins freedom for both the *Enterprise* crew and the thralls.

Starfleet Command receives a message from the U.S.S. *Horizon*, lost a century ago. The message, sent via conventional radio, suggests the ship had caused cultural contamination at planet Sigma Iotia II.

"A Piece of the Action." Kirk noted the message had been received a month prior to the episode.

Spacefaring cloud

"Obsession." Stardate 3619.2. The U.S.S. *Enterprise* encounters a cloud creature believed responsible for deaths aboard the Starship *Farragut* eleven years ago. The creature kills two *Enterprise* crew members. Kirk pursues the creature back to its home planet, Tycho IV, where it is killed by a small antimatter charge.

The U.S.S. *Enterprise* proceeds to rendezvous with U.S.S. *Yorktown* for transfer of vaccines, which the *Enterprise* then transports to the colony on planet Theta VII, where they are urgently needed.

After "Obsession." This is somewhat conjectural, but McCoy and Spock reminded Kirk of the critical situation on Theta VII, suggesting that the Enterprise would deal with the crisis immediately after leaving Tycho IV.

"The Immunity Syndrome." Stardate 4307.1. U.S.S. *Enterprise* on course to Starbase 6 for R&R, receives orders to divert for priority rescue mission to Gamma 7A system. En route, it is learned that the Starship *Intrepid* has been destroyed, and that the same agency has apparently attacked the

Gamma 7A system, killing billions of people there. Investigation reveals the destruction to have been caused by a vast spaceborne organism that creates negative particles and consumes energy from planetary systems and space vehicles. Although nonsentient, the creature is deemed a serious threat to the galaxy and is destroyed.

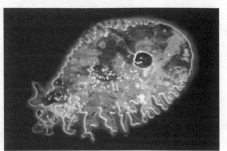

Space amoeba

The crew of the U.S.S. *Intrepid* had been entirely composed of individuals native to the planet Vulcan.

"A Piece of the Action." (No stardate given.) The U.S.S. *Enterprise* makes a follow-up visit to planet Sigma Iotia II (previously visited a century ago by the Starship *Horizon*), and discovers severe cultural contamination caused by a single book left behind by the previous expedition. In an effort to minimize further cultural damage, Kirk assists local leaders in unifying the planet under a common government.

"By Any Other Name." Stardate 4657.5. The U.S.S. *Enterprise* answers a distress call, and a landing party is captured by aliens later learned to be advance agents for the Kelvan Empire in the Andromeda galaxy. It is learned that the Kelvan hope to establish a colony in this galaxy and that they believe invasion is the only means by which this can be accomplished.

Kelvan leader Rojan and Captain Kirk

Captain Kirk negotiates an agreement with the Kelvans whereby a suitable planet can be peaceably set aside for their use. A messenger drone is sent to the Kelvan Empire to inform them of the agreement.

A Federation research station is established on planet Minara II to study a nearby star predicted to go nova in about six months. Among the station personnel are Drs. Linke and Ozaba. The star had exhibited signs of imminent collapse for some time.

Kirk examines Sargon's survival canister.

"The Empath." The station had been established six months prior to the episode.

"Return to Tomorrow." Stardate 4768.3. The Starship *Enterprise*, venturing light-years beyond explored territory, uncovers evidence of a catastrophic war a half million years ago on a previously uncharted planet. Further investigation results in discovery of canisters containing the intellects of three surviving members of the now-dead civilization. An attempt is made to provide these survivors with android bodies, but one survivor, Henoch, is destroyed when he tries to steal a living body. The remaining two survivors, Sargon and Thalassa, choose to "depart into oblivion."

"Patterns of Force." (No stardate given.) The U.S.S. *Enterprise* investigates apparent disappearance of cultural observer John Gill, stationed on planet Ekos. During orbital approach the ship is attacked by a thermonuclear weapon, the first of several discoveries that suggest severe cultural contamination. Investigation reveals that Gill, acting in violation of the Prime Directive, had engaged in a cultural experiment attempting to eliminate the planet's dangerous anarchy by imposing a government modeled after old Earth's Nazi Germany. Unfortunately, in imposing the efficiency of the Nazis, Gill created an environment in which the abuse of power also flourished. Kirk assists local inhabitants in overthrowing the Nazi government.

Captain Kirk on planet Ekos

"The Ultimate Computer." Stardate 4729.4. The U.S.S. *Enterprise* is assigned to perform field testing of the experimental M-5 multitronic computer designed by Dr. Richard Daystrom. Although initial exercises are very promising, later tests in simulated combat reveal M-5 to be unpredictable, resulting in the destruction of the Starship *Excalibur* and its crew.

Dr. Richard Daystrom

M-5 computer combat exercise

Commodore
Robert Wesley

U.S.S. Exeter *crew member, a victim of
the Omega IV bacteriological war*

Enterprise captain Kirk and task force commander Commodore Wesley aboard the U.S.S. *Lexington* are credited with quick thinking, allowing disconnection of the M-5 unit before further deaths can result. Postmission analysis suggests that despite the M-5's design goal of rendering human participation unnecessary in space exploration, it was human thinking that saved the situation.

Editors' Note: Commodore Bob Wesley was named for the pseudonym that Gene Roddenberry used when he wrote for Have Gun, Will Travel, *while still working as a police officer.*

"The Omega Glory." (No stardate given.) The U.S.S. *Enterprise* discovers the Starship *Exeter* floating derelict in orbit at planet Omega IV, all crew personnel dead. The boarding party discovers deaths to have been caused by exposure to an alien biologic agent, apparently brought to the ship from the planet surface. Evidence suggests the planet also contains biologic agents that provide immunity to the disease, so *Enterprise* boarding party personnel are transported to the surface.

Investigation on the surface of Omega IV suggests both the disease and the population's immunity are results of ancient bacteriologic warfare, perhaps over a millennium ago. Also discovered is *Exeter* captain Ronald Tracey, who survived the disease by chance because he had remained on the surface of the planet. Tracey is found to have interfered in local government, in violation of the Prime Directive, and is taken into custody.

"Assignment: Earth." (No stardate given.) The U.S.S. *Enterprise*, on historical research mission into Earth's past, encounters evidence that Earth had extraterrestrial assistance in surviving its critical nuclear age, circa 1968.

5.3 STAR TREK: THE ORIGINAL SERIES — YEAR 3

Captain James Kirk returns from a covert Starfleet mission to a Romulan ship

Melkot

"Spectre of the Gun." Stardate 4385.3. The U.S.S. *Enterprise* makes first contact with the Melkot, an alien race possessing unusual telepathic powers. After an initial period of uneasiness, Kirk persuades the Melkot of the Federation's peaceful intentions. The Melkot agree to diplomatic relations with the Federation.

"Elaan of Troyius." Stardate 4372.5. The *Enterprise* is on a diplomatic mission to the Tellun system. Assignment is to transport Elaan, the Dohlman of planet Elas, to planet Troyius as part of a peace agreement between the two warring planets. The mission is complicated by interference from Klingon interests, apparently trying to protect Klingon access to rich dilithium deposits on Troyius.

Elaan of Troyius

Editors' Note: This episode marks the first time the Klingon battle cruiser was actually used. Earlier episodes referred to this vessel, but this is the first episode that actually showed it onscreen. (In the original network airings of these episodes, "The Enterprise Incident" actually aired before "Elaan of Troyius," so the first time the audience saw the Klingon battle cruiser, it was flown by Romulans.)

"The Paradise Syndrome." Stardate 4842.6. Captain Kirk is missing from a landing party investigating the inhabitants of a Class-M planet threatened with collision from an asteroid. Search for Kirk is cut short so that U.S.S. *Enterprise* can intercept asteroid to divert it from collision. This attempt fails, resulting in severe damage to *Enterprise* warp drive systems. *Enterprise* returns to search for Kirk, who has suffered an injury resulting in memory loss. Eventually Spock discovers evidence of an ancient deflector device which is successfully employed to divert the asteroid. It is learned that Kirk, while suffering from amnesia, had married a native woman named Miramanee, who was subsequently killed in a local power struggle.

Kirk, living among the Indians

U.S.S. Enterprise *surrounded by Romulan battle cruisers*

"The *Enterprise* Incident." Stardate 5027.3. The U.S.S. *Enterprise* crosses the Romulan Neutral Zone in violation of treaty, and is captured by three Romulan battle cruisers. Captain Kirk and Commander Spock are taken into Romulan custody and accused of criminal espionage by a Romulan commander. They later escape, stealing an improved Romulan cloaking device. The *Enterprise* flees from Romulan space, and it is learned that Kirk and Spock have been conducting a covert Starfleet mission intended to gain military intelligence about the improved cloaking device. During their escape, the Romulan commander is taken prisoner aboard the *Enterprise.*

Editors' Note: The original reason for the Klingon-Romulan alliance in Star Trek*'s third season was to "explain" why the Romulans were using Klingon battle cruisers. The real reason for this was that the show had just made a major investment in designing and building the new Klingon ship. Establishing an alliance between the two adversaries created a reason to show more of the nifty new model. That ship was seen three times during the run of the original series, and the basic design was also used in the* Star Trek *features and in* Star Trek: The Next Generation.

This episode suggests Spock had been in Starfleet for 18 years, implying that he had joined in 2250, although "Journey to Babel" puts his entry into Starfleet at 2249.

Romulan commander

The capture of the Romulan cloaking device at this relatively early point in Star Trek *history raises the question of why the* Enterprise *and other Starfleet vessels have never incorporated the invisibility screen into their standard equipment. A dramatic reason for this is the writers' need to give each set of characters (i.e., the Romulans and the Federation) a different set of characteristics. Giving the Federation Starfleet the cloaking device would eliminate one of the more interesting differences between these groups. Additionally, Gene Roddenberry would in later years express the view that the men and women of the Federation Starfleet are explorers and scientists, so they "don't sneak around." We therefore assume that Federation policy prohibits the use of cloaking devices in what is primarily a nonmilitary fleet.* Star Trek: The Next Generation Technical Manual *co-author Rick Sternbach theorizes that the design of Federation starships is sufficiently different from Romulan and Klingon ships so that cloaking device usage would be energy-prohibitive.*

Gorgon

The Romulan commander is turned over to Federation authorities.

After "The Enterprise *Incident."*

"And the Children Shall Lead." Stardate 5029.5. The *Enterprise,* at planet Triacus, discovers all adult members of Starnes expedition to be dead. Surviving children show uncharacteristically little emotional impact from the tragedy. They are later discovered to be under the psychic influence of a noncorporeal being which calls itself the "Gorgan," apparently the source of legends of ancient marauders from Triacus. This entity attempts to gain control of the *Enterprise,* using the children as agents. *Enterprise* personnel help the children face their grief, thus freeing them from the Gorgan.

The survivors of the Starnes expedition tragedy on planet Triacus are taken to Starbase 4.

After "And the Children Shall Lead."

Sigma Draconis VI planetary computer device

"Spock's Brain." Stardate 5431.4. U.S.S. *Enterprise,* traveling near the Sigma Draconis system, is attacked by a spacecraft from a previously unknown civilization in that system. The only casualty is Commander

Spock, whose brain is surgically removed by the attacker. The *Enterprise* pursues the spacecraft to Sigma Draconis VI, where it is discovered that Spock's brain is being used as a vital component in a massive computer system that provides for the planet's inhabitants. Captain Kirk leads a landing party to the planet and is successful in retrieving the brain. Dr. McCoy makes use of the planetary computer's advanced knowledge to learn surgical techniques necessary to restore the brain to Spock's body. Finally, *Enterprise* personnel encourage the planet's inhabitants to learn survival without dependence on the computer system.

"Is There in Truth No Beauty?" Stardate 5630.7. The U.S.S. *Enterprise* is assigned to transport diplomatic and cultural exchange party to rendezvous with Medusan spacecraft. Among the party is Medusan Ambassador Kollos, Dr. Miranda Jones, and technical specialist Lawrence Marvick. Emotional stress, exacerbated by direct visual contact with Kollos, causes Marvick to exhibit irrational behavior, at which time he pilots the *Enterprise* across the energy barrier at the edge of the galaxy. The hazardous return trip is made possible by the navigational expertise of Ambassador Kollos. Shortly thereafter, Jones establishes a mind link with Kollos.

Dr. Miranda Jones

Editors' Note: Lawrence Marvick is described as being one of the designers of the Enterprise.

The Starship *Defiant*, in unsurveyed territory near the Tholian border, disappears without a trace.

"The Tholian Web." Kirk's log said the Defiant *had disappeared three weeks prior to the episode.*

"The Empath." Stardate 5121.5. The U.S.S. *Enterprise* on a mission to rescue personnel at the research station on planet Minara II before that planet's star goes nova. *Enterprise* landing party discovers all station personnel missing. Further investigation reveals station personnel to be dead, part of a bizarre experiment by beings called Vians, who are attempting to determine the worthiness of the planet's inhabitants to be rescued.

Gem, a member of one of the races inhabiting the Minara system

The star Minara explodes.

Just after "The Empath."

"The Tholian Web." Stardate 5693.2. The U.S.S. *Enterprise* investigates the disappearance of the Starship *Defiant* in uncharted territory, locates the *Defiant* and discovers evidence of severe violence that resulted in the death of all *Defiant* personnel. This behavior is determined to be the result of distortions to the central nervous system caused by a spatial phenomenon called interphase, a temporary overlap of two universes. The interphase phenomenon is also found responsible for the literal disappearance of the *Defiant* and for the loss of *Enterprise* captain James Kirk.

U.S.S. Enterprise *caught in Tholian tractor web*

Efforts to rescue Kirk from interspace are hampered by a severe energy drain on *Enterprise* systems by the interphase phenomenon, and by mental and behavioral disorders in *Enterprise* personnel, also caused by interphase. The rescue is further complicated by a previously unknown territorial claim on the area by Commander Loskene, representing the Tholian Assembly, although Kirk is successfully recovered before the Tholians can take decisive action against the *Enterprise*.

Editors' Note: This is the only encounter we've seen with the Tholians, although several Next Generation *episodes have referred to an ongoing conflict between the Federation and the Tholian Assembly. Spock's line*

Commander Loskene of the Tholian Assembly

about "the renowned Tholian punctuality" suggests the Federation had prior contact with the Tholians. Spock also notes that there is no record of a starship's crew ever having mutinied, although the episode "Whom Gods Destroy" (filmed after "The Tholian Web") establishes that Garth's crew mutinied some time ago when he ordered them to kill the inhabitants of planet Antos IV. Garth may have been exaggerating, of course.

Dr. Leonard McCoy is diagnosed as having xeno-polycythemia, a rare blood disorder for which there is no known cure. His condition is terminal.

Just prior to "For the World Is Hollow and I Have Touched the Sky."

Fabrini high priestess Natira and Dr. Leonard McCoy

"For the World Is Hollow and I Have Touched the Sky." Stardate 5476.3. The *Enterprise* successfully deflects an attack by technically unsophisticated missile weapons. Investigation reveals the origin of the attack to be an asteroid traveling under power as an inhabited sublight space vehicle. Course projections indicate the asteroid will impact planet Daran V in a little over a year, threatening the lives of the 3.7 million people on that world.

Transporting to the asteroid ship, Captain James Kirk, Mr. Spock, and Dr. McCoy determine the ship, called *Yonada*, to have been built by inhabitants of the Fabrina system just prior to the explosion of their sun some 10,000 years ago. The boarding party is unsuccessful in gaining the cooperation of local authorities, but Dr. McCoy, suffering from terminal xeno-polycythemia, elects to remain behind for personal reasons when Kirk and Spock return to the *Enterprise*. McCoy, having married Yonadan high priestess Natira, discovers documentation revealing technical schematics for the vehicle. Using this information, *Enterprise* personnel are successful in restoring Yonada to its intended flight path, averting the feared collision with Daran V. Also discovered among the Yonadan records is a cure for xeno-polycythemia, permitting Dr. McCoy to return to duty aboard the *Enterprise*.

The U.S.S. *Enterprise* receives a distress call from a colony on planet Beta XIIA. It is not realized at the time that the signal has been fabricated by an alien life-form, and that a Klingon battle cruiser under the command of Kang has received a similarly falsified distress call.

Just prior to "Day of the Dove."

Asteroid ship Yonada

Klingon commander Kang

"Day of the Dove." (No stardate given.) A U.S.S. *Enterprise* landing party at planet Beta XIIA discovers the distress call to have been a ruse, apparently a trick by a Klingon battle cruiser also orbiting the planet. *Enterprise* personnel, avoiding capture by a Klingon landing party, are successful in taking the Klingons captive aboard the *Enterprise*. Dangerous radiation emissions are detected aboard the Klingon vessel, and the ship is destroyed by the *Enterprise* to avoid further hazard.

Aboard the *Enterprise*, intense fighting breaks out between *Enterprise* and Klingon personnel. The situation (including the falsified distress calls) is eventually learned to have been engineered by a previously unknown energy-based life-form that thrives on the emotions of hatred and anger. *Enterprise* and Klingon personnel cooperate to drive this life-form away by generating positive emotions.

"Plato's Stepchildren." Stardate 5784.2. The *Enterprise* responds to a distress call from a previously unknown civilization. The inhabitants of this planet are discovered to have escaped nearly three millennia ago from the Sahndara star system, just before Sahndara went nova. They had stopped for a time on ancient Earth, where their leader, Parmen, had developed a

Alexander

great admiration for the philosopher Plato. Later, having settled on a planet they named Platonius, these unusually long-lived humanoids had attempted to recreate Plato's Republic.

At Platonius, *Enterprise* Chief Medical Officer Dr. Leonard McCoy declines an invitation to remain behind with the Platonians. Although the Platonians attempt to coerce McCoy to stay by using their unusual telekinetic powers, McCoy is successful in making use of local kironide chemical deposits to create similar telekinetic powers in *Enterprise* personnel, permitting their escape. One Platonian, Alexander, who had helped the *Enterprise* people, expresses a desire to leave Platonius, and is welcomed as a guest aboard the *Enterprise*.

Captain Kirk informs Starfleet Command of the Platonians and of their unusual telekinetic powers, advising other starships to take appropriate precautions before making contact with that planet.

Just after "Plato's Stepchildren."

"Wink of an Eye." Stardate 5710.5. The U.S.S. *Enterprise* responds to distress calls from planet Scalos. A landing party discovers evidence of a technically advanced humanoid civilization, but no immediately apparent life-forms. Upon the landing party's return to the *Enterprise*, a number of unexplained malfunctions are traced to the presence of previously undetected humanoid life-forms from the planet.

Scalosian queen Deela

It is learned that these humanoids are the victims of a terrible volcanic disaster which hyperaccelerated the Scalosians so that they live their lives at a much faster rate than normal. Scalosian queen Deela further reveals that their purpose in attempting to control the *Enterprise* crew is to provide breeding stock for the genetically damaged Scalosians, although the acceleration process is learned to be fatal to humans. *Enterprise* personnel are successful in preventing the takeover, in the process developing a counteragent to reverse the hyperacceleration effect.

"That Which Survives." (No stardate given.) The Starship *Enterprise* investigates an anomalous planet whose apparent geologic age is much less than the indigenous vegetation would indicate. Landing party discovers evidence of significant geologic instability, although this investigation is interrupted when the *Enterprise* is discovered to be missing from planet orbit. The ship is later found to have been transposed across some 990.7 light-years from the planet, apparently by the same agency responsible for the geologic instability.

This agency is found to be the image of a woman named Losira, who was the last surviving member of a Kalandan colony there. The planet itself is learned to be an artificial construct, the product of Kalandan technology. The image of Losira was used by the colony's still-functioning computer to defend the installation despite the fact that all colonists had been killed some years prior by disease.

Editors' Note: This episode featured the second appearance of Dr. M'Benga to the Enterprise *sickbay. M'Benga had been previously seen in "A Private Little War."*

Losira

A shuttlecraft is stolen from Starbase 4. It is later learned that the vehicle was taken by Lokai, a fugitive from the planet Cheron.

Two weeks prior to "Let That Be Your Last Battlefield."

A planetwide bacterial infection threatens life on planet Ariannus, a vital transfer point on commercial space lanes. The U.S.S. *Enterprise* is assigned to perform decontamination employing an orbital spraying technique.

Just prior to "Let That Be Your Last Battlefield."

Commissioner Bele of the planet Cheron

"Let That Be Your Last Battlefield." Stardate 5730.2. En route for planet Ariannus for decontamination mission, the U.S.S. *Enterprise* intercepts and recovers a shuttlecraft that had been stolen from Starbase 4, found to be piloted by Lokai from the planet Cheron. Shortly thereafter, a second ship intercepts the *Enterprise*. The pilot of the second ship, Commissioner Bele of the planet Cheron, reports that he has been in pursuit of Lokai for crimes against the Cheron government, and requests extradition of Lokai from Federation custody. *Enterprise* captain Kirk declines the request, citing the absence of an extradition treaty.

Upon completion of decontamination at Ariannus, the *Enterprise* is coerced to return both Lokai and Bele to Cheron, where it is discovered that their home civilization had been completely destroyed by racial hatred.

Editors' Note: The U.S.S. Enterprise *destruct command sequence, used when Kirk tries to prevent Bele's takeover of his ship, was repeated almost word for word in the film* Star Trek III: The Search for Spock. *However, the destruct sequence for the* Enterprise-D, *first seen in "11001001," was different.*

Garth and Marta, inmates at the Elba II penal colony

"Whom Gods Destroy." Stardate 5718.3. The U.S.S. *Enterprise* is assigned to deliver new medication to the penal colony on planet Elba II. One of the inmates, the former Captain Garth of Izar, is discovered to have taken over the colony, taking advantage of a cellular metamorphosis technique he had learned at Antos IV. In the process, Garth captures *Enterprise* captain Kirk and first officer Spock, and causes the death of an Orion inmate named Marta. Kirk and Spock are successful in restoring control to colony administrator Donald Corey, and early indications suggest that new treatment may be able to reverse the course of Garth's mental illness.

The government of the planet Gideon agrees to limited diplomatic contact with Federation representatives. Previous attempts at establishing diplomatic relations had been stymied by Gideon's fierce tradition of isolationism. Gideon, reported to be a near paradise, is being considered for admission into the Federation.

Prior to "The Mark of Gideon."

Odona of Gideon

"The Mark of Gideon." Stardate 5423.4. The Starship *Enterprise*, on a diplomatic mission to planet Gideon, reports Captain James Kirk missing while in transit to the planet's surface. Investigation determines Kirk to have been abducted by the Gideon council, an attempt by Gideon prime minister Hodin to use disease organisms in Kirk's bloodstream to help solve a serious overpopulation problem. Although Kirk declines to remain on Gideon to provide the disease organism, Hodin's daughter, Odona, becomes similarly infected and thus is able to fill the planet's needs.

A Federation vessel makes first contact with a spacecraft from a race calling itself "The Children of Tama." Attempts to establish communications are unsuccessful due to the unusually great difference between language types, although their behavior suggests a peaceable race. This is the first of seven such incidents over the next century, including contact by the *Shiku Maru*, whose commander, Captain Silvestri, described the Tamarians as "incomprehensible." Accounts from the other contacts are similar. As a result, no formal relations are established between the Tamarians and the Federation.

"Darmok." Data noted that Federation vessels had first encountered Tamarian ships a hundred years prior to the episode (2368).

2269

"The Lights of Zetar." Stardate 5725.3. The U.S.S. *Enterprise* is assigned to transport Lieutenant Mira Romaine to planetoid Memory Alpha, a massive archive for Federation cultural history and scientific knowledge. On final orbital approach to Memory Alpha, an energy phenomenon of unknown origin intercepts the *Enterprise*, resulting in serious neural impact on Romaine. This phenomenon subsequently attacks the Memory Alpha installation, resulting in the death of all station personnel. *Enterprise* personnel later determine that the energy is the embodiment of the survivors of the planet Zetar, destroyed many years ago. The survivors found Romaine to be a compatible life-form to serve as their corporeal body, but *Enterprise* personnel are successful in expelling the Zetar life-forms when it is found that they threaten Romaine's identity.

Mira Romaine

Lieutenant Mira Romaine returns to Memory Alpha to help rebuild the facility.

After "The Lights of Zetar."

A botanical plague threatens the vegetation on planet Merak II. The plague's devastation is expected to leave the planet's surface uninhabitable. The only known treatment requires quantities of the rare mineral zenite.

Prior to "The Cloud Minders."

Stratos administrator Plasus (Jeff Corey)

"The Cloud Minders." Stardate 5818.4. The U.S.S. *Enterprise* is on an emergency assignment to obtain mineral zenite from miners on planet Ardana. Delivery of the zenite is delayed by terrorist activity. Investigation reveals the terrorists to be driven by severe social inequities between the working class, living in the underground mines, and the upper class, living in Stratos, a cloud city. Stratos authorities defend the arrangement, citing evidence that the workers exhibit lower intelligence, but it is learned this mental impairment is due to environmental conditions. *Enterprise* captain Kirk negotiates with both parties for improved working conditions in exchange for delivery of the zenite consignment.

The Starship *Enterprise* proceeds to planet Merak II to deliver the zenite for treatment of the botanical plague.

Just after "The Cloud Minders."

Spock confers with Stratos dweller Droxine.

"The Way to Eden." Stardate 5832.3. The *Enterprise* locates the space cruiser *Aurora*, reported stolen. Intercepting the *Aurora*, the *Enterprise* takes into custody several individuals led by Dr. Severin, a noted scientist. Severin reveals he is on a quest to find the mythical planet that is the source of the legends of Eden. Severin coerces ship's personnel to locate a planet matching his criteria, using ship's computer banks to correlate astronomical data. Severin then orders the *Enterprise* to those coordinates.

At Severin's planet it is learned that although beautiful, the planet's environment is severely toxic to humanoid life, and Severin is killed from exposure to the planet's flora. Captain Kirk recommends that no legal action be taken against the remaining members of Severin's party.

Dr. Severin

Editors' Note: An earlier version of this story was written by Dorothy Fontana under the title "Joanna." The Irina character (Chekov's love interest in the aired episode) was originally Dr. McCoy's daughter, Joanna, who caught the interest of Captain Kirk in Fontana's version.

A serious epidemic of Rigelian fever breaks out onboard the Starship *Enterprise,* causing the death of three crew members and threatening the lives of 23 others. The effects of Rigelian fever resemble those of bubonic plague, killing its victims in a day. The *Enterprise* diverts to planet Holberg 917-G in the Omega system in order to obtain sufficient quantities of ryetalyn necessary for treatment of the epidemic.

Just prior to "Requiem for Methuselah."

Flint's castle on planet Holberg 917-G

"Requiem for Methuselah." Stardate 5843.7. An *Enterprise* landing party attempts to gather raw ryetalyn from the surface of Holberg 917-G, a class-M planet previously believed to be uninhabited. The ryetalyn is critically needed as an antidote to Rigelian fever, now threatening the lives of the entire *Enterprise* crew. The planet is discovered to be the abode of a reclusive individual known as Flint, who is later discovered to be a nearly immortal man, originally from Earth. Flint offers assistance in obtaining and refining the ryetalyn, but is later learned to be deliberately detaining the landing party personnel to provide experience with human interaction to a sophisticated android of Flint's construction. The android, designed as a human female called Rayna Kapec, proves incapable of withstanding the stresses of human emotions and suffers a total systems failure.

Flint and his android creation, Rayna

Flint, who is learned to have had many identities over his lifetime, claims to have been Leonardo da Vinci, Reginald Pollack, Sten from Marcus II, Brahms, Alexander, Merlin, Solomon, Lazarus, Abramson, and other historical figures. Flint ultimately provides refined ryetalyn for the successful treatment of the *Enterprise* crew, and is further discovered to have sacrificed immortality when he left Earth's ecosystems, but indicates a desire to devote the remainder of his life to improving the human condition.

Editors' Note: Rayna Kapec is apparently named for Karel Capek, the Czechoslovakian writer who first coined the term "robot" in his short story "R.U.R." The spelling of the medication "ryetalyn" is indicated in the script as "vrietalyn."

Excalbian

"The Savage Curtain." Stardate 5906.4. The U.S.S. *Enterprise* conducts scientific studies in orbit around planet Excalbia and encounters a life-form claiming to be the late President Abraham Lincoln of Earth. Captain Kirk, intrigued by the nearly perfect image of the historical figure, accepts an invitation to transport to the surface of Excalbia with Spock, where similar recreations of numerous other historical figures are encountered. Among these recreations are Surak of Vulcan, Colonel Green of Earth, and Kahless the Unforgettable from the Klingon Homeworld. The *Enterprise* crew discovers the entire situation to have been engineered by the inhabitants of Excalbia, so that they may observe and learn about the concepts of "good" and "evil." Upon completion of the drama, the Excalbians return Kirk and Spock to the *Enterprise*.

Kirk encounters the image of President Abraham Lincoln.

Editors' Note: In "Reunion," Worf tells Alexander about Kahless the Unforgettable, the leader who united the Klingon Homeworld. In "New Ground," Worf tells Alexander the Klingon legend of Kahless and his brother Morath, describing how Kahless fought him for twelve days and nights because Morath had broken his word. A sculpture in Worf's quarters of two figures wrestling depicts this heroic struggle.

"All Our Yesterdays." Stardate 5943.7. The U.S.S. *Enterprise* investigates planet Sarpeidon, hours before the predicted explosion of its star, Beta Niobe. Although earlier reports indicated Sarpeidon had been inhabited by a civilized humanoid species, sensors indicate no inhabitants remain. Investigation reveals a sophisticated time portal called the atavachron, which was used by the inhabitants to escape into their planet's past. Unfamiliarity with the atavachron results in the accidental transport of Captain Kirk, Mr. Spock, and Dr. McCoy to various points in Sarpeidon's past, although all three are recovered by Mr. Atoz, the atavachron operator. Atoz subsequently escapes into his chosen past time, and the *Enterprise* departs Sarpeidon just prior to the explosion of Beta Niobe.

Mr. Atoz

The U.S.S. *Enterprise* receives a distress call from a Federation archaeological team investigating the ruins on planet Camus II. The ship, on course to rendezvous with the Starship *Potemkin* at Beta Aurigae for gravitational studies, diverts to Camus II.

Just prior to "Turnabout Intruder."

Life entity transferrence at Camus II

"Turnabout Intruder." Stardate 5928.5. The Starship *Enterprise* conducts a rescue mission at Camus II, aiding survivors of the Federation archaeological team suffering from a serious radiation exposure accident. Upon returning to the ship, *Enterprise* captain James Kirk is discovered to be exhibiting severely aberrant behavior, resulting in the convening of a hearing to evaluate Kirk's command competency. Investigation reveals the fact that Kirk, while on Camus II, had been the victim of an abduction by Dr. Janice Lester, a member of the archaeological team. Lester had evidently employed an ancient device discovered in the ruins to transfer her consciousness into the body of James Kirk, and Kirk's consciousness into Lester's body. This mental exchange by the emotionally unstable Lester is determined to be the cause of Kirk's irrational behavior, although the transference is later found to be temporary, and both Kirk and Lester revert to their original bodies. Lester is placed in the medical care of former archaeological expedition leader Dr. Coleman.

Dr. Janice Lester

Editors' Note: Starfleet has been accused of sexism because of Janice's speech to Kirk complaining that "your world of starship captains doesn't admit women." While it is indeed possible that Starfleet did not have female captains at this point (chronologically, the first female captain we saw was the commander of the U.S.S. Saratoga *in* Star Trek IV: The Voyage Home*), we chose to interpret Janice's line as meaning that Kirk's personal world, revolving around his career as starship captain, left no room for a lasting commitment to a woman. (Gene Roddenberry apparently disagreed with this rationalization, admitting in later years that the line was simply sexist.)*

"Turnabout Intruder" was the last episode of the original Star Trek *television series.*

The U.S.S. *Enterprise* goes to Starbase 2.

Just after "Turnabout Intruder."

Enterprise undergoing refit at orbital dry dock

Kirk's five-year mission ends and the Starship *Enterprise* returns to spacedock.

Date is conjecture. Assumes the pilot episode "Where No Man Has Gone Before" was about a year into the five-year mission and that the first season was about a year after that episode. Dorothy Fontana notes that if you were to count the animated episodes (which we did not do in this chronology), this could also account for the other two years of the five-year mission.

The asteroid/spaceship *Yonada* reaches its promised land, and the Fabrini, under the leadership of high priestess Natira, begin to disembark.

"For the World Is Hollow and I Have Touched the Sky." Kirk noted that Yonada would arrive at its destination some 390 days after the episode, set in the latter half of 2268.

Admiral
James T. Kirk

Editors' Note: Kirk promised McCoy that he would arrange for the Enterprise to be there when the Fabrini reached their promised land, but since this would have been after the end of Star Trek's third season, we have no way of knowing whether or not McCoy actually managed to be there. Although Yonada's arrival is, by our reckoning, after the end of Kirk's five-year mission, there is certainly enough margin for error in the timeline that the arrival could have been before the end of that voyage.

James T. Kirk is promoted to admiral and becomes chief of Starfleet operations, accepting the promotion against the advice of his friend, Leonard McCoy.

Spock undergoes
Kohlinar dicipline
on his home
planet Vulcan.

Star Trek: The Motion Picture. Kirk said he'd been chief of Starfleet operations for two and a half years prior to the film.

2270

Spock retires from Starfleet. He returns to Vulcan to undergo the *Kohlinar* training in an effort to purge the remaining emotional influences from his intellect.

Leonard McCoy also retires, returns to Earth, and enters private medical practice, swearing he'll never return to Starfleet.

Date is conjecture. Both left Starfleet after the original Star Trek series, but before Star Trek: The Motion Picture.

Starship *Enterprise*, in San Francisco orbital dry dock, begins major refitting process. Will Decker promoted to *Enterprise* captain on Kirk's recommendation.

Dr. Leonard
McCoy

Star Trek: The Motion Picture. Scotty noted he'd spent eighteen months working on the refit project, so this is that long before the movie.

Ambassador Sarek of Vulcan begins working on treaty with the reclusive Legarans. He does not succeed until the year 2366.

"Sarek." At the time of the episode (2366), Sarek said he'd been working on the treaty for 96 years.

Ambassador
Sarek

5.4 STAR TREK MOTION PICTURES I - VI

"Remember..."

2271

Star Trek: The Motion Picture. Stardate 7412.6. Three Klingon starships and Starfleet's Epsilon 9 station are destroyed by a massive machine/organism called V'Ger. Sol sector placed on alert when V'Ger is found to be heading toward Earth at warp 7.

Refitted U.S.S. *Enterprise* returned to service to investigate the threat. Starfleet Admiral Nogura temporarily reinstates Admiral James Kirk as *Enterprise* captain, assigning former captain Decker to serve as executive officer. Commander Spock and Dr. McCoy both return to Starfleet duty.

Kirk is successful in averting the V'Ger threat to Earth, although Commander Decker and Lieutenant Ilia are reported missing in action.

Editors' Note: Decker's line about Kirk not having logged "a single star-hour in two and a half years" suggests the film is set that long after the conclusion of the first Star Trek series. Kirk's line about his having spent five years out there, dealing with unknowns, would seem to confirm that it is indeed the five-year mission they are referring to.

This film marks the first appearance of the "new and improved" Klingons, using latex makeup appliances to create their distinctive forehead ridges. Makeup artist Fred Phillips created the new designs. Phillips explained that this is what he had always wanted to do for the Klingons, but never could before because of the limitations of his television budget. Phillips and Roddenberry reportedly joked that the difference was because only "southern" Klingons were seen in the original series, but those seen in the movies were "northern" Klingons.

Klingon starships encounter V'Ger.

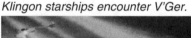

Commander Decker and Lieutenant Ilia

*Science Officer
Xon*

U.S.S. *Enterprise* embarks on Kirk's second five-year mission of deep space exploration.

Conjecture.

Editors' Note: Paramount Pictures had at one point planned a second Star Trek *television series (entitled* Star Trek II, *not to be confused with the movie of the same name) which would have depicted a second five-year mission of the* Enterprise *under the command of Captain Kirk. Most of the original* Star Trek *cast had agreed to return for this series, and new additions would have included Will Decker, Ilia, and Vulcan science officer Xon, who would have been played by actor David Gautreaux. However, just before production started, Paramount decided not to go ahead with the series and the first episode was turned into* Star Trek: The Motion Picture.

2274

Colony ship *Artemis* departs on a mission to settle planet Septimus Minor. The ship ultimately ends up at Tau Cygna V in the de Laure Belt, where one-third of the original colonists die from exposure to the hyperonic radiation in the area. Though not apparent at the time, the colony at Tau Cygna is in direct violation of the Treaty of Armens which cedes the planet to the Sheliak Corporate.

U.S.S. Enterprise *at
Spacedock in Earth orbit*

"Ensigns of Command." The ship was launched 92 years prior to the episode, and the colony had been in place for "over ninety years."

2276

Starship *Enterprise* returns from Kirk's second five-year mission of exploration.

Conjecture.

2277

Kirk at home in San Francisco

James Kirk accepts an appointment to the Starfleet Academy faculty on Earth, and moves into an apartment in San Francisco.

Commander Spock is promoted to captain, becomes member of Starfleet Academy faculty on Earth, and accepts command of Starship *Enterprise*.

Leonard McCoy is promoted from lieutenant commander to commander.

Commander Pavel Chekov assigned as first officer of U.S.S. *Reliant*.

Date is conjecture: These were after Star Trek I, *but before* Star Trek II.

Starfleet abolishes the practice of maintaining a different emblem for each starship, instead adopting the *Enterprise* symbol for the entire organization.

Conjecture. In the original series we saw different insignias for each starship, but since Star Trek: The Motion Picture, *we've seen nearly all Starfleet personnel wearing the* Enterprise *emblem.*

2278

The Starship *Bozeman*, three weeks out of starbase under the command of

Captain Morgan Bateson, disappears into what is later learned to be a temporal causality loop near the Typhon Expanse. The *Soyuz* class ship remains trapped in the causality loop until freed by the *Enterprise* in 2368.

"Cause and Effect." Captain Bateson tells Picard the year that the Bozeman embarked on its fateful trip.

Editors' Note: The registry number of the U.S.S. Bozeman, NCC-1941, was suggested by model maker Greg Jein, who did the modifications to change the Miranda class Reliant into the Soyuz class Bozeman. Greg's credits include miniatures for Steven Spielberg's movie 1941. Greg also built spaceships for Spielberg's Close Encounters of the Third Kind.

U.S.S. Bozeman

Pardek becomes a member of the Romulan Senate, representing the Krocton Segment of the planet Romulus. Pardek later meets Spock at the Khitomer Conference of 2293. He is regarded as a "man of the people" and sponsors many reforms, but is considered by the Romulan leadership to be something of a radical because of his advocacy for peace.

"Unification, Part I." Data describes Pardek's career, noting that he had served in the Romulan Senate for nine decades prior to the episode (2368).

2279

Mark Jameson

Admiral Mark Jameson is born. His celebrated Starfleet career includes a stint as commander of the starship *Gettysburg*.

"Too Short a Season." He was 85 years old at the time of the episode (2364).

2281

Saavik enters Starfleet Academy.

Date is conjecture: Saavik was taking the Kobayashi Maru test in 2285 (Star Trek II: The Wrath of Khan), suggesting she was near the end of her studies there at that time. This is four years prior to her test date, since "The First Duty" establishes the Academy to be a four-year curriculum.

Saavik

2283

McCoy's bottle of Romulan Ale, given as a birthday gift to Kirk in 2285, was of this year's vintage.

Star Trek II: The Wrath of Khan. Kirk read date off bottle.

2284

U.S.S. Enterprise

Dr. Carol Marcus presents Project Genesis proposal to the Federation. The project is funded, and her team begins work at the Regula I space station in the Mutara Sector.

Star Trek II: The Wrath of Khan. Kirk said that Carol's Genesis proposal had been made a year ago.

Starship *Enterprise* retired from exploratory service, becomes training vessel assigned to Starfleet Academy at San Francisco.

Date is conjecture: This happened after Star Trek: The Motion Picture, *but before* Star Trek II: The Wrath of Khan.

Commander Kyle is assigned to U.S.S. *Reliant.* He had served as a transporter chief aboard the *Enterprise* during Kirk's first tenure as captain.

Date is conjecture: This happened after the original Star Trek *series, but before* Star Trek II: The Wrath of Khan.

Stardate 8205.5. Starship *Excelsior* commissioned at San Francisco orbital yards. The vessel serves as experimental testbed for the unsuccessful Transwarp Development Project, but later is refitted with a standard warp drive and serves successfully as a ship of the line.

Date is conjecture: This presumably happened before Star Trek III: The Search for Spock, *because the ship was seen in that film, but also before* Star Trek II: The Wrath of Khan *because of the stardate written on the bridge commissioning plaque in* Star Trek VI: The Undiscovered Country.

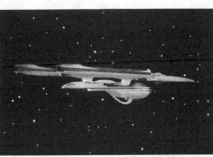

U.S.S. Excelsior, *the great experiment*

2285

U.S.S. *Reliant,* assigned to support Project Genesis, conducts search for a lifeless planetoid for third-stage experiment in the Mutara Sector. This stage would involve testing the Genesis device on a planetary scale.

Shortly before Star Trek II: The Wrath of Khan.

Star Trek II: The Wrath of Khan. Stardate 8130.3. Admiral James Kirk celebrates his 52nd birthday. Kirk and Spock, now serving as Academy instructors, later shuttle up to the *Enterprise* to participate in an inspection and cadet training exercise.

Lieutenant Saavik takes *Kobayashi Maru* test at Starfleet Academy on Earth. Saavik later pilots *Enterprise* out of spacedock on training exercise.

Federation starship *Reliant* continues survey mission to find a lifeless planet to serve as test site for Project Genesis. While surveying planet Ceti Alpha V, the *Reliant* landing party accidentally discovers the encampment of Khan Noonien Singh, the former tyrant of Earth's Eugenics Wars. Khan commandeers the *Reliant* and uses the ship to gain control of space station Regula I and the Genesis project being developed there. It is later learned that this was an effort to win vengeance on Captain James Kirk for his role in exiling Khan to Ceti Alpha V in 2267.

Although Khan is ultimately thwarted, Captain Clark Terrell is killed and his ship, the *Reliant,* is destroyed when Khan attempts to steal the Genesis device.

Captain Spock dies of severe radiation exposure during the Genesis crisis, but his actions permit the *Enterprise* to escape the detonation of the device. Khan and his followers are also reported killed in the explosion. Spock's coffin is consigned to the depths of space.

Editors' Note: The fact that Saavik was a lieutenant while still apparently an Academy cadet is consistent with the notion that Kirk apparently also held the rank of lieutenant while at the Academy.

Khan

Detonation of the Genesis device

The death of Captain Spock

Lieutenant Saavik and David Marcus assigned to U.S.S. *Grissom* for further study of the Genesis Planet in the Mutara Sector.

Between Star Trek II *and* Star Trek III.

Star Trek III: The Search for Spock. Stardate 8201.3. U.S.S. *Enterprise* returns to Spacedock in Earth orbit for repairs following battle in the Mutara Sector. Upon arrival, *Enterprise* captain James Kirk is informed by Admiral Morrow that rather than being refit, the *Enterprise* is due to be scrapped.

Marcus and Saavik study the Genesis Planet.

U.S.S. *Grissom* science team consisting of Saavik and Marcus, investigating the Genesis Planet in the Mutara Sector, discovers an extraordinary range of life-forms, including the regenerated, living body of Captain Spock. It is speculated that the torpedo serving as his coffin somehow soft-landed on the planet. During the investigation, the *Grissom* is attacked by a Klingon vessel resulting in the loss of all hands except for Saavik and Marcus, who are stranded on the planet's surface. Marcus is later killed by a Klingon landing party.

Admiral James Kirk commandeers the Starship *Enterprise*, taking it to the Mutara Sector in an effort to recover the body of Spock from the Genesis Planet so that it can be returned to planet Vulcan. During the unauthorized mission, Kirk orders the destruction of the *Enterprise* to prevent the ship from falling into Klingon hands. Kirk gains control of the Klingon vessel, using it to return Spock's now-living body to Vulcan.

The destruction of the U.S.S. Enterprise

Genesis Planet disintegrates due to protomatter used in its creation matrix.

Vulcan High Priestess T'Lar presides over the ancient *Fal-tor-pan* ceremony, re-fusing Spock's *katra,* residing in the mind of Dr. McCoy, with Spock's body, recovered from the Genesis Planet.

Editors' Note: The Enterprise *flight data recorder played for Sarek indicates the stardate of Spock's death as being 8128.7. This would seem to be inconsistent with the stardate of 8130.3 given by Saavik during her Kobayashi Maru exercise. One might rationalize that this is due to relativistic effects of spaceflight, or other peculiarities of stardate computation.*

This film establishes Dr. Leonard McCoy's middle initial to be "H," and the name of his father to be David.

T'Lar

Starship U.S.S. *Hathaway* is launched. When retired eighty years later, this *Constellation* class ship is part of a Starfleet strategic simulation exercise under the command of Captain Picard and Commander Riker.

"Peak Performance." The Hathaway *was 80 years old at the time of the episode (2365).*

Spock undergoes reeducation and retraining process at his parents' home on planet Vulcan. He rapidly assimilates his technical and scientific education, taught in the Vulcan way, but has difficulty with humanistic concepts taught by his mother, Amanda.

Between Star Trek III *and* IV. *Kirk's log in* Star Trek IV *establishes the total length of their stay (and of Spock's reeducation) is about three months.*

2286

Star Trek IV: The Voyage Home. Stardate 8390.0. Klingon Ambassador demands extradition of Admiral Kirk for alleged crimes against the Klingon

The Klingon ambassador

Dr. Gillian Taylor

nation. The Federation Council declines the request, citing pending Federation action against Kirk for violation of nine Starfleet regulations.

Alien space probe of unknown origin damages several spacecraft and wreaks environmental havoc on Earth. The probe returns to deep space after communicating with two humpback whales brought to this century by Admiral Kirk.

Cetacean biologist Gillian Taylor, originally from Earth's 20th century, becomes a scientist on a Federation science vessel.

Admiral James Kirk and his shipmates vote to return to Earth to face charges stemming from acts committed during the rescue of Captain Spock. Kirk is found guilty of disobeying direct orders and is demoted to captain, and assigned command of the Starship *Enterprise*, NCC-1701-A.

U.S.S. *Enterprise*, NCC-1701-A, the second starship to bear the name, enters service under the command of Captain James Kirk.

The Lornak clan of the planet Acamar III massacre all but five members of the clan Tralesta, ending a blood feud that had lasted for 200 years. Yuta of the clan Tralesta is one of the survivors. Her cells are altered to slow her aging so that she may have enough time to exact vengeance upon all members of the clan Lornak.

"The Vengeance Factor." Eighty years prior to the episode (2366).

The new U.S.S. Enterprise, NCC-1701-A

2287

Sybok

Star Trek V: The Final Frontier. Stardate 8454.1. U.S.S. *Enterprise* undergoes final testing and preparation for service under the direction of Engineering Officer Montgomery Scott.

Romulan, Federation, and Klingon diplomatic representatives on planet Nimbus III are seized by Sybok, Spock's half brother. The starship *Enterprise* is dispatched to parlay for their release. Negotiations are unsuccessful, and an attempt is made to free the hostages by force. The attempt is also unsuccessful, resulting in the capture of the *Enterprise* by Sybok and his followers.

Sybok commandeers the *Enterprise* in a search for the mythical planet Sha-ka-Ree, located at the center of the galaxy. The planet is eventually located, but Sybok is killed by a malevolent entity living there.

Pioneer 10 space probe, drifting in interstellar space, is destroyed by Klingon Bird of Prey under the command of Captain Klaa.

Editors' Note: Gene Roddenberry said he considered some of the events in Star Trek V *to be apocryphal. The film is included in this chronology, however, because of our desire to be as complete as possible.*

U.S.S. Excelsior, NCC-2000

Transwarp Development Project deemed unsuccessful by Starfleet Command. U.S.S. *Excelsior* is refitted with a standard warp drive and is assigned Starfleet duty. The ship, previously classified as an experimental vessel with an NX registry prefix, is redesignated as NCC-2000.

Date is conjecture, but presumably happened between Star Trek IV *and* Star Trek VI. *The date is arbitrarily biased more toward* Star Trek VI *to allow for Starfleet time to have adequately conducted its experiments and tests, while allowing enough time for the ship to have spent three years cataloging planetary atmospheres.*

A Federation starship suffers a systemwide technological failure. This is the last such occurrence prior to the Nanites' takeover of the *Enterprise*-D's main computers in 2366.

> *"Evolution." Data notes that such a failure had not happened in the past 79 years. One wonders if this incident refers to the failure of transwarp drive.*

2288

Starfleet retires *Soyuz* class of starships.

> *"Cause and Effect." Geordi notes that* Soyuz *class ships haven't been in service for 80 years prior to the episode (2368).*

> *Editors' Note: The Soyuz class U.S.S. Bozeman in "Cause and Effect" was, of course, a modification of the Miranda class U.S.S. Reliant model built for Star Trek II: The Wrath of Khan. It was originally hoped that a new model could be built for the Bozeman, but practical considerations necessitated the use of the Reliant model, so model-maker Greg Jein added some nifty outboard "sensor pods" to turn it into a different class of starship.*

Soyuz *class starship*

2290

Hikaru Sulu is promoted to captain and placed in command of the Starship *Excelsior*. The ship is assigned to scientific research in Beta quadrant, near Klingon neutral zone.

Captain Hikaru Sulu

> Star Trek VI: The Undiscovered Country. *This was three years prior to* Star Trek VI, *set in 2293, since Sulu mentions in his log that he's just finished his first mission as captain of* Excelsior, *and that the mission had lasted three years.*

Janice Rand is assigned as *Excelsior* communications officer.

Communications officer Janice Rand

> *Date is conjecture, but she served as* Excelsior *communications officer during* Star Trek VI, *although this would have been after her stint at Starfleet Command, seen in* Star Trek IV.

U.S.S. *Enterprise*, U.S.S. *Excelsior*, and other Federation starships are outfitted with improved sensors to support a scientific project cataloging planetary atmospheric anomalies.

> Star Trek VI: The Undiscovered Country. *The project had been under way for three years at the beginning of the film (2393).*

Klingon sleeper ship *T'Ong* is launched on an extended mission of exploration under the command of Captain K'Temok. They return in the year 2365, when there is peace between the Federation and the Klingon Empire.

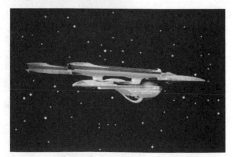

U.S.S. Excelsior

> *"The Emissary." The ship was launched 75 years prior to the episode. K'Ehleyr said the ship was from an era when the Federation and the Klingons were still at war. This is consistent with the 2290 date, which is before the Khitomer Conference in* Star Trek VI: The Undiscovered Country.

2292

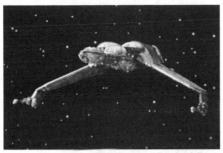

Uprated Klingon Bird-of-Prey

Klingons develop improved Bird-of-Prey capable of maintaining limited invisibility cloak while firing torpedo weapons.

Date is conjecture. This is presumably soon before Star Trek VI: The Undiscovered Country.

Editors' Note: This development raises the question of why Klingon spacecraft are still unable to use their weapons while cloaked in Star Trek: The Next Generation *episodes. The real reason, of course, is that* Next Generation *writers were not aware of this new "development" during the first four seasons of that show, before* Star Trek VI *was written. We imagine that cloaking technology, like present day "stealth" technology, is a constantly evolving race between the designers of cloaking devices and the folks who design sensors. Even though this "improved" ship could evade detection while firing, one might assume that improved sensor designs would later render this development ineffective, at least until the next advance in cloaking technology. In fact, Kirk's use of plasma sensors on photon torpedoes in* Star Trek VI *would seem to do just that.*

The alliance between the Klingon Empire and the Romulan Star Empire collapses. The two former allies become bitter enemies for at least 75 years.

"Reunion." Geordi expresses surprise at evidence of Klingon-Romulan cooperation, noting that the two powers had been blood enemies for 75 years prior to the episode (2367).

2293

Captain Montgomery Scott

Montgomery Scott buys a boat. Uhura agrees to chair a seminar at Starfleet Academy.

Just prior to Star Trek VI: The Undiscovered Country.

Klingon chancellor Gorkon

Star Trek VI: The Undiscovered Country. Stardate 9521.6. Klingon moon Praxis explodes, causing severe damage to the Klingon Homeworld of Qo'noS. Federation starship *Excelsior* also damaged by subspace shock wave from explosion.

Klingons launch major peace initiative, during which Captain Spock agrees to serve as a special envoy at the request of Ambassador Sarek. Initial talks appear encouraging, but Klingon chancellor Gorkon is assassinated while en route to Earth for a peace conference. *Enterprise* captain James T. Kirk and Dr. Leonard H. McCoy are convicted by a Klingon court for the murder, and are sentenced to life imprisonment at the Rura Penthe dilithium mines. The peace conference is rescheduled to take place at Camp Khitomer.

Kirk and McCoy are later found to be innocent of Gorkon's murder when the crime is found to be the work of Starfleet admiral Cartwright and other Federation and Klingon forces opposed to the change in the status quo. Kirk, commanding *Enterprise*, and Captain Sulu, commanding the Starship *Excelsior*, are successful in preventing another attempt by these forces to disrupt the peace conference. The Khitomer Conference becomes a major turning point in galactic politics, representing the beginning of rapprochement between the two adversaries.

Stardate 9523.1. Last mission of the Starship *Enterprise* under the command of Captain James T. Kirk.

James Tiberius Kirk

Editors' Note: At the time this chronology was compiled, it was Paramount's expressed intention that Star Trek VI *be the last film with the original crew. It is, of course, entirely possible that the studio could at some point have a corporate change of mind and produce yet another adventure with those friends, but at this writing we are accepting that this is their final mission. A sixth-season* Star Trek: The Next Generation *episode being produced at this writing ("Relics") will suggest that the* Enterprise-A *was retired approximately one year after the events in* Star Trek VI.

Dr. Leonard H. McCoy

Date of Star Trek VI *determined from Dr. McCoy's testimony that he had served aboard the* Enterprise *for 27 years. McCoy was apparently assigned to the ship in early 2266 (between "Where No Man Has Gone Before" and "The Corbomite Maneuver"). This film establishes James T. Kirk's middle name to be Tiberius, and Sulu's first name to be Hikaru. This is also the first time the Klingon Homeworld has been referred to by name, Qo'noS (pronounced "kronos.")*

Spock meets Romulan senator Pardek during the Khitomer Conference. They remain in contact, pursuing the goal of Romulan/Vulcan reunification, until the year 2368, when Pardek is exposed to be an undercover agent for the conservative Romulan government.

"Unification, Part I." Sarek said this is where Spock and Pardek met.

Camp Khitomer, site of the Khitomer Conference

2295

An outbreak of deadly plasma plague on planet Obi VI. Dr. Susan Nuress, a researcher investigating the disease, conducts at least 58 tests resulting in at least one highly virulent mutated strain.

"The Child." Pulaski noted the outbreak had taken place 70 years prior to the episode (2365).

2296

The Eastern Continental government of planet Rutia IV denies a bid for independence by the Ansata, a separatist organization. Members of the Ansata begin a long terrorist war in an attempt to force the government to grant their demands.

"The High Ground." Alexana told Riker that the Ansata had been fighting for 70 years prior to the episode (2366).

2297

First contact with the inhabitants of planet Ventax II by a Klingon expedition. The planet's culture is reported to be a peaceful agrarian economy, despite evidence of a technologically advanced society in centuries past.

"Devil's Due." Dr. Clark said the contact had taken place 70 years prior to episode (2267).

6.0 THE TWENTY-FOURTH CENTURY

The fifth Federation starship to bear the name U.S.S. Enterprise *played a key role in both exploration and diplomacy during the latter half of the 24th century.*

2302

Last Federation contact with planet Angel I prior to 2364. The contact is by a Federation vessel that reports the planet to have a technological development level similar to mid-20th-century Earth.

"Angel One." Data notes that the contact had taken place 62 years prior to episode (2364).

2305

Jean-Luc Picard

Jean-Luc Picard is born to Maurice and Yvette Picard in LaBarre, France, on Earth. He becomes captain of the fifth Federation starship to bear the name *Enterprise*.

Conjecture: This date is consistent with a Starfleet Academy graduation in 2327, as established in "The First Duty," assuming that Picard had applied unsuccessfully for the Academy at age 17, and that he was accepted when he was 18 (as suggested in "Coming of Age"). Picard's parents and place of birth are from his computer dossier file in "Conundrum." The sixth-season episode "Chain of Command, Part II" will establish Picard's mother to have been Yvette Gessard.

2307

Timicin

Timicin is born on planet Kaelon II. He becomes a scientist and plays a key role in that planet's effort to extend the life of the star Kaelon by a helium fusion ignition process.

"Half a Life." Timicin was 60 years old at the time of the episode (2367).

2311

The Tomed Incident. Thousands of Federation lives are lost. This is the last Federation contact with the Romulans prior to 2364.

"The Neutral Zone." Fifty-three years prior to episode.

Editors' Note: The episode makes it clear that the Federation and the Romulans had no contact at all during the years between this incident and "The Neutral Zone" (2364), but other episodes have suggested that there was some contact between the Romulans and the Klingons during this period, in that the Romulans apparently had been trying to destabilize the Klingon government for two decades prior to Star Trek: The Next Generation's fourth season ("Redemption, Part I," set in 2367).

The emblem of the Romulan Star Empire

2312

A life-form known as a Douwd, an "immortal being of disguise and false surroundings," who has lived in this galaxy for thousands of years, assumes the form of a human named Kevin Uxbridge. On Earth in the New Martim Vaz aquatic city in Earth's Atlantic Ocean, he falls in love with and marries a human woman named Rishon. They eventually join the 11,000 colonists in the ill-fated Delta Rana IV colony in 2361.

Kevin Uxbridge

"The Survivors." Kevin said he'd lived in human form for about 50 years prior to the episode but he and Rishon had been married for 53 years, so we are arbitrarily pegging the date he became human as 54 years prior to the episode. The Rana IV colony had existed for five years prior to the episode (2366).

2313

Gatherer Penthor Mull of planet Acamar III is accused of leading a raid on the Tralesta clan. He is killed by a microvirus carried by Yuta as part of her quest to avenge the 2286 massacre of her clan.

"The Vengeance Factor." Fifty-three years prior to episode (2366).

2314

Mark and Anne Jameson are married. The future Admiral Mark Jameson's celebrated Starfleet career includes a stint as commander of the Starship *Gettysburg.*

"Too Short a Season." Anne Jameson said they had been married for 50 years at the time of the episode (2364).

2319

The father of Mordan IV leader Karnas is assassinated by a rival tribe. Karnas seizes 65 passengers of a starliner, demanding that Starfleet provide weapons in exchange for the lives of the hostages. Two Federation mediators are killed in unsuccessful attempts to resolve the situation. Federation hostages, held by revolutionaries on planet Mordan IV, are freed thanks to negotiations conducted by Captain Jameson of U.S.S. *Gettysburg.* Although Jameson is credited with the peaceful resolution of the situation, it is later learned that this intervention included a weapons-for-hostages deal that resulted in a bloody 40-year civil war.

"Too Short a Season." Forty-five years prior to episode (2364).

2322

Jean-Luc Picard applies to Starfleet Academy, but is rejected. However, his admission test score is sufficient to allow him to reapply the following year.

Date is conjecture, assumes he was 17 years old at the time, that he was 18 years old when admitted next year, and that he graduated in 2327, as mentioned in "The First Duty." Picard confesses his early failure to gain Academy entrance to Wesley in "Coming of Age."

2323

Jean-Luc
Picard

Jean-Luc Picard enters Starfleet Academy on his second application. The superintendent of the Academy is a full Betazoid. As a freshman cadet, Picard passes four upperclassmen on the last hill of the 40-kilometer run on Danula II, becoming the only freshman ever to win the Academy marathon. One of Picard's interests is archaeology, and he studies the legendary Iconians.

Date is conjecture. Assumes Picard was 18 years old when he was admitted to the Academy, and that he graduated in 2327, as established in "The First Duty." Picard's Academy marathon win described by Admiral Hanson in "The Best of Both Worlds, Part II." Picard's interest in the Iconians from "Contagion."

2324

Dr. Beverly
Crusher

Beverly Howard, the future Beverly Crusher, is born in Copernicus City, Luna, to Paul and Isabel Howard.

"Conundrum." Date and parents' names given in computer bio screen. This is consistent with Beverly being about 40 years old during the first season, as suggested by the writers'/directors' guide.

Starfleet Academy team wins a parrises squares tournament over the heavily favored team from Minsk. The Academy team scores a dramatic victory in the last 40 seconds of the final game of the series.

"The First Duty." Boothby reminds Picard of the "parrises squares tournament in '24."

2325

Devinoni Ral is born on Earth, in Brussels, the European Alliance. He is one-fourth Betazoid, which Ral uses to his advantage as an adult in his career as a professional negotiator.

"The Price." Ral's age is given as 41 in the episode.

2327

Jean-Luc Picard graduates from Starfleet Academy. He is class valedictorian.

In later years, Picard would credit Academy groundskeeper Boothby for helping him to find the strength to make it through some difficult times.

"The First Duty." Picard reminds Boothby that he graduated in the class of '27. Robert Picard noted in "Family" that Jean-Luc had been valedictorian.

Starfleet Academy groundskeeper Boothby

2328

The Cardassian Empire annexes the Bajoran homeworld, forcing much of the native population of Bajor to resettle elsewhere, including three planets in the Valo system on the outskirts of Cardassian territory. Those who remained on Bajor were tortured and otherwise mistreated. An underground of Bajoran nationals conducts a terrorist campaign against the Cardassians for the next 40 years. The United Federation of Planets, considering this to be an internal Cardassian affair, expresses sympathy for the Bajoran people, but declines involvement in the issue until 2368.

"Ensign Ro." Admiral Kennelly noted the Cardassians had annexed Bajor 40 years prior to the episode (2368).

2331

United Federation of Planets establishes an outpost on planet Boradis III. It is the first Federation settlement in the system. This colony is among the thirteen settlements in the Boradis sector within potential striking range of the Klingon sleeper ship *T'Ong* when it returns to the area in 2365.

"The Emissary." Thirty-four years prior to episode (2365).

U.S.S. Stargazer, *NCC-2893*

2333

Captain Jean-Luc Picard assumes command of the U.S.S. *Stargazer*, embarking on a historic mission of exploration. At age 28, Picard is among the youngest Starfleet officers ever to captain a starship.

Date is conjecture, based on a reference in the Star Trek: The Next Generation Writers'/Directors' Guide that Picard's Stargazer mission was 22 years long. Also based on a reference in "The Battle" which suggests the Battle of Maxia had taken place nine years prior to that episode. Boothby, in "The First Duty," commented that Locarno would have been even younger than Picard, had he made the captaincy at age 25.

2335

William T. Riker is born in Valdez, Alaska, on planet Earth. He is the son of Kyle Riker.

"The Icarus Factor." Riker was apparently 30 years old at the time of the episode (2365) because he was 15 years old when his father left him 15 years earlier.

William T. Riker

Geordi La Forge is born in the African Confederation on planet Earth.

"Cause and Effect." Year and place of birth given in Geordi's medical records screen.

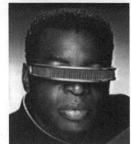

Geordi La Forge

2336

Deanna
Troi

Deanna Troi is born on Betazed. She is the child of Lwaxana Troi and Starfleet officer Ian Andrew Troi.

"Conundrum." Year given in computer bio screen. The name of Troi's father was established in "The Child."

The science colony at Omicron Theta is destroyed by what is later known as the Crystalline Entity. All life-forms on the planet are absorbed or destroyed by the Entity, apparently aided by the errant android Lore. Scientist Noonien Soong, who had constructed a second android, Data, manages to record the memories of all the colonists in the new android. Soong conceals the still-dormant android Data in an underground location, then escapes from Omicron Theta, although it is believed at the time that Soong was among the casualties at the colony.

"Datalore." Date is conjecture, but this is prior to Data's discovery by the Tripoli crew in 2338. Data said that when he was discovered, he was covered by a layer of dust, suggesting some time had passed.

2337

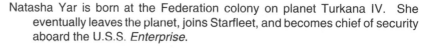

Natasha
Yar

Natasha Yar is born at the Federation colony on planet Turkana IV. She eventually leaves the planet, joins Starfleet, and becomes chief of security aboard the U.S.S. *Enterprise*.

"The Naked Now" establishes that Tasha was 15 at the time she escaped from the Turkana colony, and "Legacy" is set 15 years after her escape, meaning that Tasha would have been 30 had she been alive in 2367 (when "Legacy" is set). Tasha was 27 when she died in "Skin of Evil."

Will Riker's mother dies, leaving him to be raised by his father, Starfleet civilian adviser Kyle Riker.

"The Icarus Factor." Riker was two years old when his mother died.

Trill ambassador Odan successfully mediates a dispute between the two moons of planet Peliar Zel, although the entity later known as Odan is at the time known as Odan's father. Odan bridges the differences between the two adversaries by persuading their representatives to trade places for a week so that they can more clearly understand each other's position. During the negotiations, Alpha moon representative Kalin Trose quells a plot by radicals to assassinate the Beta moon's delegation.

"The Host." Odan, in Riker's body, describes the negotiations as having taken place 30 years prior to the episode (2367).

Android
Data

The government of the Federation colony on planet Turkana IV begins to fall apart, eventually resulting in the destruction of all the cities above ground.

"Legacy." Ishara Yar says the colony started collapsing almost 30 years prior to the episode (2367).

2338

Data is discovered at the remains of the colony on planet Omicron Theta by crew of the Federation starship U.S.S. *Tripoli*. The *Tripoli* crew reports all

colonists missing and all plant life dead. It is later discovered that the deaths had been caused by what will become known as the Crystalline Entity.

"Datalore." Data had been found 26 years prior to episode (2364). Additional attacks established in "Silicon Avatar."

2340

Worf is born on the Klingon Homeworld of Qo'noS.

"The Bonding." He was six years old at the time of the Khitomer massacre.

Editors' Note: The name of the Klingon Homeworld was established as Qo'noS (pronounced "kronos") in Star Trek VI: The Undiscovered Country.

Worf

Ro Laren is born on the planet Bajor. As an adult she serves a tour of duty aboard the Starship *Wellington*, and is court-martialed after a disastrous incident at Garon II. She later serves aboard the U.S.S. *Enterprise* under the command of Captain Jean-Luc Picard.

"Conundrum." Year of birth given in computer screen bio. Ro's back story established in "Ensign Ro."

Geordi La Forge, aged five, is caught in a fire. His parents rescue him after a couple of minutes. Although he was not hurt, Geordi would later recall that these were the longest couple of minutes of his life, and that it was some time before he would allow his parents out of earshot.

"Hero Worship." Geordi said he was five years old at the time of the fire. He also noted that he did not yet have a VISOR at this point.

2341

Data enters Starfleet Academy. The Academy had ruled that Data is a sentient life-form and thus was eligible for consideration for entry.

"Conundrum." Information from Data's bio screen. "Redemption, Part II" establishes Data had been in Starfleet for about 26 years (which should mean he joined the service in 2342). Starfleet Academy ruling on Data's sentience established in "Encounter at Farpoint."

Ishara
Yar

2342

Ishara Yar is born on planet Turkana IV. Her older sister is Natasha Yar.

"Legacy." Ishara describes her parents as having been killed "just after" she was born. (See next entry.)

Natasha Yar, a five-year-old child living in the collapsing colony on Turkana IV, is orphaned when her parents are killed by crossfire between rival gangs. She is left to care for her younger sister, Ishara.

"The Naked Now." Tasha says she was five when she was orphaned. Turkana IV established in "Legacy."

April 9. Jean-Luc Picard stands up the future Jenice Manheim in the Café des Artistes in Paris. Years later the two recreate the event in the *Enterprise* holodeck, this time with Picard keeping the rendezvous.

The future
Jenice
Manheim

City of Paris on planet Earth

"We'll Always Have Paris." Twenty-two years prior to episode (2364).

Editors' Note: The futuristic Paris cityscape seen from the Café des Artistes was the same backdrop used by production designer Herman Zimmerman for the Federation president's office in Star Trek VI: The Undiscovered Country.

Beverly Howard (the future Dr. Beverly Crusher) enters the Starfleet Academy medical school.

"Conundrum." Year given in computer bio screen.

2343

Starfleet approves early design work on *Galaxy* class starship development project. The third ship of this class will eventually become the fifth Federation starship to bear the name *Enterprise*.

Conjecture.

Geordi La Forge, aged eight, gets his first pet, a Circassian cat. Years later Geordi would recall his pet as "funny-looking."

"Violations." Geordi said he was eight when he got his pet.

2344

Enterprise
captain
Rachel Garrett

Starship *Enterprise*-C, under the command of Captain Rachel Garrett, is nearly destroyed defending a Klingon outpost on Narendra III from a Romulan attack. The rendering of assistance by a Federation starship is a key development in maintaining the path to friendly relations between the Federation and the Klingons.

"Yesterday's Enterprise.*"* Twenty-two years prior to episode (2366).

Editors' Note: Although the Khitomer Conference of 2293 (Star Trek VI: The Undiscovered Country) was depicted as a turning point in Federation-Klingon relations, it seems clear from this incident at Narendra and the Khitomer massacre of 2346 ("Sins of the Father") that peace between the two powers was gradually achieved over a period of time, involving many attempts and many breakthroughs over a number of years.

U.S.S. Enterprise, *NCC-1701-C*

Natasha
Yar

A few members of the *Enterprise*-C crew are reported to have been captured by the Romulans following the battle at Narendra III. Years later evidence is uncovered indicating that among those captured crew members was, inexplicably, a 29-year-old woman named Natasha Yar — apparently the same woman who served on the *Enterprise*-D as security chief prior to her death in 2364 at the age of 27. It is later suggested that the lives of these Starfleet personnel were spared when Natasha Yar agreed to become the consort of a Romulan official. For years, reports of the capture of *Enterprise*-C personnel are regarded only as unconfirmed rumors until the attempted Romulan hegemony into Klingon politics in 2367-68. It has been speculated that the woman captured by the Romulans had actually originated in an alternate timeline.

"Redemption, Part II." Sela described the fate of Tasha Yar to Captain Picard. We are assuming her account was substantially truthful.

Last attempt to make diplomatic contact with the Jaradans prior to 2364. The attempt is dramatically unsuccessful because of mispronunciation of a single word.

Kyle Riker

"The Big Goodbye." Twenty years prior to episode (2364).

Young William Riker goes fishing with his father, Kyle Riker, near their home in Valdez, Alaska. The younger Riker is able to hook a big fish, but his father insists on reeling it in. The incident would bother Will for many years.

"The Icarus Factor." Riker told Worf he was nine at the time.

2345

Data graduates from Starfleet Academy with honors in exobiology and probability mechanics.

"Encounter at Farpoint." Starfleet Academy was established to be a four-year institution in "The First Duty," but the 2345 graduation date disregards Data's mention of his having been part of the "class of '78." The latter date reference was written prior to the establishment of the calendar year of Star Trek: The Next Generation *late in the first season and is being ignored because it is inconsistent with the preponderance of other established dating information.*

Starfleet Academy campus at the Presidio in San Francisco

Kurn is born, son of Mogh, and brother to Worf.

"Sins of the Father." Date is conjecture, but Kurn said he was "barely a year old" when Worf left for Khitomer with their parents. Further assumes the Khitomer massacre of 2346 happened fairly shortly after their arrival.

Sela is born on Romulus. She later claims to be the child of former *Enterprise* crew member Tasha Yar and a Romulan official.

"Redemption, Part II." A year after the events in "Yesterday's Enterprise."

2346

Mogh suspects Ja'rod, a member of the powerful Duras family, of plotting with the Romulans against the Klingon emperor. He follows Ja'rod to the Khitomer Outpost. Mogh expects the trip to Khitomer to be relatively short, so he arranges for family friend Lorgh to care for his younger son, the infant Kurn. Mogh's wife and elder son, Worf, accompany Mogh to Khitomer.

Sela

"Sins of the Father." Date is conjecture, but this presumably took place between the birth of Kurn (who was "barely a year old" when Mogh left) and the Khitomer massacre. Worf's former nursemaid, Kahlest, describes Mogh's suspicions to Picard.

Romulans attack the Klingon outpost at Khitomer. The attack is successful because a Romulan collaborator had given the attackers access to secret Klingon defense codes. Four thousand Klingons are killed in the massacre. Twenty years later, Worf's father, Mogh, is posthumously accused of providing the defense codes to the Romulans, but it is ultimately learned that Ja'rod, the father of council member Duras, is guilty of the crime.

Federation starship U.S.S. *Intrepid,* responding to a distress call from Khitomer, is one of the first ships on the scene to offer aid.

One of the survivors is a six-year-old Klingon child, Worf, who is rescued by *Intrepid* warp field specialist Sergey Rozhenko. Rozhenko finds the child buried under a pile of rubble and left for dead. He adopts Worf as his son to be raised on the farm world of Gault. The only other survivor, Worf's nursemaid, Kahlest, is treated on Starbase 24 and later returned to the Klingon Homeworld. The Klingon High Command, unaware that Worf's brother, Kurn, is living with a family friend, informs Rozhenko that Worf has no living relatives, and Worf remains unaware that he does have a living biological brother.

"Sins of the Father." Twenty years prior to the episode. References to Worf's adoptive parents are from "Family." Reference to Worf's having been raised on Gault is from "Heart of Glory." Worf also mentioned that his parents were killed when he was six years old in "The Bonding."

Dr. Paul Stubbs

Astrophysicist Dr. Paul Stubbs begins a project to study the decay of neutronium expelled at relativistic speeds in a stellar explosion. He chooses a binary star system in the Kavis Alpha sector, desirable because of the predictability of its stellar bursts. He prepares and begins to test an instrumented probe for launch into the star, whose next predicted burst will occur in 2366.

"Evolution." Stubbs said he'd been working on the "egg" probe for 20 years.

2347

Worf at seven years of age gets into trouble at school on planet Gault for beating up several teenaged human boys.

"Family." Age of seven mentioned by Worf's adoptive father, Sergey Rozhenko.

Ro Laren

Ro Laren witnesses her father's brutal torture and murder at the hands of Cardassian forces.

"Ensign Ro." Ro said she was seven at the time of this incident. Assumes Ro was born in 2340, as suggested in computer bio screens in "Conundrum" and "The Next Phase."

A bottle of Chateau Picard from this year's vintage is given to Jean-Luc by Robert in 2367. Captain Picard later shares this bottle with Chancellor Durken of the planet Malcor.

"Family." Robert Picard mentions the date. Picard and Durken share the drink in "First Contact."

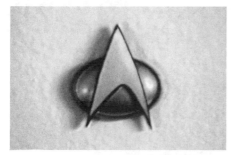

Updated Starfleet emblem

Starfleet Command orders a change in the design of the Starfleet emblem. The new, simplified design features an elliptical background field and a slightly redrawn arrowhead.

Date is conjecture, but we saw the older, feature-film version of the emblem in use on board the Enterprise-C *in 2344 ("Yesterday's* Enterprise*") and the newer version on Jack Crusher's uniform in 2349 ("Family").*

Editors Note: Producer Ronald Moore (writer of "Family") tells us that Jack Crusher's wearing of the newer insignia in that episode was purely an accident. Moore happened to be visiting the set when Jack's holographic message to Wesley was being filmed, and noticed that Jack was not wearing a Starfleet emblem on his uniform. When he pointed this out to our costumers, the only badge they could find was the Next Generation *version, so that's the one they used.*

2348

Starfleet officer Jack Crusher marries medical student Beverly Howard. Jack proposes to Beverly with a joke by giving her a book entitled *How to Advance Your Career Through Marriage*. Jack and Beverly had been introduced by Walker Keel, a close friend of Jack Crusher's and Jean-Luc Picard's, although Picard would later recall that he had not yet met Beverly at this point.

"Family." Date is conjecture, a year before their son Wesley's birth. Walker Keel established in "Conspiracy."

Jack Crusher

Marouk, the sovereign of planet Acamar III, makes an effort to reconcile her differences with her people's Gatherers. The nomadic Gatherers refuse to accept the peace that has existed on the planet for 82 years.

"The Vengeance Factor." Marouk says the last attempt to make peace with the Gatherers was 18 years prior to the episode.

Jean-Luc Picard visits his family in his hometown of Labarre, France. It is his last trip home prior to his convalescence after the Borg encounter of 2367.

"Family." Picard hadn't been home in almost twenty years.

2349

Wesley Crusher is born to Jack and Beverly Crusher. When Wesley is ten weeks old, Jack records a holographic message that he hopes Wesley will play when he reaches his 18th birthday. Although the elder Crusher hopes to record a series of messages to his son, this is the only one he will make.

"Evolution." Beverly notes Wesley was 17 during that episode (2366). Jack's holographic message was seen in "Family."

Wesley Crusher

Dr. Paul Manheim's time-gravity work begins to gain acceptance in the Federation scientific community.

"We'll Always Have Paris." Fifteen years prior to episode (2364).

Former *Enterprise* security officer Tasha Yar is reportedly executed following an attempted escape from Romulus with her daughter, Sela. The attempt fails when the child cries out for fear of being taken from her home.

"Redemption, Part II." Sela tells Picard that she was four years old at the time her mother was killed.

Tasha Yar

2350

Beverly Crusher graduates with a medical degree from Starfleet Academy.

"Conundrum." Year given in computer screen bio. Assumes that a medical degree is an eight-year program.

Kyle Riker leaves his son, William, at age 15. Will's mother had died some years earlier. The younger Riker bitterly resents being "abandoned," and the two do not speak again until 2365.

"Icarus Factor." Fifteen years prior to episode.

Kyle Riker

Sergey and Helena Rozhenko

2351

Sergey and Helena Rozhenko, along with their adopted son, Worf, and another son, move from the farm world of Gault to Earth.

Date is conjecture. The fact of the move is based on Worf's line in "Heart of Glory" that he spent his formative years on Gault, but in "Family" Guinan indicated that Worf looked toward his adoptive parents on Earth as his home. Worf spoke of a foster brother in "Heart of Glory."

2352

*Natasha Yar
at Turkana IV*

Fifteen-year-old Natasha Yar escapes from the failed colony at Turkana IV. Her younger sister, Ishara, who has joined one of the gangs on the planet, declines to leave with her. Tasha eventually joins Starfleet and becomes *Enterprise* security chief. Shortly after Tasha's departure, the colony breaks off contact with the United Federation of Planets.

"Legacy." Ishara Yar says her sister left the colony 15 years prior to the episode (2367). Her age at the time of her escape is established to be 15 in "The Naked Now."

Varria, an idealistic young woman, begins a 14-year association with unscrupulous collector Kivas Fajo, a Zibalian trader of the Stacius Trade Guild. They remain together until 2366, when she is killed by Fajo after she attempts to help Data escape from Fajo's captivity.

"The Most Toys." Varria tells Data she'd been with Fajo for 14 years.

Beverly Crusher serves a residency on planet Delos IV under Dr. Dalen Quaice.

"Remember Me." Beverly tells Data she's known Quaice for 15 years prior to the episode (2367).

Dr. Dalen Quaice

Editors' Note: This would appear to be inconsistent with the date of 2350 established in "Conundrum" for Beverly's graduation from Starfleet medical school. Maybe she had really known Quaice 17 years, and she was just rounding it off?

Scientists at the Darwin research station on planet Gagarin IV conduct an ambitious genetic experiment designed to give their children extraordinarily powerful immune systems.

"Unnatural Selection." The oldest of the super-children was twelve at the time of the episode (2365). This is a year prior to that point.

2353

Starfleet civilian adviser Kyle Riker is the sole survivor of a Tholian attack on a starbase. Afterward, Riker recovers under the care of future *Enterprise* chief medical officer Katherine Pulaski. The two become romantically involved, and Pulaski later says she would have married him "in a cold minute," but Riker had other priorities in his life. Pulaski would also later theorize that the emotional scars from the Tholian attack were the reason Kyle never remarried.

"Icarus Factor." Twelve years prior to episode (2365).

Jeremiah Rossa is born to Connor and Moira Rossa at the Federation colony on Galen IV. He is the grandson of Starfleet admiral Connaught Rossa. His parents are later killed in a Talarian attack on the colony, and he is adopted by the Talarian captain Endar, who claims the right to raise Jeremiah as his own son, naming him Jono.

"Suddenly Human." Data noted Jeremiah/Jono was 14 years old at the time of the episode (2367).

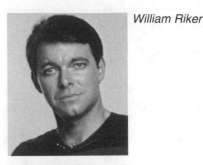
William Riker

William Riker enters Starfleet Academy. One of his friends is fellow student Paul Rice, who would eventually command the U.S.S. *Drake* prior to Rice's death at planet Minos. The superintendent of the Academy is a native of the planet Vulcan.

Date is conjecture, assumes he entered at age 18, reckoned from his birth date derived from "The Icarus Factor." Paul Rice established in "The Arsenal of Freedom." Riker mentions the superintendent in "The First Duty."

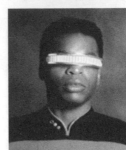
Geordi La Forge

Geordi La Forge enters Starfleet Academy at age 18. His major field of study is engineering.

"Cause and Effect." Year given in computer bio screen.

2354

Jeremy Aster

Jeremy Aster is born to Marla Aster. Jeremy's mother later becomes a crew member aboard the *Enterprise* and is killed on an archaeological research mission when an ancient artifact explodes. *Enterprise* security officer Worf adopts the orphaned boy into his family through the Klingon *R'uustai* ceremony.

"The Bonding." Jeremy's age is given as 12 in the episode (2366).

Lieutenant Jack Crusher dies on U.S.S. *Stargazer* away-team mission under the command of Captain Picard. Wesley Crusher is present when Picard brings the elder Crusher's body back to his family at a starbase. Picard accompanies Beverly as she views the body.

Date is conjecture, but the Star Trek: The Next Generation Writers'/ Directors' Guide *suggests Wesley was five years old at the time of his father's death. "Violations" shows Beverly's memory of Picard and her viewing Jack's body.*

Jean-Luc Picard and Beverly Crusher, after her husband's death

Captain Picard, aboard U.S.S. *Stargazer*, visits planet Chalna. The inhabitants call themselves the Chalnoth. Years later Picard encounters Esoqq, a native of that planet, while both are held captive by unknown aliens conducting a behavioral study.

"Allegiance." Picard said he visited Esoqq's planet 12 years prior to the episode (2366), while commanding the Stargazer. *It is unclear whether this occurred before or after Jack Crusher's death.*

2355

U.S.S. *Stargazer*, under the command of Captain Picard, is nearly destroyed in a conflict in the Maxia Zeta star system by an unknown adversary, eventually learned to be a Ferengi spacecraft. Picard would later recall that

USS Stargazer *after the Battle of Maxia*

Prosecutor Phillipa Louvois

an unidentified ship suddenly appeared and fired twice on the *Stargazer* at point-blank range, disabling the *Stargazer's* shields. Picard saves his crew by employing what is later termed the "Picard maneuver." The ship is abandoned, and the crew drifts in lifeboats and shuttlecraft for ten weeks before being rescued. It is later learned that the son of Ferengi DaiMon Bok was the commander of the attacking Ferengi vessel and was killed in what the Ferengi call "The Battle of Maxia."

"The Battle." Nine years prior to episode (2364).

Captain Picard is court-martialed for the loss of U.S.S. *Stargazer* by Starfleet prosecutor Phillipa Louvois.

"The Measure of a Man." Ten years prior to episode (2365). The fact that Picard continued to serve in Starfleet suggests that the court-martial did not result in a conviction.

Worf, aged 15, reaches Age of Ascension. This ceremony is an important step in the coming of age of a Klingon warrior.

"The Icarus Factor." In the episode (set in 2365) Worf celebrates the tenth anniversary of his Age of Ascension ceremony.

2356

A Tarellian spacecraft, believed to carry the last survivors of the planet Tarella, is destroyed by the Alcyones. The Tarellians had tried to escape their war-devastated home, but had been hunted because they were carriers of deadly biological warfare agents. Eight years later, one more Tarellian ship is discovered, attempting to make planetfall at Haven.

"Haven." The last Tarellian ship was destroyed eight years prior to episode (2364).

2357

Riker and Troi

William Riker graduates from Starfleet Academy. One of his first assignments is as a lieutenant aboard the U.S.S. *Potemkin*. At some point he is also stationed on planet Betazed, where he meets Deanna Troi. He later serves aboard the U.S.S. *Hood* and is assigned to the U.S.S. *Enterprise* in 2364.

Conjecture. Assumes Riker entered the Academy in 2353 at the age of 18. Riker's Potemkin *assignment established in "Peak Performance." He was transferred from the* Hood *to the* Enterprise *in "Encounter at Farpoint."*

Geordi La Forge graduates from Starfleet Academy with a major in engineering. One of his early assignments is aboard the Starship *Victory*.

"Conundrum." Year given in computer bio screen. His major is established in "The Child" to have been engineering. Geordi's Victory *assignment established in "Elementary, Dear Data" and "Identity Crisis."*

Worf

Worf enters Starfleet Academy. He is the first Klingon to serve in the Federation Starfleet. Worf's stepbrother also enters the Academy, but finds it not to his liking and returns to his former home on planet Gault.

"Heart of Glory." Worf described his family history to Korris, noting he was the only Klingon in Starfleet at the time of the episode (2364). Date of Worf's Academy entrance from computer bio screen in "Conundrum."

Freighter S.S. *Odin* is disabled by an asteroid collision. Some survivors escape on lifeboats, drifting for five months before ultimately ending up on planet Angel One.

"Angel One." Seven years prior to episode (2364).

Ornaran captain T'Jon assumes command of the freighter spacecraft *Sanction*. He makes critically important medical cargo run between the planets Ornara and Brekka some 27 times over the next seven years until the *Sanction* suffers a serious malfunction in 2364.

"Symbiosis." T'Jon said he'd been in command for seven years.

Federation outpost at Galen IV is attacked by Talarian forces as part of an ongoing border conflict. Most of the population of the outpost is killed. Among the casualties are Connor and Moira Rossa, whose son, Jeremiah, is rescued by Talarian captain Endar. Jeremiah had been the sole survivor.

Interplanetary freighter Sanction

"Suddenly Human." Data says the outpost was wiped out ten years and three months prior to the episode (2367). The episode also refers to a peace agreement with the Talarians, apparently reached sometime during the ten-year span between this point and the episode.

2358

Major system work progresses on the *Galaxy* class Starship *Enterprise*, under construction at Starfleet's Utopia Planitia Fleet Yards in orbit around planet Mars. The project is under the overall supervision of Commander Quinteros. Significant contributions to the design of the warp propulsion system are made by Dr. Leah Brahms, a junior member of engineering team 7, and a graduate of the Daystrom Institute. The dilithium crystal chamber is designed at Outpost Seran-T-One.

Project emblem for Galaxy *class starship development*

Date is conjecture, but Quinteros was established in "11001001," and Brahms was seen in "Booby Trap" and "Galaxy's Child." Outpost Seran-T-One mentioned in "Booby Trap."

2359

Worf and K'Ehleyr have an unresolved romantic relationship.

"The Emissary." Six years prior to the episode (2365).

A bitter civil war on planet Mordan IV is concluded. The conflict had lasted for 40 years and had been exacerbated by the improper intervention of Starfleet officer Mark Jameson in local affairs in 2319.

Worf and K'Ehleyr

"Too Short a Season." Data notes that Mordan IV had peace for five years prior to the episode (2364).

2361

Kevin and Rishon Uxbridge arrive at the Delta Rana IV colony. Rishon does not suspect that her husband, Kevin, is in reality an immensely powerful alien from a race called the Douwd, traveling in disguise as a human. The colony is later destroyed and all the colonists (except for Kevin) are killed in a Husnok attack. Among the casualties is Kevin's wife, Rishon. Reacting in anger and grief, Kevin responds by using his extraordinary powers to destroy the entire Husnok race.

"The Survivors." Five years prior to episode (2366).

Archaeologist Vash begins working as an assistant to Professor Samuel Estragon, who has spent much of his career searching for a device called the *Tox Uthat,* an artifact from the 27th century, sent back in time for safekeeping. Estragon never finds the *Uthat,* although Vash uses his notes after his death to locate the device on planet Risa.

"Captain's Holiday." Vash says she had worked for Estragon for the past five years, and she implied he had died shortly before the episode (2366).

Vash

Jeremy Aster's father dies of a Russhton infection. Jeremy's mother, Marla Aster, raises Jeremy alone. They take up residence on the U.S.S. *Enterprise* when Marla Aster becomes a staff archaeologist on the ship.

"The Bonding." Jeremy's father died five years prior to the episode (2366).

Starship *Potemkin* makes last Federation contact with the failed colony on planet Turkana IV prior to U.S.S. *Enterprise* visit in 2367. *Potemkin* personnel are warned that anyone transporting to the colony will be killed. Turkana IV is the birthplace of future *Enterprise* security chief Tasha Yar.

"Legacy." Data described the history of the colony. (See Editors' Note on page 127 regarding the relationship of the Potemkin *in "Legacy" and another ship of that name in "Turnabout Intruder.")*

2362

Dr. Dalen Quaice begins a tour of duty at Starbase 133. He remains at that posting until the death of his wife, Patricia, in 2367. Quaice had been a mentor to *Enterprise* chief medical officer Beverly Crusher during her medical residency.

"Remember Me." Beverly tells Picard that Quaice had been stationed there for six years prior to the episode (2368).

Ensign Geordi La Forge serves aboard Starship U.S.S. *Victory* under the command of Captain Zimbata. On stardate 40164.7 he and fellow *Victory* crew member Susanna Leijten are part of an away team investigating the disappearance of 49 persons at the colony on planet Tarchannan III. Five years later all members of this away team are mysteriously compelled to return to the same planet.

"Elementary, Dear Data." Geordi mentioned serving on that ship prior to his Enterprise *duty. In "Identity Crisis," Susanna describes the incident at Tarchannan III as having taken place five years prior to the episode (2367) while they were both aboard the* Victory.

2363

Federation starship *Tsiolkovsky* begins its last science mission. It is ultimately destroyed after its crew is killed by a variant of the Psi 2000 virus.

"The Naked Now." Eight months prior to episode.

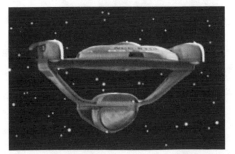

U.S.S. Tsiolkovsky, *NCC-59311*

Galaxy class Starship *Enterprise*, Starfleet registry number NCC-1701-D, is launched from Utopia Planitia Fleet Yards orbiting the planet Mars, charged with the mission "to boldly go where no one has gone before." The ship is officially commissioned on stardate 40759.5. Captain Jean-Luc Picard assumes command of the vessel, the fifth Federation starship to bear the name *Enterprise*, on stardate 41124.

"Lonely Among Us" establishes that the ship had been launched less than a year prior to the first season, and "Encounter at Farpoint" seems to imply that Picard had taken command shortly prior to that episode. Stardate and ship's motto from dedication plaque on Enterprise *bridge. Picard's date of command established in "The Drumhead."*

U.S.S. Enterprise, NCC-1701-D

2364

Nick Locarno is accepted as a cadet at Starfleet Academy on Earth. Locarno is considered one of the most promising students ever to attend that institution.

"The First Duty." Picard noted that Locarno would have graduated with that year's graduating class (2368), suggesting he had entered four years earlier.

U.S.S. *Enterprise* responds to a distress call from a colony on planet Carnel. At the rescue site, Captain Picard meets Natasha Yar, a crew member of another ship also participating in the rescue. Picard is so impressed with Yar's heroism in risking her life to save a wounded colonist that he requests she be assigned to the *Enterprise* as security chief.

Cadet Nick Locarno

"Legacy." Picard describes the incident as happening while he was in command of the Enterprise*, but it must have happened shortly before "Encounter at Farpoint" because she was already an* Enterprise *crew member by that point.*

Commander William Riker is offered the opportunity to command the Starship *Drake*, but declines the assignment in order to serve on the U.S.S. *Enterprise*. Command of the *Drake* is accepted by Riker's classmate Paul Rice. The *Drake* is later destroyed at planet Minos.

"The Arsenal of Freedom." Exact date is conjecture, but Riker told Tasha he had thought a tour aboard the Enterprise *was more advantageous, implying this was shortly prior to Riker's transfer to the* Enterprise *in "Encounter at Farpoint."*

Captain Paul Rice

Admiral Leonard McCoy travels aboard U.S.S. *Hood* to rendezvous with the *Enterprise* at Farpoint Station. Also aboard the *Hood* are Commander William T. Riker (serving as first officer), Lieutenant (Junior Grade) Geordi La Forge, Dr. Beverly Crusher, and her son Wesley Crusher, all en route to assignments on the *Enterprise*.

Prior to "Encounter at Farpoint."

Admiral Leonard McCoy

Starship *Enterprise* assigned to explore unknown space in the great stellar mass beyond planet Deneb IV.

Just prior to "Encounter at Farpoint."

6.1 STAR TREK: THE NEXT GENERATION — YEAR 1

The crew of the U.S.S. Enterprise,
NCC-1701-D

Calendar date of 2364 for first season established in "The Neutral Zone."

Farpoint Station

"Encounter at Farpoint." Stardate 41153.7. U.S.S. *Enterprise* assigned to study Farpoint Station at planet Deneb IV. Farpoint is a new starbase recently built by the Bandi for possible use as a Starfleet facility. Investigation reveals the station to have been built with the unwilling help of a spacefaring life-form capable of assuming virtually any shape or form, in this case, that of the station itself. The creature is allowed to return to deep space.

First contact with extradimensional life-form called the Q, a visitor from what it calls the Q continuum. This entity demonstrates extraordinary power to manipulate space and matter, and interferes with the execution of the Farpoint investigation mission.

Q

Commander William T. Riker, previously assigned to the U.S.S. *Hood* under the command of Captain Jonathan DeSoto, joins U.S.S. *Enterprise* crew at Farpoint Station and assumes duties of executive officer. Lieutenant (Junior Grade) Geordi La Forge joins U.S.S. *Enterprise* crew at Farpoint Station, assumes duties of flight controller (conn). Dr. Beverly Crusher joins U.S.S. *Enterprise* crew at Farpoint Station, assumes duties of chief medical officer, effective stardate 41154. Also taking up residence aboard the *Enterprise* is her 15-year-old son, Wesley.

Starfleet Admiral Leonard McCoy, traveling on Starship U.S.S. *Hood*, makes inspection visit of new U.S.S. *Enterprise*.

Editors' Note: The stardate of Beverly Crusher's assignment to the Enterprise *was established as 41154 in "Remember Me." Picard took command of the* Enterprise *on stardate 41124 ("The Drumhead"), suggesting that he had been* Enterprise *captain for only a short time prior to "Encounter at Farpoint."*

"The Naked Now." Stardate 41209.2. U.S.S. *Enterprise* assigned to rendezvous with science vessel *Tsiolkovsky*, which had been monitoring the collapse of a red giant star. A strange series of messages from the *Tsiolkovsky* suggests severe psychological disorders are threatening the crew. By the time the *Enterprise* reaches the rendezvous, all 80 crew personnel aboard the science vessel are dead. Investigation determines *Tsiolkovsky* crew suffered from a virus similar to the Psi 2000 disease that affected the crew of an earlier *Enterprise* in 2266. Contamination from the away team causes the virus to spread among the *Enterprise* crew until an appropriate treatment is developed.

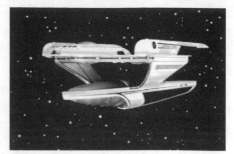

Science vessel Tsiolkovsky

Romulan Senator Pardek participates in a trade negotiations conference. Among the other participants are the Barolians.

"Unification, Part I." Data locates an archival video of Pardek in the Barolian records of the negotiations, noting that the conference had taken place four years prior to the episode (2368).

An outbreak of Anchilles fever on planet Stryris IV spreads out of control, resulting in deaths estimated in the millions.

Prior to "Code of Honor."

"Code of Honor." Stardate 41235.25. U.S.S. *Enterprise* on diplomatic mission to establish treaty with planet Ligon II and acquire a rare vaccine needed to treat the plague on planet Stryris IV. *Enterprise* security officer Yar becomes a pawn in a power struggle between Ligonian leader Lutan and his political rivals, who are ultimately successful in deposing Lutan.

Ligonian leader Lutan

U.S.S. *Enterprise* delivers critically needed vaccines to planet Stryris IV.

After "Code of Honor."

Starfleet propulsion specialist Kosinski performs warp system upgrades on Starships *Fearless* and *Ajax*. Both ships report minor performance gains.

"Where No One Has Gone Before." Exact date is conjecture, but this was fairly soon before the episode.

"Haven." Stardate 41294.5. *Enterprise* en route to planet Haven in the Beta Cassius system for shore leave, but is interrupted by urgent call for assistance. Electorine Valeda Innis of Haven, requesting Federation intervention to prevent landing of a Tarellian ship recently detected on course for Haven, explains that diplomatic efforts have failed to dissuade the Tarellians from a plan to disembark on Haven to die. Innis expresses a fear that the Tarellians, the last eight survivors of terrible biological warfare on their planet, will infect Haven with the deadly virus.

Lwaxana and Deanna Troi

Enterprise counselor Deanna Troi is informed that she must fulfill the marriage pledge with Wyatt Miller she undertook as a child. The wedding is planned to take place on board the *Enterprise*, with her mother, Lwaxana Troi, and Wyatt's parents in attendance. The wedding is canceled when Miller, an aspiring physician, chooses to take up residence with the Tarellians in hope of finding a cure for their plague.

"Where No One Has Gone Before." Stardate 41263.1. U.S.S. *Enterprise* rendezvous with Starship *Fearless* for transfer of Kosinski and his assistant, an inhabitant of planet Tau Alpha C.

U.S.S. *Enterprise* participates in a warp experiment under the supervision

The Traveler works with Wesley Crusher

of Starfleet propulsion specialist Kosinski. The tests involve modification of the ship's warp fields to gain higher engine efficiency. Initial results are extremely promising, although one test accidentally propels the ship across several million light-years, past galaxy M33. It is learned that the gains in efficiency are not due to Kosinski's modifications, but rather to the efforts of Kosinski's assistant, known as "the Traveler."

Wesley Crusher's efforts in working with the Traveler to return the *Enterprise* to the Milky Way galaxy are recognized by Captain Picard, who grants Crusher the rank of "acting ensign," effective stardate 41263.4.

The old Vulcan ship *T'Pau* is decommissioned and sent to the surplus depot Zed-15 orbiting Qualor II. The ship is later surreptitiously dismantled and smuggled out of the yard by Romulan operatives as part of a plan to place Vulcan under Romulan rule.

"Unification, Part I." Dokachin noted the T'Pau *had been logged in on stardate 41344, which would seem to place it between "Where No One Has Gone Before" and "The Last Outpost."*

Ferengi agents steal a T-9 energy converter from the unmanned monitor post on planet Gamma Tauri IV. The theft is a matter of great concern because prior to this, the Federation had virtually no direct contact with or knowledge of the Ferengi.

Prior to "The Last Outpost."

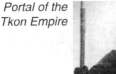

Portal of the Tkon Empire

"The Last Outpost." Stardate 41386.4. U.S.S. *Enterprise* in pursuit of Ferengi spacecraft, attempting to recover T-9 energy converter. Upon entering the Delphi Ardu star system, both ships are incapacitated by a powerful energy beam, apparently emanating from an outpost of the long-dead Tkon Empire. Diplomatic efforts are later successful in freeing both ships, with Ferengi DaiMon Taar agreeing to return the stolen energy converter.

First contact with Ferengi Alliance, as well as with the Tkon Empire.

"Lonely Among Us." Stardate 41249.3. Starship *Enterprise* on diplomatic mission to transport delegates from planets Antica and Selay in the Beta Renner system to an interstellar conference on the neutral planetoid Parliament in hope of resolving conflicts between the two antagonistic planets, both of which have applied for membership in the Federation.

U.S.S. *Enterprise* suffers a major series of malfunctions as computer system is invaded by an energy-based life-form that inhabits various crew members, then the *Enterprise* itself. The entity, which is found to be a space-borne energy cloud, is learned to be something of a kindred spirit to Picard and the crew, exploring the unknown in this manner.

Selay delegation to Parliament conference

U.S.S. *Enterprise* delivers the Antican and Selay delegations to Parliament for their conference to consider their petitions for admission to the Federation.

Just after "Lonely Among Us."

U.S.S. *Enterprise* delivers a party of Earth colonists to the Strnad star system. Shortly thereafter, ship's personnel discover another Class M planet in the adjoining Rubicun star system. This second planet is discovered to be inhabited by a peaceful humanoid species known as the Edo and is deemed suitable for shore leave by *Enterprise* personnel.

Just prior to "Justice."

Editors' Note: The Strnad star system was named for former Star Trek production staffer Janet Strnad.

Inhabitants of planet Rubicun III

"Justice." Stardate 41255.6. U.S.S. *Enterprise* personnel, on shore leave at planet Rubicun III, accidentally violate local laws. Acting Ensign Wesley Crusher commits an apparently minor transgression, but local authorities impose a death sentence for the act in accordance with planetary law. Attempts to negotiate a release for Crusher are unsuccessful because of the presence of a powerful noncorporeal spaceborne entity which the Edo worship as their god. *Enterprise* captain Picard violates the Prime Directive of noninterference by violating local laws to secure Crusher's release.

Ferengi vessel contacts U.S.S. *Enterprise* and requests a meeting in the Xendi Sabu star system. *Enterprise* waits at rendezvous point for three days, the Ferengi offering no response other than a signal to "stand by." In an apparently unrelated development, *Enterprise* captain Picard suffers from an unusually painful series of headaches.

Three days prior to "The Battle."

"The Battle." Stardate 41723.9. Ferengi DaiMon Bok, aboard a Ferengi ship at the Xendi Sabu rendezvous site, offers a gift to *Enterprise* captain Picard: The hulk of Picard's former command, the U.S.S. *Stargazer*. Examination of records aboard the *Stargazer* reveals apparently damning evidence suggesting Picard had attacked a Ferengi spacecraft some nine years ago in "The Battle of Maxia" in which the *Stargazer* was believed destroyed. The gift is found to be an elaborate ploy by Bok to gain revenge on Picard for the latter's involvement in the Battle of Maxia, during which Bok's son was killed. Bok is also discovered to have falsified the *Stargazer* records and to have attempted to injure Picard through the use of a Ferengi mind control device.

U.S.S. Stargazer

U.S.S. *Enterprise* tows the hulk of the U.S.S. *Stargazer* to Xendi Starbase 9.

Just after "The Battle."

Enterprise counselor Deanna Troi departs U.S.S. *Enterprise* on a shuttlecraft at Starbase G-6 for a visit to her home planet of Betazed.

Prior to "Hide and Q."

An explosion at the Federation mining colony on planet Sigma III injures 504 persons. An urgent call for medical assistance is transmitted to the U.S.S. *Enterprise*.

Just prior to "Hide and Q."

DaiMon Bok operates
Ferengi mind control device

"Hide and Q." Stardate 41590.5. U.S.S. *Enterprise* en route to rescue mission at Sigma III mining colony is interrupted by the reappearance of the entity known as "Q." The rescue mission is largely successful, although at least one life is lost at the colony.

Starfleet Command receives a transmission from Karnas, a leader on planet Mordan IV, reporting that terrorists have seized hostages including Federation Ambassador Hawkins. Karnas urgently requests the assistance of Starfleet Admiral Mark Jameson, noting a terrorist threat to kill the hostages if Jameson does not intervene in six days.

Two days prior to "Too Short a Season."

Rescue operations at Sigma III
mining colony

*Karnas of
Mordan IV*

"Too Short a Season." Stardate 41309.5. *Enterprise* at planet Persephone V to pick up Admiral Mark Jameson and his wife, Anne, for transport to planet Mordan IV to negotiate the release of Federation hostages. Upon arrival at Mordan IV, Jameson reveals that his celebrated negotiations (which led to release of other Federation hostages by Karnas some 45 years ago) was in fact a weapons-for-hostages deal that resulted in a bloody civil war. This conflict ended only five years ago, and it is learned that Karnas has staged the entire hostage crisis as a means of exacting retribution on Jameson for his role in exacerbating the war. Jameson, suffering from the effects of a youth drug obtained on planet Cerebus III, dies at Mordan IV after convincing Karnas to release the hostages.

Starship *Enterprise* goes to planet Isis III.

Just after "Too Short a Season."

*Picard and Data participate in Dixon Hill
holodeck simulation program*

"The Big Goodbye." Stardate 41997.7. U.S.S. *Enterprise* assigned to make diplomatic contact with the reclusive race known as the Jarada. The mission is somewhat delayed when a holodeck malfunction traps Captain Picard and other *Enterprise* personnel in an ongoing simulation program. The contact is ultimately successful in large part because of Captain Picard's precise enunciation of a formal Jaradan greeting.

U.S.S. *Enterprise* completes an assignment in the Omicron Theta star system.

Just prior to "Datalore."

"Datalore." Stardate 41242.4. U.S.S. *Enterprise,* at Omicron Theta system, takes side trip to planet where Lieutenant Commander Data was discovered. Investigation reveals remains of a Federation colony, apparently destroyed and all inhabitants killed by a powerful spaceborne Crystalline Entity of unknown origin.

*Data examines the nonfunctional
head of his brother, Lore*

Also discovered is the preserved but abandoned underground laboratory of famed cyberneticist Dr. Noonien Soong. Dr. Soong, long assumed dead, is believed to be the designer of the android Data. Among the equipment in the facility are sufficient components to assemble a second android, nearly identical to Data. Upon return to the *Enterprise*, these components are assembled, then activated. The resulting android, known as Lore, is structurally identical to Data, but with dramatically differing personality programming. This android exhibits aberrant behavior, threatening the *Enterprise*, and is eventually transported into space.

Though unknown at the time, Lore drifts in space for two years and is eventually rescued by a passing Pakled ship.

"Brothers." Lore describes his adventures to Data and Dr. Soong.

Twelve students from U.S.S. *Enterprise* participate in Quazulu field trip, accidentally bringing a respiratory virus back to the ship.

Prior to "Angel One."

U.S.S. *Enterprise* investigates disappearance of Federation freighter *Odin*, missing for seven years. The wreckage of the *Odin* is found with three escape pods missing, suggesting the possibility of survivors.

Just prior to "Angel One."

"Angel One." Stardate 41636.9. Investigation of probable flight path of *Odin* escape pods leads to planet Angel I. Survivors of the *Odin* are found to be alive on the planet's surface, having integrated themselves into the society. Local authorities request removal of survivors on the grounds they are interfering with planetary authority, but *Enterprise* captain Picard rules that the survivors have become a legitimate part of the social system and are thus immune to Prime Directive constraints.

Romulan spacecraft are detected near a Federation border post. The U.S.S. *Berlin* is dispatched to investigate. Upon completion of the *Odin* investigation, U.S.S. *Enterprise* sets course for Romulan Neutral Zone, although no direct contact with the Romulans is made at this time.

Capital city on planet Angel I

U.S.S. *Enterprise* departs toward Romulan Neutral Zone.

Just after "Angel One."

Starship *Enterprise*, at Omicron Pascal, is delayed for a week, making it late for a scheduled layover at Starbase 74.

Prior to "11001001."

"11001001." Stardate 41365.9. U.S.S. *Enterprise* at Starbase 74, orbiting Tarsas III for scheduled maintenance layover. Service and upgrades are performed by a special team from planet Bynaus. While in dock, a malfunction is reported, threatening a potentially catastrophic failure of the *Enterprise's* antimatter containment fields. As a result, all *Enterprise* personnel are evacuated, and the ship is removed from the starbase. The incident is later learned to have been engineered by the Bynars in an effort to appropriate the ship for use in restarting their home planet's main computer system in the Beta Magellan system. The Bynar planetary computer had been damaged when Beta Magellan went supernova.

Bynars

Editors' Note: At one point during the first season, "11001001" was slated to be produced before the episode "The Big Goodbye." Had the episodes been filmed and aired in that order, the modification by the Bynars to the holodeck in "11001001" would have served to explain what happened to Captain Picard when his favorite Dixon Hill simulation malfunctioned. This episode marks the first reference to the game "parrises squares" when Tasha, Worf, and two other Enterprise *personnel are off to challenge a team from the starbase.*

U.S.S. *Enterprise* has an appointment at planet Pelleus V.

Two days after "11001001."

U.S.S. Enterprise *at Starbase 74*

U.S.S. *Enterprise* begins mapping assignment at Pleiades cluster.

Prior to "Home Soil."

"Home Soil." Stardate 41463.9. U.S.S. *Enterprise* mapping assignment at Pleiades cluster is interrupted by a Federation request to investigate a loss of communication with the Federation terraforming team on planet Velara III. The *Enterprise* away team discovers that terraforming activity had been inadvertently disrupting a life-form indigenous to Velara III. This inorganic life-form exists in the narrow electrically conductive zone above the planet's water table, and was threatened by the terraforming process. The life-form is discovered to be intelligent when it responds by seizing control of the *Enterprise* computer. The crew believes that project director Mandl was aware of the intelligent nature of the Velara life-forms and that he authorized the continuation of the terraforming despite that knowledge.

Terraform team director Kurt Mandl

U.S.S. *Enterprise* evacuates Velara III terraforming station personnel and returns them to starbase.

After "Home Soil."

Benzan of the planet Straleb, and Yanar of the planet Atlec, begin a romantic relationship. Benzan gives Yanar the Jewel of Thesia, a Straleb national treasure, as a nuptial gift, this despite the fact that their respective parents are unaware of the relationship.

"The Outrageous Okona." Okona said the two had been seeing each other for about six months prior to the episode, although the exact date is conjecture.

"When the Bough Breaks." Stardate 41509.1. U.S.S. *Enterprise* discovers the mythical planet of Aldea, which had been shielded from visibility in the Epsilon Mynos system. The planet's inhabitants, found to be a technologically advanced society of artisans, use their sophisticated transporter technology to abduct several children of *Enterprise* crew members. This is discovered to be an effort by the Aldeans to reestablish their race, rendered infertile due to radiation exposure caused by damage to their ozone layer.

Although diplomatic efforts to secure the freedom of the *Enterprise* children are initially unsuccessful, the Aldeans eventually agree to their release. *Enterprise* personnel assist with the dismantling of the Aldean shielding system and perform a reseeding of the Aldean ozone layer, a move expected to reverse the sterility of the Aldean people.

"Coming of Age." Stardate 41416.2. Lieutenant Commander Dexter Remmick of the Starfleet inspector general's office conducts a thorough investigation of the U.S.S. *Enterprise* while the ship is at the Relva VII Starfleet facility. Remmick's assignment to uncover unspecified problems aboard the *Enterprise* is later explained to be a probe of Captain Picard by Admiral Gregory Quinn, a prelude to Picard's being offered the job of commandant of Starfleet Academy. Quinn's offer to Picard is coupled with a plea based on Quinn's suspicions that problems exist within the structure of Starfleet itself. Picard declines the offer, citing his belief that he can better serve the interests of the Federation as captain of the *Enterprise*.

Starfleet admiral Gregory Quinn and Inspector General Dexter Remmick

Acting Ensign Wesley Crusher undergoes Starfleet Academy entrance competition tests at Relva VII. Although Crusher fails to gain admission to the Academy, his score is sufficient to allow him to resubmit his application the following year.

U.S.S. *Enterprise* travels to Algeron IV.

Talarian freighter Batris

Just after "Coming of Age."

"Heart of Glory." Stardate 41503.7. U.S.S. *Enterprise* responds to a distress call from the freighter *Batris*, a damaged Talarian freighter. Three survivors, Klingon warriors, are rescued from the *Batris* before it explodes, although one warrior dies shortly thereafter. Investigation identifies the survivors, Korris and Konmel, to be militants opposing the Klingon government. They attempt to seize control of the *Enterprise*, but are thwarted.

"The Arsenal of Freedom" Stardate 41798.2. U.S.S. *Enterprise* at Lorenze Cluster to investigate the disappearance of the U.S.S. *Drake* at planet Minos. Although the planet Minos had been inhabited in the past, recent probes indicated no intelligent life currently on the planet. Nevertheless,

Renegade Klingons

Enterprise personnel encounter technically sophisticated weapons systems that threaten both an away team on the planet's surface, and the *Enterprise* itself. Further investigation indicates these weapons systems, still functional, were responsible for the destruction of the *Drake*, as well as for the entire Minosian culture.

Editors' Note: Riker mentions to Tasha and Picard that he had been offered command of the U.S.S. Drake, *apparently just prior to his accepting the job as executive officer on the* Enterprise.

"Symbiosis." (No stardate given in episode.) U.S.S. *Enterprise* responds to a distress call while studying solar flares at the Delos system. The distress call is found to have originated from the *Sanction*, a disabled Ornaran interplanetary freighter. Although *Enterprise* personnel are unable to save the freighter, the *Sanction*'s cargo and part of its crew are successfully rescued. It is learned that the *Sanction* had been transporting medical supplies of felicium from planet Brekka to Ornara in order to keep a 200-year-old plague in check.

Ornaran freighter Sanction

Investigation by *Enterprise* personnel reveals the medication to be a narcotic substance, no longer necessary for medical reasons. Representatives of Brekka request Federation assistance to insure delivery of these medical supplies, but Captain Picard rules that Prime Directive considerations prohibit Federation intervention. Prime Directive considerations further prevent Picard from revealing to the inhabitants of planet Ornara the exploitive nature of their dealings with Brekka for the addictive medication, but Picard believes the Ornarans will learn this for themselves.

Editors' Note: "Symbiosis" was filmed after "Skin of Evil," but is listed first because Tasha Yar, killed in the latter episode, is shown as being alive here.

Ship's counselor Deanna Troi attends a psychology conference in the Zed Lapis sector.

Just prior to "Skin of Evil."

Tasha Yar

"Skin of Evil." Stardate 41601.3. Shuttlecraft 13, carrying Deanna Troi and pilot Ben Prieto on a return flight to the *Enterprise*, is forced to make a crash-landing on planet Vagra II. Investigation by an *Enterprise* away team determines the crash to have been caused by an entity that calls itself Armus. During the investigation, *Enterprise* security chief Tasha Yar is killed by Armus.

Later efforts are successful in rescuing Troi and other *Enterprise* personnel from the planet. Captain Picard assigns Worf as acting security chief.

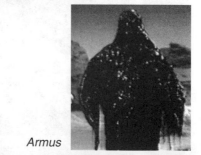

Armus

"We'll Always Have Paris." Stardate 41697.9. U.S.S. *Enterprise* is en route to planet Sarona VIII, when the ship encounters a brief temporal distortion. This phenomenon is also reported by the freighter *Lalo* and the Ilecom star system. Shortly thereafter, the *Enterprise* responds to a distress call from a science laboratory on planetoid Vandor IV. Investigation determines the temporal distortions to have been created by Dr. Paul Manheim, studying the relationship between time and gravity. Manheim suffers neurochemical injury caused by the temporal distortions, until Data is successful in repairing the temporal anomaly caused by Manheim's experiments.

Starship *Enterprise* goes to planet Sarona VIII for crew shore leave.

Just after "We'll Always Have Paris."

Temporal distortion causes Data to exist simultaneously on different planes.

*Admiral
Satie*

Admiral Norah Satie uncovers evidence of a widespread alien conspiracy infiltrating Starfleet Command. Among the evidence is a series of unusual occurrences, including a number of unusual orders, high-ranking officials backing apparently irrational orders, the evacuation of Starbase 12 for two days, and the apparently accidental deaths of Mckinney, Ryan Sipe, and Onna Karapleedeez. Satie enlists the assistance of key personnel, including captains Walker Keel, Tryla Scott, and Rixx to counter the incursion.

Prior to "Conspiracy." Satie's role in uncovering the conspiracy is described in "The Drumhead."

U.S.S. *Enterprise* is assigned to scientific investigation on planet Pacifica.

Just prior to "Conspiracy."

*Walker
Keel*

"Conspiracy." Stardate 41775.5. Mission to Pacifica is interrupted when Captain Picard receives an urgent request from Starship *Horatio* captain Walker Keel for a covert meeting at planetoid Dytallix B. Also present at this meeting are Captain Tryla Scott of the U.S.S. *Renegade*, and Captain Rixx of the U.S.S. *Thomas Paine*. At the planetoid, Keel informs Picard of his suspicion that unknown threat forces have infiltrated Starfleet Command and are responsible for recent unusual activity. Shortly thereafter, the *Horatio* is destroyed with the loss of all personnel, including Walker Keel.

*Captain
Rixx*

Picard pursues the investigation of Keel's report by taking the *Enterprise* to Earth and requesting a meeting at Starfleet Command. Keel's suspicions are borne out and Picard discovers that numerous key Starfleet personnel are being controlled by an extragalactic intelligence. Picard and Riker are successful in stopping the intelligence and neutralizing its control, but its origin and purpose remain a total mystery.

Communications are lost with Federation starbases in Sector 3-0, near the Romulan Neutral Zone. Two outposts in that area are reported destroyed.

Prior to "The Neutral Zone," contact was reported lost on stardate 41903.2.

Captain Picard attends an emergency conference at Starbase 718 to discuss the possibility of an emerging Romulan threat in the wake of the destruction of the outposts near the Neutral Zone.

Just prior to "The Neutral Zone."

Cryosatellite

"The Neutral Zone." Stardate 41986.0. Awaiting Picard's return from a Starfleet conference, Lieutenant Commander Data discovers an apparently derelict spacecraft. Investigation determines the spacecraft to contain the cryogenically preserved remains of several humans who died in the late 20th century. Three of these individuals are successfully revived because medical advances in the intervening years have rendered their maladies curable. These individuals, named Claire Raymond (who was a homemaker prior to her death), Sonny Clemons (an entertainer), and Ralph Offenhouse (a business executive), are later returned to Earth aboard the U.S.S. *Charleston*.

Federation outposts at Delta Zero Five and Tarod IX near the Romulan Neutral Zone are discovered to have been destroyed not by Romulans, but by an unknown agency that literally scooped the outposts off their planetary surfaces. This agency is later believed to be the Borg, suggesting a Borg presence near Federation space significantly earlier than 2367.

Investigating these disappearances, the *Enterprise* encounters a Romulan spacecraft studying similar occurrences on the other side of the Neutral Zone. This is the first Federation contact with the Romulans since the Tomed incident of 2311.

Editors' Note: Data gives the current calendar year in "The Neutral Zone" as 2364. This is used as a reference point from which most Star Trek: The Next Generation *dates are derived. The apparent reference to Borg activity near Federation and Romulan space appears to be inconsistent with Q's statements in "Q Who?" suggesting that the Borg are still several years away from Federation space at this point. On the other hand, it is also possible that Q did not know everything going on with the Borg.*

Claire Raymond's great-great-great-great-grandson, Thomas, whom she said looked a lot like her late husband, Donald, also bore an uncanny (and purely coincidental) resemblance to Star Trek: The Next Generation *co-producer Peter Lauritson. Raymond's family tree diagram seen on Troi's desk-top viewer also contained the (hopefully illegible) names of various characters from* The Muppet Show *and* Gilligan's Island.

The derelict spacecraft in which the 20th-century cryonauts had been lost in space was designed by Rick Sternbach and Mike Okuda. They inscribed the ship in very tiny letters with the name S.S. Birdseye. *The satellite's reactor module was labeled with the numbers 4077, an homage to* M*A*S*H, *one of Mike's favorite television shows. Inside the ship, all of the nonfunctional cryonic suspension modules (the ones containing hideously decomposed bodies) bore signs with the names of various members of the art department, as well as the name of episode director James Conway. ("The Neutral Zone" was the last episode of our very grueling first season, and the unusual number of gags described here is probably a reflection of the extraordinary level of exhaustion shared by everyone in the production company.)*

Enterprise *computer records display the face of Claire Raymond's great-great-great-great-grandson.*

6.2 STAR TREK: THE NEXT GENERATION — YEAR 2

In an important legal precedent, the android Data is ruled to be a sentient life form, thereby entitled to full constitutional rights as a citizen of the Federation.

2365

Geordi La Forge is promoted to the rank of full lieutenant and is assigned as *Enterprise* chief engineer. Lieutenant Worf is promoted to permanent chief of security, replacing the late Tasha Yar. Acting Ensign Wesley Crusher is assigned regular bridge duty, serving as flight controller (conn).

These promotions were not shown, but happened between the end of the first season and the beginning of the second.

Dr. Katherine Pulaski

Captain Picard recruits an old friend, Guinan, to serve as hostess of the Ten Forward lounge. She comes on board the *Enterprise* at Nestoriel III.

Guinan was first seen in "The Child." "Yesterday's Enterprise*" and "Redemption II" establishes that Guinan had not been aboard the* Enterprise *until sometime after Tasha's death. Data mentions Nestoriel III in "Time's Arrow, Part I."*

"The Child." Stardate 42073.1. Dr. Beverly Crusher accepts a position as head of Starfleet Medical and departs the *Enterprise*. Dr. Katherine Pulaski arrives from the U.S.S. *Repulse* via shuttlecraft as her replacement.

Deanna Troi and her son, Ian Andrew

U.S.S. *Enterprise* assigned to transport medical specimens of plasma plague from planet 'audet IX to Science Station Sierra Tango in hope that a cure can be found for an outbreak of the disease on planet Rachelis. The project is supervised by Lieutenant Commander Hester Delt, medical trustee of the Federation Medical Collection Center.

Ship's counselor Deanna Troi is impregnated by an unknown alien life form. The resulting child, which gestates and grows at a highly accelerated rate, is the product of this unknown form's desire to learn more about human life.

The entity is found to be a source of eichner radiation, compromising the safety of the storage of the deadly plasma plague specimens. Seeking to avoid harm to the *Enterprise* crew, the entity departs the ship.

Editors' Note: This episode was originally written for Captain Kirk and his crew for the Star Trek II *television series project that was never produced.*

U.S.S. *Enterprise* heads for Morgana quadrant.

After "The Child."

"Where Silence Has Lease." Stardate 42193.6. The U.S.S. *Enterprise* is updating star charts while en route to the Morgana quadrant. The voyage is interrupted when the *Enterprise* is trapped in a region of space that appears to be devoid of stars or any object other than the *Enterprise* itself. A second ship is eventually sighted, tentatively identified as the *Galaxy* class U.S.S. *Yamato*, although further investigation reveals the ship to be a fabrication. The entire situation is eventually determined to be a first-contact scenario with a noncorporeal intelligence known as Nagilum, who is attempting to understand the nature of human life.

Nagilum

U.S.S. *Enterprise* continues toward the Morgana quadrant.

Just after "Where Silence Has Lease."

The crew of the Starship *Lantree* is subjected to routine examinations at the beginning of a duty cycle. All are found to be in perfect health.

"Unnatural Selection." Pulaski noted the exams had taken place eight weeks prior to the episode.

Geordi La Forge builds a model of the ancient British sailing ship H.M.S. *Victory*, intended as a gift for Starship *Victory* captain Zimbata, under whose command La Forge served prior to his *Enterprise* assignment.

Prior to "Elementary, Dear Data."

Editors' Note: In reality, Geordi's beautiful H.M.S. Victory *model still graces the late Gene Roddenberry's office in his home.*

Starship Victory, *NCC-9754*

"Elementary, Dear Data." Stardate 42286.3. U.S.S. *Enterprise* arrives three days early for scheduled rendezvous with the *Victory*. While awaiting the *Victory*'s arrival, user error on the part of a holodeck participant results in the accidental creation of a computer software-based sentient intelligence within a simulation program. To avoid the destruction of what is apparently a self-aware life-form, Captain Picard orders the simulation program saved until a way can be found to give physical form to the synthetic intelligence.

Moriarty, a computer-generated life-form

U.S.S. *Victory* arrives for rendezvous with the *Enterprise*. Captain Zimbata receives his gift of Geordi's model.

Just after "Elementary, Dear Data."

"The Outrageous Okona." Stardate 42402.7. U.S.S. *Enterprise*, traveling through the Omega Sagitta system, offers assistance to space vehicle *Erstwhile*, an interplanetary vessel in need of guidance system repairs.

While in the Omega Sagitta system, Captain Picard mediates a dispute between planets Atlec and Straleb. Ruling families of both planets have filed claims against *Erstwhile* captain Thadiun Okona. The dispute is resolved when Benzan, son of Secretary Kushell (of the Legation of Unity of the planet Straleb) and Yanar, daughter of Debin (captain of a Straleb space vessel) agree to marry.

U.S.S. *Enterprise* responds to a distress from Kareen Brianon, assistant to noted molecular cyberneticist Dr. Ira Graves on the planet Gravesworld. Dr. Graves had been a teacher to reclusive roboticist Noonien Soong.

About eight hours prior to "The Schizoid Man."

Dr. Selar

"The Schizoid Man." Stardate 42437.5. U.S.S. *Enterprise*, en route to Gravesworld, also receives distress call from U.S.S. *Constantinople*. An away team is left on Gravesworld, while the *Enterprise* proceeds expeditiously to a successful rescue mission to the *Constantinople*. Still on Gravesworld, Dr. Ira Graves is discovered by *Enterprise* staff physician Dr. Selar to be terminally ill. Before his death Graves succeeds in recording the sum of his personal knowledge into the *Enterprise* computer system.

Editors' Note: Although this has been the only appearance of the Vulcan Dr. Selar to date, we did hear Selar being paged over the PA system of the alternate timeline Enterprise-D *in "Yesterday's* Enterprise," *and Selar was also mentioned by Dr. Crusher in "Remember Me."*

Mediator Riva

"Loud as a Whisper." Stardate 42477.2. U.S.S. *Enterprise* is unexpectedly diverted to the Ramatis star system, assigned to transport famed mediator Riva to help resolve a bitter planetary conflict on planet Solais V. Initial attempts to negotiate a cease-fire between the two combatants are unsuccessful, but Riva remains behind to continue efforts to bring the adversaries together in a quest for peace.

The first officer of the Starship *Lantree* is treated for Thelusian flu, an exotic but harmless rhinovirus.

Five days prior to "Unnatural Selection."

U.S.S. *Lantree* under the command of Captain Iso Telaka visits the Darwin genetic research station on planet Gagarin IV. It is not realized at the time that exposure to the genetically engineered children of Darwin station scientists results in hyperaccelerated aging of all *Lantree* personnel.

Three days prior to "Unnatural Selection," according to Telaka's log.

Twenty *Lantree* personnel are killed by unknown causes, leaving only six crew members alive. Captain Telaka orders course set for nearest Federation outpost.

Just prior to "Unnatural Selection," stardate 42293.1.

Darwin genetic research station

"Unnatural Selection." Stardate 42494.8. U.S.S. *Enterprise* mission to Star Station India is interrupted by a distress call from the U.S.S. *Lantree*. Responding to the call, *Enterprise* discovers all *Lantree* personnel to be dead from an unknown malady strongly resembling old age.

The source of this affliction is learned to be the Darwin genetic research station on planet Gagarin IV. Further investigation determines the aging disease to be caused by genetically engineered children at the station. These children are found to possess an unusually powerful immune system that actually attacks potential causes for infection, including other human beings. Remains of Starship *Lantree* are destroyed to eliminate risk of further contamination.

U.S.S. *Enterprise* resumes mission to rendezvous with Starfleet courier at Star Station India.

Just after "Unnatural Selection."

"A Matter of Honor." Stardate 42506.5. U.S.S. *Enterprise* at Starbase 179 to participate in new officer exchange program. Serving temporarily aboard the *Enterprise* is Ensign Mendon, a Starfleet officer from the planet Benzar. *Enterprise* executive officer William Riker is assigned duty aboard the Klingon vessel *Pagh*, the first Federation Starfleet officer to serve aboard a Klingon ship.

Benzite exchange officer Mendon

A previously unknown submicron life-form is discovered by Mendon, who reports the life-form has been detected on the hulls of the *Enterprise* and the *Pagh*. Mendon devises a successful means of removing the parasites from both ships using a tunneling neutrino beam.

"The Measure of a Man." Stardate 42523.7. U.S.S. *Enterprise* at newly established Starbase 173 for crew rotation and offloading experiment modules. Lieutenant Commander Data is assigned to Commander Bruce Maddox for study of Data's positronic neural systems to further the goal of manufacturing additional androids for Starfleet service. Data declines to accept the transfer, and Starfleet Judge Advocate General Phillipa Louvois subsequently rules that Data is indeed a life-form with full civil rights, and that he is therefore free to make his own decisions.

Judge Advocate General Phillipa Louvois

Editors' Note: This episode shows for the first time the weekly poker game that has become a fixture of off-duty life for our heroes.

Ensign Sonya Gomez is among the new crew members transferring aboard the *Enterprise* at Starbase 173.

"Q Who" establishes her assignment.

"The Dauphin." Stardate 42568.8. U.S.S. *Enterprise* assigned diplomatic mission to ferry Salia, a young planetary head of state, from planet Klavdia III to her home on Daled IV. Salia, an allasomorph, is returned to her home to accept her role of leader, and will attempt to unite the warring factions of her planet.

Anya, an allasomorph

U.S.S. *Yamato* at planet Denius III, where Captain Donald Varley, participating in an archaeological study, deciphers evidence from an ancient Iconian artifact, making it possible to determine the actual location of the Iconian homeworld, somewhere in the Romulan Neutral Zone. Varley, citing the potentially disastrous consequences should the Romulans gain access to Iconian weapons technology, orders the *Yamato* to proceed to Iconia. Near Iconia, the *Yamato* is scanned by an Iconian space probe.

Shortly prior to "Contagion," according to Varley's log.

"Contagion." Stardate 42609.1. The *Enterprise* responds to distress call from starship *Yamato* in the Romulan Neutral Zone, but is unable to save the ship or its crew from destruction due to major on-board computer malfunction. Investigation determines the *Yamato* to have been the victim of a computer software weapon surviving from the long-dead planet Iconia. This weapon is believed to have been transmitted during a sensor scan from an Iconian probe. During the investigation, the Romulan warbird *Haakona* is similarly infected by the software weapon, but assistance from the *Enterprise* averts destruction of the Romulan craft as well as an interstellar incident.

The surface of the planet Iconia, near the Romulan Neutral Zone

A passing Klingon cruiser reports discovering pieces of an unknown space vehicle in the upper atmosphere of the eighth planet in the Theta 116 system. *Enterprise* diverts from scheduled course to investigate.

Just prior to "The Royale."

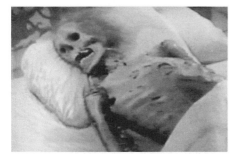

"The Royale." Stardate 42625.4. U.S.S. *Enterprise* investigates report of wreckage in orbit of the eighth planet in the previously unmapped Theta 116 system. An elaborate recreation of a 20th-century Earth environment is discovered on the otherwise uninhabitable planetary surface. Investigation determines the environment to have been created by an unknown alien intelligence in an effort to create a habitat for Colonel Steven Richey, the commander of the space vehicle *Charybdis*. That vehicle had been reported missing in 2037 after the third unsuccessful attempt to explore beyond Earth's solar system.

The remains of Charybdis *commander Steven Richey on Theta 116*

U.S.S. *Enterprise* makes layover stop at Starbase 73.

Just prior to "Time Squared."

"Time Squared." Stardate 42679.2. Mission to planet Endicor is interrupted by discovery of a duplicate of *Enterprise* shuttlepod 5, drifting in space. Discovered on board the recovered vehicle is a duplicate of Captain Jean-Luc Picard. Both the shuttle and the duplicate captain had apparently come backward in time six hours, during which the *Enterprise* had evidently been lost with all hands except the captain. The time loop is determined to have been caused by a temporal distortion. This distortion — and the impending destruction of the *Enterprise* — is disrupted when Captain Picard orders the *Enterprise* into the center of the phenomenon.

Shuttlepod El-Baz

Editors' Note: The shuttlepod seen in this episode, the El-Baz, *is named for former NASA planetary geoscientist Farouk El-Baz, currently on faculty at Brown University. Several years ago, El-Baz worked on a documentary film with* Star Trek: The Next Generation *executive producer Rick Berman.*

U.S.S. *Enterprise* resumes mission to the Endicor system.

Shortly after "Time Squared."

Lieutenant Commander Data, while performing modifications on ship's sensors, detects a radio transmission from a previously unknown life-form in the Selcundi Drema sector. Data responds to the signal. This action is later determined to be in violation of the Starfleet Prime Directive.

"Pen Pals." Exact date is conjecture, but Data tells Picard he first detected the signals about eight weeks prior to the completion of the geological survey. That survey was finished six weeks into the episode, suggesting the signals had been received about two weeks prior.

Kyle Riker

U.S.S. *Enterprise* at planet Nasreldine. A crew member contracts a flulike illness there. Afterward, minor readout anomalies require an unscheduled course change to Starbase Montgomery for engineering consultations.

Prior to "The Icarus Factor."

"The Icarus Factor." Stardate 42686.4. U.S.S. *Enterprise* at Starbase Montgomery for engineering consultations. Starfleet civilian adviser Kyle Riker, father of William Riker, is a guest aboard the *Enterprise*.

Commander William Riker is offered command of Starship *Aries*, a small scout ship serving in frontier areas, but he declines the promotion in favor of continued service aboard the *Enterprise*. This is the second time Riker declines the opportunity to command a starship.

U.S.S. *Enterprise* heads for Beta Kupsic.

Just after "The Icarus Factor."

"Pen Pals." Stardate 42695.3. U.S.S. *Enterprise* on survey mission of star systems in Selcundi Drema sector. Acting Ensign Wesley Crusher is placed in charge of planetary geophysical surveys.

Sarjenka, an inhabitant of Drema IV

Lieutenant Commander Data reports receipt of a radio signal from a lifeform on planet Drema IV. Data also acknowledges responding to the signal, even though such a response was in violation of Prime Directive protection. The signal is determined to be a distress call resulting from massive geologic instability on the planet. Captain Picard determines assistance to be appropriate, even though such intervention is a further violation of the Prime Directive. Picard further orders appropriate steps be taken to minimize cultural contamination from this action.

Starfleet receives a garbled message from the Ficus sector. The message is later found to be a distress call from a colony in the Bringloid system.

About a month prior to "Up the Long Ladder."

"Q Who?" Stardate 42761.3. U.S.S. *Enterprise* encounters the entity Q at the frontier of Federation territory. Q expresses a desire to become a member of Starfleet. When Picard declines to accept, Q sends the *Enterprise* some 7,000 light-years across the galaxy. At the previously uncharted star system J-25, evidence is found of a Class-M planet which exhibits massive surface scarring. The phenomenon is similar to that found at outposts Delta Zero Five and Tarod IX near the Romulan Neutral Zone on stardate 41986.

Borg spacecraft sighted near System J-25

At System J-25, the *Enterprise* shortly thereafter makes first contact with a Borg spacecraft. The Borg are determined to be a humanoid species making extensive use of cybernetic implants. Their spacecraft is extremely powerful, but highly decentralized, supporting a hivelike shared consciousness. First contact is a Borg incursion on the *Enterprise*, resulting in severe damage to the *Enterprise*, the loss of shuttle 06, and the death of eighteen *Enterprise* personnel.

Q, apparently satisfied with the demonstration of the hostile and powerful nature of the Borg, later returns the *Enterprise* to Federation space.

U.S.S. *Enterprise* travels to Starbase 83.

After "Q Who?"

"Samaritan Snare." Stardate 42779.1. Captain Jean-Luc Picard and Ensign Wesley Crusher take personal leave at Starbase 515. Crusher's leave is for the purpose of taking Starfleet Academy exams. Picard reports to the Starbase hospital for routine replacement of his bionic heart.

Pakled

U.S.S. *Enterprise* en route to planet Epsilon IX for astronomical survey of Epsilon Pulsar cluster when diverted to investigate a distress call from the Rhomboid Dronegar sector. The distress call is found to have been sent from a Pakled ship, the *Mondor*. Further investigation reveals the call was a ruse, an unsuccessful attempt to gain access to Federation weapons technology by capturing *Enterprise* chief engineer Geordi La Forge.

U.S.S. *Enterprise* at Starbase 73. Picard has meeting with Admiral Moore to discuss a distress call received from the Ficus sector.

Just prior to "Up the Long Ladder."

"Up the Long Ladder." Stardate 42823.2. U.S.S. *Enterprise*, having departed from Starbase 73, proceeds to the planet Bringloid V in the Ficus sector. A colony on the planet had sent a distress call because of severe solar flares in that system. At Bringloid V, *Enterprise* personnel evacuate all colonists and discover evidence of a second, previously unknown colony, in a nearby system. Investigating further, the missing colony is discovered on a nearby planet called Mariposa. It is learned that due to a disastrous crash landing of their ship, the Mariposa colony began with only five individuals who used cloning technology in an attempt to keep their society populated. The inhabitants of the colony report, however, that replicative fading threatens to make their culture nonviable. The Bringloidi colonists and the Mariposans agree to a joint settlement in an attempt to make both groups viable.

Starfleet Command begins advance planning to develop a means to defend against a possible Borg attack, based on evidence that the Borg are approaching Federation space. The project is given high priority, but little of use is forthcoming due to the extraordinary power of the Borg.

"Best of Both Worlds, Part I" Admiral Hanson said they'd been aware of the Borg and had been working on it for over a year prior to the episode.

Lwaxana Troi and her aide, Mr. Homn

"Manhunt." Stardate 42859.2. U.S.S. *Enterprise* on diplomatic mission to transport Antedian and Betazoid delegates to a conference on the planet Pacifica to consider the question of admitting planet Antede III to the Federation. The telepathic assistance of Betazed ambassador Lwaxana Troi is instrumental in exposing two Antedian delegates as assassins, intent upon disrupting the conference.

A Federation conference on planet Pacifica convenes to consider the petition of planet Antede III for admission to the United Federation of Planets.

Just after "Manhunt."

Starbase 336 receives an automated transmission from the *T'Ong,* a Klingon sleeper ship launched in 2290, now returning to Klingon space.

"The Emissary." Two days prior to the episode.

Antedean assassins

"The Emissary." Stardate 42901.3. Special Federation emissary K'Ehleyr is dispatched to the *Enterprise* with orders to intercept the Klingon sleeper ship *T'Ong* near the Boradis system before its crew is automatically revived. The *Enterprise* mission is based on fears that the *T'Ong* crew, launched prior to the Khitomer peace conference of 2293, still believes that a state of war exists between the United Federation of Planets and the Klingon Empire. K'Ehleyr's orders include the option to destroy the *T'Ong* and its crew if necessary, but Captain Picard opposes this course. Instead, he and Lieutenant Worf devise an alternate strategy in which Worf poses as *Enterprise* captain long enough to order the *T'Ong*'s crew to accept command of K'Ehleyr.

Emissary K'Ehleyr

During the *T'Ong* crisis, Emissary K'Ehleyr and *Enterprise* security chief Worf renew an old romantic relationship, although K'Ehleyr declines to take the Klingon oath of marriage. Unknown to Worf at the time, their liaison results in the conception of a child.

"Peak Performance." Stardate 42923.4. U.S.S. *Enterprise* participates in strategic simulation exercise near the Braslota star system ordered by Starfleet in preparation for possible conflict with the Borg. Also participating in the exercise is the U.S.S. *Hathaway*, an older vessel temporarily commanded by William Riker. The entire operation is overseen by Zakdorn tactician Sirna Kolrami. The exercise is briefly interrupted by the Ferengi spacecraft *Kreechta,* whose commander misinterprets the tactical importance of the obsolete *Hathaway*.

Sirna Kolrami

U.S.S. *Enterprise* returns to the nearest starbase.

Just after "Peak Performance."

Alexana Devos accepts a job as security director with the Eastern Continental government of planet Rutia IV. Two days later, a terrorist bomb destroys a shuttlebus, killing sixty schoolchildren. Operatives of the Ansata separatist movement are implicated in the incident.

"The High Ground." Exact date is conjecture, but Alexana says she started as director six months prior to the episode. She also said the shuttlebus bombing happened two days after she took the job.

U.S.S. Hathaway, *NCC-2593*

"Shades of Grey." Stardate 42976.1. U.S.S. *Enterprise* on survey mission to planet Surata IV, when Commander William Riker is injured by accidental contact with indigenous plant form.

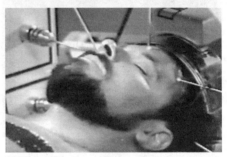

William Riker undergoes therapy following an injury on planet Surata IV.

6.3 STAR TREK: THE NEXT GENERATION — YEAR 3

Worf, son of Mogh, defends his family honor before the Klingon High Council

2366

Dr. Katherine Pulaski

Dr. Paul Stubbs

Dr. Katherine Pulaski completes her assignment on the U.S.S. *Enterprise* and is replaced by Dr. Beverly Crusher, who returns after a year at Starfleet Medical. Geordi La Forge is promoted to the rank of lieutenant commander. Worf is promoted to full lieutenant.

> *These changes occurred after the end of the second season but before the first episode of the third.*

"Evolution." Stardate 43125.8. U.S.S. *Enterprise* on astrophysical research mission for Dr. Paul Stubbs in the Kavis Alpha Sector. The mission, to deliver an instrumented probe into the Kavis Alpha neutron star, is accomplished successfully despite a systems failure aboard the *Enterprise* due to the activity of a newly evolved nanite lifeform. The Nanites, accidentally evolved from nanotechnologic robots developed for medical applications, now are found to be an intelligent species, and are granted colonization rights on planet Kavis Alpha IV.

> *Editors' Note: This episode was actually filmed after "The Ensigns of Command," but was aired first, since "Evolution" also dealt with Beverly Crusher returning to the* Enterprise *after her absence in the second season.*

Romulan admiral Alidar Jarok is censured for his arguments to the Romulan High Command that a war with the Federation would destroy the Romulan Star Empire. Jarok is reassigned to command a distant sector of the empire. It is later learned that this reassignment is part of a plan to provide the idealistic Jarok with false strategic information as a test of loyalty.

"The Defector." Exact date is conjecture; Jarok said his reassignment was four months prior to the episode.

"The Ensigns of Command." (No stardate given in episode.) U.S.S. *Enterprise* receives message from the Sheliak Corporate demanding the removal of Federation colonists on planet Tau Cygna V. The Sheliak claim the settlement exists in contravention of the Treaty of Armens, in which the Federation ceded the planet to the Sheliak. Captain Picard negotiates with the Sheliak to gain sufficient time to evacuate the colonists.

Lieutenant Commander Data transports to Tau Cygna V via shuttlepod and negotiates with colonists to evacuate their settlement in the time allowed by the Sheliak.

Editors' Note: The shuttlepod seen in this episode, the Onizuka, *was named for* Challenger *astronaut Ellison Onizuka. The shuttle* Onizuka *was recreated in floral form as part of a* Star Trek: The Next Generation *float in the 1992 Tournament of Roses Parade in Pasadena. Also part of that float was an enormous floral model of the U.S.S.* Enterprise, *and a second shuttlepod named in honor of* Star Trek *creator Gene Roddenberry.*

Shuttlepod Onizuka

U.S.S. *Enterprise* receives a distress call from the Federation colony on planet Delta Rana IV. The transmission reports the colony is under attack from an unidentified spacecraft.

Three days prior to "The Survivors."

"The Survivors." Stardate 43152.4. U.S.S. *Enterprise* is at planet Delta Rana IV in response to distress call and for possible confrontation with a hostile force. Investigation reveals that the entire colony has been destroyed, except for a single dwelling, that of Kevin and Rishon Uxbridge. The mission is interrupted by the attack of what is apparently a Husnock spacecraft. Further investigation determines that both the attack and the image of Rishon Uxbridge are illusions created by Kevin, who the crew learns is a powerful entity known as a Douwd. Kevin reveals that the colony had been destroyed by a Husnock attack some years prior, that in anger he had used his powers to destroy utterly the entire Husnock species, and that he must now live with the guilt of that act.

Kevin and Rishon Uxbridge

U.S.S. *Enterprise* heads for Starbase 133.

Just after "The Survivors."

Mintakan leader Nuria

"Who Watches the Watchers?" Stardate 43173.5. U.S.S. *Enterprise* on resupply mission to Federation anthropological observation team on planet Mintaka III. The proto-Vulcan humanoid inhabitants there are at the Bronze Age level and are thus still subject to Prime Directive protection.

The mission is complicated when the observation team's holographic duck-blind briefly fails, resulting in cultural contamination when Mintakan natives see the Federation facility. The contamination is made worse when one of the natives receives medical care from *Enterprise* personnel and interprets the experience as a fulfillment of local religious prophesy, believing Captain Picard to be a deity. Picard employs limited exposure to Starfleet personnel and technology in order to minimize the effect of the contamination by convincing Mintakan leader Nuria that he is not their god.

Editors' Note: The Mintakan tapestry given to Picard at the end of the episode can sometimes be seen in later episodes as a decoration on the back of Picard's chair in his living quarters.

Jeremy Aster and the recreated image of his mother, Marla

"The Bonding." Stardate 43198.7. U.S.S. *Enterprise* away team is on an archaeological research mission, when an explosive artifact, a bomb left over from an ancient war, kills archaeologist Marla Aster. Surviving Aster is her 12-year-old son, Jeremy. The Koinonians, a race of non-corporeal life-forms from the planet, offer to accept responsibility for the orphaned child's upbringing, but the offer is declined. *Enterprise* security officer Worf, who had commanded the mission on which Lieutenant Aster was killed, adopts Jeremy into his family through the Klingon *R'uustai* (bonding) ceremony.

Editors' Note: Producer/Writer Ron Moore named the Koinonians for his fraternity at Cornell University.

Jeremy Aster is returned to Earth to be raised by his aunt and uncle, his only living biological relatives.

After "The Bonding."

"Booby Trap." Stardate 43205.6. U.S.S. *Enterprise* is at an asteroid field in the Orelious system to chart the historic battle that resulted in the extinction of both the Menthars and Promellians. A derelict Promellian ship, apparently disabled during the battle, is discovered in the asteroid field. An energy-damping field, which drained power from the Promellian ship, is found to be still active, threatening the *Enterprise* until a means is devised to maneuver the ship from the field using minimal thruster power.

Romulan warbird

"The Enemy." Stardate 43349.2. U.S.S. *Enterprise* responds to an unidentified distress signal originating at planet Galorndon Core. Investigation reveals the signal to be from the wreckage of a small Romulan vessel. The incident is of tactical significance because of Galorndon Core's location a half light-year within Federation space.

One survivor from the downed Romulan craft is found and transported back to the *Enterprise* for medical treatment. The patient later dies because of the unavailability of Romulan-compatible ribosomes. A second survivor, Centurion Bochra, is later reported by Geordi La Forge. A Romulan warbird arrives to participate in the rescue mission, and takes custody of Centurion Bochra. Warbird commander Tomalak denies that the incursion of Bochra's ship was a treaty violation, claiming it was the result of a navigational error.

The separatist Ansata of planet Rutia IV begin the use of an interdimensional transport device in their terrorist raids. Although the nature of the process results in irreversible cellular damage to the transport subject, the Ansata terrorists continue to use the device because it is virtually untraceable and can successfully transport through force fields.

"The High Ground." Exact date is conjecture, but Alexana noted that the Ansata had begun to use the new transporter about two months prior to the episode.

Devinoni Ral

The government of the planet Barzan, under the leadership of Premier Bhavani, invites bids for control of a wormhole near Barzan. The wormhole is considered a vital natural resource due to its highly unusual stability. Bhavani hopes that fees for wormhole use will be of significant economic benefit to her people.

Prior to "The Price."

"The Price." Stardate 43385.6. U.S.S. *Enterprise* serves as host for negotiations for use of the Barzanian wormhole. Negotiator Devinoni Ral, acting on behalf of the Chrysalians, forms a strategic alliance with the Ferengi in an effort to discourage other bidders. During the negotiations, an expedition of shuttle vehicles from the *Enterprise* and the Ferengi vessel finds the wormhole to be partially unstable. The Ferengi shuttle is lost due to the instability.

"The Vengeance Factor." Stardate 43421.9. U.S.S. *Enterprise* discovers a Federation scientific outpost near the Acamarian system has been ransacked. All station personnel are discovered to have been heavily stunned by phaser fire. Investigation suggests the attack was conducted by an Acamarian outlaw group called the Gatherers. The Gatherers had been blamed for a significant number of similar incidents in recent months.

Sovereign *Marouk*

U.S.S. *Enterprise* travels to planet Acamar III to enlist local government support in discouraging the Gatherers' raids. With the assistance of Acamarian sovereign Marouk, a conference is convened at planet Gamma Hromi II with representatives of the Gatherers. The conference is disrupted when Marouk's personal servant, Yuta, attempts to murder Gatherer delegate Chorgan, a member of the clan Lornak. Yuta is discovered to be a member of the nearly extinct clan Tralesta. She is found to have been trying for 80 years to exact revenge upon the Lornack clan for the massacre of her people 80 years ago. A truce is later negotiated with the Gatherers, who agree to return to their original home planet, Acamar III.

Yuta, of the clan Tralesta

Scheduled rendezvous with Starship U.S.S. *Goddard* is postponed by new orders from Starfleet.

U.S.S. *Enterprise* goes to Starbase 343 to take on medical supplies for the Alpha Leonis system. Captain Picard authorizes shore leave for *Enterprise* personnel. A rendezvous with the U.S.S. *Goddard* is scheduled after the starbase layover.

Just after "The Vengeance Factor."

"The Defector." Stardate 43462.5. The *Enterprise*, near the Romulan Neutral Zone, detects a small Romulan scout craft within the zone in violation of treaty. Shortly thereafter, a Romulan warbird is detected in pursuit.

The pilot of the scout ship requests asylum and is taken aboard the *Enterprise*. The pilot is determined to be Romulan admiral Alidar Jarok, who claims to have defected to warn of a potentially destabilizing new Romulan outpost at planet Nelvana III, inside the Neutral Zone. Because of the gravity of the situation, Picard orders the *Enterprise* into the Neutral Zone to investigate, but determines Jarok's information to be baseless. The crew later finds that Jarok is the victim of an elaborate hoax conducted by the Romulan government, intended as a test of loyalty and an attempt to provoke an interstellar incident. The *Enterprise* withdraws with Klingon assistance. Jarok commits suicide by poison.

Romulan admiral Alidar Jarok

The government of the planet Angosia III petitions for membership in the United Federation of Planets.

Prior to "The Hunted."

"The Hunted." Stardate 43489.2. U.S.S. *Enterprise* at planet Angosia III on diplomatic mission in response to the Angosian application for membership to the Federation. The mission is interrupted when *Enterprise* captain Picard agrees to render assistance to local authorities in capturing a prisoner escaped from a high-security penal colony. The prisoner, a former Angosian soldier named Roga Danar, is successfully captured and returned to local authorities.

Roga Danar

Enterprise personnel learn that Danar is the product of intense biochemical and psychological manipulation engineered for a recent Angosian war. Upon conclusion of the war, the Angosian government imprisoned the soldiers for fear of having the warriors loose in normal society. Danar's escape is discovered to be part of an uprising by prisoners to demand rehabilitation for the veterans. Captain Picard cites Prime Directive considerations in declining Starfleet interference with the uprising. Picard agrees to further consider the Angosian petition for Federation membership, pending outcome of the uprising.

U.S.S. *Enterprise* heads for the starbase at Lya III.

Just after "The Hunted."

The government of planet Rutia IV requests Federation medical assistance following an outbreak of terrorist activity on the planet.

Prior to "The High Ground."

Ansata leader Finn

"The High Ground." Stardate 43510.7. U.S.S. *Enterprise* at planet Rutia IV to deliver medical supplies following reports of local unrest on the planet. While supervising delivery of the supplies, *Enterprise* chief medical officer Beverly Crusher is kidnapped by members of the Ansata separatist movement. Attempts to negotiate Crusher's release with Ansata operatives are unsuccessful, and the Ansata conduct additional terrorist attacks against the *Enterprise* itself. Although the first attack is thwarted, the second results in the kidnapping of Captain Jean-Luc Picard.

Rutian security director Alexana assists *Enterprise* personnel in conducting a rescue mission that succeeds in freeing both Picard and Crusher.

The United Federation of Planets signs a peace treaty with the planet Cardassia, concluding a long and bloody conflict with the Cardassians.

"The Wounded." Exact date is conjecture, but Picard's log establishes the treaty had been signed "nearly a year" prior to the episode (2367).

A large celestial body, probably a black hole, passes through the plane of the Bre'el star system, disrupting the orbit of the moon of planet Bre'el IV. The asteroidal moon's orbit begins to decay, threatening the inhabitants of Bre'el IV.

Just prior to "Deja Q."

Q

"Deja Q." Stardate 43539.1. U.S.S. *Enterprise* responds to distress call from planet Bre'el IV, and attempts to use the ship's tractor beam to alter the orbit of the descending asteroidal moon. The effort fails due to insufficient beam power. A second attempt is made with an unorthodox technique, using a low-level warp field to reduce the moon's gravitational constant. This effort is also unsuccessful.

Q once again appears on the *Enterprise*, this time claiming that he has been stripped of his powers. He requests asylum and is assigned to help develop a solution to the Bre'el crisis. Q meets with another member of the Q continuum and thereafter reports that his powers have been restored. Q uses those powers to circularize the Bre'el moon's orbit at a safe altitude.

Starship *Enterprise* heads for Station Nigala IV.

Just after "Deja Q."

Lieutenant Commander Shelby of Starfleet Tactical is placed in charge of Borg tactical analysis by Admiral J. P. Hanson. Her assignment is to develop a defense strategy against an anticipated Borg offensive.

"The Best of Both Worlds, Part I." Admiral Hanson tells Picard that Shelby had taken over the project six months before the episode.

Shelby

Stardate 43587. Crewman First Class Simon Tarses is assigned to duty in the medical department aboard the U.S.S. *Enterprise.*

"The Drumhead." The stardate given by Tarses places it between "Deja Q" and "A Matter of Perspective."

U.S.S. *Enterprise* is en route to a mission for the study of a proto-star cloud, when it is briefly diverted by a request from the Tanaga IV research station for dicosilium supplies.

Just prior to "A Matter of Perspective."

"A Matter of Perspective." Stardate 43610.4. The Starship *Enterprise* makes delivery of dicosilium to the Tanaga IV research station. Commander William Riker remains on the station while the *Enterprise* departs for 24 hours to conduct its original proto-star survey mission. Riker gathers data to evaluate the progress of Dr. Nel Apgar, a scientist believed to be on the verge of developing a technique for the use of Krieger waves for power generation. Shortly thereafter the *Enterprise* returns to pick up Riker, and the space station explodes under mysterious circumstances, resulting in the death of Dr. Apgar.

Dr. Nel Apgar and his wife

Local authorities accuse Commander Riker of murder in the incident, but Captain Picard successfully negotiates a stay of extradition pending an investigation. Research using a holodeck recreation of the events leading up to the explosion results in Riker's acquittal.

U.S.S. *Enterprise* heads for Emila II.

Just after "A Matter of Perspective."

"Yesterday's *Enterprise*." Stardate 43625.2. U.S.S. *Enterprise* personnel discover an unusual radiation anomaly in space. Investigation determines the anomaly to be a temporal rift, possibly a Kerr loop of superstring material. Initial readings suggest there may have been a spacecraft within the rift, but later indications show this reading was mistaken. A Class-1 sensor probe is launched to further investigate the phenomenon.

U.S.S. Enterprise, *NCC-1701-C*

Several years later, evidence accumulates indicating that there was indeed a space vehicle in the anomaly. The other ship may have been the *Ambassador* class starship *Enterprise*, NCC-1701-C, and its emergence from 22 years in the past may have triggered significant damage to the temporal continuum. Evidence suggests that in the alternate timeline, the Federation may have been embroiled in an extended war with the Klingon Empire, but the return of the *Enterprise*-C to its proper time apparently restored the original path of the continuum. It is later determined that in this alternate timeline, *Enterprise* security officer Tasha Yar did not die at Vagra II, and instead traveled back in time with the *Enterprise*-C into a common past, about 2344. In this past Yar was captured by Romulans, and eventually gave birth to a daughter, Sela, who grew up to become a Romulan operative.

Tasha Yar

U.S.S. *Enterprise* travels to planet Archer IV.

Just after "Yesterday's Enterprise.*"*

Lieutenant Commander Data attends a cybernetics conference, learning of recent advances in submicron matrix transfer technology. Upon returning to the *Enterprise*, Data uses the new techniques to attempt the transfer of his neural net programming into a positronic brain similar to his own. Commander Riker temporarily leaves the *Enterprise* to take personal leave while the ship conducts a routine mapping mission in sector 396. He returns to the *Enterprise* shortly after stardate 43657.0.

Data

Prior to "The Offspring."

"The Offspring." Stardate 43657.0. Lieutenant Commander Data announces that his efforts to program a positronic brain have been a result of his desire to create a child. He further reveals that he has constructed an android body for the child, and that he has activated it, giving it the name Lal, from the Hindi word meaning "beloved."

*Data's
android child,
Lal*

Upon being notified of the development, Starfleet Research at the Galor IV annex of the Daystrom Institute expresses an interest in Data's work, and requests the transfer of Lal to the Daystrom Institute for study. Data declines the request on grounds that he does not wish to give up custody of his child. Starfleet Admiral Anthony Haftel, citing the disastrous M-5 tests of 2268, renders an administrative ruling requiring Data to relinquish custody, but Captain Picard orders Data not to comply, citing issues of personal liberty. The question becomes moot when a malfunction in Lal's neural matrix cascades into a systemwide failure, resulting in her death.

Kova Tholl, an inhabitant of planet Mizar II, is abducted by unknown aliens as part of a behavioral study. Tholl is a public servant, assistant to the regent of Pozaron, the third-largest city on Mizar II. Tholl is replaced by a near-perfect replica.

"Allegiance." Tholl said he had been kidnapped about twelve days prior to the episode.

Worf faces his accusers

"Sins of the Father." Stardate 43685.2. U.S.S. *Enterprise* conducts a cometary cloud and asteroid survey. Klingon commander Kurn serves aboard the Starship *Enterprise* as part of the continuing exchange program. Kurn informs Lieutenant Worf that the two are brothers, having been separated shortly before the Khitomer massacre of 2346. He further informs Worf that the Klingon High Council has judged their father, Mogh, to be a traitor for his alleged role in the Khitomer massacre 20 years ago.

High Council Leader K'mpec

Captain Picard orders the *Enterprise* to the Klingon Homeworld so that Worf can challenge the allegations against his father. Although initial evidence appears to be damning, comparison against sensor logs from the U.S.S. *Intrepid* suggests the data files had been tampered with. It is later revealed that Worf has uncovered information implicating Ja'rod, the father of council member Duras, of betrayal just prior to the Khitomer massacre. Kurn is injured in an ambush, apparently by Duras family operatives attempting to dissuade Worf from presenting these findings, but Picard agrees to fulfill the ceremonial role of *cha'DIch* so that the inquiry can continue. Council leader K'mpec refuses to admit the new evidence, citing the political implications of exposing the powerful Duras family. A compromise is reached in which Worf accepts discommendation from the council for his father's alleged acts, but is allowed to go free.

U.S.S. *Enterprise* assists in eradicating an outbreak of Phyrox plague on planet Cor Caroli V. Starfleet classifies the incident as "secret."

Just prior to "Allegiance."

"Allegiance." Stardate 43714.1. U.S.S. *Enterprise* proceeds to rendezvous with U.S.S. *Hood* for terraforming project on planet Browder IV.

Esoqq of planet Chalna

Captain Picard is abducted by unidentified alien scientists, who employ the captain to conduct a behavioral study into the nature of authority. Also abducted for the study is Kova Tholl of the planet Mizar II, and Esoqq of the planet Chalna. All three individuals are replaced with near-perfect replicas, who conduct additional studies in their subjects' natural environments. The study is discontinued when Captain Picard and his fellow captives refuse to participate.

Editors' Note: The fake participant in the study, Cadet Haro, is described as a "Bolian," from planet Bolarus IX. This race of aliens, first seen as Captain Rixx in "Conspiracy," was named after director Cliff Bole, who directed that episode.

U.S.S. *Enterprise* resumes course for rendezvous with U.S.S. *Hood* for Browder IV terraforming project.

Just after "Allegiance."

U.S.S. Hood *NCC-42296*

U.S.S. *Enterprise* at planet Gemaris V, where Captain Picard serves as mediator in a trade dispute between the Gemarians and their nearest neighbor, the Dachlyds.

At least two weeks before "Captain's Holiday." Riker notes that the conference had lasted for two weeks.

"Captain's Holiday." Stardate 43745.2. At the recommendation of Chief Medical Officer Crusher, Captain Picard takes shore leave on the resort planet of Risa while the *Enterprise* departs to Starbase 12 for a week of routine maintenance. While on shore leave, Picard works with archaeologist Vash in an effort to continue Dr. Samuel Estragon's search for the Tox Uthat, a 27th-century artifact hidden in the past. The device is believed to have enormous potential as a weapons system. Although the search for the Uthat is successful, the artifact is destroyed to prevent it from falling into the hands of two 27th-century Vorgon criminals (possibly poets) who have also traveled back to this time.

Vorgon criminals from the 27th-century

U.S.S. *Enterprise* undergoes a maintenance layover at Starbase 12.

Editors' Note: In "Captain's Holiday," Riker asks Picard to bring him a souvenir, a Hor'gon *statuette. Picard does so, and in later episodes the Hor'gon can often be seen in Riker's quarters.*

The unmanned *Vega IX* probe returns scientific data from the star Beta Stromgren, a star beyond Federation space, believed to be on the verge of exploding into a supernova. Among the data is evidence of a small object, possibly a spaceborne organic life-form. The object, believed to be of significant strategic importance, is code-named Tin Man.

Prior to "Tin Man."

"Tin Man." Stardate 43779.3. U.S.S. *Enterprise* is en route to mission to prepare detailed exospheric charts of planets in the Hayashi system. The

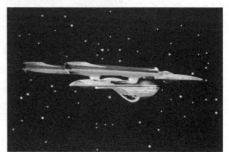

Tin Man

Tam
Elbrun

mission is interrupted by a priority rendezvous with U.S.S. *Hood*, relaying classified orders to investigate the newly discovered Tin Man. Also conveyed aboard the *Hood* is Tam Elbrun, a Federation specialist in communication with unknown life-forms. Elbrun, a full Betazoid, had earlier been a patient of Deanna Troi's at the University of Betazed.

Despite interference from a Romulan expedition wishing to utilize Tin Man for Romulan interests, mission specialist Elbrun is successful in establishing a symbiotic rapport with the previously unknown creature. Elbrun elects to remain with Tin Man (which refers to itself as Gomtuu) and is successful in propelling the *Enterprise* and a *D'Deridex* class Romulan warbird to safety just prior to the explosion of Beta Stromgren.

Editors' Note: Engineer Russell, who works with Geordi to reroute the ship's power and get the sensors working in the episode, is named for Russell Bailey, the son of "Tin Man" cowriter Dennis Bailey.

U.S.S. *Enterprise* goes to Starbase 152 for inspection and repairs to damage resulting from the Gomtuu encounter.

Just after "Tin Man."

Lt. Reginald
Barclay

Lieutenant Reginald Barclay III, a systems diagnostics engineer, transfers from the U.S.S. *Zhukov* to serve aboard the U.S.S. *Enterprise*. Barclay is highly recommended by *Zhukov* captain Gleason, despite Barclay's tendencies toward reclusive behavior.

Prior to "Hollow Pursuits."

"Hollow Pursuits." Stardate 43807.4. U.S.S. *Enterprise* accepts a shipment of special tissue samples donated by the Mikulaks for shipment to planet Nahmi IV. It is hoped the samples will help develop a cure for an outbreak of Correllium fever on that planet. A number of serious systems malfunctions aboard the *Enterprise* are later traced to contamination from invidium used in the Mikulak sample containers. The invidium contamination is rendered inert by exposure to cryogenic temperatures.

Lieutenant Barclay receives an unsatisfactory performance rating for his work in the *Enterprise* engineering department. Barclay's rating is further jeopardized by revelations that he had been surreptitiously creating holodeck simulations of his crewmates, in violation of protocol. Counselor Troi reports this behavior to be due to Barclay's feeling of social awkwardness. Later, his performance improves when given support from his superiors. Barclay is credited with being instrumental in diagnosing and resolving the malfunctions resulting from the Mikulak invidium contamination.

U.S.S. *Enterprise* proceeds to Starbase 121 for complete systems and bio decontamination.

Just after "Hollow Pursuits." One also assumes they went to planet Nahmi IV as well.

Fajo's
companion,
Varria

Serious tricyanate contamination threatens the subsurface water supply for the Federation colony on planet Beta Agni II. The U.S.S. *Enterprise* is ordered to lend assistance.

Prior to "The Most Toys."

"The Most Toys." Stardate 43872.2. U.S.S. *Enterprise* procures 108 kilograms of hytritium compound from the Zibalian trader Kivas Fajo. The hytritium is required to treat the tricyanate contamination at planet Beta Agni II. Because of the risks inherent in beaming such a dangerously unstable substance, the hytritium is transported via shuttlepod piloted by Data. An apparent failure in a hytritium containment vessel results in the destruction of the shuttle, along with its pilot, en route to the *Enterprise*.

The remaining hytritium compound is deemed sufficient to neutralize the Beta Agni II groundwater contamination, and the treatment is performed without incident. Postmission analysis suggests that the tricyanate contamination may have been deliberate sabotage, and further investigation implicates Kivas Fajo. It is later learned that Fajo was indeed responsible for the Beta Agni II contamination, and that he had staged the entire incident as a ruse to abduct Data, who was not killed in the shuttle explosion as previously believed. U.S.S. *Enterprise* intercepts Fajo's ship, the *Jovis*, and extracts Data from Fajo's custody with the assistance of Varria. Fajo himself is placed under arrest for kidnapping and theft.

Editors' Note: The shuttlepod piloted by Data in this episode, the Pike, *was named for the former* Enterprise *captain seen in "The Menagerie." Fajo was named for* Star Trek *production staffer Lolita Fatjo.*

"Sarek." Stardate 43917.4. U.S.S. *Enterprise* on diplomatic mission to host a conference between Federation Ambassador Sarek and a delegation from Legara IV. Preparations for the conference are disrupted by outbreaks of unexplained violence among the *Enterprise* crew. Investigation suggests that Ambassador Sarek may be suffering from Bendii syndrome, and that the violent incidents may be the side effects of that ailment.

Sarek of Vulcan

Further investigation supports the theory that Sarek is indeed afflicted with Bendii syndrome, which causes the gradual and irreversible degeneration of intellectual capacity and emotional control. Sarek is found to have deteriorated to the point where his ability to conduct the Legaran conference is in doubt. At the suggestion of Sarek's wife, Perrin, Captain Picard agrees to a mind-meld with Sarek in hope of reinforcing the ambassador's emotional control for a brief time. The mind meld, though painful for Picard, is successful, and the Legarans indeed agree to diplomatic relations with the Federation. This agreement is hailed as the final triumph of Sarek's distinguished career.

Perrin, Sarek's wife

Editors' Note: Except for a brief cameo by DeForest Kelley as Admiral McCoy in "Encounter at Farpoint," "Sarek" marks the first major "crossover" involving a character from the original Star Trek *series.*

Sarek, Perrin, and the Vulcan delegation return to Vulcan on board the Starship *Merrimac*.

After "Sarek."

"Menage à Troi." Stardate 43930.7. U.S.S. *Enterprise* is in attendance at the biennial Trade Agreements Conference on Betazed. In attendance at closing banquet held aboard ship is Betazed delegate Lwaxana Troi along with a Ferengi delegation headed by DaiMon Tog.

DaiMon Tog

U.S.S. *Enterprise* departs Betazed for a stellar mapping mission in the Gamma Erandi Nebula, during which time Counselor Troi and Commander Riker take shore leave on Betazed. Riker, Troi, and Lwaxana Troi are abducted by DaiMon Tog from the surface of Betazed to the Ferengi vessel *Krayton*. Tog offers Lwaxana Troi a partnership designed to take advantage of her Betazoid telepathic abilities in trade negotiations. Lwaxana declines the proposal.

Upon the *Enterprise*'s return from the Gamma Erandi mapping mission, Betazed authorities inform Captain Picard of the abduction, and the *Enterprise* gives chase to the *Krayton*. Lwaxana Troi is successful in negotiating the release of her daughter and Riker from Ferengi custody, and Picard is able to negotiate freedom for Lwaxana.

*Acting Ensign
Wesley Crusher*

Acting Ensign Wesley Crusher receives the results of his Starfleet Academy application. He is accepted, but misses his opportunity for transport aboard the U.S.S. *Bradbury* to Starfleet Academy due to his assistance with the search for the Ferengi vessel. Although Admiral Hahn at the Academy indicates Crusher is welcome to apply again next year, Picard recognizes Crusher's sacrifice by granting him a field promotion to full ensign.

Editors' Note: Author Ray Bradbury, for whom the unseen U.S.S. Bradbury was named, was a friend of Star Trek creator Gene Roddenberry's and was a speaker at the memorial service following Gene's death in 1991. This episode was cowritten by Gene Roddenberry's longtime assistant, Susan Sackett (with Fred Bronson).

U.S.S. *Enterprise* proceeds to Xanthras system for rendezvous with the Starship *Zapata*.

Just after "Menage à Troi."

*"John Doe,"
prior to his
transformation*

"Transfigurations." Stardate 43957.2. U.S.S. *Enterprise* is charting an unknown star system in the Zeta Gelis cluster, when the wreckage of a small space vehicle is discovered on one of the planets in the region. One survivor is discovered in critical condition, and chief medical officer Crusher is successful in stabilizing his condition by using Geordi La Forge's neural system to regulate that of the patient.

The survivor, referred to as "John Doe," is found to possess extraordinary recuperative powers, and Doe is fully recovered in a very short time. Dr. Crusher expresses some concern over what appears to be a progressive mutation of Doe's cells, his apparent loss of memory, and his subsequent inability to recall his origin or the circumstances of his crash.

Analysis of wreckage from Doe's vehicle indicates a probable origin point. En route to that point, an alien vessel is encountered that identifies itself as Zalkonian. The captain of the Zalkonian vessel identifies himself as Sunad, and claims custody of Doe for crimes against his people. Doe, whose cellular mutation has been accelerating, is found to be undergoing a metamorphosis into an energy-based being, and it is learned that Sunad's mission is to prevent this evolution by killing all individuals undergoing the change. Once Doe's transfiguration is complete, he departs the *Enterprise* to live in free space, beyond Sunad's ability to harm him.

Editors' Note: Sunad (spell it backward) was named for former Star Trek story editor Richard Danus.

Starfleet Command offers *Enterprise* executive officer William Riker a promotion to captain of the Starship *Melbourne*. This is the third command offer made to Riker, who eventually declines the promotion.

Prior to "Best of Both Worlds, Part I."

*Commander
William
Riker*

The New Providence colony on planet Jouret IV sends a distress call. The U.S.S. *Enterprise* proceeds to Jouret IV in response.

About twelve hours prior to "Best of Both Worlds, Part I."

"The Best of Both Worlds, Part I." Stardate 43989.1. U.S.S. *Enterprise* at Jouret IV finds the New Providence colony to have been totally destroyed, with no sign of the colony's 900 inhabitants. Surface conditions are almost identical to those found at System J-25 on stardate 42761.3, suggesting that the New Providence colony had been attacked by the Borg. Admiral J. P. Hanson of Starbase 324 assigns Lieutenant Commander Shelby to the *Enterprise* to assist with tactical preparations.

Remains of the New Providence colony at planet Jouret IV

Hanson reports a distress signal has been received at Starbase 057 from Starship *Lalo* near Zeta Alpha II, indicating a probable Borg sighting in Federation space. Contact with the *Lalo* is subsequently lost, and the ship is believed destroyed by a Borg vessel. Further readings indicate the Borg vessel to be headed to Sector 001 at high warp speeds. Admiral Hanson orders every available Starfleet ship to rendezvous at Wolf 359 to mount a defense. A request is also made to the Klingon High Command to provide additional ships for this engagement.

Diverted to engage the Borg in advance of the fleet, efforts are made by *Enterprise* personnel to improvise improvements to existing defenses and weapons for the anticipated encounter. These preparations are unsuccessful in preventing the abduction of Captain Picard by the Borg. Picard is subjected to extensive surgical modification to incorporate him into the Borg collective consciousness.

Admiral Hanson

6.4 STAR TREK: THE NEXT GENERATION — YEAR 4

Locutus of Borg

2367

Borg spacecraft

"The Best of Both Worlds, Part II." Stardate 44001.4. A powerful deflector-based weapon devised by *Enterprise* personnel is unsuccessful in disabling the Borg vessel, which continues at high speed toward Earth. The use of the improvised deflector weapon temporarily incapacitates the *Enterprise*.

An armada of 40 Federation and Klingon starships is nearly annihilated at Wolf 359 by the Borg. Eleven thousand personnel (including Admiral J. P. Hanson) and 39 starships are lost. It is believed that the involuntary cooperation of Captain Jean-Luc Picard, then known as Locutus of Borg, played a significant role in this terrible defeat. The Borg ship proceeds to Earth, and is met by the *Enterprise*, whose drive systems are once again functional. A rescue mission is successful in recovering Captain Picard, and a study of Picard's Borg modifications yields information making it possible to trigger a self-destruct command on the Borg vessel.

Editors' Note: Casualty figures from the battle of Wolf 359 are from "The Drumhead."

U.S.S. Enterprise *at McKinley station*

U.S.S. *Enterprise* arrives at Earth Station McKinley for an estimated six weeks of repair work. Captain Picard also undergoes extensive medical treatment and therapy for the Borg surgical modifications and implants. Unknown to anyone at the time, a defective hatch is installed on the dilithium chamber of the *Enterprise* warp drive system. Undetectable submicron fractures in the casing cause a near-disastrous failure several months later, shortly before stardate 44765.2.

After "Best of Both Worlds, Part II." Failure of the dilithium chamber hatch described in "The Drumhead."

"Family." Stardate 44012.3. Repair work on the *Enterprise* at Earth Station McKinley is completed a week early. While in dock, Captain Picard takes shore leave at his family home in Labarre, France, visiting his brother and sister-in-law, Robert and Marie Picard. There, Picard declines an offer to serve as director of the Atlantis Project, choosing instead to remain with Starfleet. Sergey and Helena Rozhenko visit their adoptive son, Worf, aboard the *Enterprise*. Wesley Crusher views a holographic message from his late father, recorded when Wesley was only ten weeks old.

Editors' Note: Transporter chief Miles Edward O'Brien is given a first and middle name in this episode when he introduces himself to Worf's parents. O'Brien had been a recurring character since "Encounter at Farpoint" (he was battle bridge conn, not referred to by name), but he had not been referred to by first or middle name prior to this point.

"Family" was actually the fourth episode filmed during the fourth season. It is listed second because it is a direct continuation of the story line from "Best of Both Worlds, Part II," and as such was the next episode aired.

Captain Jean-Luc Picard is reunited with his family in Labarre, France.

U.S.S. *Enterprise* at planet Ogus II for crew shore leave. The two-day layover is cut short when a child's practical joke endangers the life of his brother, Willie Potts, necessitating an emergency medical evac to Starbase 416.

Enterprise chief engineer Geordi La Forge performs dilithium vector calibrations on the ship's warp propulsion system. Although the system can remain on line during the calibration, this procedure requires maximum warp velocity to be restricted during the operation.

Just prior to "Brothers."

Dr. Beverly Crusher cares for young Willie Potts in medical isolation.

"Brothers." Stardate 44085.7. En route to Starbase 416 for emergency medical treatment of Willie Potts, Lieutenant Commander Data exhibits severely aberrant behavior, commandeering the *Enterprise* to a distant planet. Beaming down to the planet, Data discovers he had been summoned by his creator, Dr. Noonien Soong, long thought to be dead. Also arriving is Lore, Data's android brother, who was thought destroyed in 2364 near Omicron Theta. Soong informs his two creations that he is dying, but attempts unsuccessfully to install a new circuit chip in Data, a modification which would have permitted Data to experience human emotions. An *Enterprise* away team investigating Soong's lab reports Soong to have died and Lore to have departed. Data, having fulfilled his creator's command, returns to normal operation.

Dr. Noonien Soong and his android creation Lore

U.S.S. *Enterprise* proceeds to Starbase 416 for emergency care of Willie Potts. The treatment is successful in restoring Potts to health.

"Suddenly Human." Stardate 44143.7. U.S.S. *Enterprise* in sector 21947 in response to a distress call from a Talarian observation craft. Among the survivors is a young human, Jeremiah Rossa, found to be the grandson of Starfleet admiral Connaught Rossa. Investigation determines that Jeremiah had been raised by a Talarian captain, Endar, in keeping with a Talarian tradition permitting a warrior to claim the son of a slain enemy. Admiral Rossa requests her grandson be returned to her care, but *Enterprise* captain Picard rules the child's interests would be better served by returning him to his adoptive family, since Jeremiah now considers Endar to be his father.

Talarian captain Endar and his son, Jono, also known as Jeremiah Rossa

"Remember Me." Stardate 44161.2. U.S.S. *Enterprise* at Starbase 133 for crew rotation. Also on board for passage to planet Kenda II is Dr. Dalen Quaice, mentor to Dr. Beverly Crusher. Upon departing for planet Durenia

The Traveler

IV, a freak accident in a warp field experiment causes Dr. Crusher to be trapped for several hours inside a static warp bubble. She is rescued, unharmed, by the efforts of her son, Ensign Wesley Crusher, with the assistance of the individual called the Traveler, a native of planet Tau Alpha C. The Traveler had previously participated in a warp propulsion system experiment aboard the *Enterprise* in 2364.

Editors' Note: Picard notes the ship's complement at the end of the episode is 1,014 people.

"Legacy." Stardate 44215.2. U.S.S. *Enterprise* bypasses a scheduled archaeological survey of planet Camus II in response to a distress call from Federation freighter *Arcos*, in orbit around planet Turkana IV. Upon arrival at Turkana, two survivors from the *Arcos* are discovered to have landed on the planet surface. The two are discovered to have been captured by one of two rival gangs now in control of the colony. One of the gangs offers assistance in the person of Ishara Yar, sister to the late *Enterprise* security chief. The rescue is successful, although Yar is discovered to be using the operation to attempt to gain an advantage over her rival gang.

Ishara Yar

Editors' Note: The bypassed archaeological survey of planet Camus II referred to in Picard's opening log was intended as an "inside" joke, a salute to the original Star Trek television series. The seventy-ninth and final episode of that show, "Turnabout Intruder," involved an archaeological expedition on Camus II. "Legacy" is the eightieth episode of Star Trek: The Next Generation. The gag was the brainchild of executive producer Rick Berman, actor Jonathan Frakes, and script coordinator Eric Stillwell. The reference to the Starship Potemkin (See 2361), also mentioned in the last episode of the original Star Trek, is another such inside joke.

K'Ehleyr

"Reunion." Stardate 44246.3. U.S.S. *Enterprise* investigating radiation anomalies in the Gamma Arigulon system reported by the Starship *LaSalle*. The study is cut short when the *Enterprise* is met by a *Vor'cha* class Klingon attack cruiser bearing Klingon high council leader K'mpec, who requests a meeting with Captain Picard. Also aboard the attack cruiser is Klingon emissary K'Ehleyr, who comes aboard the *Enterprise* with a child, Alexander. K'Ehleyr informs Lieutenant Worf that Alexander is his son from their encounter during her previous visit to the *Enterprise*.

K'mpec reveals that he has been fatally poisoned by political enemies, and appoints Picard to mediate the rite of succession. K'mpec explains the highly unusual request on the basis of his fears that factions within the Klingon High Council may plunge the empire into civil war. Picard accepts, and K'mpec dies shortly thereafter.

Picard hears claims from council member Duras and political newcomer Gowron as part of the *ja'chuq* (succession) process. Emissary K'Ehleyr uncovers suppressed evidence that Duras's father had betrayed the Klingon people at the Khitomer massacre of 2346. Duras murders K'Ehleyr in an attempt to prevent her from reporting these findings, but Worf later claims the right of vengeance and kills Duras. Gowron remains as the sole contender for leadership of the Klingon High Council and is subsequently installed in that position. Worf is officially reprimanded by Captain Picard for his actions in the death of Duras.

Worf and his son, Alexander

U.S.S. *Enterprise* at Starbase 73. Lieutenant Worf is met by his adoptive parents, Sergey and Helena Rozhenko, who take custody of Worf's son, Alexander. They return to Earth to raise the child.

After "Reunion."

"Future Imperfect." Stardate 44286.5. U.S.S. *Enterprise* is conducting a security survey of the Onias sector near the Romulan Neutral Zone. Evidence of activity at planet Alpha Onias III, a barren and inhospitable Class-M world, necessitates an away mission to the planet's surface. Commander William Riker is diverted during the beam-up process, and detained by an alien called Barash. The alien eventually agrees to release Riker and to be a guest on the *Enterprise*.

Riker celebrates his 32nd birthday.

Commander Riker and the alien Barash

Captain Picard is asked to mediate a dispute among the salenite miners on planet Pentarus V.

Wesley Crusher is accepted to Starfleet Academy when a position opens up in the current year's class.

Prior to "Final Mission."

Dirgo and Picard defend the shuttle party following the crash of the Nenebek.

"Final Mission." Stardate 44307.3. U.S.S. *Enterprise* receives a distress call from planet Gamelan V. Gamelan chairman Songi reports an unidentified spacecraft has entered orbit around her planet, resulting in significant increases in atmospheric radiation levels. Commander Riker orders the *Enterprise* diverted to Gamelan V, and determines the spacecraft to be an ancient freighter carrying unstable nuclear wastes. *Enterprise* personnel are successful in sending the freighter through the Meltasion Asteroid Belt and into the Gamelan sun, although the operation entails hazardous radiation exposure to the *Enterprise* crew.

Captain Picard departs for Pentarus V, aboard the Pentaran mining shuttle *Nenebek*. Also aboard the shuttlecraft is pilot Dirgo and Ensign Wesley Crusher. A malfunction of the shuttle's propulsion system forces a crash landing on Lambda Paz, a moon of Pentarus III. Although no one is immediately killed in the crash, Dirgo dies in an attempt to secure water for the survivors before the *Enterprise* can locate them.

Emblem of Starfleet Academy

Wesley Crusher leaves the *Enterprise* to enroll in Starfleet Academy on Earth.

After "Final Mission."

"The Loss." Stardate 44356.9. U.S.S. *Enterprise*, on course for planet T'lli Beta, delays to investigate anomalous sensor readings. While studying the area, a warp drive malfunction is detected, apparently caused by a school of two-dimensional life-forms discovered nearby. Attempts to restore engine function are unsuccessful until it is determined that the life-forms are attempting to return to a nearby cosmic string fragment. The *Enterprise* main deflector is used to simulate the string's natural harmonics in a successful effort to guide the life-forms to the string, apparently their natural home.

A side effect of the presence of the two-dimensional life-forms is the temporary loss of empathic powers by *Enterprise* counselor Deanna Troi.

Editors' Note: Planet T'lli Beta was named by episode writer Hillary Bader for her grandmother, Tillie Bader.

U.S.S. *Enterprise* arrives at designated coordinates for rendezvous with U.S.S. *Zhukov*.

Just before "Data's Day."

Ambassador T'Pel, aka Subcommander Selok

Miles and Keiko O'Brien

Data and his pet cat, Spot

Starship Enterprise

"Data's Day." Stardate 44390.1. U.S.S. *Enterprise* rendezvous with U.S.S. *Zhukov* to transport Vulcan ambassador T'Pel to the Romulan Neutral Zone for negotiations. T'Pel is apparently killed in a transporter accident while beaming over to the Romulan ship *Devoras.* Investigation reveals the accident to have been staged by the Romulans, and it is later revealed that T'Pel is in reality Romulan subcommander Selok, who had been an undercover agent in Federation territory. The incident had been staged in order to facilitate her return to Romulan space.

Enterprise crew member Francisca Juarez gives birth to a baby boy. The child's father, Alfredo Juarez, is also a member of the *Enterprise* crew. Chief Miles Edward O'Brien is married to botanist Keiko Ishikawa in a ceremony held in the Ten Forward lounge. Captain Jean-Luc Picard officiates, and Lieutenant Commander Data serves as father of the bride.

Long-range sensors continue to gather scientific data on the Murasaki Quasar.

Lieutenant Commander Data records personal log for transmission to Commander Bruce Maddox, Cybernetics Division, Daystrom Institute. The recording is made to provide information on Data's programming.

Editors' Note: This episode marks the first appearance of Data's pet cat, whose name is later established to be Spot. Captain Picard's introduction to the O'Brien wedding ceremony is an homage by writer Ron Moore to a similar speech given by Captain Kirk at the Tomlinson wedding in "The Balance of Terror." In "Data's Day," we also get our first glimpse of the Enterprise *barbershop. The Murasaki Quasar was a reference to the original series episode "The Galileo Seven."*

Data notes that this episode marks the 1550th day since the commissioning of the Enterprise. *We tried to project this back to determine when the ship was commissioned. Our theory was this: With* Next Generation *stardates, you can sometimes get a pretty good idea of when an episode theoretically occurs within a given year by treating the last three digits as measuring thousandths of a year. (This means that a stardate with the last three digits of 500 would be about halfway through a given year.) The resulting date is a rough estimate at best, given the number of cases where things don't line up properly. (See Appendix D for more on stardates.) Nevertheless, we tried it anyhow.*

Given a stardate of 44390, this yields an estimated date of late May 2367 for the episode. Subtracting 1550 days gives an approximate commissioning date of late February 2363. This might be inconsistent with the first season episode, "Lonely Among Us," which suggests the ship was launched in the latter half of 2363 (because of Picard's line that the Enterprise *is less than a year old in that episode). We rationalize that the ship was commissioned in February but officially launched several months later.*

For whatever it's worth, the dedication plaque on the bridge bears a launch stardate of 40759.5, corresponding to an approximate calendar date of October 4, 2363. It's no coincidence that the launch of Sputnik I, *which many regard as the dawn of the Space Age, was on October 4, 1957.*

U.S.S. *Enterprise* travels to planet Adelphous IV.

Just after "Data's Day."

A Cardassian science station in the Cuellar system is destroyed by the U.S.S. *Phoenix* under the command of Captain Benjamin Maxwell. The action is in violation of the peace treaty between the Cardassians and the Federation, although Captain Maxwell claims to have evidence that the science station was in fact a military transport facility.

Two days before "The Wounded."

"The Wounded." Stardate 44429.6. U.S.S. *Enterprise*, on mapping survey near Cardassian space, is attacked by a Cardassian *Galor* class warship, the *Trager*. The commander of the attacking vessel informs *Enterprise* captain Picard that the attack is in response to the destruction of the Cardassian station in the Cuellar system two days ago. Captain Picard is instructed by Starfleet admiral Haden to investigate Maxwell's attack.

Captain Ben Maxwell

Picard determines Maxwell's actions against Cardassian forces to be due to Maxwell's theory that the Cardassians are about to launch an unprovoked military offensive against the Federation. Captain Picard, acting under direct orders from Starfleet, prevents Maxwell from taking further action against the Cardassians. Two Cardassian spacecraft are destroyed before Maxwell is relieved of his command. While Maxwell is placed in custody, Picard instructs Cardassian officer Gul Macet to inform his government that Starfleet is aware that Maxwell's charges of covert military preparations have a basis in fact.

Cardassian Gul Macet

Editors' Note: This episode marks the first appearance of the Cardassians, a group of adversaries that would recur in Star Trek: The Next Generation *episodes as well as in* Star Trek: Deep Space Nine. *(The back story established in "The Wounded" suggests, however, that hostilities between the Federation and the Cardassians had existed for at least several years prior to the episode. Picard notes he had fled from the Cardassians while in command of the* Stargazer, *suggesting these hostilities had existed earlier than 2355, when the* Stargazer *was destroyed.)*

"The Wounded" also marks the first appearance of the Nebula *class starship, although an earlier preliminary "study model" of the* Nebula *class design might be spotted among the wreckage in the spaceship "graveyard" in "The Best of Both Worlds, Part II" and in the junkyard from "Unification." A second study model of that ship graced Captain Riker's desk in his imaginary ready room in "Future Imperfect."*

U.S.S. Phoenix, *NCC-65420*

Starship *Phoenix* returns to Starbase 211.

Just after "The Wounded."

Inhabitants on planet Ventax II are terrified by visions of the mythical figure Ardra, coinciding with legends predicting Ardra would return to Ventax a thousand years after her earlier visit, a millennium ago. The visions of Ardra are accompanied by a series of geologic tremors in Ventaxian cities.

Several days before "Devil's Due."

"Ardra"

"Devil's Due." Stardate 44474.5. U.S.S. *Enterprise* responds to emergency transmission from Federation science station on planet Ventax II. Station director Howard Clark reports widespread panic among the local population, due to the anticipated arrival of Ardra, a legendary supernatural being. A humanoid identifying herself as Ardra does arrive at Ventax II, but *Enterprise* captain Picard is able to convince local authorities that this individual is not the legendary supernatural figure and that they are therefore not bound by an ancient contract with Ardra.

Editors' Note: This episode was originally written back in 1978 for Kirk and company for the Star Trek II *television series that was never produced. It is the second script from that project to have been resurrected for* Star Trek: The Next Generation. *(The first was "The Child.")*

U.S.S. *Enterprise* completes a mission at planet Harrakis V ahead of schedule, permitting Captain Picard to grant extra personal time for many of the crew.

Just prior to "Clues."

"Clues." Stardate 44502.7. Starship *Enterprise* passing through the Ngame Nebula to a diplomatic assignment to the Evadne system. While en route, a T-tauri–type star with a single Class-M planet is discovered. While investigating this anomalous planet, the *Enterprise* accidentally passes through an unstable wormhole, displacing the ship approximately 0.54 parsecs from previous position. *Enterprise* captain Picard orders a hazard advisory issued to Starfleet regarding the wormhole, and orders course resumed for Evadne IV.

Unstable wormhole discovered near the Ngame Nebula

Editors' Note: The main story of "Clues," the Enterprise *encounter with the reclusive Paxans and their efforts to erase all human and computer memories of the incident, is not described above because we assume the second attempt at erasing the memories of* Enterprise *personnel was successful. A historical record that includes information based on* Enterprise *records would therefore have no mention of this incident. (Data does retain a memory of the encounter, but he was ordered by Captain Picard never to reveal this information, not even to Picard or the authors of this book.)*

U.S.S. *Enterprise* goes to planet Evadne IV.

After "Clues."

The unmanned Argus subspace telescope array, located near the edge of Federation space, mysteriously stops relaying its information. This is later discovered to be due to a probe from the Cytherians.

"The Nth Degree." Picard's log notes the array had stopped transmitting nearly two months prior to the episode.

Argus subspace telescope array

U.S.S. *Brattain* issues a distress call, the last known signal from the ship. It is later learned that the *Miranda* class starship was trapped in a Tyken's Rift.

"Night Terrors." The distress call was sent 29 days prior to the episode.

Enterprise botanist Keiko O'Brien and her husband, Miles, conceive a child.

"Disaster." Date is conjecture, but about eight months prior to the episode, given the suggestion that Molly's delivery was premature.

Commander Riker disguised for covert surveillance on planet Malcor III

U.S.S. *Enterprise* at planet Malcor III to conduct covert sociological surveillance as prelude to possible first contact. Malcor III is currently under Prime Directive protection, but is believed to be on the verge of developing interstellar spaceflight capability and may therefore be eligible shortly for first contact. Commander William Riker is transported to the planet's surface as part of the observation team.

Prior to "First Contact."

"First Contact." (No stardate given in episode.) Commander Riker is injured on the surface of planet Malcor III while participating in covert sociological surveillance. He is cared for in a local medical facility, but examination by indigenous persons uncovers evidence that he is an extraterrestrial and threatens the security of the surveillance operation. Local authorities are alerted of the Federation presence, and plead with *Enterprise* captain Picard that contact with the outworlders will cause serious cultural shock at this point in the planet's social development. Picard concurs, and orders the contact postponed indefinitely.

Malcorian science minister Mirasta Yale elects to remain on board the *Enterprise*.

Editors' Note: The bottle of Chateau Picard shared by the captain and Chancellor Durken was given to Picard by his brother, Robert, in "Family."

Barclay as Cyrano

Lieutenant Reginald Barclay joins Dr. Beverly Crusher's acting workshop aboard the U.S.S. *Enterprise*. Their first project is a performance of *Cyrano de Bergerac*.

"The Nth Degree." Geordi notes that Barclay had been taking lessons for six weeks prior to the episode.

"Galaxy's Child." Stardate 44614.6. U.S.S. *Enterprise* at Starbase 313 to pick up scientific equipment for a Federation outpost in the Guernica system, as well as a visitor, Dr. Leah Brahms, for an inspection tour. Brahms had earlier served on one of the design teams responsible for the propulsion system of the U.S.S. *Enterprise* at Utopia Planitia, and has since been promoted to senior design engineer of the Theoretical Propulsion Group.

Dr. Leah Brahms

Unusual energy readings from the unexplored Alpha Omicron system result in a diversion to that system for further research. An object is discovered orbiting planet Alpha Omicron VII, and is determined to be a spaceborne life-form. During the investigation, a low-level phaser burst is employed in an attempt to discourage a potentially hazardous radiation field from the creature, but the attempt proves lethal to the life-form. Later study of the creature's remains reveals an unborn child, which is delivered with the assistance of *Enterprise* personnel. The child appears to regard the *Enterprise* as a source of nurturing, drawing power from the ship's engines until a means can be found to urge it to join a school of its fellow creatures.

Starship *Enterprise* resumes its mission to the Guernica system.

Just after "Galaxy's Child."

Infant spaceborne creature whose mother was accidentally killed by U.S.S. Enterprise personnel

"Night Terrors." Stardate 44631.2. U.S.S. *Enterprise* passing through an uncharted binary star system discovers the derelict U.S.S. *Brattain*, reported missing 29 days ago. Investigation reveals only one survivor from the *Brattain* crew; the remaining 34 having died under violent but unexplained circumstances. During the investigation, the *Enterprise* becomes trapped in a Tyken's Rift, causing failure of ship's power systems. Cooperation with an unknown intelligence on the other side of the rift permits the *Enterprise* and the unknown intelligence to escape. Proximity to the alien intelligence is found to be responsible for severe dream deprivation of all *Enterprise* personnel, a side effect of a successful attempt to communicate by the aliens. This dream deprivation is believed to be the cause of the insanity that claimed the lives of most of the *Brattain* crew.

U.S.S. *Enterprise* heads for Starbase 220.

Just after "Night Terrors."

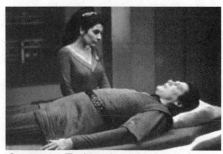

Counselor Troi tends to the sole survivor of the Brattain crew.

Emilita Mendez, a crew member aboard the Starship *Aries*, steals the shuttlepod *Cousteau* and heads for planet Tarchannan III. Her crewmates later report that she was last seen an hour before her disappearance from the *Aries* and that she seemed completely normal at the time.

Prior to "Identity Crisis."

Lieutenant Paul Hickman, missing in a stolen shuttlecraft, is reported sighted by a Federation supply ship en route to planet Tarchannen III.

A day before "Identity Crisis."

Susanna Leijten

Lieutenant Commander Susanna Leijten, formerly of the U.S.S. *Victory*, is assigned temporarily to the *Enterprise* to investigate aberrant behavior on the part of ex-*Victory* personnel who participated in an away mission to planet Tarchannan III in 2362. Among the former *Victory* crew members are Emilita Mendez, Paul Hickman, Ensign Brevelle, and Geordi La Forge.

Prior to "Identity Crisis," after Hickman is sighted near Tarchannan III.

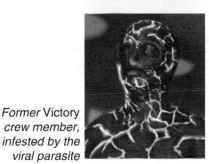

Former Victory *crew member, infested by the viral parasite*

"Identity Crisis." Stardate 44664.5. U.S.S. *Enterprise* is at planet Tarchannen III investigating aberrant behavior by former U.S.S. *Victory* personnel, attempts to intercept a stolen shuttlecraft piloted by former *Victory* crew member Paul Hickman. The shuttle is incinerated on atmospheric entry before the *Enterprise* can reach tractor or transporter range.

Research of old *Victory* records and on-site investigation at the old Tarchannan III colony uncovers evidence of an indigenous life-form that reproduces by means of a viral parasite. This life-form is determined to have infected members of the *Victory* away team in 2362, compelling them to return to Tarchannan III, where their DNA is altered to match that of the parasite. The transformation is deemed irreversible for most of the ex-*Victory* personnel, but the parasite is successfully removed from Leijten and La Forge.

Warning beacons are placed in orbit around planet Tarchannan III and on the planet's surface.

Just after "Identity Crisis."

Lieutenant Reginald Barclay

"The Nth Degree." Stardate 44704.2. U.S.S. *Enterprise* at the edge of Federation space to investigate the apparent failure of the Argus Subspace Telescope Array. An alien space probe is discovered in the vicinity of the array. Initial studies of the alien probe are uninformative, although the probe is found to be emitting radiation that causes significant damage to computer systems of a shuttlecraft assigned to the investigation.

Lieutenant Reginald Barclay, part of the shuttlecraft crew, is discovered to have experienced unusual side effects from the probe radiation. His intellectual capacities are found to have dramatically increased by at least two orders of magnitude. This expanded intelligence is of significant value in saving the Argus Array from a series of critical malfunctions, and later allows Barclay to devise an extraordinary modification of the *Enterprise* warp drive system. Acting against direct orders from Captain Picard, Barclay pilots the *Enterprise* some 30,000 light-years toward the galactic core. This is learned to be due to the efforts of a previously undiscovered race called the Cytherians, who use such techniques to bring visitors to their world for cultural exchange. Picard agrees to such an exchange with the Cytherians, who then return the *Enterprise* to Federation space.

"Qpid." Stardate 44741.9. *Enterprise* at planet Tagus III to serve as host of the Federation Archaeology Council's annual symposium. *Enterprise* captain Picard delivers the keynote address on the ancient Tagus ruins.

The entity known as Q reappears, transporting Captain Picard, his staff, and Archaeology council member Vash into an imaginary environment. Upon their return, Vash agrees to enter into a partnership with Q.

Worf, cast by Q into the role of Will Scarlet

Klingon exobiologist J'Ddan, serving on board the *Enterprise* as part of an exchange program, accesses restricted technical information on the ship's dilithium chamber design. The incident is routinely recorded by the ship's computer system.

"The Drumhead." A week before the Romulans got the technical data.

Stardate 44765.2. U.S.S. *Enterprise* is crippled by an explosion in the ship's dilithium chamber. No one is killed, but two members of the engineering staff are hospitalized with radiation burns. No apparent cause is immediately discovered, and sabotage is suspected.

Four days prior to "The Drumhead."

Starfleet Command receives intelligence reports that schematic drawings of the *Galaxy* class starship dilithium chamber have fallen into Romulan hands. Klingon exchange technician J'Ddan is implicated in the breach of security.

"The Drumhead." About the same time as the Enterprise *dilithium chamber explosion.*

"The Drumhead." Stardate 44769.2. Admiral Norah Satie visits *Enterprise* for investigation of possible sabotage in the dilithium chamber explosion. Klingon exchange exobiologist J'Ddan is discovered to have been responsible for the transmission of technical schematics to the Romulans, but is found innocent of sabotaging the dilithium chamber. J'Ddan is arrested and referred to Klingon authorities on charges of espionage. Also implicated but found innocent is crewman First Class Simon Tarses, although Tarses is found to have falsified his Starfleet application in an attempt to conceal the fact that his grandfather is Romulan.

Admiral Norah Satie

Admiral Satie continues to pursue her belief that a conspiracy is responsible for the *Enterprise* explosion despite evidence that the explosion was an accident. Admiral Thomas Henry rules Satie's investigation unconstitutional in the absence of evidence, and orders it discontinued.

U.S.S. *Enterprise* security officer Jenna D'Sora breaks off a romantic relationship with fellow *Enterprise* crew member Jeff Arton.

"In Theory." About six weeks prior to the episode.

"Half a Life." Stardate 44805.3. U.S.S. *Enterprise* at planet Kaelon II to assist in an experiment to demonstrate the practicality of a helium ignition process designed to extend the life of their star. Initial tests under the guidance of Kaelon scientist Timicin at the Praxillus system fail when unanticipated neutron migration causes Praxillus to explode. During postmission analysis, further avenues of experimentation are uncovered, and Timicin decides to postpone his scheduled return to his homeworld so that he can pursue these developments. His failure to return, despite the Kaelon tradition of "Resolution" (voluntary suicide at age 60), threatens a diplomatic incident until Timicin reverses his decision. Lwaxana Troi accompanies Timicin to his home to join in the celebration of his Resolution.

Scientist Timicin

Editors' Note: Timicin's daughter was played by actor Michelle Forbes, who would later portray the character of Ensign Ro.

Ambassador Odan occupying a Trill host body

Federation ambassador Odan is assigned diplomatic duty aboard the U.S.S. *Enterprise* to help mediate a dispute between the two moons of the Peliar Zel system.

About ten days prior to "The Host."

Wesley Crusher sends a letter from Starfleet Academy to his mother, Beverly Crusher, aboard the U.S.S. *Enterprise*. The younger Crusher reports he is doing well in exobiology, but that he is still having difficulties in his ancient philosophies class.

Just prior to "The Host."

"The Host." Stardate 44821.3. U.S.S. *Enterprise* en route to planet Peliar Zel, transporting Ambassador Odan to a diplomatic assignment there. Dr. Beverly Crusher works with Ambassador Odan to study effects of the controversial magnetic energy tap employed by the people of Peliar Zel Alpha, one of two moons in the system. En route to the conference, Odan's shuttlecraft is attacked by unknown forces, resulting in apparently fatal injuries to Odan. The ambassador is learned to be a member of a joined species, the Trill, and the symbiotic parasite living in Odan's body is discovered to be the actual intelligence known as Odan.

Ambassador Odan occupying the body of Commander William Riker

Commander William Riker volunteers to serve as temporary host to Odan until a new permanent Trill host body can arrive. The surgical procedure is accomplished by Dr. Beverly Crusher, a task made difficult by an emotional attachment she has developed for Odan. The ambassador, now in the new host body, is able to mediate the talks between Peliar Zel Alpha and Beta.

Kriosian rebels, seeking independence from the Klingon Empire, launch at least two attacks on neutral freighters, one Ferengi, the other Cardassian. The attacks are staged near the Ikalian asteroid belt, believed to be a hiding place for the rebels.

Sometime prior to "The Mind's Eye."

Governor Vagh of the Klingon Kriosian colonies charges the Federation with aiding rebel forces. Vagh cites Federation phaser rifles in rebel hands as evidence of such interference. Klingon special emissary Kell is assigned by the High Council to investigate these charges. Kell requests transport aboard the *Enterprise* to the Kriosian system and the assistance of *Enterprise* captain Jean-Luc Picard in the investigation.

Just before "The Mind's Eye."

Geordi undergoes Romulan mental reprogramming

"The Mind's Eye." Stardate 44885.5. *Enterprise* chief engineer Geordi La Forge transports via shuttlepod to planet Risa to attend an artificial-intelligence seminar. Unknown to the *Enterprise* crew, he is abducted en route by Romulan operatives, under the supervision of Sela, who employ sophisticated mental programming to plant commands in La Forge's brain.

Klingon special emissary Kell, aboard the U.S.S. *Enterprise*, meets with Kriosian governor Vagh to discuss allegations of Federation interference in Kriosian affairs. Close examination of purported Federation phaser rifles reveals the weapons to be of Romulan manufacture, suggesting the Kriosian rebel attacks to have been the result of Romulan hegemony. This theory is given further weight when Commander La Forge, acting under the influence of Romulan mental reprogramming, is apprehended in the act of attempting to assassinate Kriosian governor Vagh. Further investigation reveals Emissary Kell to be a Romulan collaborator responsible for triggering La Forge's implanted programming.

Editors' Note: The mysterious Romulan woman in the shadows during Geordi's brainwashing is, of course, later revealed to be Sela, the half-Romulan daughter of former Enterprise *security officer Tasha Yar. Her identity is not revealed until "Redemption, Part I," two episodes later. The actor seen as Sela in "The Mind's Eye" was* not *Denise Crosby, although Crosby did dub in Sela's voice during postproduction.*

Counselor Troi works with Geordi La Forge to help reconstruct his memories that were altered by the Romulan mental reprogramming.

After "The Mind's Eye."

"In Theory." Stardate 44932.3. The *Enterprise* enters Mar Oscura nebula on scientific investigation mission. An unusual preponderance of dark matter in the nebula is found to result in small but dangerous subspace anomalies. These anomalies are found to threaten the structure of the *Enterprise* as well as the operation of its systems. A shuttle piloted by Captain Jean-Luc Picard is sent ahead of the ship as a scout to help navigate out of the region.

Lieutenant Commander Data, as part of his ongoing effort to experience humanity, attempts to establish a romantic relationship with security officer Jenna D'Sora.

Lieutenant Commander Data and security officer Jenna D'Sora

Starship *Enterprise* heads for Starbase 260.

Just after "In Theory."

"Redemption, Part I." Stardate 44995.3. U.S.S. *Enterprise* en route to the Klingon Homeworld for the installation of Gowron as leader of the High Council. Prior to arrival at the Homeworld, the *Enterprise* is intercepted by Gowron aboard the Klingon attack cruiser *Bortas*. Gowron requests Starfleet assistance in preventing an anticipated ploy by the family of the late Duras to block Gowron's scheduled ascension to leadership of the Klingon High Council. *Enterprise* captain Picard declines, noting that such action would be beyond his role as arbiter of the succession. Additionally, Picard later orders Lieutenant Worf not to use his position as a Starfleet officer to influence the Klingon political process.

The Great Hall of the Klingon Homeworld

A challenge to Gowron's claim to the council is made by Toral, son of Duras. It is suspected and later confirmed that other Duras family members have been secretly working with Romulan operatives to assure Toral's ascendency. Captain Picard, as arbiter, rules Toral's claim inadmissible under Klingon law.

Gowron, son of M'Rel, assumes leadership of the Klingon High Council, and restores honor to the family of Mogh in exchange for the support of Worf and his brother, Kurn. Worf, seeking to avoid a conflict of interest, resigns his Starfleet commission and assumes the post of weapons officer aboard the Klingon attack cruiser *Bortas*.

Klingon attack cruiser Bortas

6.5 STAR TREK: THE NEXT GENERATION — YEAR 5

Romulan operative Sela

2368

*Klingon High
Council leader
Gowron*

*Tamarian
Captain
Dathon*

Gowron's forces are successful in destroying the Duras supply bases in the Mempa sector.

About three weeks prior to "Redemption, Part II."

Three major engagements between forces loyal to Gowron and those of the Duras family result in significant losses to Gowron. Starfleet continues to resist involvement in what is principally an internal Klingon matter.

Within two weeks of "Redemption, Part II."

A Tamarian spacecraft arrives at planet El-Adrel IV. The vessel transmits a subspace signal toward Federation space. The signal is determined to contain a standard mathematical progression, which Starfleet interprets as an attempt to start a dialog with the Federation.

"Darmok." Picard notes the ship apparently arrived nearly three weeks prior to the episode.

"Redemption, Part II." Stardate 45020.4. U.S.S. *Enterprise* at Starbase 234, where Fleet Admiral Shanthi authorizes Captain Jean-Luc Picard to lead an armada of 23 starships in an attempt to blockade a Romulan convoy suspected of being the source of supplies to forces loyal to the Duras family. Such Romulan interference is believed to threaten the stability of the Gowron regime.

Among the vessels assigned to the blockade are the *Enterprise, Excalibur,* and the *Sutherland.* Due to limited available personnel, *Enterprise* executive officer William Riker is assigned to temporary command of the

Excalibur, and *Enterprise* operations manager Data is placed in charge of the *Sutherland*. Gowron's forces are reported in full retreat from the Mempa sector, this despite the fact that the Duras supply bases in that sector had been destroyed three weeks before.

Ambassador *class starship* Excalibur, *NCC-26517*

Utilizing a tachyon network technique developed by Geordi La Forge, Picard's armada is successful in detecting a cloaked Romulan warbird, whose commander requests a meeting with Captain Picard. The commander identifies herself as Sela, the daughter of former *Enterprise* security officer Tasha Yar, claiming that Yar had been sent into the past and had been captured after the destruction of the *Enterprise*-C some 24 years ago. Sela further claims that she is the product of a union between Yar and a Romulan general, who spared the lives of the surviving *Enterprise* personnel when Yar agreed to become his consort. Later, La Forge's tachyon network is further successful in detecting additional Romulan spacecraft attempting to run the blockade line. The ships turn back after being located, and the Federation vessels also return to their home territory.

In the absence of Romulan support, the Duras family challenge to leadership of the High Council fails, marking the end of the Klingon civil war. Although Toral, son of Duras, is convicted of treason, Worf, eldest son of Mogh, declines to exercise his right to take Toral's life for wrongfully having brought disgrace to Worf's family. Captain Jean-Luc Picard accepts Worf's request for reinstatement as a Starfleet officer.

Worf

Editors' Note: Other ships in Picard's armada included the U.S.S. Tian An Men *(a remembrance of those who died for Chinese freedom, much as the U.S. Navy has a* Lexington*, commemorating the first battle of the American Revolution), the* Endeavour *(named for NASA's new space shuttle orbiter), the* Akagi *and the* Hornet *(two ships that fought against each other in the Battle of Midway, now serving side by side), and the* Sutherland *(named for the ship commanded by C. S. Forester's fictional Horatio Hornblower, one of Gene Roddenberry's inspirations for the character of Captain Kirk). These names were all selected by writer-producer Ron Moore.*

"Darmok." Stardate 45047.2. U.S.S. *Enterprise* en route to the uninhabited El-Adrel star system, near the territory of the enigmatic race known as the Children of Tama. Previous attempts at establishing communication with these people had been unsuccessful, and attempts by *Enterprise* personnel to communicate with the Tamarians are similarly unsuccessful, even with use of the universal translator.

Enterprise captain Picard is abducted by the Tamarians, and transported to the surface of planet El-Adrel IV, along with Tamarian captain Dathon. The abduction, initially believed to be a hostile act, is later learned to be an attempt at communication by Captain Dathon. The Tamarian gives his life in this attempt to bridge the communication gap between the Tamarians and the alien captain of the *Enterprise*. Because of Dathon's actions, it is learned that the Tamarian language is based on metaphors derived from Tamarian mythology, marking the first successful attempt at communication between the two dissimilar cultures.

Captain Dathon attempts to communicate through the use of metaphors from Tamarian mythology.

A terrorist attack destroys the Federation settlement on planet Solarion IV. The attack is blamed on Bajoran terrorists seeking to involve the Federation in the Bajoran dispute with the Cardassian Empire.

Prior to "Ensign Ro."

A Cardassian liaison meets with Starfleet Admiral Kennelly, requesting assis-

Cardassian

tance in tracking down Bajoran terrorists, which the Cardassian describes as their "mutual enemy."

About a week prior to "Ensign Ro," but after the Solarion IV attack. Kennelly said he'd met with the Cardassian liaison "last weekend."

Admiral Kennelly visits Ensign Ro Laren, in prison on Jaros II for the *Wellington* disaster at Garon II. He offers an administrative pardon in exchange for her agreement to undertake a special mission aboard the *Enterprise* to help resolve the Bajoran terrorist issue. It is later learned that Ro's orders from Kennelly included the offering of illegal weapons to the Bajoran terrorists for use against the Cardassians.

Admiral Kennelly

Prior to "Ensign Ro," after Kennelly's meeting with the Cardassian liaison.

"Ensign Ro." Stardate 45076.3. Starship *Enterprise* at Lya Station Alpha with survivors from planet Solarion IV. Admiral Kennelly assigns *Enterprise* to seek out Bajoran terrorist leaders to dissuade them from further violence. Ensign Ro Laren is assigned as mission specialist because of her knowledge of Bajoran culture.

*Ensign
Ro Laren*

At the Valo star system, Ro assists in locating Bajoran leader Orta on the third moon of planet Valo I. Orta meets with Picard, presenting convincing evidence that the attack at Solarion IV was not the work of Bajoran terrorists. It is later learned that the Solarion attack had been staged by the Cardassians in an effort to gain Federation assistance in locating Bajoran leaders. It is further determined that Admiral Kennelly had acted improperly by permitting the Cardassians to destroy a Bajoran *Antares* class sublight cruiser in an unsuccessful attempt to eliminate Orta.

Ensign Ro elects to remain aboard the *Enterprise* as a crew member at the invitation of Captain Picard. She is assigned to the position of flight controller (conn).

Editors' Note: This episode marks the first appearance of Ensign Ro Laren. The class name of the Bajoran cruiser, Antares, *was suggested by writer Naren Shankar as an homage to the old freighter by the same name that was destroyed in "Charlie X."*

U.S.S. *Enterprise* conducts survey assignment in sector 21305.

Just after "Ensign Ro."

Editors' Note: The end of "Ensign Ro" suggests the Enterprise *will be returning to Lya Station Alpha in "a few weeks" after the survey in sector 21305, but it is not clear if this is before or after the next episode. It is possible that this is where the* Enterprise *went while the away team was assisting at Melona IV during "Silicon Avatar."*

U.S.S. *Enterprise* drops off a contingent of personnel to assist with preparations for a colonization project on planet Melona IV, then departs from the area.

About a day before "Silicon Avatar."

*Colonist
Carmen Davila,
killed by the
Crystalline
Entity*

"Silicon Avatar." Stardate 45122.3. At planet Melona IV, an *Enterprise* away team headed by Commander William Riker assists with survey preparations for construction of a colony. The planet's surface is devastated by an unprovoked attack by a powerful spaceborne life-form known as the Crystalline Entity. This is believed to be the same entity that destroyed the colony at Omicron Theta in 2336. Two colonists, including Carmen Davila, are killed in the attack before a secure shelter can be found.

Upon detecting the presence of the Crystalline Entity, Captain Picard orders the *Enterprise* to return to Melona IV ahead of schedule to rescue the survivors. Starfleet Command, notified of the incident, assigns xenologist Dr. Kila Marr to assist with the study of the entity. The mission is to locate and establish communication with the entity, but Marr, who lost her son in the attack at Omicron Theta, suggests that destruction of the entity would be a preferable course of action. Marr cites records suggesting the entity had been responsible for at least eleven attacks since 2338.

Dr. Kila Marr

During the investigation, it is learned that the transport ship *Kallisko* had been pursued and later destroyed by the Crystalline Entity, which has since departed Melona IV. Upon intercepting the entity near the Brechtian Cluster, *Enterprise* personnel attempt communication, using a modulated graviton beam. The attempt is interrupted by an unauthorized modification of the beam control program by Dr. Marr. This action, apparently motivated by Marr's desire for revenge for her son's death, creates a continuous graviton beam, resulting in the destruction of the Crystalline Entity.

Starship *Enterprise* completes a mission to planet Mudor V several days ahead of schedule, affording the crew a respite before their next assignment.

Prior to "Disaster."

Three children of *Enterprise* crew personnel, Jay Gordon, Marissa Flores, and Patterson Supra, win the ship's primary school science fair. Their prize is a tour of the ship to be personally conducted by Captain Picard.

Just prior to "Disaster."

Enterprise science fair winners

"Disaster." Stardate 45156.1. U.S.S. *Enterprise* suffers major systems damage from collision with a quantum filament. The ship's main computer, warp drive, antimatter containment, and other key systems are affected. Counselor Deanna Troi, temporarily in command of the vessel, orders emergency procedure Alpha 2, bypassing computer control and placing key systems on manual. Indications are detected of a potential breach of the antimatter containment system, but Chief O'Brien and Ensign Ro Laren are successful in assisting engineering personnel in averting an explosion despite a major power failure in the engineering section.

Enterprise botanist Keiko O'Brien gives birth to a baby girl. Assisting with the delivery is security chief Worf. The child is named Molly.

Editors' Note: The name of the O'Brien child is not established until "The Game," when Wesley asks how Molly is doing. Molly was named for former Star Trek *production staffer Molly Rennie.*

Keiko O'Brien and her newborn daughter

Captain Picard takes the three winners of the *Enterprise* science fair on a tour of the ship that includes visits to the battle bridge and the torpedo bay. U.S.S. *Enterprise* proceeds to Starbase 67 for major systems repair.

After "Disaster."

Ambassador Spock mysteriously disappears from his home on Vulcan. He has wrapped up his affairs very carefully, but has given little clue as to his plans.

"Unification, Part I." Admiral Brackett said Spock had disappeared three weeks prior to the episode. Perrin implied that Spock's residence was on planet Vulcan.

Starship *Enterprise* on scientific mission to conduct studies at the previously uncharted Phoenix Cluster. Several science teams are transported from the starship *Zhukov* to assist in the project. Although the exploration had been scheduled to last five weeks, a diplomatic mission to Oceanus IV has cut the available time to only two weeks.

Just prior to "The Game."

Editors' Note: Sensor scans of luminescent asteroids within the Phoenix cluster were apparently unsuccessful in locating the whereabouts of Lieutenant Talby.

Etana and Riker on Risa

Cadet Wesley Crusher

"The Game." Stardate 45208.2. Commander William Riker takes shore leave on planet Risa. He meets a woman named Etana, who is later learned to be a military operative for the Ktarans. Riker returns to the *Enterprise* with a small recreational device, which he replicates for distribution to his crewmates. It is later learned that these devices employ sophisticated neural-optical conditioning techniques to control the behavior of the *Enterprise* crew, part of a Ktaran attempt to gain control of the Federation Starfleet. Lieutenant Commander Data and Cadet Wesley Crusher, on leave from Starfleet Academy, are successful in developing an optical deprogramming technique to counteract the effects of the Ktaran devices. Mission specialist Robin Lefler is also credited with helping to identify the threat posed by the Ktarans.

U.S.S. *Enterprise* rendezvous with U.S.S. *Merrimac*, transferring Wesley Crusher for transport back to Starfleet Academy. *Enterprise* thereafter proceeds to Oceanus IV for diplomatic mission.

After "The Game."

A Ferengi cargo shuttle crashes in the Hanolin asteroid belt near Vulcan. Wreckage is recovered from over 100 square kilometers. Parts of a derelict Vulcan spacecraft, concealed in crates labeled as containing medical supplies, are found among the debris. The parts are sent to Vulcan for identification, and U.S.S. *Enterprise* personnel are later asked to assist.

Sometime prior to "Unification, Part I."

Ambassador Spock

Starfleet Intelligence reports Ambassador Spock, missing for nearly three weeks, has been sighted on Romulus. The unauthorized visit is of great concern to Starfleet Command because of the tremendous potential for damage to Federation security in the event that Spock has defected.

Two days prior to "Unification, Part I."

U.S.S. *Enterprise* terraforming mission to planet Doraf I is canceled, ship is recalled to Starbase 234 by Fleet Admiral Brackett.

Just prior to "Unification, Part I."

"Unification, Part I." Stardate 45233.1. U.S.S. *Enterprise* is assigned by Fleet Admiral Brackett to investigate Spock's disappearance. At the suggestion of Ambassador Sarek, Captain Picard and Lieutenant Commander Data journey to Romulus to seek out Romulan senator Pardek. Despite initial reluctance by Klingon authorities, Klingon council leader Gowron agrees to the loan of a Bird-of-Prey for the purpose of a covert trip to Romulus. Picard later discovers that the Klingon reluctance to lend assistance was due to selective editing of the historical record by Gowron, intended to downplay the aid of the Federation in the recent Klingon civil war.

En route to Romulus, it is learned that Ambassador Sarek has died from Bendii syndrome, a degenerative brain disorder, at his home on Vulcan. He is survived by his wife, Perrin, and his son, Spock. Sarek was 203.

Ambassador Sarek

Enterprise personnel, assisting Vulcan authorities in investigating debris recovered from a recently crashed Ferengi shuttle, uncover evidence that unknown agents, possibly Ferengi, had been attempting to smuggle Vulcan spacecraft components to an unknown destination. The components are traced to a decommissioned Vulcan ship, the *T'Pau*, sent four years ago to the surplus depot at Qualor II. Investigation at the depot shows the *T'Pau* was removed under mysterious circumstances, probably by an unidentified spacecraft detected at Qualor II. The vehicle is reported to have self-destructed, apparently to avoid further investigation.

Picard and Data, working undercover on Romulus, are successful in making contact with Romulan senator Pardek and Federation ambassador Spock near the Krocton Segment.

Captain Picard in Romulan disguise near the Krocton Segment

Editors' Note: The death of Sarek is an important milestone in Star Trek *history, marking the first occasion when a major continuing character has died and not been resurrected. (Of course, it is possible that a younger Sarek might yet be seen in a feature film or other project set in* Star Trek's *earlier era.)*

The surplus depot at Qualor II uses many wrecked ships originally built for the graveyard scene in "The Best of Both Worlds, Part II." Some additional ships may be seen by those with a discerning eye and a good VCR or a laserdisk: Several study models, originally designed by Nilo Rodis, Bill George, and their colleagues at Industrial Light and Magic as possible designs for the U.S.S. Excelsior *in* Star Trek III: The Search for Spock, *are among the ships in the junkyard, as is a replica of the Klingon battle cruiser originally built for* Star Trek: The Motion Picture. *Even more intriguing are two study models for a proposed* Enterprise *redesign by Ralph McQuarry. These models were made in the mid '70s for a proposed* Star Trek *movie project that was never produced.*

"Unification, Part II." Stardate 45245.8. Captain Picard is informed by Spock of his purpose on Romulus: To support the cause of reunification between the Vulcan and the Romulan peoples. Picard informs Spock of Federation objections to his presence on Romulus, but Spock cites the support of Romulan senator Pardek as evidence that such reunification may succeed.

Capital city on Romulus

U.S.S. *Enterprise*, still at Qualor II, continues to investigate the theft of a Vulcan ship. It is learned by Commander Riker that the *T'Pau* had been delivered to a Barolian freighter at Galorndon Core, near the Romulan Neutral Zone.

Spock, meeting with Romulan proconsul Neral, is given assurances of support for the reunification movement. Later, Spock and Picard learn that this support, along with the support of Senator Pardek, had been part of a Romulan attempt to conquer Vulcan. This plan, under the direction of Romulan operative Sela, is discovered to involve use of the pretext of reunification to cover the movement of a Romulan invasion force to Vulcan. The invasion force is carried in three stolen Vulcan ships, including the *T'Pau*. Once discovered, the Vulcan ships are destroyed by Romulan forces to avoid their capture.

Romulan senator Pardek

Despite the absence of official support in the Romulan government, Spock elects to remain on Romulus to continue his work for Vulcan/Romulan reunification.

Jev

Ullian telepathic researcher Jev, on a research project to two planets in the Nel system, commits two acts of telepathic rape, although the victims are mistakenly diagnosed as suffering from Iresine syndrome.

"Violations." Geordi's research indicated Jev was in the Nel system between stardates 45321 and 45323, apparently between "Unification, Part II," and "A Matter of Time."

A Type-C asteroid impacts on planet Penthara IV. Although the asteroid has hit an unpopulated continent, scientists on the planet predict the resulting dust clouds may result in disastrous global cooling because of increased planetary albedo.

Just prior to "A Matter of Time."

Professor Berlinghoff Rasmussen

"A Matter of Time." Stardate 45349.1. U.S.S. *Enterprise*, proceeding to planet Penthara IV, encounters a time/space distortion, followed by the appearance of an individual identifying himself as Professor Berlinghoff Rasmussen, a researcher from the late 26th century.

Upon arrival at Penthara IV, *Enterprise* personnel attempt to counter global cooling by employing the ship's phasers to release massive underground pockets of volcanic carbon dioxide. It is hoped that the additional CO_2 will increase the amount of solar heat retained in the planet's atmosphere. Although initial results of the attempt are encouraging, seismic activity is much greater than anticipated, resulting in a massive release of volcanic dust, exacerbating the original problem. A second attempt successfully employs the *Enterprise* to trigger a massive electrostatic discharge to vaporize the dust particles, then directing the resulting energy surge harmlessly into space.

Investigating reports of numerous small items discovered missing by *Enterprise* personnel, Lieutenant Commander Data searches Rasmussen's time-travel pod, and discovers Rasmussen to be the culprit. Upon questioning, Rasmussen confesses to being a time traveler not from the future, as previously claimed, but from the past. Rasmussen, who admits his goal was to return to the 22nd century with articles of 24th-century technology, is placed in custody.

U.S.S. *Enterprise* goes to Starbase 214 to turn Rasmussen over to authorities.

After "A Matter of Time."

Helena Rozhenko, upon hearing that the *Enterprise* is in the sector, secures passage aboard the transport vessel *Milan* for herself and Worf's son, Alexander. The *Milan* will intercept the *Enterprise*.

Prior to "New Ground."

Alexander Rozhenko, son of Worf

"New Ground." Stardate 45376.3. U.S.S. *Enterprise* meets with transport ship *Milan* for transfer of passengers Helena Rozhenko and Alexander Rozhenko. Helena informs her adoptive son, Worf, that his son, Alexander, has been having difficulty adjusting to life on Earth. Worf agrees to take custody of his son aboard the *Enterprise*.

U.S.S. *Enterprise* at planet Bilana III to participate in an engineering test of the soliton wave development project. The test is initially successful in accelerating a test payload to warp 2.35, but subspace instabilities result in destruction of the payload. *Enterprise* is successful in overtaking the wavefront, and employs photon torpedoes to disperse the soliton wave.

Editors' Note: Solitons are real. They are nondispersing waves used in fiber-optic communications. Episode writer (and physicist) Naren Shanker observed the study of electromagnetic (but not subspace) soliton wave packets by Dr. C. R. Pollock while a graduate student at Cornell University.

Research vessel Vico, NAR-18834

Starbase 514 loses contact with research vessel S.S. *Vico*, on a mission to explore the interior of a black cluster. The U.S.S. *Enterprise* is assigned to investigate the disappearance.

Two days before "Hero Worship."

"Hero Worship." Stardate 45397.3. U.S.S. *Enterprise* locates the *Vico* inside the black cluster. The *Vico* is discovered to have been severely damaged, and an away team is able to rescue only a single survivor. The survivor, a young boy, Timothy, has been severely traumatized by the tragedy, but he is helped by Counselor Troi and Lieutenant Commander Data.

Data helps care for young Timothy.

Immediately following the rescue mission, the *Enterprise* is buffeted by gravitational distortions within the black cluster. It is determined that a similar phenomenon caused the destruction of the Vico, and Timothy's recollection of the *Vico*'s final moments are instrumental in devising a means to avoid a similar fate for the *Enterprise*.

"Violations." Stardate 45429.3. While on a mapping survey mission, U.S.S. *Enterprise* is assigned to transport a delegation of Ullians to planet Kaldra IV. The Ullians, conducting a research project to catalog telepathically retrieved memories from individuals on several planets, are linked to a series of unexplained neurological disorders resembling Iresine syndrome reported in several *Enterprise* crew members. Further investigation reveals one Ullian, Jev, to be responsible for the disorders. It is learned that Jev had been committing a form of rape involving memory invasion, and he is returned to Ullian authorities for prosecution and rehabilitation.

Enterprise stops at Starbase 440, where the Ullian delegation disembarks.

After "Violations."

A stellar core fragment, believed to be from a disintegrated neutron star, is detected in the Moab sector. U.S.S. *Enterprise* diverted to monitor possible disruption of planetary systems in the sector.

Colony on planet Moab IV, a genetically engineered society

Just prior to "The Masterpiece Society."

"The Masterpiece Society." Stardate 45470.1. U.S.S. *Enterprise*, while tracking the stellar core fragment, discovers a previously unknown human colony on planet Moab IV, near the fragment's trajectory. Engineering analysis indicates the colony would be unable to withstand the resulting seismic disruption, although colony authorities decline assistance, citing an aversion to outside cultural influences. An agreement is later negotiated in which a limited number of *Enterprise* personnel are allowed within the colony to assist in structural reinforcement. Simultaneously, the *Enterprise* uses its tractor beam to partially deflect the core fragment, and thus reduce its seismic effect on Moab IV.

Scientist Hannah Bates

The effort is largely successful, although colony authorities express disapproval at the decision of 23 colonists, including scientist Hannah Bates, to leave their home and accept passage aboard the *Enterprise*. Colony authorities, explaining that their society had been planned as a sealed, self-contained biosphere, express further concern that *Enterprise* assistance may have thereby caused irreparable damage to the society.

"Conundrum." Stardate 45494.2. On a mission to investigate a series of subspace signals indicating possible intelligent life in the Epsilon Silar system, the Starship *Enterprise* is ambushed by what is later identified as a Satarran vessel. The attack employs a sophisticated energy weapon that disrupts *Enterprise* communication systems, selectively damages and alters *Enterprise* computer records, and erases the identities and short-term memories of all *Enterprise* personnel. The Satarran ship is believed to have self-destructed immediately after the attack.

Captain Picard with Keiran MacDuff, a Satarran operative

Enterprise crew members are successful in retrieving information on their identities and their mission from the ship's computer. Unknown to the crew at the time, this information includes deliberate disinformation planted by the Satarrans. The altered computer records falsely identify a Satarran, apparently from the destroyed ship, as *Enterprise* executive officer Keiran MacDuff. They also indicate that the Federation is currently at war with the Lysian Alliance and that the *Enterprise*'s mission is to destroy the Lysian military command center.

Complying with the fraudulent Starfleet orders, *Enterprise* personnel engage and easily destroy a Lysian spacecraft, resulting in the deaths of approximately 53 Lysians. Tactical analysis of remaining Lysian forces indicates a weapons potential substantially inferior to that of the *Enterprise*.

Troubled by the extreme selectiveness of the damage to ship's records and crew memories and by the limited weapons technology of the Lysians, Captain Picard refuses to obey orders to destroy the command center. *Enterprise* personnel subsequently learn that the orders to act against the Lysians had been falsified by the Satarrans in an effort to use Federation weaponry against the Satarrans' enemies.

On the *Enterprise*'s subsequent course to Starbase 301, crew memories are restored using a medical technique developed by Dr. Beverly Crusher in which the activity of the medial temporal region of the brain is artificially increased.

Ensign Ro Laren

Editors' Note: This episode establishes significant biographical details about many of the ship's senior officers in the form of a computer display of the ship's crew manifest. A careful examination would reveal many personal facts like birth dates and years of graduation listed elsewhere in this chronology.

This episode is also notable for introducing one of the few romantic liaisons between continuing characters, as Ensign Ro Laren successfully seduces Commander Will Riker.

Cadet Wesley Crusher and Cadet Joshua Albert participate in a ski trip to Calgary. Joshua forgets his sweater, so Wesley loans him one of his.

"The First Duty." Wesley remembered that he and Josh had gone on the ski trip two months prior to the episode.

Cadet Wesley Crusher

"Power Play." Stardate 45571.2. U.S.S. *Enterprise* responds to a distress call originating from an unexplored Class-M moon of planet Mab-Bu VI. Due to electromagnetic disturbances in the moon's atmosphere, transporter use is not advised, and a shuttlepod piloted by Commander William Riker, along with Lieutenant Commander Data and Counselor Troi, is sent to investigate. Unexpectedly severe storms force the craft down on the surface, and a rescue mission effected by Chief O'Brien is successful in recovering the shuttle crew. Upon their return to the *Enterprise*, O'Brien, Data, and Troi exhibit severely aberrant behavior, blockading themselves in the Ten-Forward lounge and taking *Enterprise* crew personnel as hostages. The crew determines that this behavior is the result of control by alien life-forms, later learned to be convicted criminals, exiled to Mab-Bu VI some 500 years ago from the Ux-Mal system.

Enterprise captain Picard is successful in securing an agreement with the Ux-Mal terrorists to release *Enterprise* personnel and return to the Mab-Bu moon's surface.

"Ethics." Stardate 45587.3. U.S.S. *Enterprise* is en route to Sector 37628 for survey mission, but is diverted upon receipt of a distress call from the transport ship *Denver*. The ship had struck a gravitic mine left over from the Cardassian war, resulting in heavy damage and many injuries. Responding at high warp speed, the *Enterprise* arrives at the accident site in under seven hours. All three *Enterprise* shuttlebays are converted to emergency triage and evac centers, allowing treatment of *Denver* crew and colonists.

Dr. Toby Russell

Lieutenant Worf is seriously injured by an accident in the cargo bay, resulting in the shattering of seven vertebrae, and the crushing of his spinal cord. Although the prognosis suggests permanent paralysis, *Enterprise* chief medical officer Crusher consults Dr. Toby Russell, a neurogeneticist. Russell proposes an experimental genetronic replication technique that is successful in replacing Worf's spinal column and restoring virtually all of his muscular function. Crusher expresses objections to Russell's use of experimental procedures in a manner that Crusher characterizes as taking unnecessary and unethical risks with patients' lives.

Starship *Enterprise* drops off survivors from *Denver* accident, then proceeds to its survey mission at Sector 37628.

Lieutenant Worf

After "Ethics."

"The Outcast." Stardate 45614.6. U.S.S. *Enterprise* is at the J'naii planet to help search for a missing J'naii spacecraft. A survey conducted by *Enterprise* commander William Riker and J'naii pilot Soren is able to map the anomalous null space pockets in the J'naii system. Shortly thereafter, a rescue attempt is successful in retrieving the crew of the J'naii shuttle.

The J'naii government expresses appreciation of the assistance lent by *Enterprise* personnel, but later accuses Soren of aberrant behavior, alleging a socially unacceptable sexual relationship with Commander Riker. *Enterprise* captain Picard, citing Prime Directive considerations, refuses to intervene with the J'naii judiciary in the Soren matter. Soren is found guilty of forbidden behavior and is rehabilitated, restoring one to social norms in accordance with local laws.

Pilot Soren

U.S.S. *Enterprise* proceeds to Phelen system to negotiate a trade agreement.

Just after "The Outcast."

"Cause and Effect." Stardate 45652.1. The U.S.S. *Bozeman*, a *Soyuz* class Federation starship under the command of Captain Morgan Bateson, reported lost in 2278 near the Typhon Expanse, unexpectedly emerges from a rift in the space-time continuum, nearly colliding with the U.S.S. *Enterprise*.

Compelling evidence suggests a collision between the two ships did in fact occur, in which the *Bozeman* impacted the *Enterprise*'s starboard warp nacelle, resulting in the destruction of the *Enterprise*, with loss of all hands.

U.S.S. Bozeman, *NCC-1941*

*Captain
Morgan Bateson
of the U.S.S.
Bozeman*

The magnitude of the explosion, however, appears to have thrown the *Enterprise* into a recursive causality loop in which the events leading up to the collision were repeatedly experienced by those aboard the ship. Verification with Federation Timebase Beacons indicate the outside universe had experienced the passage of 17.4 days while the *Enterprise* was trapped in several iterations of the causality loop. The *Bozeman* had apparently been caught in a similar causality loop for approximately 80 years.

The hypothesized disaster was apparently averted on the final cycle as the result of a message transmitted via dekyon field to Lieutenant Commander Data by the *Enterprise* crew on its penultimate cycle. During that final cycle, numerous crew members reported phenomena that appear to have been "echoes" of previous passes through the time loop.

Ensign Wesley Crusher and four fellow cadets at Starfleet Academy are involved in a serious flight accident involving a collision of trainer spacecraft at the Academy range near Saturn. Cadet Joshua Albert is reported killed in the collision, and all five spacecraft are reported destroyed. The remaining cadets, all members of Nova Squadron, are able to transport safely to the emergency evac station on Mimas. No cause for the accident is immediately revealed.

*Cadets Wesley Crusher
and Nick Locarno*

Just prior to "The First Duty."

"The First Duty." Stardate 45703.9. U.S.S. *Enterprise* en route to Earth, where Captain Jean-Luc Picard is scheduled to deliver the commencement address at Starfleet Academy. Just prior to arrival, Picard is notified of the accident involving Wesley Crusher.

At the Academy, an investigation is convened by Superintendent Brand in an effort to determine the cause of the accident that claimed the life of Cadet Joshua Albert. Initial testimony by members of Nova Squadron suggests the collision was due to pilot error, but this is later found to be inconsistent with telemetric data. A statement by Cadet Wesley Crusher reveals the cause of the crash to be an unauthorized attempt to perform a Kolvoord Starburst, a maneuver prohibited because of its extreme risk. The board of review expels Nova Squadron leader Nick Locarno for his role in the accident and for attempting to conceal information from the board. All three remaining Nova Squadron members are reprimanded, and their academic credits for the year are voided.

*Admirals Brand and Setlek presiding
over the Nova Squadron inquiry*

"Cost of Living." Stardate 45733.6. U.S.S. *Enterprise* destroys an asteroid to avoid a disastrous impact on planet Tessen III. Unknown to the crew, the asteroid had been rich in metallic nitrium, and that the nitrium had been a food source to parasitic nonsentient life-forms that had lived in the asteroid. The crew later discovers that these life-forms had settled on the *Enterprise* hull in the aftermath of the asteroid's destruction, resulting in significant damage to the ship's structure and systems.

U.S.S. *Enterprise* serves as the site for a wedding between Minister Campio of planet Kostolain and Ambassador Lwaxana Troi of planet Betazed. Just prior to the ceremony, Campio's protocol adviser, Erko, recommends cancellation of the wedding due to what he regards as irreconcilable differences between Kostolain and Betazed customs.

U.S.S. *Enterprise* picks up a group of miners stranded at planet Harod IV, resulting in a slight delay in the ship's arrival at planet Krios.

Prior to "The Perfect Mate."

"The Perfect Mate." Stardate 45761.3. U.S.S. *Enterprise* arrives at planet Krios to pick up a Kriosian delegation for a critical Ceremony of Reconciliation between planets Krios and Valt Minor, in an effort to bring an end to a centuries-old war. En route to the ceremony site, U.S.S. *Enterprise* responds to a distress call from a Ferengi shuttle vehicle, successfully rescuing a crew of two before the shuttle explodes.

Kamala

Preparations for the reconciliation ceremony are disrupted when a Kriosian gift to Chancellor Alrik of Valt is accidentally released from stasis. The "gift" is learned to be a humanoid female named Kamala, a Kriosian sexual "metamorph" intended as the mate of Alrick. Preparations for the ceremony are further complicated when Kriosian ambassador Briam is injured in an altercation with Ferengi personnel. *Enterprise* captain Picard is successful in finalizing preparations for the ceremony during Briam's convalescence. The Ceremony of Reconciliation is performed without incident, although Ambassador Briam would later express astonishment at Picard's ability to work so closely with Kamala without succumbing to her sexual attraction.

"Imaginary Friend." Stardate 45852.1. While on a scientific survey mission of nebula FGC-47, U.S.S. *Enterprise* accidentally encounters a previously undiscovered life-form. The entity materializes aboard the *Enterprise* in the form of a human child. The appearance of this entity on the ship is later found to correlate with an unexpectedly high drag coefficient encountered when passing through the nebula. It is eventually discovered that the entity is indigenous to the nebula, and is attempting to evaluate the potential of the *Enterprise* as an energy source. The spaceborne entity, which has befriended young Clara Sutter, departs the ship when made aware of its negative impact on the child.

Clara Sutter's imaginary friend

A Borg scout craft crash-lands on a small moon in the Argolis cluster. Four of the five crew members on board the ship are killed in the impact.

Shortly prior to "I, Borg."

"I, Borg." Stardate 45854.2. U.S.S. *Enterprise* charts six star systems in the Argolis cluster as a possible prelude to colonization. A distress signal is detected from what investigation determines to be a Borg scout craft that had crashed on a small moon in the region. A single survivor, an adolescent Borg, is recovered from the wreckage.

Third of Five, aka Hugh Borg

Under the instructions of *Enterprise* captain Picard, analysis of the Borg survivor's biochip implants yields information on the Borg collective intelligence's command structure and interface protocols. This information is used to develop an invasive programming sequence believed capable of destroying the entire Borg race if introduced into the Borg system.

During the development of the invasive programming software, *Enterprise* personnel observe that the Borg, now cut off from access to the collective intelligence, exhibits behavioral characteristics of an individual. Deeming it unethical to use a sentient individual as a weapon of mass destruction, Picard orders the Borg, now known as Hugh, to be returned to the crash site for rescue by a second Borg scout craft. Engineer Geordi La Forge, observing Hugh's rescue at the crash site, later reports his belief that Hugh has retained his individuality despite reassimilation into the Borg collective.

A Romulan scout ship experiences a serious malfunction of its propulsion system and issues a distress call. U.S.S. *Enterprise* responds to the signal.

Just prior to "The Next Phase."

Ro Laren

"The Next Phase." Stardate 45892.4 U.S.S. *Enterprise*, on rescue mission to crippled Romulan ship, assists in safe ejection of malfunctioning engine core and provides temporary replacement components, permitting maintenance of life support and propulsion.

During the rescue operation, an apparent transporter malfunction results in the apparent loss of Lieutenant Commander Geordi La Forge and Ensign Ro Laren. Both La Forge and Ro are later found not to be dead, but rather suspended in an area of interspace rendering them effectively invisible. This interphase phenomenon is found to have been caused by an experimental Romulan cloaking device, and exposure to an anionic beam is successful in restoring both La Forge and Ro back to normal space.

U.S.S. *Enterprise* heads for planet Garadius IV for an urgent diplomatic mission.

Just after "The Next Phase."

Starship *Enterprise* conducts a magnetic wave survey of the Parvenium sector, then proceeds to Starbase 218 for a scheduled meeting with Fleet Admiral Gustafson.

Prior to "The Inner Light."

"The Inner Light." Stardate 45944.1. En route to Starbase 218, U.S.S. *Enterprise* encounters a space probe of unknown origin. A low-level nucleonic particle beam from the probe is successful in penetrating the *Enterprise*'s shields, interacts with Captain Picard, rendering him comatose. Upon regaining consciousness, Picard reports having experienced a lifetime of memories from a native of planet Kataan. The crew determines that the purpose of the probe was to transmit these memories from that long-dead civilization in hope of perpetuating a portion of the Kataan culture.

Data's head, discovered buried beneath the city of San Francisco

Work crews excavating beneath the city of San Francisco on Earth discover artifacts suggesting an extraterrestrial presence in that city during the late 19th century. Among the artifacts discovered is an object identified as the head of Lieutenant Commander Data, decayed from having been buried for some 500 years.

Just prior to "Time's Arrow."

"Time's Arrow." Stardate 45959.1 U.S.S. *Enterprise* is recalled to Earth on a priority mission to investigate discovery of Data's remains in San Francisco. Analysis of artifacts found at the dig site suggest origination from planet Devidia II in the Marrab Sector.

Proceeding to Devidia II, *Enterprise* personnel discover humanoid life-forms existing on an asynchronous temporal plane, rendering the humanoids nearly undetectable. Evidence is uncovered that suggests these life-forms may have threatened 19th-century Earth. While investigating these life-forms, Lieutenant Commander Data is accidentally entrapped in a temporal vortex, which transports him back to Earth in the 19th century. Recreating the vortex, an away team consisting of Picard, Riker, Data, Troi, Crusher, and La Forge follow Data into the past in an effort to prevent the Devidia II life-forms from threatening Earth, and in the hope of preventing Data's death.

Data seeks information from a 19th-century San Francisco native.

7.0 THE FAR FUTURE

The Andromeda Galaxy,
home of the Kelvan Empire

26TH CENTURY

A researcher from this century travels back to New Jersey, Earth, in the 22nd century, where his time pod is stolen by an individual named Berlinghoff Rasmussen. The unscrupulous Rasmussen uses the pod to travel to the 24th century.

"A Matter of Time." Rasmussen confessed his past to Data.

Berlinghoff
Rasmussen

27TH CENTURY

Scientist Kal Dano invents the *Tox Uthat,* a quantum phase inhibitor with enormous weapons potential because of its ability to halt all nuclear reactions within a star. An attempt is made to steal the *Uthat* by two Vorgon criminals, so Dano travels back in time to the 22nd century, hiding the device on planet Risa. The device remains there until unearthed by archaeologist Vash, whereupon it is destroyed by *Enterprise* captain Picard in 2366.

"Captain's Holiday." The Vorgons related the tale.

33RD CENTURY

Vorgon criminals attempting to
steal the Tox Uthat

Radiation levels in the Andromeda galaxy are expected to reach intolerably high levels within ten millennia, according to scientists of the Kelvan Empire. Agents of the Kelvan Empire were dispatched aboard a multigenerational spacecraft to explore our Milky Way galaxy for possible colonization.

"By Any Other Name." Rojan described the predicted radiation to Kirk.

APPENDIX A: UNDATABLE EVENTS AND OTHER UNCERTAINTIES

There is a significant number of events in *Star Trek* history for which there are no reliable time references. In certain cases there were enough clues to narrow the range sufficiently so we could arbitrarily suggest dates for some events in the main body of this chronology. In others, however, the range of possible dates is too wide, or there is simply too little evidence to even hazard a guess. This section is a compilation of some of these undatable events, along with notes on whatever dating information was available.

We think these notes will be of general interest to *Star Trek* enthusiasts, and hope that perhaps they may someday serve as springboards for writers of future *Star Trek* projects. Note that *Star Trek: The Next Generation* is still in production as this is being written, and Paramount is still apparently thinking about yet another *Star Trek* feature film with the original cast. This means that by the time you read this, it is entirely possible that one or more of these items may have been addressed by the show. Further, the new *Star Trek: Deep Space Nine* series could well give more answers, and will undoubtedly raise more questions.

MAJOR CHARACTERS

In most cases, we do not know the fates of the principal characters from the original *Star Trek* series. This is apparently being left somewhat vague to allow for the possibility of future projects with those characters, but we do know a few data points.

James T. Kirk. We believe that Kirk was born in 2233, and that he attended Starfleet Academy from 2250 to 2254. Kirk's Starfleet record as of 2267 included the following commendations: Palm Leaf of Axanar Peace Mission, Grankite Order of Tactics, Class of Excellence, Preantares Ribbon of Commendation, Classes First and Second. His awards of Valor include the Medal of Honor, Silver Palm with Cluster, Starfleet Citation of Conspicuous Gallantry, Kragite Order of Heroism. No dates are given for these, but they would have had to have been awarded after Kirk's entry into the Academy in 2250, but before 2267, when the events in "Court Martial" are set. "Whom Gods Destroy" suggests that Kirk visited Axanar as a "new fledged cadet," which would seem to suggest the Palm Leaf of Axanar commendation was earned early in his career.

Sometime prior to "Where No Man Has Gone Before," Kirk and Gary Mitchell were on planet Dimorus, where they encountered rodentlike life-forms who threw deadly poisoned darts. Gary took one of the darts intended for Kirk, and nearly died as a result. This would have happened sometime between Kirk's entry into the Academy in 2250, and 2265, when the events in "Where No Man Has Gone Before" are set.

Kirk once suffered from a serious bout of Vegan choriomeningitis, a rare disease that can cause death in 24 hours if not treated. Although Kirk survived, his blood continued to carry the disease organisms, which the council of the planet Gideon attempted to use to control the overpopulation on their world ("The Mark of Gideon").

Kirk's relationships with Ruth, Janet, Areel, Janice, and Carol: James Kirk apparently had several major romances prior to his assignment to the *Enterprise*. Ruth (no last name given, seen in "Shore Leave") had apparently been close to Kirk during his days at Starfleet Academy. Endocrinologist Janet Wallace (seen in "The Deadly Years") eventually married Theodore Wallace because both she and Kirk were inflexible in their career choices. Areel Shaw served as Kirk's prosecutor when he was accused of causing Ben Finney's death ("Court Martial"). Janice Lester and Kirk evidently shared a year together when Kirk was attending Starfleet Academy ("Turnabout Intruder"). Finally, Carol Marcus and James Kirk conceived a child, David Marcus, in 2261 (*Star Trek II,* assumes that David was 24 at the time of the movie, 2285). There has been speculation that Carol Marcus may have been the "blond lab technician" that Kirk nearly married under Gary Mitchell's guidance while they attended Starfleet Academy (circa 2250, "Where No Man Has Gone Before"). Of course, this lab technician just as easily could have been Janet Wallace, or some other woman we have not seen.

Kirk once visited the cloud city of Stratos prior to 2269 ("The Cloud Minders") but noted it was only a brief visit and he didn't have time to look around.

We do not know the fate of Captain James Kirk, although Gene Roddenberry did once express an opinion that he thought Kirk was probably dead by the time of *Star Trek: The Next Generation* (2364).

Spock. Computer records in "Court Martial" establish that as of 2267, Spock had earned the Vulcanian Scientific Legion of Honor, and had twice been decorated by Starfleet Command. We conjecture that Spock was born in 2230, and that he graduated from Starfleet Academy in 2253.

Spock apparently does have a first name. It has never been established, although he once told Leila Kalomi that "you couldn't pronounce it" ("This Side of Paradise"). Amanda told Kirk that she could pronounce Sarek's family name after many years of practice ("Journey to Babel").

Spock's marriage: The episode "Sarek" has Picard mentioning that he attended the wedding of Sarek's son. There is no specific time reference to peg the date of this event, but Picard mentioned that he was a "young lieutenant" at the time. This would seem to suggest the wedding took place sometime between 2327 (when Picard graduated from the Academy) and 2333 (when Picard took command of the *Stargazer*, and was therefore apparently a captain). Although the episode does not make clear if this son is Spock, Gene Roddenberry indicated that he was sure it was. This view is supported by Picard's mention in "Unification, Part I" that he had met Spock once prior to that episode. It is not made clear if Spock is still married at the time of "Unification."

Spock was last seen as a Federation ambassador working undercover for Vulcan-Romulan reunification on Romulus in "Unification, Part II" (2368). We do not know of his fate beyond this point.

Leonard H. McCoy. Based on McCoy's age of 137 in "Encounter at Farpoint" (2364), we believe the good doctor was born in 2227. A large number of uncertainties exist regarding McCoy's early years, prior to his service aboard the first Starship *Enterprise*. We conjecture that he entered college or medical school in 2245 (assuing he was 18 at the time) and that he graduated in 2253 (assuming an eight-year medical program). Significant questions remain, however, as to whether or not those years were spent at Starfleet Academy or if he attended another school.

The main uncertainty surrounds a back story developed for McCoy by Dorothy Fontana and Gene Roddenberry in which McCoy had married, but that marriage ended in a bitter divorce. In this scenario, the emotional aftermath of this divorce was what drove McCoy to abandon a private medical practice and join Starfeet. This back story would have been described in an episode written by Fontana called "Joanna," which would have shown McCoy's grown daughter coming on board the *Enterprise*. (The episode was never produced, and was extensively rewritten, eventually becoming "The Way to Eden.") Because none of this material was ever incorporated into any aired episodes, we have not included it in the main body of this chronology. We mention it here because it offers some fascinating insight into the McCoy character, and because it does not significantly conflict with any aired material.

There is some possibility, however, that at least some of these points may be someday proven wrong if the *Star Trek: The Academy Years* film project is ever produced. This script, written by David Loughery to be produced by Harve Bennett, would depict the early days of our heroes, and would contradict the notion that McCoy did not attend the Academy until after his college days. In many other respects, however, this story would be reasonably consistent with other established information, although based on evidence from the episodes and films, it is difficult to tell which (if either) scenario is more likely to be "correct."

McCoy's father: *Star Trek V: The Final Frontier* establishes that sometime after McCoy had earned his medical degree, his father, David (name established in *Star Trek III: The Search for Spock),* suffered from a terminal disease that caused the elder McCoy terrible pain. Leonard "pulled the plug" on his father out of compassion, but was horrified when, shortly thereafter, a cure was discovered for the affliction.

McCoy had been briefly stationed on planet Capella IV apparently as part of a Starfleet mission sometime prior to his assignment to the *Enterprise* (2265). McCoy would later recall that the Capellans were totally uninterested in medical aid or hospitals because of a cultural belief that only the strong should survive ("Friday's Child"). Sometime prior to "Court Martial" (set in 2267), McCoy had earned the Legion of Honor and had been decorated by Starfleet surgeons.

Dr. McCoy survives at least until the first season of *Star Trek: The Next Generation* (2364), since he made an inspection tour of the *Enterprise*-D in "Encounter at Farpoint" at the age of 137.

Montgomery Scott. We speculate that Scotty was born in 2222. This would make him 44, the same age as actor James Doohan during the first season of the original *Star Trek* series (2266). Scotty served as an engineering adviser on a couple of freighting runs to the miners in the asteroid belt of the Denevan system ("Operation: Annihilate!"). This was apparently before his duty aboard the *Enterprise* (which began around 2265). A sixth-season *Next Generation* episode ("Relics") being planned at this writing will establish that Scotty disappeared around 2294, only to reappear in 2369.

Uhura. Remarkably little has been established about Uhura's past (she doesn't even have a first name), although we speculate she was born in 2239, which would have made her 27 at the time of the original *Star Trek*'s first season. This, too, matches the age of the actor portraying the role.

Sulu. Almost as little is known about Sulu, although he did at least get a first name (Hikaru) in *Star Trek VI,* and his hometown was established as San Francisco in *Star Trek IV.* We speculate he was 29 at the time of *Star Trek*'s first season, suggesting a birth date of 2237.

Pavel Chekov. Prior to Chekov's assignment to the *Enterprise*, he was romantically involved with a woman named Irina Galliunin. At the time, both had apparently been in Starfleet, although Irina subsequently resigned because she felt uncomfortable in what she felt was too regimented an organization ("The Way to Eden"). Chekov said he was 22 years old in "Who Mourns for Adonais" (2267), suggesting a birthdate of 2245.

Sarek. "Journey to Babel" establishes Sarek's age at the time (2267) to be 102, suggesting a birth date of 2165. Among Sarek's many distinguished achievements are the Coridan admission to the Federation ("Journey to Babel," 2268), the Klingon alliance *(Star Trek VI: The Undiscovered Country,* 2293), the Legaran conference ("Sarek," 2367), as well as the treaty of Alpha Cygnus IX. This last item was not dated, nor were any other details established. The episode "Sarek" also refers to Spock's mother, Amanda, as having died sometime prior to the episode. This date is not established, nor is a date set forth for Sarek's marriage to Perrin.

Star Trek V: The Final Frontier establishes (perhaps apocryphally) that prior to his marriage to Amanda (conjecturally set in 2230), Sarek had been married to a Vulcan princess and that they had a son, Sybok. Spock noted that Sybok's mother died shortly after Sybok's birth, which may have taken place in 2224, seven years prior to Spock's birth. (For that matter, it is not made clear if he had one or more other marriages in the intervening years between Amanda and Perrin. On the other hand, Picard's log in "Sarek" notes that Perrin, "like his first wife, is from Earth," which would appear to contradict the Vulcan princess back story.)

Sarek met a young lieutenant Picard once prior to the episode "Sarek," at Sarek's son's wedding. This was apparently between 2327 and 2333. (See note on Spock in this section.)

Sarek died at the age of 203 in "Unification, Part I" (2368), making him the only major character from the original *Star Trek* series whose fate we do know.

Jean-Luc Picard. We conjecture that Picard was born in 2305, which is consistant with an Academy graduation date of 2327 ("The First Duty"), assuming he tried unsuccessfully for admission at age 17 ("Coming of Age").

In "Where No One Has Gone Before," Picard referred to his mother in the past tense, implying she was no longer alive. This is reinforced by "Family," which has Picard returning to his family home in France, no longer occupied by his parents. In "Night Terrors," Picard recalls that as a young man, he saw his "grandfather deteriorate... from a powerful, robust figure... to a frail wisp of a man, who couldn't even remember how to make his way home." Picard's aunt Adele made ginger tea with honey, very hot, as a cure for the common cold. Picard remembered this and offered it to his guests aboard the *Enterprise* when they had a similar affliction ("Ensign Ro"). (Aunt Adele was named for *Star Trek: The Next Generation* assistant director Adele Simmons.) Picard once recalled (in "Conspiracy") that his "oldest and closest friends were Jack Crusher, may he rest in peace, and Walker Keel." Keel was later killed when the alien bluegills blew up the Starship *Horatio* in that episode.

Picard's heart transplant: Captain Jean-Luc Picard is established to have gotten into a fight at the Bonestell Recreation Facility at Farspace station Earhart some years ago. He apparently picked a fight with three Nausicaans, and nearly died from a stab wound to the heart (described in "Samaritan Snare"). Picard survived with the aid of a bionic heart. The date of this incident was not established, although Picard describes himself as being a young Starfleet officer at the time. If Picard was attending the Academy when he got into the fight, this could be the dark incident that Boothby alluded to in "The First Duty."

William T. Riker. "The Icarus Factor" establishes that Riker had not seen his father for 15 years prior to the episode (2365), and that he was 15 years old at the time his father left him, suggesting a birth date of 2335.

Riker served aboard the Starship *Hood* under the command of Captain Jonathan DeSoto prior to his assignment to the *Enterprise* ("Encounter at Farpoint"). His service aboard the *Hood* would have been sometime after his graduation from Starfleet Academy, probably around 2357, and 2364, the date for "Farpoint." Prior to the *Hood*, he served aboard the U.S.S. *Potemkin* as a lieutenant ("Peak Performance"), although little has been established to determine a date for this. Riker was also stationed on the planet Betazed prior to his *Enterprise* assignment ("Menage à Troi").

At some unspecified point during his service aboard the *Hood*, Riker, as first officer, refused to allow Captain DeSoto to beam down to planet Altair III, citing the danger involved. While DeSoto apparently disagreed with Riker's judgment, Riker was acting in accordance with his duty to protect the life of his captain from unnecessary risk ("Encounter at Farpoint").

The relationship between Will Riker and Deanna Troi. Some years prior to *Star Trek: The Next Generation*'s first season, Riker served on Troi's home planet of Betazed. At that time they became romantically involved, and Troi still occasionally calls him *Imzadi*, which is Betazoid for "beloved." Neither the exact dates nor the specifics of this relationship have been given, although "Menage à Troi" establishes that Riker was a junior lieutenant assigned to Betazed and that Troi was a psychology student at the time.

Data. The crew of the U.S.S. *Tripoli* activated Data 26 years prior to "Datalore" (2364), suggesting an activation date of 2338. The computer record in "Measure of a Man" establishes that Data had been honored with the Decoration for Gallantry, the Medal of Honor with Clusters, the Legion of Honor, and the Star Cross. No dates were associated with any of these awards, although they were presumably awarded prior to the episode's date of 2365.

Data was once on the Starship *Trieste*, where he passed through an unstable wormhole. This event, mentioned in "Clues," was apparently prior to 2367, but nothing else is known about it or about Data on the *Trieste*.

Deanna Troi. The computer bio screen in "Conundrum" establishes that Troi was born in 2336. We have established that Deanna Troi's father, Ian Andrew Troi, was a human Starfleet officer who married Deanna's Betazoid mother, Lwaxana. Troi's father is further established to be deceased ("Half a Life," et al.), but the time and circumstances of his death have not been established. When Troi was studying psychology at the University of Betazed, Tam Elbrun, who later became a Starfleet specialist in contact with alien life, was her patient ("Tin Man").

When Deanna was a child, she was genetically bonded with Wyatt Miller, a human, who is the son of Steven Miller, close friend of Deanna's father. The exact ages of Deanna and Wyatt were not established, but such bonding at childhood is still a common Betazoid custom, and generally results in marriage when both children reach adulthood. The marriage was never performed ("Haven").

Beverly C. Crusher. The episode "Conspiracy" establishes that *Horatio* captain Walker Keel was one of Picard's closest friends and that he introduced Beverly to Jack Crusher. No date is given for this, although this would have to had been sometime prior to Wesley Crusher's birth in 2349.

Beverly's biographical data screen in "Conundrum" suggests her maiden name was Beverly Howard and that she was born in 2324. This has yet to be established in dialog.

Geordi La Forge. "Imaginary Friend" establishes Geordi's father to have been an exozoologist, and his mother to have been a command officer, both members of Starfleet. Geordi recalled that his parents were always on the move, sometimes living together, other times separately. As a child, Geordi spent time with his father, studying invertebrates in the Modean system. He also lived with his mother on an outpost near the Romulan Neutral Zone. Geordi's bio screen in "Cause and Effect" suggests his parents are (or were) Edward M. and Alvera K. La Forge, and that he was born in 2335.

In "The Next Phase," Picard mentions that the first time he met La Forge was when Geordi was a young officer assigned to pilot Picard on an inspection tour. Picard recalled having made an offhanded remark about the engine, and Geordi stayed up all night that evening refitting the shuttle's fusion initiators. Picard was so impressed by this that he knew he wanted Geordi on his next command. This was presumably before Picard's assignment to the *Enterprise* in 2364.

Worf. The first Klingon in Starfleet was six years old at the time of the Khitomer massacre (2346), suggesting a birth date of 2340. Much has been established about Worf's early years, but little is known about his adoptive human brother. This brother, the natural son of Sergey and Helena Rozhenko, was mentioned in "Heart of Glory," but virtually nothing has been established beyond the fact of his existence and the fact that they spent their formative years on the farm world of Gault, prior to moving to Earth. Note that this is not the same person as Kurn, who is Worf's natural Klingon brother, established in "Sins of the Father."

Natasha Yar. Tasha said she was 15 years old at the time she escaped from the failed colony at Turkana IV ("The Naked Now"), and "Legacy" (set in 2367) is 15 years after that escape, suggesting a birth date of 2337.

Wesley Crusher. Wesley was 17 years old in "Evolution," set in 2366, suggesting a birth date of 2349.

Miles Edward O'Brien. Prior to his duty aboard the *Enterprise*, O'Brien served as tactical officer aboard the U.S.S. *Rutledge* under the command of Captain Ben Maxwell. Open hostilities existed between the Federation and the Cardassians at this point, and both O'Brien and Maxwell were present shortly after a Cardassian attack on a Federation settlement at Setlik ("The Wounded"). The time of this tour of duty (or the attack) is not known, although it would have had to have been prior to 2364, because O'Brien was first seen as battle bridge conn in "Encounter at Farpoint." (The *Enterprise* was apparently launched in late 2363.) O'Brien and Maxwell met again when Maxwell commanded the U.S.S. *Phoenix* in "The Wounded."

Ensign Ro Laren. Ensign Ro served aboard the U.S.S. *Wellington* prior to her assignment to the *Enterprise*. She was court-martialed after a mission to Garon II in which she disobeyed orders and eight members of the *Wellington* away team were killed. Ro was released from prison on Jaros II after agreeing to duty aboard the *Enterprise* in 2368 on a crucial diplomatic mission with Bajoran terrorists. ("Ensign Ro.") No time frame has been established for her *Wellington* assignment or her subsequent court-martial. These events clearly had to take place prior to "Ensign Ro," but after 2364, since her computer bio screen in "Conundrum" gave this as the date of her graduation from Starfleet Academy.

Guinan. The mysterious hostess of Ten Forward remains a significant unknown, although we know she is at least five hundred years old, since we saw her younger self on Earth in Samuel Clemens's era ("Time's Arrow"). Guinan said she'd been in serious trouble once, and had extricated herself only because she'd trusted Captain Picard. This was presumably before her joining the *Enterprise*, perhaps even before her travels aboard the *Stargazer* with Picard. Guinan once mentioned she had several children and an uncle named Terkim, her mother's brother ("Hollow Pursuits").

Katherine Pulaski. The former *Enterprise* chief medical officer was married three times prior to her *Enterprise* tour of duty ("The Icarus Factor," 2365). She noted that she remains good friends with all three exes. Pulaski also once wrote a ground-breaking scientific paper entitled "Linear Models of Viral Propagation" ("Unnatural Selection").

Keiko Ishikawa O'Brien. The *Enterprise* botanist once recalled, under hypnotic suggestion, that her grandmother was very skilled at Japanese brush writing. Young Keiko's job was to fill a cup with water, and bring it to the table where her grandmother would create her art ("Violations"). Keiko's father is (or was) named Hiro ("Disaster").

U.S.S. *ENTERPRISE* AND THE STARFLEET:

The spaceship *Enterprise*. In *Star Trek: The Motion Picture,* Decker shows Ilia a display in the recreation room of various ships called *Enterprise*. Besides the wooden frigate, the aircraft carrier, the space shuttle, and the original television series starship, there is another spaceship *Enterprise* that appears to predate the starship. One can probably assume that this vessel was not designated as a starship, because the *Enterprise*-D has been established as the fifth starship to bear the name, and the previous four starships have all been accounted for. Nothing else has been officially established for this vessel, although we understand the design had actually been developed for a proposed Gene Roddenberry television project that never reached the production stage.

The original Starship *Enterprise*. This ship was apparently commissioned in 2245, a date derived from working backward from the 2266 date for the first season of the original series, taking into account such past events as Spock's tenure with Pike ("The Cage" and "The Menagerie") as well as a conjectural five-year mission under the command of Captain Robert April.

The *Enterprise*-A. The second starship to bear the name. (The first was, of course, the ship seen in the original *Star Trek* series and the first three movies.) This second ship was launched in 2286 *(Star Trek IV: The Voyage Home)* under the command of Captain Kirk. Although Kirk apparently retired as commander, and the ship was to be decommissioned in 2293 *(Star Trek VI: The Undiscovered Country)*, there is still some doubt that either actually happened, as the folks at Paramount (those clever devils!) seem to have left this somewhat ambiguous to allow for the possibility of another *Star Trek* feature film or some other project with the original ship or crew.

The *Enterprise*-B. The third starship to bear the name, an *Excelsior* class vessel, remains a significant unknown. This ship apparently did not yet exist in 2293 (the year in which *Star Trek VI* is set). It would have to have been decommissioned or destroyed quite some time prior to 2344, when its successor, the *Enterprise*-C was destroyed ("Yesterday's *Enterprise*"). Nothing has been established about this ship's captain, crew, or missions.

The *Enterprise*-C. The fourth starship to bear the name. This ship was an *Ambassador* class vessel, and was established to have been destroyed in 2344 while defending the Klingon outpost at Narendra III ("Yesterday's *Enterprise*"). It was apparently launched after the decommissioning or destruction of the *Enterprise*-B, but there is nothing further to establish the date. Just prior to its destruction, the *Enterprise*-C was commanded by Captain Rachel Garrett.

Captain Christopher Pike. Little is known about Kirk's predecessor other than the fact that he was born in Mojave, on Earth, and that he eventually went to live among the Talosians on Talos IV ("The Cage"). Pike evidently commanded two five-year missions of exploration aboard the *Enterprise* and later served as fleet captain before being seriously injured in an explosion on a training ship in 2266.

Captain Garth of Izar. The episode "Whom Gods Destroy" establishes former Fleet Captain Garth to have been a major figure in Starfleet history. Garth led a major Federation victory at Axanar, and, in another battle, Garth used something called a Cochrane deceleration maneuver to defeat a Romulan vessel near Tau Ceti. It is unclear when any

of this occurred, but Kirk, noting that Garth was his hero, said that he had read all about Garth at the Academy, suggesting some of this took place prior to Kirk's admission to the Academy in 2250. Garth's Romulan encounter would have had to have happened after 2266 (when "Balance of Terror" established the Neutral Zone had not been crossed for a century) and 2269 (when "Whom Gods Destroy" is set). One of Kirk's early missions as a cadet was a peace mission to Axanar, for which Kirk was awarded the Palm Leaf of the Axanar Peace Mission (as mentioned in "Court Martial"). In later years Garth was seriously injured in an unknown accident, but he was treated by the inhabitants of planet Antos IV, who taught him the technique of cellular metamorphosis (even before Michael Jackson and Arnold Schwarzenegger learned about morphing). Unfortunately, either the accident or the treatment left Garth mentally disturbed, and he tried to destroy the Antos people. Garth's starship crew refused to obey his orders, and Garth was eventually confined to the penal colony on Elba II for psychiatric treatment.

Boothby. The wise old groundskeeper at Starfleet Academy, mentioned in "Final Mission" and "The Game," was reunited with Picard in "The First Duty." Boothby alluded to some incident during Picard's Academy days in which Picard was involved in a fight and thereafter nearly resigned from Starfleet. It is not clear, but this may have been the fight mentioned in "Samaritan Snare" at Farspace station Earhart in which Picard is so seriously injured that his heart is replaced with a bionic implant. Boothby said he was then about as old as Picard is at the time of "The First Duty," suggesting Boothby is around 105 years old at that point (2368).

SCIENTIFIC AND EXPLORATORY MILESTONES:

First contact by humans with extraterrestrial life. No *Star Trek* episode or film has yet told the story of Earth's first contact with alien life, even though this event is an important implied cornerstone of the *Star Trek* scenario. This must have happened at least a hundred years before the first season of the first *Star Trek* series (set in 2266), because that show made several references to hundred-year-old missions to other planets. The Romulan wars push that point back at least several years past the century mark. One can probably assume, therefore, that the first contact took place after our present day, but significantly before the year 2160.

First contact with Vulcan. Gene Roddenberry said that at the time of the first *Star Trek* series' first season, Spock was the only Vulcan serving in Starfleet. (The second season episode "The Immunity Syndrome" established a Starfleet vessel with a Vulcan crew.) One might speculate from this that first contact with Vulcan was a fairly recent event, perhaps within a generation of Spock's birth.

First Earth-Saturn space probe. Colonel Shaun Geoffrey Christopher, son of U.S. Air Force Captain John Christopher, commanded this historic mission, according to Spock's computer research. No date is given for this flight, although the younger Christopher had apparently not yet been conceived in 1969 ("Tomorrow Is Yesterday").

The invention of the transporter. In "Masterpiece Society," Geordi suggests that the transporter had been invented "over a century" prior to the episode, set in 2368. On the other hand, the transporter would have had to have been invented prior to "The Cage," set in 2254, because we saw Captain Pike and company beam down to planet Talos IV. On the third hand, it might be reasonable to assume the transporter had been invented by the time the *Enterprise* itself was launched, which would push the invention date back to at least before 2245. A sixth-season episode being planned at this writing ("Realm of Fear") may establish that the transporter was initially developed around 2158, but that it was not until around 2219 that the system was considered safe for routine use with human subjects. This episode may show that significant difficulties were encountered during the initial use of the transporter with human subjects around 2209. It is unclear as to exactly when the transporter-based replicator came into use. This device is clearly in widespread use in *Star Trek: The Next Generation,* but it is not certain if it had been invented or was in use during the first *Star Trek* series.

Invention of subspace radio. Although faster-than-light warp drive was apparently developed by Zefram Cochrane around 2061, the invention of subspace radio had not occurred as late as 2168, when the Starship *Horizon* made contact with planet Sigma Iotia II. As a result, a message from that ship was not received by Starfleet for a century.

Development of hyronalyn. According to Dr. McCoy in "The Deadly Years," adrenaline-based treatments had been used for radiation sickness early in the atomic age. Although early research had been highly promising, adrenaline was abandoned shortly after the invention of hyronalyn. Hyronalyn was the treatment of choice by the year 2267, and is still in use by Starfleet in the 24th century, as evidenced by Dr. Crusher's treatment of *Enterprise* personnel in "Final Mission."

MAJOR CULTURAL AND POLITICAL DEVELOPMENTS:

The Vulcan Reformation. At some time in the distant past, the Vulcan people were emotional and violent, so much so that their passions threatened to destroy them. Surak ("The Savage Curtain") led the Vulcan people to the philosophy of logic and peace. We conjecture the Reformation took place as much as 2,000 years ago (based on the age of Spock's family ceremonial grounds in "Amok Time"), although Gene Roddenberry once speculated it might have been as recently as 700 years before the original series. One might speculate that this event may also have triggered the schism between the Vulcans and the Romulans, in which the Vulcan ancestors of the Romulans left Vulcan to form what eventually became the Romulan Star Empire. (See "Unification, Parts I and II.")

Establishment of the Prime Directive. One of the most important principles of the Federation Starfleet is the prohibition against interference in the normal development of any

society. This rule, also known as Starfleet General Order Number One, was apparently instituted before Kirk took command of the *Enterprise* in 2264, but it is unclear exactly when this happened, or what events led to the adoption of the directive. The episode "A Piece of the Action" establishes that the Prime Directive had not yet been instituted in 2168, when the U.S.S. *Horizon* made contact with planet Iotia.

Fundamental Declarations of the Martian Colonies. Samuel T. Cogley cited this document, along with the Bible, the Code of Hammurabi, and the Constitution of the United States as a historic milestone in the development of legal systems that protect individual rights. Also cited were the Tribunals of Alpha III. No date was given for either document ("Court Martial").

Romulan alliance with dissident Klingons. "The *Enterprise* Incident" establishes that some measure of cooperation existed between the two empires during the third season of the original *Star Trek* series, c. 2268. At this point, the two powers were allied against what they perceived as a threat from the United Federation of Planets. However, by 2292 (just prior to *Star Trek VI*), relations between the Romulans and Klingons had deteriorated significantly (from Geordi's line in "Reunion" that suggests the two powers had become "blood enemies" 75 years prior to that episode). The Romulans attacked the Klingon outpost at Narendra III in 2344 ("Yesterday's *Enterprise*"), and in 2346 the Romulans also attacked the Khitomer Outpost near the Romulan border, killing thousands of Klingons. "Sins of the Father" and "Redemption, Part II" show, however, that the Romulans have been working with at least some factions of the Klingon government in an effort to overthrow K'mpec's regime. The dates and circumstances of this Romulan alliance with dissident Klingons are unclear.

World government on Earth. In "Up the Long Ladder" Data notes that the establishment of a political entity called the European Hegemony was a step toward the establishment of a world government on Earth in the 22nd century.

Kahless the Unforgettable. The legendary leader who united the Klingon Homeworld at some time in the planet's past history, Kahless is also considered responsible for that planet's history of aggression ("The Savage Curtain"). Klingon legend has it that Kahless was a highly honorable individual, so much so that he once fought his brother, Morath, for twelve days and nights because Morath had broken his word and brought shame to his family ("New Ground").

WARS AND OTHER DISASTERS:

Nuclear holocaust on Earth. Several references have been made to a third world war at some point between our present day and *Star Trek*'s time. These references have included Spock's mention in "Bread and Circuses" that 37 million humans died in World War III. Other references have included Q's description in "Encounter at Farpoint" of a barbaric period on Earth during the "postatomic horror" during which all the lawyers were killed sometime before 2079, at which time "all 'united Earth' nonsense [had been] abolished." Further, a line in "A Matter of Time" suggests that Earth suffered a "nuclear winter" during the twenty-first century. There isn't much else to determine a more accurate time frame for this war, but it does seem to be a distinctly different event than the Eugenics Wars ("Space Seed"), which were over by 1996. ("Space Seed" also has Spock describing the third world war as having taken place during the mid-1990s, although he admits that records from that period are "fragmentary.") Colonel Green, seen in "The Savage Curtain," was described as having led a genocidal war on Earth during the twenty-first century.

Cardassian wars. "The Wounded" establishes that an uneasy truce between the Cardassians and the Federation was signed sometime in 2367, and that hostilities had existed for at least several years prior. "The Wounded" also establishes that Chief Miles O'Brien had served under Captain Ben Maxwell on the Starship *Rutledge* some unspecified number of years ago during some brutal hostilities between the two parties at Setlik III. Maxwell's family, along with about a hundred other civilians, were killed in the incident. The *Rutledge* arrived at Setlik a day later. (The Cardassian Glinn Daro said in "The Wounded" that the Setlik massacre had been a terrible mistake on the part of the Cardassians, who believed the outpost was to be used as a launching point for a massive attack by the Federation.) "Unification, Part I" establishes that Ambassador Sarek had been involved in negotiations with the Cardassians, although Spock publicly opposed his position. Hostilities with the Cardassians extend at least as far back as 2355 (the year the *Stargazer* was destroyed) because Picard noted in "The Wounded" that the last time he was near Cardassian space, he was on the *Stargazer*, running away at warp speed from a Cardassian ship. Picard added that he had been sent to make preliminary overtures for a truce.

Tholian wars. Relations between the Federation and the Tholian Assembly are shown to be less than friendly during the episode "The Tholian Web," set in 2268. The episode "Peak Performance" establishes that Riker, during an Academy simulation, calculated a sensory blind spot on a Tholian vessel, suggesting that relations between the Federation and the Tholians were at least somewhat strained during Riker's Academy days. Riker's father, Kyle, was injured in 2353 (the same year that William entered Starfleet Academy) during a Tholian attack on a starbase ("The Icarus Factor"). This suggests that there were open hostilities at that point. In "Reunion" (set in 2367), K'Ehleyr expressed fear that internal Klingon conflicts could escalate to involve other powers, including the Tholians.

Romulan wars. Although we estimate that the Romulan wars were concluded around the year 2160, we have no information to suggest the time frame (or events) that led to the beginning of this conflict, or for first contact with the Romulan Star Empire itself ("Balance of Terror"). We do know that between the end of the Romulan wars (2160) and the episode "Balance of Terror" (2266), the Neutral Zone treaty remained unbroken. We also know that there was no contact between the Federation and the Romulans between the Tomed Incident (2311) and the events of "The Neutral Zone" (2364).

Altarian conflict. Admiral Komack, in his communiqué to the *Enterprise*, explains that the Altair system was in the process of putting itself together after a long interplanetary conflict. The inauguration of a new president just after that episode was expected to stabilize the entire system, demonstrating friendship and strength, and causing ripples clear to the Klingon Empire ("Amok Time").

Tarellian war. Tarellia, a Class-M planet with intelligent humanoid life, suffered a terrible crisis when hostilities between inhabitants of two land masses culminated with the use of a biological warfare weapon. This weapon caused the death of the entire culture, estimated to have reached a technological level similar to Earth's late-20th century. A few Tarellians escaped, but they carried the deadly disease, causing numerous deaths on the planets they reached. Eventually, almost all Tarellians were hunted down and destroyed. The last known Tarellian ship was detected near planet Haven in 2364 ("Haven").

Station Salem One. Neither the date, the adversary, nor the circumstances of this incident are made clear, but in "The Enemy," Station Salem One is described by Picard as being the site of a Pearl Harbor-like sneak attack that set the stage for a bloody war.

Ersalrope wars. Unspecified conflict during which the now-dead inhabitants of the planet Minos gained notoriety as interstellar arms merchants. The Minosians were apparently all killed when one of their weapons systems proved too advanced for their own good ("The Arsenal of Freedom").

New data: The *Star Trek* timeline is constantly growing and evolving with the addition of each new episode or movie. During the months when this volume was in preparation, it was interesting to note the number of items from this list of undatable events that had to be deleted because they were in fact established. Most of these deleted items have since shown up in the main body of the chronology. Among these were the date for incorporation of the United Federation of Planets (established in "The Outcast" to have taken place in 2161), and birth dates and Academy graduation dates for several members of the *Enterprise*-D crew (established in "The First Duty," "Conundrum," and others.)

APENDIX B: ALTERNATE TIMELINES

A number of *Star Trek*'s episodes and movies have involved time travel. In many cases, these stories have involved the efforts of our heroes to repair the damage that caused the alternate (and presumably improper) timelines, thus restoring the flow of history to "normality." Because of this, some of the following story lines are not entirely incorporated into the main body of this chronology, since many of the alternate timelines never "really" happened.

"Tomorrow Is Yesterday." This episode involved the *Enterprise*, under the command of Captain Kirk, accidentally thrown into the past, to Earth in the year 1969. While attempting to avoid detection by the U.S. Air Force, *Enterprise* personnel accidentally destroyed an Air Force fighter aircraft, and were forced to bring the pilot, Captain John Christopher, to the starship. These events created an alternate timeline in which the U.S. Air Force made a confirmed, documented UFO sighting in 1969. Additionally, the capture of Captain Christopher would have prevented Christopher from fathering a child. According to historical records, that child, Shaun Geoffery Christopher, commanded the first Earth-Saturn probe. The history of space exploration in this timeline would presumably have followed a significantly different course than the one described in this chronology. This alternate timeline was eliminated when the *Enterprise* returned to the 23rd century, restoring John Christopher and an Air Force security guard to their original coordinates before they were beamed to the *Enterprise*. It is not clear if, in the "repaired" timeline, either Christopher or the guard retain memory of their stay aboard the *Enterprise*.

"City on the Edge of Forever." Traveling into Earth's past through the Guardian of Forever, Dr. McCoy prevented a fatal traffic accident involving social worker Edith Keeler in 1930. This created an alternate timeline in which Keeler became a factor in American politics, delaying that nation's entry into the Second World War long enough for Adolf Hitler's scientists to develop the atomic bomb. In this alternate timeline, Nazi Germany won the Second World War, becoming Earth's dominant power in the 20th century. This alternate timeline was excised when Kirk and Spock followed McCoy into the past, preventing McCoy from saving Keeler in that critical traffic accident.

"Assignment: Earth." This episode does not exactly involve an alternate timeline, but deals with Kirk and Spock on Earth in 1968 working to prevent what they fear is interference from future aliens. In fact, the alien "interference" was from an individual named Gary Seven, who was found to be part of the "normal" events in that day. Thus, it appears that no alternate timeline was created in the episode.

Star Trek IV: The Voyage Home. An alternate timeline was apparently created in this film in 1986 when Kirk and company visited San Francisco to find two humpback whales. In this timeline, two humpback whales disappeared near San Francisco, a mysterious stranger was captured on the Navy aircraft carrier U.S.S. *Enterprise* and later disappeared, Dr. Nichols of Plexicorp invented transparent aluminum, and Dr. Gillian Taylor disappeared, never to be seen again. This alternate timeline was not "corrected," and we might therefore conclude that the entirety of *Star Trek* history from that point is in that continuum. It is also possible, therefore, that an "original" timeline exists in a parallel continuum in which neither the humpbacks nor Taylor disappeared.

It is interesting to note that an early draft of the *Star Trek IV* script had one of the questions in Spock's memory test establish that Dr. Nichols had invented transparent aluminum back in 1986. Since this was "prior" to our heroes traveling back in time, this would have implied that an alternate timeline was not created, but that Kirk and his crew were simply part of "proper" past history.

"Time Squared." Captain Picard evidently made a decision that resulted in the destruction of the *Enterprise*. Just before the ship was destroyed, however, Picard departed the vessel aboard a shuttle. The force of the starship's explosion threw the shuttle back in time by several hours. As a result, an alternate timeline was created in which the *Enterprise* was not destroyed. All subsequent *Star Trek* episodes have apparently been set in this alternate timeline.

"Yesterday's *Enterprise*." This is one of the strangest and most complicated alternate timeline stories in *Star Trek* history. The triggering event here was a photon torpedo explosion back in 2344, fired by the *Enterprise*-C, which accidentally opened a temporal rift, sending that ship into the future. Once removed from its "proper" time, an alternate timeline was created in which the *Enterprise*-C did not attempt to help defend the Klingon outpost at Narendra III. Later, tensions between the Federation and the Klingons escalated, and an extended war ensued. The *Enterprise*-C emerged from the temporal rift in the year 2366, by which time the Federation was on the verge of defeat. The crew of the *Enterprise*-C, once made aware of the impact of their removal from the original timeline, returned back in time to 2344, where they were nearly destroyed rendering assistance to the Klingons at Narendra III. Although his act restored the timeline to its original form, or nearly so, *Enterprise*-D security chief Tasha Yar — who in the alternate timeline did not die at Vagra II — elected to join the crew of the *Enterprise*-C when it returned to the past.

"Captain's Holiday." This is another complicated one. Vorgon criminals from the 27th century traveled back to Picard's time in an effort to locate a valuable artifact, the *Tox Uthat*. The Vorgons knew from historical records that Picard would be involved with the discovery of the *Uthat*, and also that Picard would later destroy the artifact. The criminals from the future therefore tried to steal the *Uthat* before Picard was able to destroy it. Although they were unsuccessful, the Vorgons traveled back in time again to make another attempt to acquire the object.

It may be that no significant alternate timelines were created in this episode, although it seems possible that the Vorgons could continue *ad infinitum* to steal the *Uthat*, and that they would be eventually successful. If this is the case, then each attempt might be considered a different alternate timeline. (In fact, the script as originally written ended with a repeat of the first scene! Had the episode been shown in that form, savvy viewers could have concluded that the Vorgons would eventually succeed in their effort.)

"Redemption, Parts I and II." In these episodes, we learn that the alternate Tasha did not die in the battle at Narendra III. Instead, she and her crewmates were captured by Romulans, and Tasha won the lives of her crewmates by agreeing to become the consort of a Romulan official. A year later, Yar gave birth to a daughter, Sela, who later became a powerful Romulan operative. According to Sela, Yar was killed trying to escape when Sela was four years old.

Even though this version of Yar originated in an alternate timeline, she returned to the past with the *Enterprise*-C, and thus continued to exist, even after the timeline was restored. This raises the interesting question of whether this past Tasha had existed prior to the creation of the alternate timeline. In other words, it would have been interesting if the *Enterprise*-D, prior to "Yesterday's *Enterprise*," had traveled into the past to Romulus. Would they have met Yar and Sela? If not, one might reasonably argue that the entire *Star Trek* scenario since "Yesterday's *Enterprise*" is an alternate (or at least an altered) timeline.

"A Matter of Time." A researcher from the 26th century went back to the 22nd century, where he or she had the misfortune of encountering Professor Berlinghoff Rasmussen. The unethical professor stole the researcher's time machine and attempted to use it for his own gain. An alternate timeline was apparently created here when the 26th-century researcher met Rasmussen in the past.

Other episodes: Time travel elements were also part of such episodes as "The Naked Time" and "Cause and Effect." In most of these cases, the time travel was either a one-way trip forward, or a recursive loop, which did not appear to create an alternate timeline.

About time: The question of whether or not the time continuum is ultimately fixed or mutable in the *Star Trek* universe has never been definitively addressed. Every time a terrible change occurs, our people have been pretty much able to restore the "proper" flow of history, suggesting that both the change and the restoration were "normal." Every time a change is not restored, we are left with the possibility that the change is simply what was "supposed" to have happened.

If these suppositions are true, we may be left with the conclusion that very few of the items listed here are in fact truly alternate timelines. However, if time is truly changeable, each of the events here may have created a completely independent, parallel universe.

On the other hand, if time is changeable, but parallel timelines cannot exist, we are faced with the possibility that the continuum may have been altered an infinite number of times, and that there is no way that we can know what the "original" timeline was like.

It is the authors' opinion that time travel stories almost never stand up under close scrutiny. Questions such as those posed here ultimately become questions about the nature and mechanics of time travel, and therefore become questions about the rules of time travel in the *Star Trek* universe. One might suppose that those mechanics might vary with the specific time-travel method used in a particular story ("slingshot" effect, temporal rift, Guardian of Forever, et cetera.)

Those interested in further examination of the mechanics of time travel and its ramifications may enjoy the novel *The Man Who Folded Himself* by David Gerrold. Also highly recommended for the same reasons is the classic short story "All You Zombies" by Robert Heinlein.

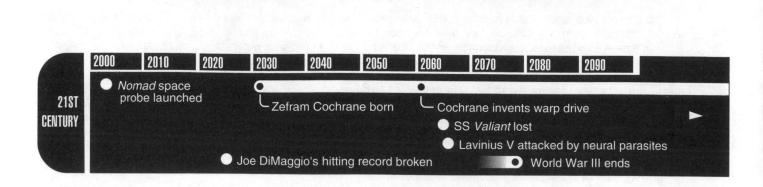

21ST CENTURY

| 2000 | 2010 | 2020 | 2030 | 2040 | 2050 | 2060 | 2070 | 2080 | 2090 |

- *Nomad* space probe launched
- Zefram Cochrane born
- Cochrane invents warp drive
- SS *Valiant* lost
- Lavinius V attacked by neural parasites
- Joe DiMaggio's hitting record broken
- World War III ends

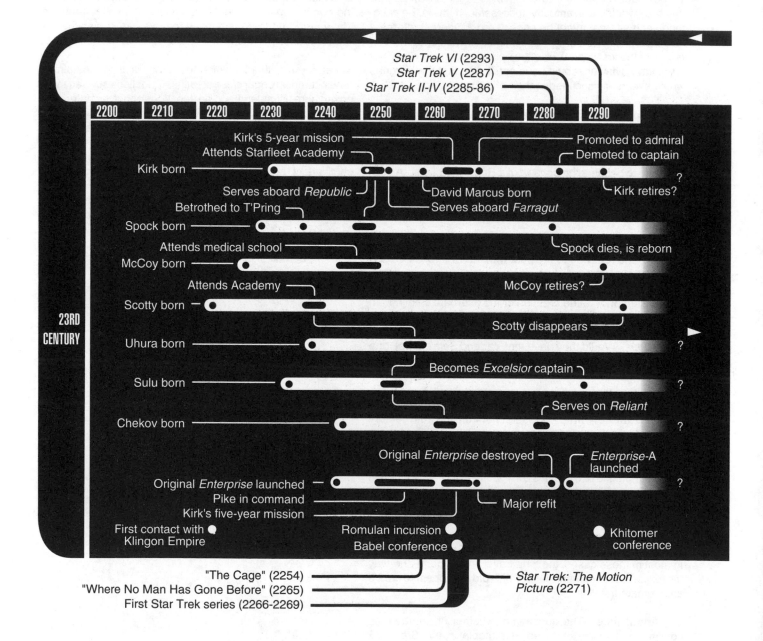

Star Trek VI (2293)
Star Trek V (2287)
Star Trek II-IV (2285-86)

| 2200 | 2210 | 2220 | 2230 | 2240 | 2250 | 2260 | 2270 | 2280 | 2290 |

23RD CENTURY

- Kirk's 5-year mission
- Attends Starfleet Academy
- Kirk born
- Promoted to admiral
- Demoted to captain
- Serves aboard *Republic*
- David Marcus born
- Kirk retires?
- Betrothed to T'Pring
- Serves aboard *Farragut*
- Spock born
- Spock dies, is reborn
- Attends medical school
- McCoy born
- McCoy retires?
- Attends Academy
- Scotty born
- Scotty disappears
- Uhura born
- Becomes *Excelsior* captain
- Sulu born
- Serves on *Reliant*
- Chekov born
- Original *Enterprise* destroyed
- *Enterprise*-A launched
- Original *Enterprise* launched
- Pike in command
- Kirk's five-year mission
- Major refit
- First contact with Klingon Empire
- Romulan incursion
- Babel conference
- Khitomer conference

"The Cage" (2254)
"Where No Man Has Gone Before" (2265)
First Star Trek series (2266-2269)

Star Trek: The Motion Picture (2271)

22ND CENTURY

2100 | 2110 | 2120 | 2130 | 2140 | 2150 | 2160 | 2170 | 2180 | 2190

Zefram Cochrane disappears

Sarek of Vulcan born

USS *Archon* lost

Treaty of Algeron
Battle of Cheron

USS *Horizon* visits Iotia

USS *Essex* lost

Romulan war

United Federation of Planets founded

Star Trek: Deep Space Nine (2369)

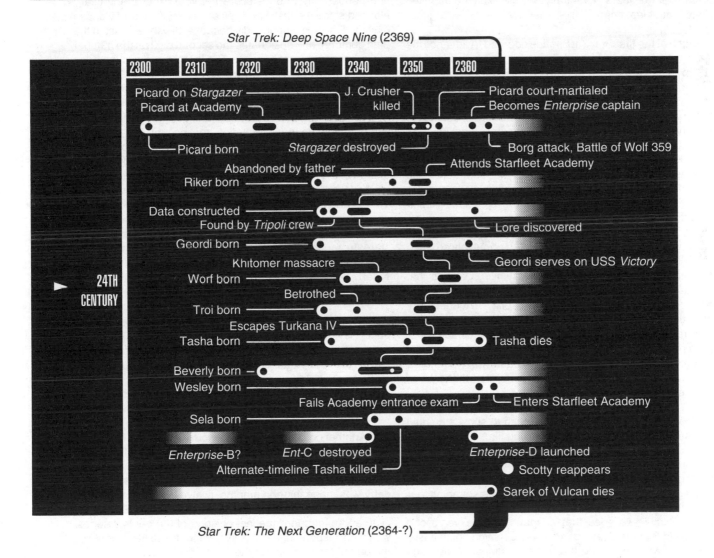

24TH CENTURY

2300 | 2310 | 2320 | 2330 | 2340 | 2350 | 2360

Picard on *Stargazer*
Picard at Academy

J. Crusher killed

Picard court-martialed
Becomes *Enterprise* captain

Picard born
Stargazer destroyed
Borg attack, Battle of Wolf 359

Abandoned by father
Riker born

Attends Starfleet Academy

Data constructed
Found by *Tripoli* crew
Lore discovered

Geordi born
Geordi serves on USS *Victory*

Khitomer massacre
Worf born

Betrothed

Troi born

Escapes Turkana IV
Tasha born
Tasha dies

Beverly born

Wesley born

Fails Academy entrance exam
Enters Starfleet Academy

Sela born

Enterprise-B?
Ent-C destroyed
Enterprise-D launched

Alternate-timeline Tasha killed
Scotty reappears

Sarek of Vulcan dies

Star Trek: The Next Generation (2364-?)

APPENDIX D: REGARDING STARDATES

Gene Roddenberry said he invented stardates primarily as a means to remind us that the show was set in the future. We thought about trying to derive a formula to convert stardates to our present Gregorian calendar, but we quickly discovered that several different methods were apparently used to determine stardates over the history of the show. It became clear that stardates were never intended to be examined too closely, and that many errors have crept into the system over the years. (Naturally, we *did* examine them too closely, but at least now you've been warned.)

Much of the first *Star Trek* series seemed to advance the stardate an average of about 57 units each episode, from 1512 in "The Corbomite Maneuver" to 5928 in "Turnabout Intruder." Within a given episode, an increase of one unit (i.e., 1312 to 1313) seemed to correspond to about 24 hours. Additionally, there were a few episodes in which stardates apparently went backward from the previous week's show. The real reason for this is that the *Star Trek* production staff didn't always know which order the network would air the episodes. Dorothy Fontana also notes that some episodes were filmed out of intended order when writers were late in completing their scripts. (Ms. Fontana was diplomatic enough to avoid naming any names.)

Nevertheless, enough people asked about this so Gene Roddenberry came up with an explanation in Stephen Whitfield's *The Making of Star Trek,* which explains that stardates "adjust for shifts in relative time which occur due to the vessel's speed and space warp capability." Roddenberry added that "the stardate specified in the log entry must be computed against the speed of the vessel, the space warp, and its position within our galaxy in order to get a meaningful reading." (Gene also admitted that he wasn't quite sure what that explanation meant, and that he was glad that a lot of people seemed to think it made sense.)

The *Star Trek* feature films also tried to show a gradual increase in stardates in each succeeding film. The numbers seem to have been arbitrarily determined, since the apparent value of each stardate unit seemed to vary widely in the gaps between movies. *Star Trek VI: The Undiscovered Country* was an even stranger case. This picture was set about four years after *Star Trek V* (stardate 8454). We've seen from the original *Star Trek* series that a span of three years can correspond to an increase of 4416 units, which could easily have put *Star Trek VI* into the five-digit range. A five-digit stardate seemed inappropriate for a *Star Trek* movie with the original *Enterprise* crew, since the longer stardates have been the province of the *Next Generation.* For this reason, the stardate for *Star Trek VI* was arbitrarily set at 9523, since this was near the upper limit of four-digit numbers. (We have a bit of insight into this selection process as *Star Trek VI* cowriter Denny Martin Flinn consulted with chronology coauthor Mike Okuda on this matter.)

Yet another method for stardate computation is employed for episodes of *Star Trek: The Next Generation.* Gene Roddenberry made *Next Generation* stardates five-digit numbers, apparently to underscore the years that theoretically elapsed since the first *Star Trek* series. He arbitrarily chose 4 as the first digit (supposedly because this show is set in the 24th century), and designated the second digit as the number of the show's current season. The last three digits increase unevenly from 000 at the beginning of a season, to 999 at the end. This means that a stardate of 43999 would be the last day of the third season of *Star Trek: The Next Generation.* (Of course, given this setup, the last four digits of a stardate would not contain enough information to account for an entire century.) As with the original series, an increase of a single unit within an episode corresponds to about 24 hours, even though this is inconsistent with a 365-day year. (We rationalize that relativistic time dilation makes up the difference.) *Star Trek: The Next Generation* script coordinator Eric Stillwell served as the show's keeper of stardates during the first five seasons. Every year, Eric issued a memo listing suggested stardate ranges for each upcoming episode. This memo served as a guide to help our writers keep their stardates in order. Still, as we noted earlier, stardates were never intended to stand up under close scrutiny.

Several methods of deriving stardates from calendar dates have been developed by *Star Trek* fans. One of the most popular systems arranges the year, month, and date so that a calendar date of July 20, 1969, corresponds to a stardate of 6907.20. Although this does not correspond to the stardates used on the show, many fans enjoy using them anyway.

Another conjectural theory espoused by some fans theorizes that stardates relate only to the length of the ship's current voyage. For example, a stardate of 1312 (as in "Where No Man Has Gone Before") would indicate that the log entry was made thirteen months, twelve days since the ship left port. By coincidence or design, stardate 5928, given in "Turnabout Intruder," the last episode of the original series, would correspond under this system to the sixtieth month or the end of the fifth year of the *Enterprise*'s mission.

APPENDIX E: WRITING CREDITS

The authors of this book wish to acknowledge the writers of the *Star Trek* television episodes and motion pictures, from whose work this document has been derived.

StarTrek: Original Series Year 1 (originally aired 1966-67)
"The Cage." Written by Gene Roddenberry.
"Where No Man Has Gone Before." Written by Samuel A. Peeples.
"The Corbomite Maneuver." Written by Jerry Sohl.
"Mudd's Women." Teleplay by Stephen Kandel. Story by Gene Roddenberry.
"The Enemy Within." Written by Richard Matheson.
"The Man Trap." Written by George Clayton Johnson.
"The Naked Time." Written by John D. F. Black.
"Charlie X." Teleplay by D. C. Fontana. Story by Gene Roddenberry.
"Balance of Terror." Written by Paul Schneider.
"What Are Little Girls Made Of?" Written by Robert Bloch.
"Dagger of the Mind." Written by S. Bar-David.
"Miri." Written by Adrian Spies.
"The Conscience of the King." Written by Barry Trivers.
"The Galileo Seven." Teleplay by Oliver Crawford and S. Bar-David. Story by Oliver Crawford.
"Court Martial." Teleplay by Don M. Mankiewicz and Steven W. Carabatsos. Story by Don M. Mankiewicz.
"The Menagerie, Part I." Written by Gene Roddenberry.
"The Menagerie, Part II." Written by Gene Roddenberry.
"The Squire of Gothos." Written by Paul Schneider.
"Arena." Teleplay by Gene L. Coon. From a story by Fredric Brown.
"The Alternative Factor." Written by Don Ingalls.
"Tomorrow Is Yesterday." Written by D. C. Fontana.
"The Return of the Archons." Teleplay by Boris Sobelman. Story by Gene Roddenberry.
"A Taste of Armageddon." Teleplay by Robert Hamner and Gene L. Coon. Story by Robert Hamner.
"Space Seed." Teleplay by Gene L. Coon and Carey Wilber. Story by Carey Wilber.
"This Side of Paradise." Teleplay by D. C. Fontana. Story by Nathan Butler and D. C. Fontana.
"The Devil in the Dark." Written by Gene L. Coon.
"Errand of Mercy." Written by Gene L. Coon.
"The City on the Edge of Forever." Written by Harlan Ellison.
"Operation: Annihilate!" Written by Steven W. Carabatsos.

StarTrek: Original Series Year 2 (originally aired 1967-68)
"Catspaw." Written by Robert Bloch.
"Metamorphosis." Written by Gene L. Coon.
"Friday's Child." Written by D. C. Fontana.
"Who Mourns for Adonais?" Written by Gilbert Ralston.
"Amok Time." Written by Theodore Sturgeon.
"The Doomsday Machine." Written By Norman Spinrad.
"Wolf in the Fold." Written by Robert Bloch.

"The Changeling." Written by John Meredyth Lucas.
"The Apple." Written by Max Ehrlich.
"Mirror, Mirror." Written by Jerome Bixby.
"The Deadly Years." Written by David P. Harmon.
"I, Mudd." Written by Stephen Kandel.
"The Trouble with Tribbles." Written by David Gerrold.
"Bread and Circuses." Written by Gene Roddenberry and Gene L. Coon.
"Journey to Babel." Written by D. C. Fontana.
"A Private Little War." Teleplay by Gene Roddenberry. Story by Jud Crucis.
"The Gamesters of Triskelion." Written by Margaret Armen.
"Obsession." Written by Art Wallace.
"The Immunity Syndrome." Written by Robert Sabaroff.
"A Piece of the Action." Teleplay by David P. Harmon and Gene L. Coon. Story by David P. Harmon.
"By Any Other Name." Teleplay by D. C. Fontana and Jerome Bixby. Story by Jerome Bixby.
"Return to Tomorrow." Written by John Kingsbridge.
"Patterns of Force." Written by John Meredyth Lucas.
"The Ultimate Computer." Teleplay by D. C. Fontana. Story by Laurence N. Wolfe.
"The Omega Glory." Written by Gene Roddenberry.
"Assignment Earth." Teleplay by Art Wallace. Story by Gene Roddenberry and Art Wallace.

StarTrek: Original Series Year 3 (originally aired 1968-69)
"Spectre of the Gun." Written by Lee Cronin.
"Elaan of Troyius." Written by John Meredyth Lucas.
"The Paradise Syndrome." Written by Margaret Armen.
"The *Enterprise* Incident." Written by D. C. Fontana.
"And the Children Shall Lead." Written by Edward J. Lakso.
"Spock's Brain." Written by Lee Cronin.
"Is There in Truth No Beauty?" Written by Jean Lisette Aroeste.
"The Empath." Written by Joyce Musket.
"The Tholian Web." Written by Judy Burns and Chet Richards.
"For the World Is Hollow and I Have Touched the Sky." Written by Rik Vollaerts.
"Day of the Dove." Written by Jerome Bixby.
"Plato's Stepchildren." Written by Meyer Dolinsky.
"Wink of an Eye." Teleplay by Arthur Heinemann. Story by Lee Cronin.
"That Which Survives." Teleplay by John Meredyth Lucas. Story by Michael Richards.
"Let This Be Your Last Battlefield." Teleplay by Oliver Crawford. Story by Lee Cronin.
"Whom Gods Destroy." Teleplay by Lee Erwin. Story by Lee Erwin and Jerry Sohl.
"The Mark of Gideon." Written by George F. Slavin and Stanley Adams.
"The Lights of Zetar." Written by Jeremy Tarcher and Shari Lewis.

"The Cloud Minders." Teleplay by Margaret Armen. Story by David Gerrold and Oliver Crawford.

"The Way to Eden." Teleplay by Arthur Heinemann. Story by Michael Richards and Arthur Heinemann.

"Requiem for Methuselah." Written by Jerome Bixby.

"The Savage Curtain." Teleplay by Gene Roddenberry and Arthur Heinemann. Story by Gene Roddenberry.

"All Our Yesterdays." Written by Jean Lisette Aroeste.

"Turnabout Intruder." Teleplay by Arthur H. Singer. Story by Gene Roddenberry.

StarTrek movies (originally released 1979-1991)

Star Trek: The Motion Picture. Screenplay by Harold Livingston. Story by Alan Dean Foster.

Star Trek II: The Wrath of Khan. Screenplay by Jack B. Sowards. Story by Harve Bennett and Jack B. Sowards.

Star Trek III: The Search for Spock. Written by Harve Bennett.

Star Trek IV: The Voyage Home. Story by Leonard Nimoy and Harve Bennett. Screenplay by Steve Meerson & Peter Krikes and Harve Bennett & Leonard Nimoy.

Star Trek V: The Final Frontier. Story by William Shatner & Harve Bennett & David Loughery. Screenplay by David Loughery.

Star Trek VI: The Undiscovered Country. Story by Leonard Nimoy and Lawrence Konner & Mark Rosenthal. Screenplay by Nicholas Meyer & Denny Martin Flinn.

StarTrek:The Next Generation Year 1 (first aired 1987-88)

"Encounter at Farpoint, Part I." Written by D. C. Fontana and Gene Roddenberry.

"Encounter at Farpoint, Part II." Written by D. C. Fontana and Gene Roddenberry.

"The Naked Now." Teleplay by J. Michael Bingham. Story by John D. F. Black and J. Michael Bingham.

"Code of Honor." Written by Katharyn Powers & Michael Baron.

"Haven." Teleplay by Tracy Tormé. Story by Tracy Tormé & Lan Okun.

"Where No One Has Gone Before." Written by Diane Duane & Michael Reaves.

"The Last Outpost." Teleplay by Herbert Wright. Story by Richard Krzemien.

"Lonely Among Us." Teleplay by D. C. Fontana. Story by Michael Halperin.

"Justice." Teleplay by Worley Thorne. Story by Ralph Wills and Worley Thorne.

"The Battle." Teleplay by Herbert Wright. Story by Larry Forrester.

"Hide and Q." Teleplay by C. J. Holland and Gene Roddenberry. Story by C. J. Holland.

"Too Short a Season." Teleplay by Michael Michaelian and D. C. Fontana. Story by Michael Michaelian.

"The Big Goodbye." Written by Tracy Tormé.

"Datalore." Teleplay by Robert Lewin and Gene Roddenberry. Story by Robert Lewin and Maurice Hurley.

"Angel One." Written by Patrick Barry.

"11001001." Written by Maurice Hurley & Robert Lewin.

"Home Soil." Teleplay by Robert Sabaroff. Story by Karl Guers & Ralph Sanchez and Robert Sabaroff.

"When the Bough Breaks." Written by Hannah Louise Shearer.

"Coming of Age." Written by Sandy Fries.

"Heart of Glory." Teleplay by Maurice Hurley. Story by Maurice Hurley and Herbert Wright & D. C. Fontana.

"The Arsenal of Freedom." Teleplay by Richard Manning & Hans Beimler. Story by Maurice Hurley & Robert Lewin.

"Skin of Evil." Teleplay by Joseph Stefano and Hannah Louise Shearer. Story by Joseph Stefano.

"Symbiosis." Teleplay by Robert Lewin and Richard Manning and Hans Beimle. Story by Robert Lewin.

"We'll Always Have Paris." Written by Deborah Dean Davis and Hannah Louise Shearer.

"Conspiracy." Teleplay by Tracy Tormé. Story by Robert Sabaroff.

"The Neutral Zone." Television story & teleplay by Maurice Hurley. From a story by Deborah McIntyre & Mona Glee.

StarTrek:The Next Generation Year 2 (first aired 1988-89)

"The Child." Written by Jaron Summers & Jon Povill and Maurice Hurley.

"Where Silence Has Lease." Written by Jack B. Sowards.

"Elementary, Dear Data." Written by Brian Alan Lane.

"The Outrageous Okona." Teleplay by Burton Armus. Story by Les Menchen & Lance Dickson and David Landsberg.

"The Schizoid Man." Teleplay by Tracy Tormé. Story by Richard Manning & Hans Beimler.

"Loud as a Whisper." Written by Jacqueline Zambrano.

"Unnatural Selection." Written by John Mason & Mike Gray.

"A Matter of Honor." Teleplay by Burton Armus. Story by Wanda M. Haight & Gregory Amos and Burton Armus.

"The Measure of a Man." Written by Melinda M. Snodgrass.

"The Dauphin." Written by Scott Rubenstein & Leonard Mlodinow.

"Contagion." Written by Steve Gerber & Beth Woods.

"The Royale." Written by Keith Mills.

"Time Squared." Teleplay by Maurice Hurley. Story by Kurt Michael Bensmiller.

"The Icarus Factor." Teleplay by David Assael and Robert L. McCullough. Story by David Assael.

"Pen Pals." Teleplay by Melinda M. Snodgrass. Story by Hannah Louise Shearer.

"Q Who?" Written by Maurice Hurley.

"Samaritan Snare." Written by Robert L. McCullough.

"Up the Long Ladder." Written by Melinda M. Snodgrass.

"Manhunt." Written by Terry Devereaux.

"The Emissary." Television story and teleplay by Richard Manning & Hans Beimler. Based on an unpublished story by Thomas H. Calder.

"Peak Performance." Written by David Kemper.

"Shades of Grey." Teleplay by Maurice Hurley and Richard Manning & Hans Beimler. Story by Maurice Hurley.

StarTrek:The Next Generation Year 3 (first aired 1989-90)

"The Ensigns of Command." Written by Melinda M. Snodgrass.

"Evolution." Teleplay by Michael Piller. Story by Michael Piller and Michael Wagner.

"The Survivors." Written by Michael Wagner.

"Who Watches the Watchers?" Written by Richard Manning & Hans Beimler.

"The Bonding." Written by Ronald D. Moore.

"Booby Trap." Teleplay by Ron Roman and Michael Piller & Richard Danus. Story by Michael Wagner & Ron Roman.

"The Enemy." Written by David Kemper and Michael Piller

"The Price." Written by Hannah Louise Shearer.

"The Vengeance Factor." Written by Sam Rolfe.

"The Defector." Written by Ronald D. Moore.

"The Hunted." Written by Robin Bernheim.

"The High Ground." Written by Melinda M. Snodgrass.

"Deja Q." Written by Richard Danus.

"A Matter of Perspective." Written by Ed Zuckerman.

"Yesterday's *Enterprise*." Teleplay by Ira Steven Behr & Richard Manning & Hans Beimler & Ronald D. Moore. From a story by Trent Christopher Ganino & Eric A. Stillwell.

"The Offspring." Written by Rene Echevarria.

"Sins of the Father." Teleplay by Ronald D. Moore & W. Reed Moran. Based on a teleplay by Drew Deighan.

"Allegiance." Written by Richard Manning & Hans Beimler.

"Captain's Holiday." Written by Ira Steven Behr.

"Tin Man." Written by Dennis Putman Bailey & David Bischoff.

"Hollow Pursuits." Written by Sally Caves.

"The Most Toys." Written by Shari Goodhartz.

"Sarek." Television story and teleplay by Peter S. Beagle. From an unpublished story by Marc Cushman & Jake Jacobs.

"Menage à Troi." Written by Fred Bronson & Susan Sackett.

"Transfigurations." Written by René Echevarria.

"The Best of Both Worlds, Part I." Written by Michael Piller.

StarTrek:The Next Generation Year 4 (first aired 1990-91)

"The Best of Both Worlds, Part II." Written by Michael Piller.

"Suddenly Human." Teleplay by John Whelpley & Jeri Taylor. Story by Ralph Phillips.

"Brothers." Written by Rick Berman.

"Family." Written by Ronald D. Moore.

"Remember Me." Written by Lee Sheldon.

"Legacy." Written by Joe Menosky.

"Reunion." Teleplay by Thomas Perry & Jo Perry and Ronald D. Moore & Brannon Braga. Story by Drew Deighan and Thomas Perry & Jo Perry.

"Future Imperfect." Written by J. Larry Carroll & David Bennett Carren.

"Final Mission." Teleplay by Kasey Arnold-Ince and Jeri Taylor. Story by Kasey Arnold-Ince.

"The Loss." Teleplay by Hilary J. Bader and Alan J. Alder & Vanessa Greene. Story by Hilary J. Bader.

"Data's Day." Teleplay by Harold Apter and Ronald D. Moore. Story by Harold Apter.

"The Wounded." Teleplay by Jeri Taylor. Story by Stuart Charno & Sara Charno and Cy Chermax.

"Devil's Due." Teleplay by Philip Lazebnik. Story by Philip Lazebnik and Willian Douglas Lansford.

"Clues." Teleplay by Bruce D. Arthurs and Joe Menosky. Story by Bruce D. Arthurs.

"First Contact." Teleplay by Dennis Russell Bailey & David Bischoff and Joe Menosky & Ronald D. Moore and Michael Piller. Story by Marc Scott Zicree.

"Galaxy's Child." Teleplay by Maurice Hurley. Story by Thomas Kartozlan.

"Night Terrors." Teleplay by Pamela Douglas and Jeri Taylor. Story by Sheri Goodhartz.

"Identity Crisis." Teleplay by Brannon Braga. Based on a story by Timothy DeHaas.

"The Nth Degree." Written by Joe Menosky.

"QPid." Teleplay by Ira Steven Behr. Story by Randee Russell and Ira Steven Behr.

"The Drumhead." Written by Jeri Taylor.

"Half a Life." Teleplay by Peter Allan Fields. Story by Ted Roberts and Peter Allan Fields.

"The Host." Written by Michel Horvat.

"The Mind's Eye." Teleplay by René Echevarria. Story by Ken Schafer and René Echevarria.

"In Theory." Written by Joe Menosky & Ronald D. Moore.

"Redemption, Part I." Written by Ronald D. Moore.

StarTrek:The Next Generation Year 5 (first aired 1991-92)

"Redemption, Part II." Written by Ronald D. Moore.

"Darmok." Teleplay by Joe Menosky. Story by Philip Lazebnik and Joe Menosky.

"Ensign Ro." Teleplay by Michael Piller. Story by Rick Berman and Michael Piller.

"Silicon Avatar." Teleplay by Jeri Taylor. From a story by Lawrence V. Conley.

"Disaster." Teleplay by Ronald D. Moore. Story by Ron Jarvis and Philip A. Scorza.

"The Game." Teleplay by Brannon Braga. Story by Susan Sackett & Fred Bronson and Brannon Braga.

"Unification, Part I." Teleplay by Jeri Taylor. Story by Rick Berman and Michael Piller.

"Unification, Part II." Teleplay by Michael Piller. Story by Rick Berman and Michael Piller.

"A Matter of Time." Written by Rick Berman.

"New Ground." Teleplay by Grant Rosenberg. Story by Sara Charno and Stuart Charno.

"Hero Worship." Teleplay by Joe Menosky. Story by Hilary J. Bader.

"Violations." Teleplay by Pamela Gray and Jeri Taylor. Story by Shari Goodhartz and T. Michael and Pamela Gray.

"The Masterpiece Society." Teleplay by Adam Belanoff and Michael Piller. Story by James Kahn and Adam Belanoff.

"Conundrum." Teleplay by Barry Schkolnick. Story by Paul Schiffer.

"Power Play." Teleplay by Rene Balcer and Herbert J. Wright & Brannon Braga. Story by Paul Ruben and Maurice Hurley.

"Ethics." Teleplay by Ronald D. Moore. Story by Sara Charno & Stuart Charno.

"The Outcast." Written by Jeri Taylor.

"Cause and Effect." Written by Brannon Braga.

"The First Duty." Written by Ronald D. Moore & Naren Shankar.

"Cost of Living." Written by Peter Allan Fields.

"The Perfect Mate." Teleplay by Gary Perconte and Michael Piller. Story by René Echevarria and Gary Perconte.

"Imaginary Friend." Teleplay by Edithe Swensen and Brannon Braga. Story by Jean Louise Matthias & Ronald Wilkerson and Richard Fliegel.

"I, Borg." Written by René Echevarria.

"The Next Phase." Written by Ronald D. Moore.

"The Inner Light." Teleplay by Morgan Gendel and Peter Allan Fields. Story by Morgan Gendel.

"Time's Arrow." Teleplay by Joe Menosky and Michael Piller. Story by Joe Menosky.

INDEX

Acamarian System; nearby Federation*
outposts are attacked, 116
Adams, Dr. Tristan; director of Tantalus V*
penal colony, 40;
developer of neural neutralizer*, 44
Akaar, Leonard James; new Cappellan*
leader, 52
Aldebaron Colony; from which Dehner*
comes aboard, 39
Alexander; jester to Platonians*, 64
Alexander; son of Worf and K'Ehleyr*. See
Rozhenko, Alexander
aliens. *See also* Betazoid; Borg;
Cardassians; Ferengi; Klingons;
Romulans; Vulcans
Alcyones; race which destroys last
Tarellian* ship, 91
Aldeans; seek anonymity, 7;
kidnap children from the
Enterprise-D *, 101
allasomorph; Salia* is an, 108
Archons, the; 25
Bajorans; Ro*'s people, 3, 82, 138-39,
154
Bandi; build Farpoint Station*, 95
Barolians; Pardek* participates in
talks with, 96
Bolians, 120
Bynars; engineer theft of the
Enterprise-D*, 100
Capellans; 52, 152
Chalnoth; inhabitants of Chalna*, 90
"Children of Tama, The". *See*
Tamarians
Chrysalians; Ral* negotiates for, 116
Crystalline Entity; destroys Omicron
Theta* colony, 83, 99, 84;
attacks Melona IV*, 139-40
Dachlyds; Picard,* mediates dispute
between Gemarians* and, 120
Douwd; begins living as human, 80;
Uxbridge, Rishon* does not
know Kevin* is a, 92;
Uxbridge, Kevin* turns out to be
a, 114
Edo; race found in Rubicun star
system*, 97;
worship a spaceborne god, 98
Fabrini; flee exploding star, 5;
encounter *Enterprise*, 63;
disembark from *Yonada*, 69
Gatherers, The; attack Federation*
outposts, 116;
outcasts of Acamar III*, 45
Gemarians; Picard* mediates dispute
between Dachlyds* and, 120
Gomtuu; space-faring organism, aka
Tin Man*, 5, 121
Gorn, space vehicle of is incapacitated by the Metrons*, 8
first contact between Federation*
and, 47
Horta; critter which begins cycle of
rebirth, 4;
discovered on Janus VI*, 50

Husnok; encountered, 114;
destroy Delta Rana colony*, 92;
Uxbridge, Kevin* destroys all the,
92–93
Iconians; beings known as "demons
of air and darkness", 4
favorite interest of Picard*, 81
Jarada; race contacted by *Enterprise*-
D*, 99;
last contact with prior to 2364, 86
J'naii, the; androgynous species, 146
Kalandans; construct a small planet, 5
Kataans; launch a probe containing
memories of their planet, 9
Koinonians; offer to accept responsi-
bility for Aster, Jeremy*, 115
Melkot; *Enterprise* first contacts, 60
Menthars; fight a devastating war with
the Promellians*, 9;
battle of the, 115
Metrons; one is born, 8;
Enterprise makes first contact
with the, 47
Mikulaks; use invidium*, 121
Nagilum; *Enterprise*-D meets, 106
Nanites; mechanical life form, 113
Nausicaans; Picard fights, 153
Old Ones, The; ancient civilization on
Exo III*, 3
Organians; impose peace treaty, 50
Paxans; *Enterprise*-D encounters, 131
Platonians; race found on Platonius, 7
Preservers, The; alien anthropologists
who visit Earth*, 10
Progenitors, The; race which installs a
cloaking device on Aldea, 7
Promellians; fight with Menthars*, 9;
battle of the, 115
proto-Vulcan humanoids; live on
Mintaka III*, 114
Satarrans; falsify orders in *Enterprise*-
D*'s computers, 145
Scalosians; hyper-accelerated beings,
64
Sheliak Corporate; last contact with
prior to 2366, 36;
claims Tau Cygna V* under
treaty, 71;
Federation* receives message
from, 114
Talarians; peace agreement with, 92;
Enterprise-D* encounters
Talarian ship, 101, 126
Talosians; survive by living under
ground, 3;
Enterprise visits, 35;
Spock* acts on behalf of, 47;
Pike* lives among the, 155
Tamarians; aka "Children of Tama"*,
65–66;
have no formal relation with the
Federation*, 66;
all attempts to communicate with
have failed, 138;
spacecraft of the arrives at El-

Adrel IV*, 137;
communication of is based on
metaphors, 138
Thasians; first contact with the, 43;
care for Evans, Charles, 34
Tin Man; Federation* name for
Gomtuu*, 5;
discovered near Beta
Stromgren*, 120
Trill, The; is a joined species, 5
Odan* is one of, 135
Ullians; telepathic researchers, 144
Vians; test Gem*, 62
Vorgons; travel in time to find the *Tox
Uthat*, 120, 150, 159
Zakdorn; master strategists; 112
alien spores, 50
Alpha Centauri; star system in which
Cochrane* lived, 19, 22
Alpha Leonis system, 116
Altairian conflict, 157
Amanda. *See* Grayson, Amanda
Amazing Detective Stories Magazine;
publishes Dixon Hill* stories, 12, 13
Anchilles Fever; breaks out on Stryris IV*,
96
Andorian terrorism; apparent, 56
androids. *See:* Data; Korby, Roger; Kapec,
Rayna; Norman; Ruk; Lal; Lore.
Andromeda Galaxy, 55, 58, 150
Angosian war; in which Danar* was a
soldier, 117
animated episodes, 68
Ansata Separatists,19, 78, 112, 115, 117
Apgar, Dr. Nel; head of Tanaga IV*
research station, 118
Apollo; alien known as Greek god, 6, 53
April, Capt. Robert; first commander of the
Enterprise, 31, 34, 155
Archons, the, 25
Ardra; supernatural being which visits
Ventax II, 8;
not, 130
Armens, Treaty of; between the Federa-
tion* and the Sheliak Corporate*, 36
Armstrong, Neil; first human to walk on
Earth's moon, 14
Armus; evil entity found on Vagra II*, 102
Ascension, Age of; Worf* reaches, 91
Assignment: Earth; unproduced television
show, 14
Aster, Jeremy; 115;
born, 90;
father dies of russhton infection*, 93;
returns to live with relatives, 115
Aster, Marla; mother to Aster, Jeremy*, 90;
widowed, 93;
killed, 115;
Atavachron; time portal on Sarpeidon*, 6,
68
Atlantis Project; Picard* declines director-
ship, 126
Atoz, Mr.; recovers Kirk* and company
from Sarpeidon*'s past, 68
Ayelborne; an Organian, 2

Babel Conference; concerning Coridan*'s admission to the Federation*, 38

Bailey, Lt.; assigned to duty aboard the *Fesarius**, 41

Bajoran Nationals; conduct terrorist campaign, 82, 138–39, 154

Balok, Commander; of the *Fesarius**, 41

Barclay, Reginald; transfers from the *Zhukov* *to the *Enterprise*-D, 121; assists in resolving malfunctions, 121; helps contact Cytherians*, 133

Bateson, Capt. Morgan; commands the *Bozeman**, 72, 146–47

Battle of Maxia, The; at which the *Stargazer** is nearly destroyed , 91

Bele, Commissioner; pursues Lokai* from Cheron*, 4; coerces *Enterprise* to Cheron*, 65

Benbeck; head of Moab IV* colony, 26

Bendii Syndrome; Sarek* suffers from, 122; Sarek* dies from, 142, 153

benjasidrine; drug prescribed for Sarek*'s heart condition, 56

Benton; miner on Rigel XII*, 38

Benzan; has relationship with Yanar*, 101, 107

Berthold rays; endanger Sandoval expedition*, 39, 50

Beta Aurigae; star system in which *Enterprise** meets the *Potemkin**, 68

Beta Cassius system; Haven located in, 96

Beta Five Computer; Seven, Gary*'s computer, 6

Beta Geminorum system; where *Enterprise** meets Apollo*, 53

Beta Magellan system; location of Bynaus*, 100

Beta Niobe; Sarpeidon*'s star, about to go nova, 68

Beta Portolan System; overcome by mass insanity, 10, 51

Beta quadrant; *Excelsior** assigned to, 76

Beta Renner system; location of Antica* and Selay*, 97

Beta Stromgren; *Vega IX* probe** studies the star, 120

Betazoid; Picard,*'s supervisor is, 81; delegates, Enterprise-D* is assigned to transport, 111

Bhavani, Premier; of Barzan*, 115

Big Bang, the, 1

bionic heart; Picard,* has a, 153;

Bochra, Centurion; Romulan discovered by LaForge*, 115

Bok, DaiMon; presents gift to Picard,*, 98; son of attacks the *Stargazer**, 91

Bonestall Recreation Facility; at Farspace station Earhart*, 153

Boothby; groundskeeper at Starfleet Academy*, 153, 155; discusses parrises squares*, 81; discusses Locarno*, 82; credited by Picard* with helping him graduate, 82

Boradis Sector; contains 13 Federation settlements, 82

Boradis system; *Enterprise*-D* intercepts *T'Ong* nearby, 111

Borg, the; home world of, 17; destroy Guinan*'s home planet, 40; encountered by Picard*, 88;

believed to have destroyed Neutral Zone* outposts, 103; and Q*'s statements about, 104; Starfleet* plans against, 111; simulation prepares for arrival of, 112; Shelby* in charge of tactical analysis for, 118; New Providence colony* attacked by, 124; abduct Picard*, 124; modifications, made to Picard*, 125

Brack, Mr.; aka Flint*, 7; purchases Holberg 917-G*, 30

Brahms, Dr. Leah; contributes to warp engine design of *Enterprise*-D*, 92; visits *Enterprise*-D*, 132

Brain parasite; infects Deneva*, 151

Braslota star system, 112

Bre'el star system; through which a celestial body passes, 117

Brianon, Kareen; sends distress call to *Enterprise*-D*, 107

Bringloid system; in Ficus Sector*, 110

Brown, Dr.; Korby*'s assistant, 44

Burke, John; maps space including Sherman's Planet*, 21

Cafe des Artistes; where Picard* stands up Manheim, Jenice*, 84; used as backdrop in *Star Trek VI**, 85

Campio; to marry Troi, Lwaxana*, 147

Cardassian Empire, the; annexes Bajor*, 82; forces, torture and murder Ro*'s father, 87; liaison meets with Kennelly*, 138–39; science station is destroyed, 129–30; Wars, 157

Cardassians, 154; nearly destroy culture on Bajor*, 3; pursue the *Stargazer**, 157; Bajoran nationals* conduct a terrorist campaign against the, 82

Cartwright, Adm.; responsible for Gorkon*'s murder, 77

cats, 85, 129

causality loop. *See:* temporal causality loop

cellular metamorphosis; used by Garth*, 65

cha'DIch; Klingon term for second, Picard* becomes Worf*'s, 119

Chapel, Christine; fiancée of Korby*, 44; first appearance of, 44

Chateau Picard; wine produced by Picard family, 87

Chekov, Pavel A.; born, 31, 152; involved with Galliunin, Irina*, 152; not yet part of crew, 50; discusses Sherman's Planet*, 21; incarcerated by Earth's military authorities, 15; becomes first officer of *Reliant**, 31–32;

Cheron, Battle of; ends Romulan wars*, 23

Chicago Mobs of the 'Twenties; is published in New York, Earth, 16; left on Sigma Iotia II*, 25, 58

Childress, Ben; begins mining on Rigel XII*, 38

Chorgan; member of Lornack Clan*, Yuta* tries to murder, 116

Christianity; begins on Earth, 7; evolves on 892-IV*, 56

Christopher, Capt. John; of the United

States Air Force, 155–56; captured by *Enterprise**, 14, 48, 158

Christopher, Capt. Shaun Geoffrey; son of Christopher, John*, 158; commands first Earth-Saturn probe*, 18, 48, 155–156;

Circassian cat; La Forge, Geordi*'s first pet, 85

Clark, Dr.; discusses Ventax II*, 78

Clemens, Samuel; meets Data* in Earth's past, 11, 154

Clemonds, L. Q. "Sonny"; 20th century entertainer, 20, 103

cloaking devices; Aldean, 7, 101; Klingon, 15, 77; Romulan; discovered, 43; Kirk* and Spock* steal, 61; experimental interphase version, 149

cloud creature encountered by *Enterprise**. *See* Vampire cloud

Cochrane, Zefram; inventor of warp drive, 18, 35–36, 156; born, 19; is six at *Charybdis** launch, 20; successfully demonstrates lightspeed propulsion, 20; departs for parts unknown, 22; lives on planetoid in Gamma Canaris* system, 22, 52; meets Kirk.* et al., 52

Cogley, Samuel T., 156; defends Kirk* during court-martial, 46

Coleman, Dr., assumes care of Lester*, 68

Colony 5; Evans* to be transferred to, 43

Companion, The; friend to Cochrane*, 22, 52

computer software weapon; discovered on Iconia*, 108

C-111 Star System; location of Beta III*, 25

Copernicus City, Luna; birthplace of Crusher, Beverly*, 81

cordrazine; McCoy* accidentally overdoses on , 51

Corellium Fever, 121

Corey, Donald; colony administrator, 65

Crater, Nancy; ends relationship with McCoy*, 36; arrives at planet M-113*, 37; is killed by creature on M-113*, 37, 39; creature lives in the form of, 42

Crater, Professor Robert,; arrives at planet M-113*, 37; last shape-shifter lives with, 39; creature kills, 42

Crusher, Beverly; (née Howard, Beverly) 16, 81, 117, 126–27, 154, 156; born, 81, 154; enters medical school, 85; graduates from Starfleet Academy*, 88; marries Crusher, Jack*, 88; has son, Crusher, Wesley*, 88; serves residency under Quaice*, 89, 93; views her husband's body, accompanied by Picard*, 90; travels aboard the *Hood** to meet *Enterprise*-D*, 94; becomes Chief Medical Officer aboard *Enterprise*-D*, 95; leaves *Enterprise*-D* to accept

*Items marked with an asterisk are also listed elsewhere as main entries. Individual **episodes** can be found alphabetically under "episodes." Look for **aliens**, **ships**, and **planets**, grouped alphabetically under those general headings.

Crusher, Beverly (CONTINUED)
    position at Starfleet Medical*,
        105;
    returns to Enterprise-D*, 113
Crusher, Lt. Jack; 87, 126, 153, 154
    marries Beverly Howard, 88
    dies on the Stargazer*, 90
Crusher, Wesley, 154;
    born, 88, 154;
    Crusher, Jack* creates holographic
        message for, 87;
    is 5 years old when father dies, 90;
    travels aboard the Hood* to meet the
        Enterprise-D*, 94;
    moves onto Enterprise-D* with his
        mother, 85;
    Picard* confesses Starfleet Academy*
        entrance failure to, 81;
    fails Starfleet Academy entrance
        exam, 87;
    appointed acting ensign, 101;
    is assigned regular bridge duty, 105;
    leads geological survey, 110;
    promoted to full ensign, 123;
    takes leave for Starfleet Academy*
        exams, 110;
    accepted to Starfleet Academy*, 123;
    views holographic message from his
        father, 126;
    enrolls in Starfleet Academy*, 128;
    repeats sophomore year at Starfleet
        Academy*, 147
Custodian, The; computer controller
    on Aldea*, 7

Danar, Roga; soldier from Angosia*, 116,
    117
Dar, Caithlin; Romulan ambassador to
    Nimbus III*, 57
Daro, Glinn; Cardassian*, 157
Darwin genetic research station; source of
    aging disease, 107;
    super-children developed at, 89
Data, 153;
    constructed by Soong*; 83;
    is activated, 153;
    discovered on Omicron Theta*, 83–
        84, 99;
    is thrown back into Earth's past, 11;
    discusses television, 20;
    ruled sentient by Starfleet*, 84;
    enters Starfleet Academy*, 84;
    graduates from Starfleet Academy*,
        86;
    abducted by Fajo*, 122;
    locates video of Pardek*, 96;
    successfully repairs temporal anomaly
        caused by Manheim*, 102
    states calendar date from which Star
        Trek: The Next Generation is
        based, 104;
    assigned to Maddox*, 108;
    ruled to be sentient, 84, 108;
    hijacks Enterprise-D*, 126;
    is taken over by an alien, 145–46;
    commendations, 153
Davila, Carmen; killed by Crystalline
    Entity*, 139–40
Daystrom, Dr. Richard; born, 28;
    invents duotronic computers, 31;
    designs M-5 computer*, 58;
    wins Nobel* and Zee-Magnees*
        prizes, 31
Daystrom Technological Institute; named
    for Daystrom*, 31;
    warp design for the Enterprise-D*

done here, 92;
    Galor IV Annex, Starfleet Research,
        expresses an interest in Data*'s
        work, 119
Debin, father of Yanar*, 107
Decker, Commodore Matt, commands
    Constellation*, 53
Decker, Will; takes command of the
    Enterprise*, 69;
    assigned as executive officer, 70;
    reported missing in action, 70;
    character would have appeared in
        second TV series, 71
Deela; Scalosian* queen, 64
Deep Space Station K-7; Enterprise*
    summoned to, 55
Dehner, Dr. Elizabeth; joins Enterprise*
    crew, 39
de Laure Belt; location of Tau Cygna V*, 71
Delos system; Enterprise-D* studies solar
    flares in, 102
Delphi Ardu star system; Enterprise-D* is
    incapacitated in, 97
Delt, Hester; medical trustee, 105
delta-ray; exposure to severely injures
    Pike, Christopher*, 44
Delta Vega Mining Facility; Enterprise*
    attempts to quarantine Mitchell* at, 39
DeSoto, Jonathan; captain of the Hood*
    when Riker* was first officer, 95, 153
destruct command sequence of Enter-
    prise*; same in ST III* and original
    series, 65
Devos, Alexana; discusses Ansata
    Separatists*, 78;
    accepts job as security director on
        Rutia IV*, 112;
    assists in recovering Crusher,
        Wesley* and Picard* 117
dicosilium, 118
dilithium; crystals (previously lithium
    crystals*) use of in Enterprise*, 40;
    Enterprise* sent to secure mining
        rights to, 54;
    Klingons protect access to, 60;
    chamber designed, 92;
    chamber, defective hatch installed in,
        125;
    vector calibrations, performed by
        LaForge*", 126;
    chamber explodes, 134
DiMaggio, Joe; hitting record of is broken,
    19
discommendation; Worf* accepts, 119;
    Worf*'s honor restored, 136
"Doe, John"; survivor found, 123
Dohlman; Elaan* is the, 60
Dokachin; discusses T'Pau*, 97
doomsday machine; planet-killing device,
    4, 53
Duana; discusses the building of The
    Custodian*, 7
duotronic computer technology;
    invented by Daystrom*, 28, 31
Duras; Klingon, son of Ja'rod*, 86;
    seeks to lead Klingon Council, 127;
    murders K'Ehleyr*; killed by Worf*,
        127;
    family of, 86
Durken, Chancellor; Picard,* shares
    Chateau Picard* with, 87

Earth, 24;
    first single-celled organisms evolve
        on, 2;
    visited by "Preservers"*, 10;

humans taken to be raised by aliens,
    6;
visited by the Platonians*, 6, 7;
Flint* originated on, 7, 67;
United Nations* chartered on, 13;
adopts nuclear test ban treaty, 13;
launches Pioneer 10, 15;
launches Viking I, 15;
Eugenics Wars* on, 16, 49, 157;
Khan* is dictator over one quarter of,
    16, 49;
launches Voyager 6*, 17;
launches Nomad*, 18;
first contact with extraterrestrial life,
    155;
first contact with Vulcan*, 155;
Charybdis* launched from, 20;
nuclear war, 21, 156-57;
nuclear winter on, 157;
at war with Romulans, 23, 24;
colonizes Moab-IV*, 26;
home of Grayson, Amanda*, 28;
birth planet of Kirk*, 29;
birth planet of Uhura*, 30;
birth planet of Sulu*, 30;
San Francisco Yards Facility* in orbit
    near, 31;
Enterprise* travels into past of, 59;
Platonians* visited, 63–64;
threatened by V'ger*, 70;
environmental havoc wreaked on, 75;
Gorkon* en route to, 77;
threatened by the Borg*, 125;
Earth Colony Two; Kirk, George Samuel*
    wanted to transfer to, 51;
Earth Station McKinley; Enterprise-D* is
    repaired at, 125, 126
Earth-Saturn probe; Christopher, John*'s
    son to head, 48, 155–56, 158
Einstein, Albert; publishes special theory of
    relativity, 12
Elaan; the Dohlman* of Elas*, 60
Elbrun, Tam; Betazoid specialist in alien
    contact, 121, 153;
    notes how long Tin Man* has been
        wandering, 5
Eminiar Star System; war begins in the, 10
Endar; Talarian* captain who adopts
    Rossa, Jerimiah*, 90, 92, 126
Endicor; mission to this planet was
    disrupted, 109
energy barrier; Valiant* encounters this at
    the edge of the galaxy, 20
    Enterprise* encounters, 39, 62
Enterprise (space shuttle); first space ship
    so named, undergoes flight testing, 15
Enterprise, U.S.S. (NCC-1701); 35,154–55;
    commissioned, 155;
    computers based on duotronic
        technology*, 31;
    launched from San Francisco Yards
        with April* in command, 31;
    returns from first 5-year mission, 34;
    leaves on its second 5-year mission,
        34;
    ends its second 5-year mission (under
        Pike*), 36;
    embarks on and completes its third 5-
        year mission (under Pike*), 37;
    embarks on its fourth 5-year mission,
        (the first under Kirk*), 38–39;
    begins routine star mapping, 40;
    goes across energy barrier*, 62;
    destruct command sequence of, 65;
    returns to San Francisco orbital
        drydock*, 68, 69;

undergoes refitting, 69;
returned to service to investigate
  V'ger*, 70;
embarks on and returns from its fifth
  5-year mission, the second
  under Kirk*, 71;
retired from active service; becomes
  training vessel, 72–73;
commanded by Spock*, 71;
comandeered by Kirk*, 74;
due to be scrapped, 74;
destroyed, 74

Enterprise-A (NCC-1701A), 155;
  enters service under Kirk*, 75, 155;
  undergoes refitting, 75;
  captured by Sybok* and company, 75;
  helps to save peace conference, 77;
  final mission (?) of, 78
Enterprise-B (NCC-1701B); *Excelsior*
  class* vessel, 155
Enterprise-C (NCC-1701C);
  Ambassador class* vessel, 155;
  nearly destroyed defending Klingon
    outpost, 85;
  opens a temporal rift, 158–59;
  unable to render assistance to
    Narendra III*, 159
Enterprise-D (NCC-1701D); 154–55;
  early design work begun on, 85
  system work progresses on, 92
  launched from Utopia Planitia Fleet
    Yards*, 94;
  complement of is 1, 014, 127;
  destruct sequence of, 65;
  first contact with the Q*, 95
  first contact with the Tkon Empire*, 97
  first contact with the Ferengi*, 97
  discovers mythical planet Aldea*, 101
  first contact with Romulans since
    2311, 103
  first contact with the Borg*, 110
  takes part in strategic simulation, 112
  collides with the *Bozeman**, 146-47
  recreated in flowers, 114

episodes (**Boldfaced** pages have main
  synopsis for that episode.)
  "Allegiance", 90, 119, **120;**
  "All Our Yesterdays", 6, 8, **68;**
  "Alternative Factor, The", **48;**
  "Amok Time", 7, 29, 30, 42, **53,** 156,
    157;
  "And the Children Shall Lead", **61;**
  "Angel One", 79, 92, **99–100;**
  "Apple, The", 5, 33, **54;**
  "Arena", 8, **47–48;**
  "Arsenal of Freedom, The", 90, 94,
    101–2, 157;
  "Assignment: Earth", 6, 14, **59,** 158;
  "Balance of Terror", 8, 23, 24, **43,**
    155, 157;
  "Battle, The", 82, 91, **98;**
  "Best of Both Worlds, The, Part I",
    111, 118, **124;**
  "Best of Both Worlds, The, Part II", 81,
    125, 126;
  "Big Goodbye, The", 13, 19, 86, **99,**
    100;
  "Bonding, The", 84, 87, 90, 93, **115;**
  "Booby Trap", 9, 92, **115;**
  "Bread and Circuses", 8, 21, 34, 37,
    56, 156 ;
  "Brothers", 99, **126;**
  "By Any Other Name", **58;**

  "Cage, The", 3, 29, 31, **35,** 37, 44,
    46, 155, 156;
  "Captain's Holiday", 31, 93, **120,** 159;
  "Catspaw", **52;**
  "Cause and Effect", 72, 76, 82, 90,
    146–47, 154, 159;
  "Changeling, The" 17, 18, **54;**
  "Charlie X", 9, 24, 32, 34, **43;**
  "Child, The", 78, 83, **105–6;**
  "City on the Edge of Forever, The", 1,
    12, 19, **51,** 158;
  "Cloud Minders, The", 9, **66,** 151;
  "Clues", **131,** 153;
  "Code of Honor", **96;**
  "Coming of Age", 79, 81, **101;**
  "Conscience of the King, The", 24, 32,
    37, **45;**
  "Conspiracy", 88, **103,** 153, 154;
  "Contagion", 4, 81, **108;**
  "Conundrum", 79, 81, 83, 84, 85, 87,
    88, 91, **145,** 153, 154, 157;
  "Corbomite Maneuver, The", 40, **41,**
    78, 162;
  "Cost of Living", **147;**
  "Counter Clock Incident, The", 31;
  "Court Martial", 24, 33, 34, 38, **46,**
    151, 152, 155, 156;
  "Dagger of the Mind", 40, **44;**
  "Darmok", 65–66, **138;**
  "Datalore", 35, 83, 84, **99,** 153;
  "Data's Day", 31, **129;**
  "Dauphin, The", 10, **108;**
  "Day of the Dove", 27, 31, 50, **63;**
  "Deadly Years, The", 29, 38, **55,** 151,
    156;
  "Defector, The", 23, 113–14, **116;**
  "Deja Q", **117–18;**
  "Devil in the Dark, The", 4, 48, **50;**
  "Devil's Due", 9, 78, **130–31;**
  "Disaster", **140,** 154;
  "Doomsday Machine, The", 4, 44, **53;**
  "Drumhead, The", 24, 35, 94, 95, 103,
    118, 125, **134;**
  "Elaan of Troyius", **60;**
  "Elementary, Dear Data", 91, 93, **106;**
  "Emissary, The", 76, 82, 92, **111;**
  "Empath, The", 58, **62;**
  "Encounter at Farpoint", 19, 21, 28,
    84, 91, 94, **95,** 122, 126, 152,
    153, 154, 156–157;
  "Enemy, The", **115,** 157;
  "Enemy Within, The", 42
  "Ensign Ro", 3, 82, 84, 87, **139,** 153,
    154;
  "Ensigns of Command, The", 36, 71,
    113, **114;**
  Enterprise Incident, The", 8, 60, **61,**
    156;
  "Errand of Mercy", 2, **50–51;**
  "Ethics", **146;**
  "Evolution", 26, 76, 87, 88, **113,** 154;
  "Family", 82, 87, 88, 89, **126,** 153;
  "Final Mission", 21, **128,** 155, 156;
  "First Contact", 27, 87, **131–32;**
  "First Duty, The", 24, 35, 56, 72, 79,
    81, 82, 86, 90, 94, **147,** 153, 155,
    157;
  "For The World Is Hollow and I Have
    Touched the Sky", 5, **63,** 69;
  "Friday's Child", **52,** 152;
  "Future Imperfect", **128;**
  "Galaxy's Child", 92, **132;**
  Galileo Seven, The", **45–46;**

  "Game, The", **141,** 155;
  "Gamesters of Triskelion, The", **57;**
  "Half a Life", 8, 79, **134,** 153;
  "Haven", 91, **96,** 153–54, 157;
  "Heart of Glory", 87, 89, 91, **101,** 154;
  "Hero Worship", 84, **144;**
  "Hide and Q", **98;**
  "High Ground, The", 19, 115, 78, 112,
    117;
  "Hollow Pursuits", **121,** 154;
  "Home Soil", **100;**
  "Host, The", 5, 11, 83, **135;**
  "Hunted, The", **116–17;**
  "I, Borg", **148;**
  "I, Mudd", **55;**
  "Icarus Factor, The", 82, 83, 86, 88,
    89, 90, 91, **109–10,** 154, 157;
  "Identity Crisis", 91, 93, **133;**
  "Imaginary Friend", **148,** 154;
  "Immunity Syndrome, The", **57–58,**
    155;
  "Inner Light, The", 9, **149;**
  "In Theory", 134, **136;**
  "Is There in Truth No Beauty?", 31,
    62;
  "Joanna", earlier verson of "Way to
    Eden, The", 67, 152 ;
  "Journey to Babel", 24, 28, 30, 32, 35,
    38, **56,** 61, 151, 152;
  "Justice", 97, **98;**
  "Last Outpost, The", 2, **97;**
  "Legacy", 83, 84, 89, 93, 94, **127,** 154;
  "Let That Be Your Last Battlefield", 4,
    23, 64, **65;**
  "Lights of Zetar, The", 9, **66;**
  "Lonely Among Us", 94, **97;**
  "Loss, The", **128;**
  "Loud as a Whisper", 8, 9, **107;**
  "Manhunt", **111;**
  "Man Trap, The", 36, 37, 39, **42;**
  "Mark of Gideon, The", **65–66,** 151;
  "Masterpiece Society, The", 26, **144,**
    156;
  "Matter of Honor, A", **108;**
  "Matter of Perspective, A", **118;**
  "Matter of Time, A", 21, **143,** 157, 159;
  "Measure of a Man, The", 31, 91, **108,**
    153;
  "Menage a Troi", **122–23,** 153;
  "Menagerie, The, Part I", 3, 31, 34,
    35, 37, 38, 44, **46,** 122, 155;
  "Menagerie, The, Part II", **46–47;**
  "Metamorphosis", 19, 22, **52;**
  "Mind's Eye, The", **135–36;**
  "Miri", 14, 24, **44–45;**
  "Mirror, Mirror", 42, **54–55;**
  "Most Toys, The", 89, **121–22;**
  "Mudd's Women", 38, 39, 40, **41–42;**
  "Naked Now, The", 43, 83, 84, 89, 93,
    96, 154;
  "Naked Time, The", **42–43,** 159;
  "Neutral Zone, The", 16, 20, 80, **103;**
  "New Ground", 67, **143,** 156;
  "Next Phase, The", 87, 148–**149,** 154;
  "Night Terrors", **132,** 153;
  "Nth Degree, The", **133;**
  "Obsession", 33, 35, 36, **57;**
  "Offspring, The", 31, **119;**
  "Omega Glory, The", **59;**
  "11001001", 65, 92, **100;**
  "Operation: Annihilate!", 10, 21, 25,
    29, 40, 45, **51;**
  "Outcast, The", 24, **146,** 157;

*Items marked with an asterisk are also listed elsewhere as main entries. Individual **episodes** can be found alphabetically under "episodes."
Look for **aliens**, **ships**, and **planets**, grouped alphabetically under those general headings.

episodes (CONTINUED)

"Outrageous Okona, The", 101, **106**;
"Paradise Syndrome, The", 10, **60**;
"Patterns of Force", 33, 55, **58**;
"Peak Performance", 74, 91, **112**, 153, 157;
"Pen Pals", 27, **110**;
"Perfect Mate, The", **148**;
"Piece of the Action, A", 16, 25–26, 57, **58**, 156;
"Plato's Stepchildren", 7, **63–64**;
"Power Play", 11, 25, 26, **145–46**;
"Price, The", 81, **115–16**;
"Private Little War, A", 36, 45, **56–57**, 64;
"Qpid", 2, 4, **134**;
"Q Who?", 17, 25, 40, 104, 108, **110**;
"Redemption, Part I", 80, **136**, 159;
"Redemption, Part II", 15, 84, 85, 86, 88, 105, **137–38**, 156, 159;
"Remember Me", 89, 93, 95, 107, **126–27**;
"Requiem for Methuselah", 7, 30, **67**;
"Return of the Archons", 6, 25, **49**;
"Return to Tomorrow", 2, 3, **58**;
"Reunion", 67, 77, **127**, 156, 157;
"Royale, The", 19, 20, 21, **109**;
"Samaritan Snare", **110**, 153, 155;
"Sarek", 42, 56, 69, **122**, 152–53;
"Savage Curtain, The", 8, **67**, 156, 157;
"Schizoid Man, The", **107**;
"Shades of Grey", **112**;
"Shore Leave", 34, **47**, 151;
"Silicon Avatar", 84, **139–40**;
"Sins of the Father", 85, 86, 87, **119**, 154, 156;
"Skin of Evil", 83, **102**;
"Space Seed", 16, 18, **49–50**, 54, 157;
"Spectre of the Gun", **60**;
"Spock's Brain", 6, **61–62**;
"Squire of Gothos, The", **46, 47**;
"Survivors, The", 80, 92–93, **114**;
"Symbiosis", 24, 92, **102**;
"Taste of Armageddon, A", 10, 24, 27, **49**;
"That Which Survives", 5, 57, **64**;
"This Side of Paradise", 38, 39, **50**, 151;
"Tholian Web, The", **62–63**, 157;
"Time's Arrow", 11, 105, **149**, 154;
"Time Squared", **109**, 158;
"Tin Man", 5, **120–21**, 153;
"Tomorrow is Yesterday", 14, 18, 24, 43, **48–49**, 155–56, 158;
"Too Short a Season", 72, 80–81, 92, 98, **99**;
"Transfigurations", **123**;
"Trouble with Tribbles, The", 21, 30–31, **55–56**, 151;
"Turnabout Intruder", **68**, 93, 127, 151, 162;
"Ultimate Computer, The", 28, 31, **58–59**;
"Unification, Part I", 8, 29–30, 72, 78, 96, 97, **141–42**, 152, 156, 157;
"Unification, Part II", 8, **142**, 156;
"Unnatural Selection", 89, 106, **107**, 154;
"Up the Long Ladder", 22–23, **111**, 156;
"Vengeance Factor, The", 21, 45, 75, 80, 88, **116**;
"Violations", 85, 90, 143, **144**, 154;
"Way to Eden, The", **66–67**, 152;

"We'll Always Have Paris", 84–85, 88, **102**;
"What Are Little Girls Made Of?", 3, 29, 37–38, **44**, 51;
"When the Bough Breaks", 7, **101**;
"Where No Man Has Gone Before", 17, 20, 27, 30, 31, 33, 34, **39**, 40, 49–50, 68, 78, 151;
"Where No One Has Gone Before", **96–97**, 153;
"Where Silence Has Lease", **106**;
"Whom Gods Destroy", 23, 32, 33, 63, **65**, 151, 155;
"Who Mourns for Adonais?" 6, 31, **53**, 152;
"Who Watches the Watchers?" **114**;
"Wink of an Eye", **64**;
"Wolf in the Fold", 12, 15, 21, 22, 23, 41, **54**;
"Wounded, The", 117, **130**, 154, 157;
"Yesterday's *Enterprise*", 85, 86, 87, 105, 107, **118**, 155, 158–59;
"Yesteryear", **29–30**;

Epsilon Mynos System; location of Aldea*, 7, 101
Epsilon 9 Station; destroyed by V'ger*, 70
Epsilon Pulsar cluster; *Enterprise*-D* to do survey of, 110
Ersalope Wars, 157
Esoqq; Picard* meets, 90, 120
Estragon, Professor Samuel; employer of Vash*, 93, 120
Eugenics Wars; of Earth, 16, 158; *Botany Bay*￼ seeks refuge from, 49
European Hegemony, 156
Evans, Charles; is born, 32; sole survivor of space ship crash, 34; rescued from Thasus*, 43
Exo; star which begins to fade, 3

Fabrini System; in which sun goes nova, causing *Yonada* to be built, 5, 63
Fajo, Kivas; Zibalian trader, 89, 121, 122
Fal-tor-pan; Vulcan ceremony, 24, 74
Famous Spock Nerve Pinch (FSNP). *See:* Vulcan nerve pinch
Farpoint Station, 95
Farspace station Earhart, 155
Federation. *See* United Federation of Planets
Felicium; addictive drug used to halt plague on Onara*, 24
Ferengi; first contact with, 97; steal an energy converter, 97; negotiate for wormhole, 116; spacecraft nearly destroys *Stargazer*, 90–91; neural control device, Bok* uses one on Picard*, 98; interfere with strategic simulation, 112; kidnap Troi*, 122
Ferris, Galactic High Commissioner; supervises transfer of vaccines, 45
Ficus Sector; location of Bringloid* and Mariposa*, 22, 110, 111
Finnegan; friend of Kirk*, 34
Finney, Benjamin; befriends midshipman Kirk*, 33; reported killed, 46, 151
Finney, Jamie; daughter of Finney, Benjamin*, named after Kirk, James T.*, 33
Flint, 30; born in Mesopotamia, 7; identities of, 67

Fontana, Dorothy C., predicts day of moon launch, 14; chooses name for Christopher, John*'s son, 18; discusses UESPA*, 24; discusses Spock*'s age, 29; writes "Yesteryear"*, 30; discusses Kirk*'s middle name, 39–40 discusses dilithium* crystals, 40; discusses "Naked Time"* and "Tomorrow Is Yesterday"*, 43; discusses *Enterprise*'s computer, 48; comments on Klingons and Romulans, 51; and "Joanna"*, 67; discusses animated episodes, 68; discusses McCoy*'s marriage and divorce, 152; discusses episodes being filmed out of order, 162
Fox, Ambassador, 49
FSNP (Famous Spock Nerve Pinch). *See* Vulcan nerve pinch
Fundamental Declarations of the Martian Colonies, 156

Gaetano; *Galileo*￼ crewmember killed on Taurus II*, 46
Gagarin, Yuri; first human to travel in space, 13
Galaxy M33; *Enterprise*-D* ends up in, 97
Galileo; builds first astronomical telescope, 10
Galliunin, Irina; Chekov*'s love interest, 67, 152
Galorndon Core; *Enterprise*-D* responds to distress call from, 115; Vulcan ship sent to, 142
Gamma Arigulon System; *Enterprise*-D* investigates radiation anomalies in the, 127
Gamma Canaris System; Cochrane, Zefram* ended up in the, 22; Kirk* *et al.* crash in the, 52
Gamma Erandi Nebula; *Enterprise*-D* departs to the, 122
Gamma 7A System; *Enterprise** ordered to, 57; attacked by space creature, 57–58
Garrett, Capt. Rachel; captain of *Enterprise*-C*, 85, 155
Garrovick, Capt.; Kirk* assigned to serve with, 35, 36
Garth, Fleet Capt.; leads Axanar* peace mission, 33; crew of mutinies, 63; takes over colony, 65; Kirk*'s personal hero, 32, 33
General Order 7; *Enterprise*￼ is in violation of, 46
Genesis Device; Khan* attempts to steal the, 73
Genesis Project; *Reliant*￼ investigates Ceti Alpha V* for, 54; 73 proposal presented to Federation, 72; *Reliant*￼ assigned to the, 73; Khan* steals the, 73
Gill, John; one of Kirk*'s instructors, 32, 33; Federation* loses contact with, 55, 58; violates Prime Directive*, 58
Gleason, Capt.; captain of the *Zhukov*￼, 121
Gomez, Sonya; comes aboard *Enterprise*-D* at Starbase 173, 108
Gorgan; entity which attemps to control *Enterprise*￼, 61

Gorkon; Klingon chancellor, 77
Gossett; begins mining on Rigel XII*, 38
Gowron; succeeds K'mpec* as head of
	Klingon council, 127, 136, 137, 141
Graves, Dr. Ira; Brianon* assistant to, 107
Grayson, Amanda; 32, 151;
	marries Sarek*, 28;
	mother to Spock*, 29;
	opposes heart operation for Sarek*,
		56;
	oversees Spock*'s retraining, 74;
	dies, 153;
	appears in Star Trek features, 56
Green, Colonel; of Earth, being calling itself
	is found on Excalbia*, 67, 157
Guardian of Forever; time gate, 158–59,
	created billions of years ago, 1;
	McCoy* goes through the, 12;
	used as method of time travel, 159
Guinan, 154;
	age of, 154;
	has several children, 154;
	meets Data* in Earth's past, 11;
	encounters Q*, 25;
	home planet is destroyed by the
		Borg*, 40;
	serves on the Stargazer*, 154;
	recruited to tend Ten Forward
		Lounge*, 105

Haftel, Adm. Anthony; requires Data* to
	turn Lal* over to Starfleet*, 119
Hahn, Adm.; says Crusher, Wesley* will be
	welcome at Starfleet Academy* one
	year later, 123
Halkan System; Enterprise* visits, 54
Hanson, Adm. J. P.; plans defenses
	against Borg* attack, 111;
	assigns Shelby* to Enterprise-D* in
		charge of defense tactics against
		Borg*, 124, 118;
	lost at battle of Wolf 359*, 125
Haro, Cadet; Bolian*, 120
Haskins, Dr.; talks to Tylor*, 35
Have Gun, Will Travel, 59
Hawkins; Federation* ambassador seized
	on Mordan IV*, 98
Hayashi System; Enterprise-D* en route to
	120
Hedford, Commissioner Nancy; crashes
	with Kirk* et al., 52;
	merges with the Companion*, 22
helium fusion ignition; Timicin* uses, 79
Hengist; carries nasty entity to Argelius*
	from Rigel IV*, 41
Henoch; Sargon*'s enemy, 58
Hickman, Paul; serves on the Victory*, 133
Hill, Dixon; stories are published, 13;
	simulation malfunctions, 100
Hitler, Adolph; develops atom bomb, 158;
	wins World War II, 12, 157
Hodin, prime minister of Gideon*, 65
holodeck; malfunction traps Picard*, 99;
	used to recreate events on research
		station, 118
Hor'gon; Risa*n sculpture with erotic
	connotation; Riker* asks Picard,* to
	bring him one, 120
Hotel Royale; book found on Theta VIII*,
	20
Howard, Beverly. See Crusher, Beverly
Howard, Isabel; mother of Crusher,
	Beverly*, 81

Howard, Paul; father of Crusher, Beverly*,
	81
How to Advance Your Career Through
	Marriage; how Crusher, Jack*
	proposes to Crusher, Beverly*, 88
Humpback whales (Megaptera
	novaeangliae); brought to 23rd
	century by Kirk* et al., 75, 158
hyper-acceleration; what Scalosians* suffer
	from, 64
hyperonic radiation; kills one-third of
	colonists from Artemis*, 71
hyronalyn; used to treat radiation sickness,
	156
hytritium compound; Enterprise-D*
	procures from Fajo*, 121–22

I-chaya; name of Spock*'s pet sehlat*, 29
Ilecom star system; reports temporal
	distortion, 102
Ilia, Lt.; reported missing in action, 70;
	would have appeared in second TV
		series, 71
Imzadi; Betazoid* term for "beloved", 153
Innis, Valeda; Electorine of Haven*, 96
inter-dimensional transport device; Ansata
	separatists* begin using, 115
interphase phenomenon; causes loss of
	Defiant* and Kirk*, 62;
	basis for experimental Romulan
		cloaking device, 149
invidium; contamination causes system
	malfunctions aboard the Enterprise-
		D*, 121
Iowa, Earth; birthplace of Kirk*, 29
Ireland, reunification of, 19
Irina. See Galliunin, Irina
Ishikawa, Hiro; O'Brien, Keiko*'s father,
	154
Ishikawa, Keiko. See O'Brien, Keiko*

ja'chuq, Klingon rite of succession
	overseen by Picard*, 127, 136
Jameson, Adm. Mark; born, 72;
	commands Gettysberg*, 80–81;
	actions exacerbated civil war on
		Mordan IV*, 92;
	Karnas* requests assistance from, 98,
		99
Jameson, Ann; marries Jameson, Adm.
	Mark*, 80
Jared; leader of Ventax II*, 9
Ja'rod; accused of treason by Klingon High
	Council* member, 119;
	father of Duras*, 86, 119;
	discovered to have plotted with
		Romulans, 86
Jarok, Adm. Alidar; Romulan admiral;
	defects to Enterprise-D* to save
		Romulans from themselves, 23,
		113–14, 116. See also Setal
Jev; commits telepathic rapes, 143, 144
Jewel of Thesia; Benzan* gives Yanar* the,
	101
Jones, Dr. Miranda; links minds with
	Kollos*, 62;
	joins law firm, 444
Jono, aka Rossa, Jerimiah*, 90
Justman, Robert; his gag about
	Roddenberry, Gene* became "May
	the Great Bird of the Galaxy ...", 42

Kaelon, Timicin*; tries to extend life of a

star, 79
Kahless the Unforgettable; united the
	Klingon homeworld*, 156;
	being calling itself found on Excalbia*,
		67
Kahlest; Worf*'s nursemaid, 86;
	survives Khitomer Massacre*, 87
Kahs-wan; Vulcan survival ordeal, 29
Kalandan Colony, 64
Kalomi, Leila; romantically attracted to
	Spock*, 38, 151
Kang; Klingon commander, 63
Kapec, Rayna; android companion to
	Flint*, 67
Karapleedeez, Onna; dies, 103
Karidian, Anton; aka Kodos the Execu-
	tioner*, 32;
	performs on Planet Q*, 45
Karidian, Lenore; born, 32
	responsible for series of murders, 45
Karidian company; theatrical, begins official
	tour, 37
Karnas; leader of Mordan IV*, 80
	reports terrorists have seized
		hostages on Mordan IV*, 98
katra; Vulcan concept of the soul; Spock*'s
	returned from McCoy*, 74
Kavis Alpha neutron star; detonates, 26;
	Stubbs* to deliver a probe into, 113
Kavis Alpha sector; location of Kavis Alpha
	neutron star*, 87, 113
Keel, Capt. Walker; Satie* enlists aid of,
	103;
	introduces Crusher, Beverly* and
		Crusher, Jack*, 88, 154;
	killed, 153
Keeler, Edith; social worker, 19, 157;
	McCoy* prevents death of, 12, 158;
	Kirk* et al. discover she must die, 51
K'Ehleyr, Klingon emissary, 157;
	has unresolved relationship with
		Worf*, 92;
	resumes relationship with Worf*;
		conceives a child, 111;
	comes aboard Enterprise-D* with
		Rozhenko, Alexander*, her son,
		127
	murdered by Duras*, 127
Kelvin Empire; first contact with, 58;
	may become uninhabitable, 150
Kennelly, Adm.; meets with Cardassians*,
	138–39
Kesla; murderous entity on Rigel IV*, 41
Khan, Zor; Sarpeidon leader who exiles
	Zarabeth, 6
Khan Noonien Singh; rises to power and is
	overthrown, 16;
	attempts to take over Enterprise*, 49;
	heads colony at Ceti Alpha V*, 49, 54;
	discovered on Ceti Alpha V*, 73;
Kirk, Aurelan; talks about arrival of parasite
	critters, 45;
	dies, 10, 51
Kirk, George Samuel; brother to Kirk,
	James T.*, 29;
	has three sons, 51;
	killed, 51
Kirk, James T., 151;
	born, 29;
	middle initial was "R", 39–40;
	survives massacre committed by
		Kodos*, 32;
	enrolls in Starfleet Academy*, 32;

*Items marked with an asterisk are also listed elsewhere as main entries. Individual **episodes** can be found alphabetically under "episodes."
Look for **aliens**, **ships**, and **planets**, grouped alphabetically under those general headings.

Kirk, James T. (CONTINUED)
meets Finney, Benjamin*, 33;
meets Mitchell, Gary*, 33;
meets Finnegan*, 33–34;
becomes Chief of Starfleet Operations, 69;
commandeers *Enterprise*, 74;
commands Klingon Bird of Prey*; returns to Earth's past, 15;
romantically involved with Ruth, 34, 151;
serves as ensign on *Republic*, 33;
is lieutenant on *Farragut*, 33, 35, 36;
commands first planet survey, 36;
graduates from Starfleet Academy*, 35;
awarded commendations, 35, 151;
romantically involved with Wallace, Janet*, 38;
promoted to *Enterprise* captain, 38;
embarks on his first 5-year mission, 38–39;
and Areel Shaw, 38, 46;
has a son, Marcus, Dr. David*, 37;
is court martialed, 46, 75;
discusses Kirk, George Samuel*'s (his brother's) children, 51;
brother and sister-in-law killed on Deneva, 10, 51;
meets Cochrane, Zefram*, 22, 52;
marries Miramanee*, 60;
his first 5-year mission ends, 68;
promoted to admiral, 69;
reinstated as captain of *Enterprise*, 70;
embarks on and returns from second 5-year mission, 71;
accepts appointment to Starfleet Academy*, 71;
Khan* attempts vengeance on, 73
informed *Enterprise* is to be scrapped, 74;
demoted to Captain; assigned to *Enterprise*-A*, 75;
brings two Humpback whales* back to 23rd century, 75;
sent to penal colony Rura Penthe'*, 77;
last mission of (?), 78;
suffers Vegan choriomeningitis, 151;
dies (?), 151
Kirk, Peter; nephew of Kirk, James T.*; survives parasite critter attack; has two brothers, 51
Kitchen sink; of *Enterprise*-D, inexplicably excluded from book but indexed anyway, 1701
Klaa, Capt.; commands Klingon Bird of Prey*, 75
Klingon Empire; first contact with, 27;
Federation relations degenerate, 28;
fights Donatu V * battle with Federation*, 30;
dispute with Federation* peaks, 50;
Federation* negotiations with break down, 28, 50;
Spock* negotiates peace between Federation* and, 29;
claims Sherman's Planet*, 55–56;
diplomatic representative of is seized by Sybok*, 75;
and peace with Federation*, 76;
alliance with Romulans collapses, 77;
embroiled with war with Federation* in alternate timeline, 118, 159;

alliance with the Federation*, 152;
ambassador; demands extradition of Kirk*, 74–75;
expedition; makes first contact with Ventax II*, 78;
government; settles Nimbus III* in joint venture with Romulans and the Federation*, 57;
Romulans try to destabilize, 80;
High Command; informs Rozhenko, Sergey* that Worf* has no living relatives, 87;
High Council; accuses Mogh* of conspiring with the Romulans, 119;
Homeworld; 119. *See also* Qo'noS;
Kahless* unites the, 67, 156;
Kahlest* returns to, 87
Klingon-Romulan Alliance; explained, 61;
collapses, 77
Klingons;
first contact with, 27;
first appearance of, 51;
relations with Federation* deteriorate, 28;
develop Bird of Prey with new firing capabilities, 77;
launch a peace initiative, 77;
have contact with Romulans between 2311 and 2364, 80;
changes in appearance of, 51, 70;
civil war, 136-138
K'mpec; Klingon High Council leader, 156;
refuses to admit new evidence, 119;
requests meeting with Picard,*, 127;
is fatally poisoned, 127
Kobayashi Maru; Starfleet Academy* test, 35, 73
Kodos the Executioner; seizes power on Tarsus IV*, 32;
revealed to be Karidian, Anton*, 45
Kohlinar; Vulcan mental training, 69
Kollos; Medusan ambassador, 62
Kolrami, Serna; Zakdorn tactician, 112
Komack, Adm., 157
Konmel; Klingon renegade, 101
Koon-ut-kal-if-fee; Vulcan mating challenge, 53
Korby, Dr. Roger; does research on Exo III*, 3;
puts his personality into an android body, 44;
last message received from, 37–38
Korris; Klingon renegade, 91, 101
Kosinsky; supervises tests of *Enterprise*-D* warp systems, 96, 97
Krieger waves; Apgar, Dr.* believed to be developing, 118
Krioisian colonies; rebel attacks of are backed by Romulans, 135–36
Krocton Segment; represented by Pardek*, 72,
K'Temok; commands *T'Ong*, 76
Kurn, 154;
Worf*'s brother; is born, 86;
is left in Lorgh*'s care, 86;
Klingon High Command unaware of, 87;
comes aboard *Enterprise*-D*, 119;
honor is restored to family by Gowron*, 136
Kushell, Secretary; of Straleb*, 107
Kyle, Cmdr.; assigned to *Reliant*, 73

LaBarre, France, Earth; birthplace of Picard,*, 79;

Picard,* visits, 88, 126
La Forge, Alvea; La Forge, Geordi*'s mother, 154
La Forge, Edward M.; La Forge, Geordi*'s father, 154
La Forge, Geordi; born, 82, 154
did not have VISOR* at age 5, 84;
is caught in fire, 84;
gets a cat, 85;
enters Starfleet Academy*, 90;
graduates from Starfleet Academy*, 91;
serves aboard the *Victory*, 93, 133;
travels on the *Hood* to meet *Enterprise*-D*, 94;
begins service on *Enterprise*-D*, 154;
assumes duties of conn, 95;
promoted to full lieutenant; becomes Chief Engineer, 105;
builds model of the sailing ship *Victory*, 106;
promoted to lt. cmdr., 113;
is brainwashed by Romulans, 135–36
Lal; Data*'s android daughter, 119
Lambda Paz; third moon of Pentarus III*, 128
Landru; leader who builds computer to care for his people after his death, 5-6;
his planet-running computer system, 5–6, 25, 49
Latimer; *Galileo* crewmember, killed on Taurus II*, 46
Lazarus; dual entity causes space/time discontinuity, 48
Lefler, Robin; mission specialist, 141
Legaran Conference; placed in doubt by Sarek*'s illness, 122
Legarans; agree to dipolomatic relations with the Federation*, 122, 152;
Sarek* begins negotiations with, 69
Leighton, Dr. Thomas; one of 9 survivors of Tarsus IV*, 32;
calls *Enterprise* to Planet Q*, 45;
killed, 45
Leijten, Lt. Cmdr. Susanna; fellow crewmember of LaForge* on the *Victory*, 93;
viral parasite removed from, 133
Leka, Governor; of Peliar Zel*, 11
Lester, Dr. Janice; abducts Kirk*, 68, 151
Lincoln, Abraham; *Enterprise* encounters being calling itself, 67
Lincoln, Roberta; assistant to Seven, Gary*, 14
Lindstrom; *Enterprise* sociologist; remains on Beta III*, 49
Linke, Dr.; Federation* researcher on Minara II*, 58
lithium crystals (later dilithium*); *Enterprise* use of, 40, 41
lithium miners; Kirk* deals with; women elect to stay with, 41, 42
Llangon Mountains; on Vulcan*, Spock* went to as a child, 29
Locarno, Nick; accepted into Starfleet Academy*, 94;
expelled from Starfleet Academy*, 147;
Boothby* discusses, 82
Locutus of Borg; aka Picard, Jean-Luc*, 125
Lokai; leads a revolution on Cheron*, 4;
steals shuttlecraft; coerces *Enterprise* to* return to Cheron*, 64, 65
London Kings; shortstop of breaks

DiMaggio, Joe*'s hitting record, 19
Lore; Data*'s brother; helps Crystalline Entity* to destroy Omicron Theta*, 83; discovered disassembled , 99; returns, 126
Lorenze Cluster; Minos* located in the, 101–2
Lorgh; will take care of Kurn*, 86
Lornack Clan; of Acamar III* begins a bitter feud, 21; massacre Tralesta Clan*, 21, 75
Losira; last surviving Kalandan*, 64
Loskene, Commander; Tholian* commander, 62
Louvois, Phillipa; prosecuted Picard,* for loss of the Stargazer*, 91; Judge Advocate General; rules Data* to be sentient, 108
Lutan; Ligonian* leader, 96
Lya Station Alpha; Enterprise-D* takes survivors of Solarion IV* attack to, 139

M-5 multitronic computer; testing of, 58–59
M-5 tests; are reason why Data* must relinquish Lal*, 119
MacDuff, Keiran; Satarran* who poses as Enterprise-D* executive officer, 145
Macet, Gul; Cardassian* officer, 130
Maddox, Cmdr. Bruce; Data* is assigned to, 108; Data* records personal log for, 129
Mallory; helps Kirk* get into Starfleet Academy*, 32, 33
Malurian System; is attacked, 54
Mandl; director of terraforming project on Velara III*, 100
Manheim, Dr. Paul; scientist, 88; creates temporal distortion during experiments, 102
Manheim, Jenice; is stood up by Picard,*, 84
Manway, Dr.; is killed, 54
Marcus, Dr. Carol; gives birth to Marcus, David*, 37, 151; presents Genesis Project*, 72
Marcus, Dr. David; son of Kirk, James T.*,is born, 37, 151; killed by Klingons, 74
Mar Oscura Nebula; Enterprise-D* enters on a scientific mission, 136
Marouk, Sovereign; attempts to reconcile her people, 88; sovereign of Acamar III*, 116; discusses peace, 45
Marr, Dr. Kila; loses her son in an attack on Omicron Theta*, 140
Marrab Sector, 149
Marta; inmate killed by Garth*, 65
Marvick, Lawrence; designer of Enterprise*, 31, 62
Maxia, Battle of, 82, 98
Maxia Zeta Star System; Stargazer* nearly destroyed in, 90–91
Maxwell, Capt. Benjamin; captain of the Phoenix*, 129–30, 154, 157 captain of the Rutledge*, 154
"May the Great Bird of the Galaxy Bless your Planet", 42
M'Benga, Dr; Enterprise* staff physician, 57, 64
McCoy, David; father of McCoy, Leonard H.*, 28, 74, 152

McCoy, Joanna; daughter of McCoy, Leonard H.*, 67, 152
McCoy, Leonard H., 152; goes into Sarpeidon*'s past, 6; born, 28, 152; enters medical school, 32, 152; graduates from medical school, 35, 152; ends romantic relationship, 36; is assigned to the Enterprise*, 40; has baby named after him, 52; says Spock* must return to Vulcan* or die, 53; treats Sarek* for heart attack, 56; replaces Spock*'s brain, 62; cured of xeno-polycythemia*, 63; marries Natira*, 63; retires from Starfleet*, enters private practice, 69; returns to duty, 70; promoted to full Commander, 71; Spock*'s katra* removed from, 74; length of service on Enterprise*, 78; travels aboard the Hood* , 94; commendations, 152; tours Enterprise-D*, 95; daughter McCoy, Joanna*, 67, 152; and appearance in "Encounter at Farpoint"*, 122;
McGivers, Marla; Enterprise* historian, 18; elects to stay with Khan*, 49
McKinney*; death of related to conspiracy in Starfleet*, 103
Meltasion Asteroid Belt; Enterprise-D* tows freighter through the, 128
Mempa Sector; Duras*' family bases are destroyed in, 137; Gowron*'s forces retreat from the, 138
Mendez, Commodore; discusses Pike, Christopher*'s accident, 44; investigates return of Enterprise*, 46
Mendez, Emilita; formerly of the Victory*; steals a shuttlepod and heads for Tarchannan III*, 133
Mendon, Ensign; officer from Benzar*, 108
Merrick, R. M.; meets Kirk* at Starfleet Academy*, 34; captain of Beagle*, 37, 56
Mesopotamia; Flint* is born in, 7;
Miller, Steven, father of Miller, Wyatt*, 153–54;
Miller, Wyatt; Troi, Deanna*'s betrothed, 96, 153–54
Minara; star which explodes, 62
Miramanee; Kirk* marries, 60; killed, 60
Miri; 14; Enterprise* landing party aided by, 44
Mitchell, Gary, 17; meets Kirk, James T.*, 33; mutated by energy barrier, 39
Modean System; La Forge, Geordi* lives in the, 154
Mogh; Worf*'s and Kurn*'s birth father, 86, 119; suspects Ja'rod* of plotting with the Romulans, 86; accused of conspiring with the Romulans at Khitomer*, 119; Gowron* restores honor to the family of, 136
Mojave, Earth; birthplace of Pike*, 155
Morath; Kahless*'s brother, 67, 156

Morgana Quadrant; 106
Morrow, Adm.; and age of Enterprise*, 31; informs Kirk* that the Enterprise* is to be scrapped, 74
M'rel; Gowron* is son of, 136
M24 Alpha System; Triskelion* is located in the, 57
Mudd, Harcort Fenton; 41, 55; convicted, 39; is turned over to Federation* authorities, 42
Mull, Penthor; accused of leading a raid on the Tralesta Clan*, 80
Mullen, Steven; first officer of the Essex*, 25
Murasaki Quasar, 46, 129
Mutara Sector, 50; Botany Bay* found near the, 49, 50; Regula 1 space station* located in the, 72; Reliant* patrols the, 73; Genesis Planet* located in the, 74

Narsu, Adm. Uttan; of Starbase 12, 25
Natira; Yonada*'n high priestess, marries McCoy*, 63; leads Fabrini* off Yonada*, 69
Nazi Germany; recreated on Ekos*, 58; wins World War II* in alternate timeline, 158
Nebula FGC-47; Enterprise-D* investigates the, 148
Nel System; Jev* commits rape in the, 143
Neral; Romulan proconsul, 142
neural neutralizer; Van Gelder* suffers adverse effects from, 44
Neutral Zone, Klingon, 76
Neutral Zone, Romulan; 43, 55, 61, 103–4, 110, 157; establishment of, 23; Iconia* located in, 108
Neutral Zone outposts; Delta Zero 5, 110; Tarod IX, 110; 2–4, destroyed in apparent Romulan attack, 34, 43
New Jersey, Earth; Rasmussen* is from, 150
New Martim Vaz aquatic city; Uxbridge, Kevin* and Uxbridge, Rishon* meet at, 80;
New Paris Colonies; plague threatens the, 45, 46
New Providence colony; on Jouret IV*, 123 found destroyed, 124
New United Nations; rules Earth citizens, 19
Ngame Nebula, 131
Nichols, Dr.; invents transparent aluminum, 15, 158
Nobel Prize; won by Daystrom*, 28, 31
Noel, Helen; investigates Tantalus V* with Kirk*, 44
Nogura, Adm.; reinstates Kirk* as captain of the Enterprise*, 70
Norman; android, assumes control of Enterprise*, 55
Nova Squadron; Crusher, Wesley* belongs to; suffers a flight accident, 147
Nuclear Age; of Earth, 59
Nuclear Test Ban Treaty; adopted on Earth, 13
null space pockets; found near the J'naii

*Items marked with an asterisk are also listed elsewhere as main entries. Individual **episodes** can be found alphabetically under "episodes." Look for **aliens**, **ships**, and **planets**, grouped alphabetically under those general headings.

planet*, 146
Number One, 44
Nuress, Dr. Susan; conducts experiments
  on Plasma Plague*, 78
Nuria; leader on Mintaka III*, 114

O'Brien, Keiko (née Ishikawa, Keiko); 154;
  marries O'Brien, Miles Edward*, 129;
  conceives a child, 131;
  gives birth to O'Brien, Molly*, 140;
O'Brien, Miles Edward; 126, 140;
  serves on the *Rutledge*, 154, 157;
  marries Keiko Ishikawa, 129;
  conceives a child, 131;
  is taken over by an alien, 145–46
O'Brien, Molly; daughter of O'Brien, Miles
  Edward* and O'Brien, Keiko*, born,
  140
Odan; Trill* Ambassador, 11;
  Crusher, Beverly*'s love interest, 83,
  135
Odona; daughter of Hodin*, 65
Offenhouse, Ralph, 103
Okona, Thadiun; discusses Jewel of
  Thesia, 101;
  claims filed against, 106–7
Omega Sagitta System, 106–7
Omega System; location of Holberg 917-
  G*, 30, 67
Omicron Delta Region; new planet found in
  the, 47
Omicron Theta system; where Data was
  buillt, 99
Onias Sector; near Neutral Zone, 128
Orelious System; *Enterprise*-D at, 115
Organian Peace Treaty; imposed, 50–51
Orion terrorism, 56, 65
Orta; Bajoran* terrorist leader, 139
Outpost Seran-T-One; *Enterprise*-D*
  dilithium chamber designed at, 92
Ozaba, Dr.; Federation* researcher on
  Minara II*, 58

Palm Leaf of Axanar; Kirk* is awarded the,
  33, 155
Pardek; Romulan senator, 72, 96, 141,
  142;
  exposed as Romulan operative, 78
Paris, France; Earth, Federation*
  president's office is located in, 24;
  Café des Artistes in, 84, 85
Parmen; leader of the Platonians*,
  Philiana*'s husband, 7, 63–64
parrises squares; game; Starfleet* wins
  tournament of, 81, 100
Parvenium Sector; *Enterprise*-D at, 149
Peliar Zel system; Odan* mediates at, 135
Pergium; mineral mined on Janus VI*, 48,
  50
Perrin; Sarek*'s second human wife, 122,
  153;
  implies Vulcan is where Spock* lives,
  140;
  survives Sarek*, 142
Phelen System; *Enterprise*-D goes to, 146
Philiana; Parmen*'s wife, 7
Phoenix Cluster; *Enterprise*-D surveys, 141
Phyrox plague, 120
Picard, Jean-Luc, 153;
  born, 79, 153;
  relatives of, 153;
  becomes only freshman to ever win
    Starfleet Academy marathon, 81;
  enters Starfleet Academy*, 81;
  graduates from Starfleet Academy*,
    81–82, 153;

credits Boothby* with helping him to
  graduate, 82, 155;
has heart replaced, 110, 153, 155;
attends marriage of Sarek's son, 152;
begins 22-year mission aboard the
  Stargazer, 82, 90–91;
stands up Manheim, Jenice*, 84;
is close friend of Keel*, 88;
fled from Cardassians* while aboard
  the *Stargazer*, 130;
Crusher, Jack* dies under command
  of, 90;
is courtmartialed for loss of the
  Stargazer, 91;
meets Yar, Tasha* on Carnel*, 94;
assumes command of the *Enterprise*-
  D*, 94, 95;
violates the Prime Directive*, 98;
is offered job as Commandant of
  Starfleet Academy*, 101;
recruits Guinan* to tend Ten Forward
  lounge*, 105;
duplicate discovered, 109;
believed to be a deity, 114;
becomes Worf*'s *cha'DIch*, 119;
meets Sarek*, 153;
melds minds with Sarek*, 122;
is abducted by the Borg*, 124;
Borg* use him to defeat armada, 125;
visits LaBarre*, 88, 126, 153;
appointed arbiter of succession by
  K'mpec*, 127;
conducts O'Brien* wedding, 129;
as arbiter of succession, rules Toral*'s
  claim inadmissible, 136;
accepts Worf*'s request for reinstatement, 138;
invites Ro Laren* to remain as
  crewmember, 139;
to deliver commencement address at
  Starfleet Academy*, 147
Picard, Marie; Picard, Robert*'s wife;
  Picard, Jean-Luc*'s sister-in-law, 126
Picard, Maurice; Picard, Jean-Luc* and
  Picard, Robert*'s father, 79
Picard, Robert; Picard, Jean-Luc*'s
  brother, 82, 87, 126
Picard, Yvette; Picard, Jean-Luc* and
  Picard, Robert*'s mother, 79, 153
Picard maneuver; Picard,* uses to save the
  Stargazer, 91
Pike, Christopher, 36, 155, 156;
  Spock* served with, 29, 31, 34;
  begins *Enterprise*'s second 5-year
    mission (his first), 34;
  ends his first 5-year mission on
    Enterprise, 36;
  completes his second 5-year mission,
    37;
  promoted to Fleet Captain, 38;
  is injured in accident, 44;
  kidnapped by Spock*, 46–47;
  and Vina*, 3, 29;
  remains on Talos IV*, 47
Piper, Dr. Mark, replaced by McCoy* as
  Medical Officer of *Enterprise*, 40
planet killer, aka doomsday machine, 4, 53
**planets. *See also*: Cardassia; Earth;
Khitomer; Qo'noS; Romulus;
Vulcan**
Acamar III, 116;
  home of the Lornack* and the
    Tralesta* clans, 21, 75;
  peace is established on, 45;
  home of Mull, Penthor*, 80;
  home of Marouk*, 88;

Enterprise-D * goes to, 116;
Aldea; once thought to be mythical,
  discovered by *Enterprise*-D*, 7,
  101;
Alderaan; never visited by the
  Enterprise, 2001;
Alfa 177; geological survey is
  performed on, 42;
Algeron IV; visited by *Enterprise*-D*,
  101;
Alpha Eridani II; on which two women
  are murdered, 23;
Altair III; DeSoto* visits, 153;
Altair VI; *Enterprise** on a diplomatic
  mission to, 53;
Angel 1, 79, 92, 100;
Angosia III; petitions for admission
  into the Federation*, 116–17;
Antede III; petitions for admission into
  the Federation*, 111;
Antica; *Enterprise*-D * transports
  delegates from, 97;
Antos IV; inhabitants of are killed, 63,
  65;
Archer IV; *Enterprise*-D goes to, 119;
Ardana; a cloud city is built on, 9, 66;
Argelius II; on which killings occur,
  14–15, 21, 22, 23, 41, 54;
Ariannus; decontaminated, 65;
Atlec; birthplace of Yanar*, 101;
  Picard* mediates dispute with,
  106–7;
'audet IX; from which *Enterprise*-D
  transfers plasma plague*
  specimens, 105;
Axanar; visited by Kirk*, 33, 151, 155;
Babel; planetoid, 56;
Bajor; on which civilization flourished
  500,000 years ago, 3;
  remaining population of is
    tortured by Cardassians*,
    82;
  birthplace of Ro Laren*, 84, 82
Barzan; location of wormhole, 115–16
Benzar; birthplace of Mendon*, 108;
Beta Agni II; contamination threatens
  water supply on, 121, 122;
Beta III; Landru*'s planet, 5, 25;
  Archon* disappears nearby, 49;
Beta IV; *Enterprise** goes to on a
  supply mission, 47;
Beta Kupsic; *Enterprise** goes to, 110;
Beta XIIA; visited by *Enterprise**, 63;
Betazed; birthplace of Troi, Deanna*,
  83;
  Troi* visits, 98;
  trade conference is held on, 122;
Bolarus IX; Haro*'s home, 120;
Boradis III; first Federation* outpost in
  Boradis system*, 82;
Bre'el IV; whose moon's orbit is
  disrupted by a black hole, 117;
Brekka; on which felicium is manufac-
  tured, 24, 92, 102;
Bringloid V; 22, 111;
Browder IV; on which *Enterprise*-D*
  participates in terraforming
  mission, 120;
Bynaus; of the Bynars*, 100;
Camus II; on which archaeological
  survey is conducted, 68, 127;
Canopius Planet; home of the poet
  Tarbolde*, 17;
Capella IV; visited by *Enterprise**, 52;
Carnel; Enterprise-D* responds to
  distress call from; 94;

planets (CONTINUED)

Cerebus III; source of youth drug, 99;

Cestus III; outpost is destroyed on, 47, 48;

Ceti Alpha V; on which Khan* and followers are left, 49;
    Starfleet* never informed (?) of the colony on, 50;
    orbit disrupted by explosion of Ceti Alpha VI*, 54;
    Reliant survives Genesis explosion near, 73;

Ceti Alpha VI; explodes, 54;

Chalna; visited by Picard* and *Stargazer*, 90
    birthplace of Esoqq*, 120;

Cheron; revoltution on, 4;
    Lokai* and Bele* are from, 64;
    Enterprise coerced to go to, 65;

Cor Caroli V; on which *Enterprise*-D* eradicates Phyrox plague*, 120;

Coridan; Babel Conference* concerns, 38;
    admission to Federation* discussed and approved, 56, 152;

Cygnet XIV; *Enterprise* puts in for repairs at, 48;

Cygnia Minor; famine on, 45;

Daled IV; upon which civil war starts; rotates only once per year, 10;
    Enterprise-D* transports Salia* to, 108;

Danula II; where Starfleet Academy* marathon is held, 81;

Daran V; collision with *Yonada* and is averted, 63;
    Yonada's inhabitants will disembark on planet near the star, 5;

Delos IV; where Crusher, Beverly* does residency, 89;

Delta Rana IV; the Uxbridges* join this colony, 80, 92;
    Enterprise-D* gets a distress call from, 114;

Deneb IV; *Enterprise*-D* is assigned to explore space beyond, 94;
    location of Farpoint Station*, 95;

Deneva; is colonized, 25 ;
    overcome by same insanity that took Beta Portolan*, 10, 21, 45, 51;

Denius III; source of evidence about Iconia*, 4;
    Yamato participates in archaeological studies at, 108;

Dimorus; Kirk* and Mitchell* at, 151;

Donatu V; battle of; fought near Sherman's Planet*, 30;

Drema IV; from which Data* receives radio transmissions, 110; *See also:* Selcundi Drema;

Durenia IV; *Enterprise*-D at, 126–27;

Dytallix B; Picard,* meets Keel* on, 103;

Eden; Severin* is in search of, 66;

892-IV; has society which develops like that of Earth's ancient Rome, 8;
    on which the Beagle * crashes, 37, 56;

Ekos; where Gill* is stationed, 55, 58;

El-Adrel IV; Tamarian ship at, 137;

Elas; where Elaan* is from, 60;

Elba II; penal colony on, 65;

Emila II; *Enterprise*-D at, 118;

Eminiar VII; at war with Vendikar*, 10, 27;
    contacted by *Valiant*, 27;
    contacted by *Enterprise*, 49;

Epsilon Canaris II; shuttlecraft picks up Hedford* on, 52;

Epsilon IX; *Enterprise*-D goes to, 110;

Excalbia; *Enterprise* studies, 67;

Exo III; becomes uninhabitable, 3;
    Korby* does his research on, 3, 37–38;
    visited by *Enterprise*, 44;

Gagarin IV; planet; location of Darwin research station*, 89, 107;

Galen IV; birth of Rossa, Jerimiah*, 90, 92;

Gamelan V; radioactive freighter orbits, 21;

Gamma Hromi II; *Enterprise*-D* visits the planet, 116;

Gamma Hydra IV; *Enterprise* visits, 55;

Gamma II; planetoid, 57;

Gamma Tauri IV; Ferengi* steal an energy converter from, 97;

Gamma Trianguli VI; home of the machine god Vaal, 5, 54

Garon II; Ro Laren* courtmartialed after disaster on, 84, 154;

Gault; farm planet where Worf* is raised, 87, 154;
    Rozhenkos* move from, 89;
    Worf*'s step-brother returns to, 91;

Gemaris V; *Enterprise*-D* visits, 120;

Genesis Planet; *Grissom* assigned to study , 74;
    disintegrates, 74;

Gideon; limited Federation* contact agreed to by, 65, 151;

Gothos; Trelane*'s planet, 47;

Gravesworld; *Enterprise*-D* leaves landing party on, 107;

Haven; Tarellian* spacecraft attempts to make planetfall on, 91;
    Enterprise-D* en route to, 96

Holberg 917-G; purchased by Brack*, 30;
    Enterprise diverts to, 67;

Iconia; on which civilization flourished 200,000 years ago, 4;
    Varley* locates the planet, 108;

Ingraham B; attacked by parasite critters, 40, 51;
    struck by same insanity that took Deneva, 10;
    vessel from transfers parasite critters, 45;

Isis III; *Enterprise*-D* visits the planet, 99;

Janus VI; home of the Horta*, 4, 48, 50, 51;

Jaros II; Ro Laren* is in prison on, 154;

Jouret IV; location of New Providence colony*, 123, 124;

Kaelon II; which adopts the custom of the Resolution*, 8;

Timicin* born on, 79;

Kataan; which suffers a drought and its sun going nova, 9;

Kavis Alpha IV; Nanites* granted rights to colonize, 113;

Kenda II; Quaice* goes to, 126

Klavidia II; *Enterprise*-D* transports Salia* from, 108;

Lavinius V; struck by same insanity that took Deneva, 10, 21, 51;

Legara IV; Sarek* goes to, 122;

Ligon II; *Enterprise*-D* to establish treaty with, 96;

Lya III; *Enterprise*-D* heads for starbase at, 117;

Mab-Bu VI, 145;
    criminals are imprisoned on the moon of, 11;
    Essex is lost on, 25;

Makus III; *Enterprise* to transfer vaccines from, 45, 46;

Malcor II; Durken* is from, 87;
    Enterprise-D* visits for covert observation, 131–32;

Mariposa; *Enterprise*-D* discovers another colony on, 111;

Mars; *Viking I* lands on, 15;
    Utopia Planitia Fleet Yards* orbit, 94;

Melona IV; *Enterprise*-D* assists in survey of, 139, 140;
    attacked by Crystalline Entity*, 139–40;

Memory Alpha; all personnel killed on; Romaine, Lt.* returns to, 66;

Merak II; botanical plague threatens , 66;

Mimas; to which Nova Squadron* is evacuated, 147;

Minara II; sun of explodes, 58, 62;

Minos, 157;
    Rice* dies on, 90;
    Drake destroyed at, 94, 101–?;

Mintaka III; *Enterprise* visits, 114;

Miri's planet, 14;
    Federation* sends help to, 45;

Mizar II; Tholl, Kova*'s home planet, 119, 120;

Moab IV; colonized, 26, 144;

M-113; Crater, Nancy* and Crater, Robert* arrive on, 37;
    Crater, Nancy* is killed on, 37, 39;
    Enterprise visits, 42;

Mordan IV; Federation* hostages are held on, 80–81;
    civil war ends on, 92;
    Jameson*s are transported to, 99;

Mudor IV, 140;

Nahmi IV, 121;

Narendra III; *Enterprise*-C* crew captured on, 85;
    incident on is a turning point in Klingon/Federation relations, 85, 156;
    Yar, Tasha* did not die on, 159;
    Enterprise-C* unable to render aid to, 159;
    Enterprise-C* is destroyed at, 155;

Nasredine; *Enterprise*-D visits, 109;

Nelvana III; Romulan outpost reported

---

*Items marked with an asterisk are also listed elsewhere as main entries. Individual **episodes** can be found alphabetically under "episodes."
Look for **aliens**, **ships**, and **planets**, grouped alphabetically under those general headings.

planets (CONTINUED)
on, 116;
Nestoriel III; Guinan* comes aboard
Enterprise-D* at, 105;
Neural; early-draft name of Tyree*'s
planet, 36;
Nimbus III; "Planet of Galactic Peace",
is settled in joint venture
between Klingons, Romulans,
and the Federation, 57;
diplomatic representatives
seized on, 75;
Obi IV; plasma plague* breaks out
on, 78;
Oceanus IV, 141;
Ogus II, 126;
Omega IV; Exeter lost at, 59;
Omicron Ceti III; settled by Sandoval
expedition*, 38, 39, 50;
Omicron Pascal, 100;
Omicron Theta; Soong* escapes from,
83;
Data* is discovered on, 83–84 ;
Lore* believed destroyed near,
126;
Crystalline Entity* destroyed
colony on, 139;
Onara, 24;
Ophiucus III, Mudd*'s women
originally bound for, 41–42
Orelious IX; war near, 9;
Organia; inhabitants transform
into beings of pure energy, 2;
invaded by Klingons, 50;
Ornara; plague on, 24, 92, 102;
Pacifica, 103, 111;
Parliament; planetoid, 97;
Peliar Zel, 10–11, 135;
two moons of have a dispute, 83;
Alpha, moon, 135;
Beta, moon, 135;
Pelleus V, 100;
Pentarus II; Nenebek* crashes on
third moon of, 128;
Penthara IV, 143;
Persephone V, Enterprise-D at, 99;
Planet Q; home of Leighton, 45;
Platonius; settled by the Platonians, 7,
64;
Pollux IV; where Greek-god aliens
settle after leaving Earth, 6, 53;
Psi 2000, 42–43;
Pyris VII; home of aliens with ability to
transmute matter, 52;
Qualor II; location of Surplus Depot
Zed-15*, 97;
the T'pau* should be at, 142;
Rachelis; has outbreak of plasma
plague disease, 105;
Remus; one of the home planets of
the Romulans, 23;
Rigel VII; Pike* visits, 35;
Rigel XII; lithium mining on, 38, 41–
42;
Risa; pleasure planet;
Tox Uthat* is hidden on, 93, 150;
Picard,* takes shore leave on,
120;
La Forge,* is en route to when
captured by Romulans,
135;
Romii; alternate name for Remus*, 23;
Romulus; one of the home planets of
the Romulans; 23;
Rubicun III; home of the Edo, 98;
Rutia IV; Ansata separatists* are

located on, 19, 78, 112, 115,
117;
Sarona VIII, Enterprise-D visits, 102;
Scalos; home of hyper-accelerated
beings, 64;
Selay; seeks admission to Federation,
97;
Selcundi Drema; begins to disinte-
grate, 27;
Septimus Minor; Artemis* was
supposed to go to the planet, 71
Sha-ka-Ree; at center of galaxy, 75;
Sherman's Planet; first mapped, 21;
Donatu V* battle is fought near,
30;
under dispute, 55;
Sigma Draconis VI; to which Spock's
brain is taken, 6, 61–62;
Sigma III; has mining colony, 98;
Sigma Iotia II, 58, 156;
culture of is created from book
left on, 16, 25;
message from the Horizon*
comes from, 57;
Solais V; war begins on, 8;
Riva* transported to, 107;
Solarian IV; attacked by terrorists,
138, 139;
Straleb; birthplace of Benzan*, 101;
Picard* mediates dispute with,
106–7;
Stryris IV; Anchilles Fever* breaks out
on, 96;
Surata IV; where Riker* stubs his toe,
112;
Tagus III, 134;
civilization flourished here two
billion years ago, 2;
first archaeological expedition
was 25,000 years ago, 4;
Talos IV, 35, 46;
war on, 3;
Columbia* crashes on, 29;
Pike, Christopher* greets
survivors on, 39, 156;
Tanaga IV; location of Dr. Apgar's
research station, 118;
Tantalus V; penal colony, 44;
Van Gelder* assigned to, 40;
Tarchannan III; colonists disappear
on, 93;
Mendez* and Hickman* head for,
133;
Tarellia; plague planet, 91, 157;
Tarsas III; location of Starbase 74*,
100;
Tarsus IV; site of Kodos*' executions,
32;
Tau Alpha C; Kosinski*'s assistant,
the Traveler*, is from, 96, 127;
Tau Cygna V; ceded to the Sheliak*,
36;
Artemis* lands on, 71;
Federation* colonists must be
removed from, 114;
Taurus II; Galileo* crashes on, 46;
Tessen III; threatened by asteroid,
147;
Thasus, 32, 34, 43;
inhabitants of evolved into forms
of pure energy, 9;
Theta VII; needs vaccines, 57;
T'lli Beta; two-dimensional life forms
discovered near, 128;
Triacus, and Starnes expedition, 61;
Triskelion; home of gamesters, 57;

Troyius; at war with Elas*, 60;
Turkana IV; birthplace of Yar, Tasha*,
83;
birthplace of Yar, Ishara*, 84;
Yar, Tasha* escapes from, 89,
154;
Potemkin* makes last contact
with prior to 2367, 93;
Arcos* crew lands on, 127;
Tycho IV; vampire cloud at, 36, 57;
Tyree's planet; Klingons attempt to
influence politics on, 45;
Vagra II; shuttlecraft crashes on, 102;
Yar, Tasha* dies on, 118, 159;
Yar, Tasha* does not die on in
alternate timeline, 118, 159;
Valo I; Orta* is located on the third
moon of, 139;
Valt Minor; new home of Kamala, 148;
Vandor IV; planet, source of temporal
distortion, 102;
Velara III; planet, 100, 101;
life forms of are threatened by
terraforming project, 100;
Vendikar; at war with Eminiar VII*, 10,
27, 49;
Ventax II; believes in Ardra, 78;
visited by Ardra*, 8, 78, 130;
Wolf 359; armada meets the Borg*
vessel at, 124;
armada destroyed at, 125;
Zeta Alpha II; Lalo* is located near,
124;
Zetar; nearly all life is destroyed on, 9,
66
plasma plague; breaks out on Obi VI*, 78;
Enterprise-D* transports specimens
of, 105
Plato; inspiration for Parmen* and
Platonians*, 7, 64
Pleiades Cluster; star system, 100
Plexicorp; where transparent aluminum* is
invented; Nichols, Dr.* is plant
manager of, 15, 158
poker, played on Enterprise-D*, 108
Pon farr; Spock* experiences, 53
Potts, Willie; his brother's practical joke
endangers the life of, 126
Pozaron; city on Mizar II*, 119
Praxillus system; Helium Fusion Ignition*
process tried in the, 134
Praxis; Klingon moon, explodes, 77
Prieto, Ben; pilot of shuttle which crashes
on Vagra II*, 102
Prime Directive; Starfleet General Order
Number One, 56, 102, 117, 131, 146,
156;
not yet instituted, 25;
violated, 58, 59, 98, 109, 110;
does not apply, 100
Project Genesis. See Genesis Project
Project Ozma; one of Earth's first attempts
to search for extraterrestrial life, 13
Psi 2000 infection, 43;
kills crew of Tsiolkovsky*, 93, 96
psycho-simulator test, Merrick* fails a, 56
Pulaski, Katherine, 154;
married three times, 154;
discusses plasma plague*, 78;
cares for Riker, Kyle*, 89;
assumes position of Chief Medical
Officer aboard Enterprise-D*,
105;
leaves Enterprise-D*, 113;
falls down elevator shaft, 444

Q; extra-dimensional being, 2, 19, 156–57;
    has encounter with Guinan*, 25;
    first contact with, 95;
    wants to join Starfleet*, 110;
    is stripped of his powers, 117;
    enters into partnership with Vash*, 134
Q Continuum, 95;
    Q meets with another member of the, 117
quadrotriticale; grain tribbles* like to eat, 55
Quaice, Dr. Dalen; Crusher, Beverly* does residency with, 89;
    begins tour of duty on Starbase 133, 93;
    Crusher, Beverly*'s mentor, 126
quantum filament; *Enterprise*-D* collides with, 140
Quazulu; field trip to, 99
Quinn, Adm. Gregory; orders investigation of *Enterprise*-D*, 101
Quinteros, Cmdr.; supervises construction of *Galaxy*-class starships*, 92

Ral, Devinoni; born, 81;
    negotiates for wormhole purchase, 115–16
Ramart, Capt.; rescues Evans*, 43
Ramatis Star System; ruling family lacks gene for hearing; chorus of interpreters is developed, 9, 107
Rand, Janice; assigned to *Excelsior*￼ as Communications Officer, 76
Rashella; discusses cloaking shield on Aldea*, 7
Rasmussen, Berlinghoff; comes aboard the *Enterprise*-D*, 143;
    meets a time traveler from the 26th century, 150, 159
Raymond, Claire, 104;
    dies, 16;
    found cryogenically frozen on derelict ship, 103
Raymond, Donald; has wife frozen cryogenically, 16
Regula I space station; Marcus, Dr. Carol* begins work at, 72;
    Khan* takes control of, 73
Remmick, Lt. Cmdr. Dexter; conducts investigation of *Enterprise*-D*, 101
replicative fading; threatens Mariposa*, colony*, 111
replicator; transporter-based, 156
Resolution, The; ritualistic suicide custom adopted on Kaelon II*, 8;
    Timicin* refuses, then complies with, 134;
Rhomboid Dronegar sector, 110
Rice, Paul; Riker*'s fellow student, 90;
    accepts command of the *Drake*, 94
Richey, Colonel Stephen; *Royale*￼ created for, 109;
    commands the *Charybdis*, 20;
    patch on space suit, 19;
    dies on Theta VIII*, 21
Rigel Colonies; doomsday machine* headed for the, 53
Rigellian Fever; breaks out on *Enterprise*￼, 67
Riker, Kyle; Starfleet* civilian advisor, 109;
    Riker, William T.*'s father, 82;
    is widowed and left to raise Riker, William T.*, 83;

leaves son, 88;
    sole survivor of Tholian* attack, 89, 157
Riker, William T., 153;
    born, Valdez, Alaska, Earth*, 82, 153;
    mother of dies, 83;
    goes fishing with his father, 86;
    is left by father, 88;
    enters Starfleet Academy*, 90, 157;
    graduates from Starfleet Academy*, 91;
    stationed on Betazed*, 153;
    is romantically involved with Troi, Deanna*, 153;
    serves aboard the *Potemkin*, 153;
    serves as First Officer on the *Hood*￼, 94, 153;
    is offered command of the USS *Drake*, 94;
    assigned to *Enterprise*-D* as first officer, 95;
    assigned temporary duty aboard the *Pagh*, 108;
    offered command of the *Aries*, 109–110;
    commands the *Hathaway*, 112;
    offered captaincy of the *Melbourne*, 123;
    celebrates 32nd birthday, 128;
    as an extraterrestrial, 132–32;
    assigned temporary command of the *Excalibur*, 137–38;
    takes shore leave on Risa*, 141;
    has romantic encounter with Ro Laren*, 145
Riley, Lt. Kevin; gets Psi 2000 virus, 43;
    one of nine survivors of Tarsus IV*, 32
    murder attempt made on, 45
Riva; mediator, 107;
Riva's Chorus; trio of interpreters, 9;
Rixx, Capt.; Bolian*, 120;
    is present on Dytallix B*, 103;
    Satie* enlists the aid of, 103
Roddenberry, Gene; *Star Trek* creator and executive producer, 75;
    writes "Nightingale Woman", 17;
    discusses Nomad* and the Borg*, 17;
    discusses events in *Star Trek V*, 28;
    on *Enterprise*￼ history, 31;
    is fond of the name "Tiberius", 39–40;
    known as the "Great Bird of the Galaxy", 42;
    named Wesley, Commodore Bob* for his psuedonym used during *Have Gun, Will Travel*, 59;
    works as police officer, 59;
    comments on cloaking device*, 61;
    discusses sexism in Starfleet*, 68;
    discusses Klingons, 70;
    HMS *Victory* model graces office of, 106;
    shuttle is named for, 114;
    Bradbury, Ray is long-time friend of, 123;
    Horatio Hornblower was his inspiration for Kirk*, 138;
    on the fate of Kirk*, 151;
    discusses Spock*'s marriage, 152;
    discusses McCoy*'s marriage and divorce, 152;
    on the Vulcan reformation*, 156;
    on stardates, 162
Ro Laren, 154;

born, 84;
    witnesses her father's torture and murder, 87;
    graduates from Starfleet Academy*, 154;
    serves aboard the *Wellington*, 154;
    elects to remain on *Enterprise*-D*, 139;
    meets with Kennelly, Adm.*, 139;
    has romantic encounter with Riker*, 145;
Romaine, Lt. Mira; is injured in attack, 66;
    returns to rebuild Memory Alpha*, 66
Romulan
    ale, 72;
    convoy, Picard,*'s armada attempts to blockade a, 137;
    diplomatic representative is seized by Sybok*, 75;
    expedition attempts to capture Tin Man*, 121
    High Command, censures Jarok*, 113;
    invasion force, sent to Vulcan, 142
    Neutral Zone, treaty signed establishing, 23;
    peace treaty. *See* Treaty of Algernon;
    Senate; Pardek* becomes member of, 72;
    Vulcan reunification, Spock* and Pardek* pursue, 78;
    wars, 23, 24, 155, 157;
        end at Cheron, Battle of*, 2;
        between Earth and Romulans, 23, 24
Romulan Star Empire; formation of, 8, 156;
    and war with Earth, 23;
    settle Nimbus III* in joint venture with Klingons and Federation*, 57;
    alliance with Klingons collapses, 77;
    and the Tomed Incident, 80;
    first contact with since the Tomed Incident*, 104, 157;
    Federation* would go to war with, 113
Romulans; came from Vulcan, 8;
    home planets are Romulus* and Remus*, 23;
    test Federation* resolve, 43;
    fly Klingon Battle Cruisers, 60, 61;
    last Federation* contact with, 80;
    capture crewmembers of *Enterprise*-C*, 85;
    alliance with dissident Klingons, 156;
    attack Khitomer*, 86;
    attempt to conquer Vulcan, 142;
    steal the *T'pau*￼ in plot to rule Vulcan, 97;
    first Federation* contact with since 2311, 104;
    capture Yar, Tasha*, 118;
    Fontana comments on the, 51
Rossa, Connaught; grandmother of Rossa, Jeremiah*, 90, 126;
Rossa, Connor; father of Jeremiah*, 90;
    killed at Galen IV*, 92
Rossa, Jeremiah, is born, 90;
    discovered on the Talarian* craft, 126;
    rescued by Endar*, 92
Rossa, Moira; mother of Rossa, Jeremiah*, 90;
    killed at Galen IV*, 92
Roykirk, Jackson; designed *Nomad*, 18
Rozhenko, Alexander; son of Worf* and

*Items marked with an asterisk are also listed elsewhere as main entries. Individual **episodes** can be found alphabetically under "episodes." Look for **aliens**, **ships**, and **planets**, grouped alphabetically under those general headings.

Rozhenko, Alexander (CONTINUED)
K'Ehleyr*; Worf* first meets, 127;
learns about Kahless*, 67;
goes to Earth with Rozhenko, Sergey*
and Rozhenko, Helena*, 127;
goes aboard the Milan* with
Rozhenko, Helena*, 143;
comes to live aboard the Enterprise-
D*, 143
Rozhenko, Helena; Worf*'s foster mother,
154;
moves to Earth, 89;
visits Enterprise-D*, 126;
meets Worf* at Starbase 73 to take
Rozhenko, Alexander* home,
127;
comes aboard Enterprise-D* with
Rozhenko, Alexander* 143
Rozhenko, Sergey, Worf*'s foster father,
154;
rescues Worf* at Khitomer*, 87;
informed by Klingon High Command*
that Worf* has no living relatives,
87;
moves to Earth from Gault*, 89;
visits Enterprise-D*, 126;
meets Worf* at Starbase 73* to take
Rozhenko, Alexander* home,
127
Rubicun star system; home of the Edo, 97
Ruk; android built by the Old Ones, 3
Rura Penthe' dilithium mines; Kirk* and
McCoy* are sentenced to, 77
Russell, Dr. Toby; attempts to cure Worf*
with experimental procedure, 146
russhton infection; Aster, Jeremy*'s father
dies of , 93
Ruth; romantically involved with Kirk*, 34
R'uustai ceremony; Klingon ceremony of
bonding; Worf* and Aster, Jeremy*
participate in, 90, 115
ryetalyn; drug needed to cure Rigellian
fever*, 67

Saavik, Lt.; enters Starfleet Academy*, 72;
promoted to Lieutenant while at
Starfleet Academy*, 73;
takes Kobayashi Maru* test, 72, 73;
assigned to Grissom*; investigates
Genesis Planet*, 74
Sahndara star system, 7, 63;
Sakuro's Disease; Hedford* contracts, 52
salenite miners; Picard asked to mediate a
dispute among the, 128
Salia; head of state of Daled IV*, 108
Sandoval, Elias; leads expedition to
Omicron Ceti III*, 38, 39
San Francisco, Earth
Data* visits in 1893, 11;
Kirk*, et al. visit in 1986, 15;
United Federation of Planets* Council
is located in, 23–24
Sulu*'s birthplace, 30;
Yards Facility, Enterprise* launched
from, 31;
orbital drydock, Enterprise* under-
goes refitting at the, 69;
Data*'s head is found beneath, 149
Sarek; Vulcan ambassador, 25, 151, 152;
born, 24, 152;
marries a Vulcan princess*, 28, 153;
Sybok*'s father, 28;
marries Grayson, Amanda*, 28;
Spock*'s father, 28, 29;
marries Perrin*, 153;
disapproves of Spock*'s career

choice, 32, 38;
has heart attacks, 56;
works on Legaran treaty*, 69;
meets young Picard*, 153;
asks Spock* to serve as envoy to the
Klingons, 77;
discusses meeting of Spock* and
Pardek*, 78;
mind melds with Picard, 122;
suggests that Picard* meet Pardek*,
141;
suffers and dies of Bendii Syndrome*,
122, 142, 153;
achievements of, 152;
first time mentioned by name, 56;
appears in Trek features and in Star
Trek: The Next Generation, 56;
death discussed, 142
Sargon; discusses the destruction of his
planet, 3;
his people explore the galaxy, 2;
disappears, 58
Sarpeidon; planet which experiences an
ice age, 6, 68
Satie, Adm. Norah; investigates conspiracy
infiltrating Starfleet*, 103;
investigates possible sabotage of
Enterprise-D*'s dilithium
chamber, 134
Science Station Sierra Tango; Enterprise-
D* transports plasma plague*
specimen to, 105
Scott, Montgomery, 152;
born, 28, 152;
supervises refit of Enterprise-A*, 75;
buys a boat, 77;
disappears and reappears, 152
Scott, Tryla; present on Dytallix B*; Satie*
enlists aid of, 103
Second World War. See: World War II
Sector; 001; Earth located in; Borg*
heading for, 124;
3-0; communications lost with
outposts in, 103;
396; Enterprise-D* conducts mapping
mission in, 119;
21305; Enterprise-D* goes there for
survey assignment, 139;
21947; Talarian vessel* is found in,
126;
37628; Enterprise-D surveys, 146
sehlat; Spock*'s childhood pet, 29
Sela; claims to be offspring of Yar, Tasha*
and a Romulan general, 138;
born, 86, 118, 159;
Yar, Tasha* tries to escape with, 88,
159;
supervises La Forge*'s brainwashing,
135;
comes aboard Enterprise-D*, 138;
directs Romulan force to conquer
Vulcan, 142;
describes fate of Yar, Tasha*, 85;
is woman in shadows, 159;
Selar, Dr.; discovers Graves* to be ill, 107
Selcundi Drema sector; radio signals come
from, 109, 110
Selok, Romulan subcommander; formerly
Vulcan T'Pel*, 129
Setal; Jarok* masquerades as, 23
Setlik; Cardassians* attack, 154, 157
Seven, Anan; official of Eminiar VII*, 10, 49
Seven, Gary; describes mission to the
computer, 6;
meets Kirk*, 14;
alien interference from, 158

Seventh Guarantee, The; included in
Federation* Constitution, 24
Severin, Dr.; is killed, 66
Shanthi, Fleet Adm.; Picard,* meets with,
137
Shaw, Lt. Areel, 38, 151
prosecutes Kirk, James T.*, 46
Shelby, Lt. Cmdr.; is put in charge of Borg*
tactical analysis, 118;
assigned to Enterprise-D*, 124
shields; transporters don't work when in
place, 48
ships. See also: Enterprise-A; Enter-
prise-B; Enterprise-C; Enterprise-
D; Enterprise.
Borg ships
scout craft; crashes, 148;
spacecraft, Enterprise-D* first
encounters, 110;
vessel, believed to have
destroyed the Lalo*, 124;
vessel, heads for Earth, 125;
Earth ships
Artemis; colony ship, 71;
Challenger, NASA space
shuttle, has major
malfunction, 15;
Charybdis; flag on wreckage
discussed, 19;
launched by NASA, 20;
arrives at Theta VII*, 20;
commanded by Richey*, 21,
109;
Columbia; space shuttle,
makes its first orbital flight,
15;
Eagle; dedication on lunar
lander, 14;
Enterprise; space shuttle,
undergoes flight
testing, 15;
Pioneer 10; first probe to leave
solar system, 15;
V'ger, massive machine
organism, 70;
Victory, HMS; LaForge* builds a
model of the, 106;
Viking I; lands on Mars, 15;
Vostok I; first Earth manned
spacecraft, 13;
Voyager 6; is launched from
Earth, 17 ;
Klingon ships
Battle Cruiser; first use of, 60;
flown by Romulans, 60, 61;
one is destroyed, 63;
Bird of Prey; destroys Pioneer
10*, 15, 75;
new type developed, 76;
is piloted by Kirk, et al., 15
cruiser,109;
Pagh; Klingon vessel Riker*
serves aboard, 108;
starships; 3 destroyed by V'ger*,
70;
T'Ong; Klingon sleeper ship; 76,
111;
threatens Boradis Sector*,
82;
vessel; attacks and destroys
Grissom*, 74;
Kirk* gains control of, 74;
Vor'cha class Klingon cruisers,
127
Other
Antares; spaceship, 43;

ships (CONTINUED)

Aurora; space cruiser, 66;
Batris; Talarian* freighter, 101;
Erstwhile; Okona, Thadiun*'s ship, 106–7;
Fesarius; ship of the First Federation, 41;
Jovis; Fajo*'s ship, 122;
Krayton; Ferengi vessel pursued by *Enterprise*-D*, 122, 123;
Kreechta; Ferengi vessel, 112;
Lysian spacecraft; *Enterprise*-D* destroys a, 145;
Medusan spacecraft; *Enterprise** meets, 62;
Mondor, Pakled* ship, 110;
Nenebek; mining shuttle from Pentarus III, 128;
Pakled ship; Lore* picked up by a, 99;
Promellian ship; discovered, 115;
Sanction; T'Jon* assumes command of the, 92;
Satarran vessel; attacks *Enterprise*-D*, 145;
Trager, Cardassian* Galor-class* warship, 130;
Yonada; giant space ark built by the Fabrini*, 5, 63;
reaches promised planet, 69;
Zalkonian vessel, 123

Probes

Class one sensor probe, 118;
Iconian space probe; *Yamato** scanned by, 108;
Nomad; space probe, is constructed in early 2000s, 17;
is launched from Earth, 18;
discovered, 54;
Tan Ru; alien probe which merged with *Nomad**, 54;
Vega IX probe; returns from Beta Stromgren*, 120;

Romulan ships

battle cruisers, 61;
cloaking device, 43, 61, 149;
Haakona; Romulan warbird saved by *Enterprise*-D, 108;
scout craft, 116, 148;
spacecraft, 55, 100, 103–4;
capable of sub-light speeds only, 43;
vessel, wreckage of found, 115;
warbird, 115, 116, 138;
D'deridex class, 121

Starfleet and Federation ships

Ajax, U.S.S.; Kosinski* performs warp system upgrades on the, 96;
Ambassador class starships, 155;
Archon, U.S.S.; 24, 25, 49
Arcos; Federation* freight ship, 127;
Aries, U.S.S.; ship on which Riker* is offered command, 109;
Beagle, S.S.; crashes on 892-IV*, 37;
wreckage of found, 56;

Berlin, U.S.S.; near Neutral Zone, 100;
Botany Bay, S.S.; DY-100 class sleeper ship;
Khan* escapes in the, 16;
found by *Enterprise**; 49;
Bozeman, U.S.S.; disappears near Typhon Expanse*, 71–72;
emerges from a rift, 146–47;
discussion of registry number, 72;
modification of *Reliant**, 76;
Bradbury, U.S.S.; slated to take Crusher, Wesley* to Starfleet Academy*, 123;
Brattain, U.S.S.; caught in Tyken's Rift*, 131;
Charleston, U.S.S.; Raymond*, Clemons*, and Offenhouse* return to Earth on, 103;
Columbia, S.S.; crashes on Talos IV*, 29, 35, 36;
Constantinople, U.S.S.; *Enterprise*-D* receives distress call from, 107;
Constellation, U.S.S.; nearly destroyed by doomsday machine*, 53;
Constellation-class starships; *Hathaway** was one of the, 74;
Constitution-class starships; *Enterprise** is one, 31;
only 12 exist, 48–49;
Daedalus-class starships;
*Essex** was one of the, 25;
*Horizon** and *Archon** are possibly of the, 25;
withdrawn from service, 26;
Defiant, U.S.S.; disappears with no trace, 62;
Drake, U.S.S.; Rice* commands the, 90;
Riker* offered command of the, 94;
Enterprise-D* investigates disappearance of the, 101–2;
weapons on Minos* responsible for the destruction of the, 102;
DY-100; interplanetary space vehicle, 49;
El-Baz; shuttlepod; named after Farouk El-Baz, 109;
Endeavour; starship named for NASA space shuttle, 15;
Enterprise. See separate listings for each Starship *Enterprise*;
Essex, U.S.S.; 24;
destroyed over moon of Mab-bu VI*, 25;
Excalibur, U.S.S., destroyed by M-5* computer, 58;
Excelsior, U.S.S., Sulu* is captain of, 30, 76;
commissioned, 73;
refitted with standard warp drive, redesignated NCC-2000, 75–76;

fitted with improved sensors, 76;
damaged in Praxis* explosion, 77;
helps to save peace conference, 77;
Excelsior-class vessels, 155;
Exeter, U.S.S.; discovered in derelict condition, 59;
Farragut, U.S.S.; Kirk* serves on as lieutenant, 33, 34, 35;
Kirk* meets vampire cloud* while serving on, 36, 57;
Fearless, U.S.S.; Kosinski* performs warp upgrades on, 96;
Galaxy class starship development project; is begun by Starfleet*, 85;
Galileo; shuttlecraft, 45–46;
crashes on Taurus II*, 46;
crashes on planetoid, 52;
Gettysburg, U.S.S.; Jameson, Mark* commands, 72, 80–81;
Goddard, U.S.S.; *Enterprise*-D* to rendezvous with, 116;
Grissom, U.S.S.; attacked by Klingon vessel, investigates Genesis Planet*, 74;
Hathaway, U.S.S.; launched, 74;
commanded by Riker*, 112;
Hood, U.S.S.; Adm. McCoy travels on the, 94;
Riker* assigned to before serving on *Enterprise*-D*, 91, 95;
Horatio, U.S.S.; Keel* captain of; destroyed, 103, 153;
Horizon, U.S.S., 24, 25, 57, 156;
visits Sigma Iotia II*; leaves book, accidentally contaminating culture, 16, 58;
Intrepid, U.S.S.; has all-Vulcan crew, 58;
destroyed, 57-58;
Intrepid, U.S.S.; one of the first ships to render aid at Khitomer*, 86;
Enterprise-D* compares data logs from, 119;
Kobayashi Maru; simulation; Kirk* is the only cadet to ever beat the, 35;
Saavik* attempts, 72, 73;
Lalo, U.S.S.; freighter; reports temporal distortion, 102;
sights Borg*; is lost, 124;
Lantree, U.S.S.; 106;
crewmembers of die of premature old age, 107;
LaSalle, U.S.S.; reports radiation anomalies, 127;
Lexington, U.S.S.; Wesley, Bob* is aboard, 59;
Mariposa, S.S.; launched for Ficus Sector, 22;
crashes on Mariposa*, 22–23;
Melbourne, U.S.S.; Riker*

*Items marked with an asterisk are also listed elsewhere as main entries. Individual **episodes** can be found alphabetically under "episodes." Look for **aliens**, **ships**, and **planets**, grouped alphabetically under those general headings.

ships (CONTINUED)

offered captaincy of, 123;

Merrimac, U.S.S.; Sarek* *et al.* return to Vulcan aboard the, 122;

meets the *Enterprise*-D*, 141;

Milan S.S.; Rozhenko, Helena* books passage on the transport ship, 143;

Miranda class starships; *Reliant** is of the, 72; *Brattain** is of the, 131;

Nebula class starships, first appearance of, 130;

Odin, S.S.; ship, 92, 99, 100;

Onizuka, shuttle; is named for Ellison Onizuka, 114;

Phoenix, U.S.S.; 154 destroys a Cardassian* station, 129–30; returns to Starbase 211, 130;

Pike; shuttle, named for Pike, Christopher*, 122;

Potemkin, U.S.S., 68; makes last Federation* contact with Turkana IV*, 93; one of Riker*'s first assignments, 91;

Reliant, U.S.S., 50; Chekov* serves on the, 31, 71; investigates Ceti Alpha V*, 54; commandeered by Khan*, 73; searches for planet for Genesis Project*, 73; Kyle* assigned to the, 73; destroyed, 73; modifications made to model by Jein, 72, 76;

Renegade, U.S.S.; Scott, Tryla* is captain of the, 103;

Republic, U.S.S.; 46; Kirk* serves on while at Starfleet Academy*, 33; Kirk*'s service after, 34;

Repulse, U.S.S.; Pulaski* arrives on the, 105;

Rutledge, U.S.S.; O'Brien, Miles Edward* serves on, 154, 157;

Saratoga, U.S.S.; first female capatain commanded the, 68;

Shiku Maru, ship; makes contact with Tamarians*, 65;

shuttlecraft; lack of discussed, 42;

Shuttlecraft 13; crashes on Vagra II*, 102;

Shuttlepod 5; discovered adrift in space, 109;

Shuttle 6; lost in encounter with the Borg*, 110;

Sleeper ships, 16; become obsolete, 18;

Soyuz class starships; *Bozeman** is one of the, 72; are retired, 76;

Stargazer, U.S.S., 157; Picard,* assumes command

of the, 82;

Crusher, Jack* dies on the, 90;

is nearly destroyed at Maxia Zeta Star System*, 90–91;

hulk of the is presented to Picard*, 98;

Sutherland, U.S.S.; part of the armada, 137, 138; Data* placed in temporary command of the, 138;

Thomas Paine, U.S.S.; Rixx* is captain of the, 103;

Tian An Men, U.S.S.; ship of the armada, 138;

T'pau; ship decommissioned; sent to Qualor II*, 97; debris of, 142; part of Romulan invasion force, 142;

Trieste, U.S.S.; 153;

Tripoli, U.S.S.; discovers Data*, 83–84, 153;

Tsiolkovsky; U.S.S., 96; begins last science mission, 93;

Valiant, S.S.; 20, 39

Valiant, U.S.S.; 27, 49–50

Vico, S.S.; science ship, 144

Victory, U.S.S.; one of La Forge*'s early assignments, 91, 93; Leijten* and Hickman* served on the, 133;

Wellingon, U.S.S.; Ro Laren* serves on the, 84, 139;

Yamato, U.S.S.; illusion of the, 106; destroyed, 108;

Yorktown, U.S.S., 57;

Zapata, U.S.S., 123;

Zhukov, U.S.S.; 121, 128, 129, 141

ShirKahr; Spock*'s home city, 29

Shumar, Capt. Bryce; commander of the *Essex**, 25

Sigma Draconis system, 61

Silarian Sector; location of Kataan*, 9

Silvestri, Capt.; captain of the *Shiku Maru**, 65

Singh, Khan Noonien. *See* Khan Noonien Singh

Sipe, Ryan; dies, 103

Skon; Sarek*'s ancestor, 24, 25

slingshot effect; method of time travel, 159

Sol; begins to form, 2

Sol sector; location of Earth, 70. *See also* Sector 001

Solkar; Sarek*'s ancestor, 24, 25

Songi; Gamelan V* chairman, 128

Soong, Dr. Noonien; Graves* is a teacher of, 107; puts colonists' memories into Data*, 83; escapes from Omicron Theta*, 83; Data* summoned by, 126; underground laboratory of, 99; attempts to install chip into Data* to allow him to feel emotions, 126; dying, 126;

Soren; J'naii* pilot; Riker*'s love interest, 146

Spacedock; *Enterprise** returns to, 74

Spock, 61, 151; ancestors adopt a ceremonial ground,

7;

has half brother, Sybok*, 75;

born, 29;

first name of, 151;

disappears into the Llangon Mountains* on Vulcan, 29;

is telepathically bonded to T'pring*, 29, 30;

goes into Sarpeidon*'s past, 6, 68;

goes into Earth's past to find McCoy, Leonard H.*, 12;

discusses hostilities between Klingons and the Federation*, 28;

studies with Gill*, 32;

graduates from Starfleet Academy*, 35, 151;

enters Starfleet*, 32, 61, 155;

serves aboard *Enterprise** with Pike, Christopher*, 31, 34;

visits parents on Vulcan, 38;

is promoted to Commander, 46;

is court-martialed for kidnapping Pike, Christopher*, 46–47;

experiences *Pon farr**, 53;

donates blood to Sarek*, 56;

has brain removed, 61–62;

commendations of, 151;

retires from Starfleet*; returns to Vulcan to start *Kohlinar** training, 69;

returns to Starfleet*, 70;

promoted to Captain; assigned to Starfleet Academy*; accepts command of the *Enterprise**, 71;

dies of radiation exposure, 73;

inconsistencies with stardate of his death, 74;

Kirk* attempts to recover body of, 74;

Katra* of is reunited with regenerated body; undergoes retraining on Vulcan, 74;

friends of face charges for rescue of, 75;

marries, 152;

agrees to serve as special envoy to the Klingons, 77;

meets Pardek*, 78;

mysteriously disappears from Vulcan, 140;

is sighted on Romulus*, 141, 152;

informs Picard,* of his purpose for being on Romulus*, 142;

survives Sarek*, 142

Spock, mirror, moves his society in more humane direction, 55;

spores, alien; offer protection from Berthold rays, 50;

Spot, Data*'s pet cat, 129

Sputnik I; is launched from Earth, 13; *Enterprise*-D*'s dedication plaque bears stardate to coincide with launch of, 129

Starbases
057; receives distress call from the *Lalo**, 124;

2; *Enterprise** goes to after "Turnabout Intruder"*, 68;

4; shuttlecraft is stolen from, 61; survivors of the Starnes expedition* are taken to, 64, 65;

6; *Enterprise** is on course to for R&R, 57;

9; *Enterprise** is on course to, 48;

10; *Enterprise** takes Stocker* to, 55;

11; Kirk* stands trial at, 38, 46;

*Enterprise** returns to, 46;
12; Narsu* is from, 25;
evacuated, 103;
*Enterprise** undergoes maintenance at, 120;
24; Kahlest* is treated at, 87;
67; *Enterprise*-D* visits for major systems repair, 140;
73; *Enterprise*-D* has layover at, 109;
Picard,* meets with Moore at, 111;
Worf* gives Rozhenko, Alexander* to his foster parents at, 127;
74; *Enterprise*-D* has scheduled layover at, 100;
83; *Enterprise*-D* goes to after "Q Who?"*, 110;
121; *Enterprise*-D* has systems and biodecontamination at, 121;
133; Quaice has tour of duty at, 93 *Enterprise*-D* heads for, 114 *Enterprise*-D* is at for crew rotation, 126;
152; *Enterprise*-D* visits for damage repair, 121;
173; Gomez* comes aboard *Enterprise*-D* at, 108;
179; Mendon* comes aboard *Enterprise*-D* at, 108;
211; *Phoenix** returns to, 130;
214; Rasmussen* turned over to authorities at, 143;
218; *Enterprise*-D* is en route to, 149;
220; *Enterprise*-D* heads to after "Night Terrors"*, 132;
234; *Enterprise*-D* meets Shanthi* at, 137;
Enterprise-D* is recalled to, 141;
260; *Enterprise*-D* heads to after "In Theory"*, 136;
301; *Enterprise*-D* heads to after "Conundrum"*, 145;
313; *Enterprise*-D* picks up equipment from, 132;
324; Hanson* is located at, 124;
336; receives automated transmission from the *T'Ong**, 111;
343; *Enterprise*-D* picks up medical supplies at, 116;
416; Potts* is evacuated to, 126;
440; Ullian* delegation disembarks at, 144;
514; loses contact with the *Vico**, 144;
515; Picard,* and Crusher, Wesley* take personal leaves at, 110;
718; Picard,* attends emergency conference at, 103;
G-6; Troi, Deanna* departs at to visit Betazed*, 98;
Montgomery; *Enterprise*-D* has engineering consultation at, 109
Star Cluster NGC 321; location of Eminiar VII* and Vendikar*, 27, 49
stardates; discussed, 129, 162;
fans' methods of determining, 162
Starfleet; established, 23, 24;
Charter of, 23;
before institution of Prime Directive*, 25;
withdraws *Daedalus* -class* starships, 26;
Sulu* has distinguished career in, 30;

Spock* enters, 32;
why they lack a cloaking device, 61;
first female Captain to appear from, 68;
retires *Soyuz*-class** starships, 76;
starts work on *Galaxy*-class* starships, 85;
resists involvement in Klingon civil war, 137;
term first used, 24;
discussion of sexism in, 68;
abolishes different symbols for each ship, 71;
Starfleet Academy; Kirk* enrolls in, 32;
Kirk* meets Finney, Benjamin* at, 33;
Kirk* serves as Ensign while at, 33;
Spock* graduates from, 35;
Kirk* and Merrick* meet at, 56;
Kirk* assigned to, 71;
Saavik* enters, 72;
*Enterprise** is assigned to, 72;
Saavik* takes *Kobayashi Maru** test at, 73;
Uhura* agrees to chair seminar at, 77;
wins parrises squares* tournament, 81;
rejects Picard*'s first application, 81;
Picard* graduates from, 81;
Data* enters, 84;
Data* graduates from, 86;
Crusher, Beverly* graduates from, 88;
Riker* graduates from, 91;
Locarno* accepted into, 94;
Crusher, Wesley* takes entrance exams for, 101;
Crusher, Wesley* enters, 128;
Crusher, Wesley* on leave from, 141;
established as 4-year institution, 56;
Starfleet armada; annihilated by Borg* vessel, 125
Starfleet Command
alternate terms for, 24;
Uhura* serves at, 30;
ends transwarp development, 75;
Satie* investigates conspiracy infiltrating, 103;
begins panning for Borg* attack, 111;
is concerned about Spock*'s defection, 141;
term first used, 46, 49;
orders change in Starfleet* emblem, 71, 87;
Starfleet General Order Number One. See Prime Directive, The
Starfleet Inspector General's Office; Remmick* is assigned to, 101
Starfleet Medical; Crusher, Beverly* accepts position at, 105;
Crusher, Beverly* returns from a year at, 113
Starfleet Tactical; Shelby* is from, 118
Starnes expedition, survivors are taken to Starbase 4*, 61
starships; Individual ships listed under "ships." See also *Enterprise*.
Star Station India; 107, 108
Star system J-25; Q* transports *Enterprise*-D* to, 110
Star Trek features; 151, 162;
Star Trek: The Academy Years, 152;
Star Trek: The Motion Picture, 17, 42, 69, 70, 71, 73;
Star Trek II: The Wrath of Khan, 16,

31, 35, 37, 49–50, 54, 71, 72, 73–74, 76, 151;
Star Trek III: The Search for Spock, 24, 25, 28, 30, 31, 65, 73–74, 152;
Star Trek IV: The Voyage Home, 16, 24, 29, 30, 68, 73–74, 75, 76, 155, 158;
Star Trek V: The Final Frontier, 15, 28, 57, 75–76, 152, 153, 162;
Star Trek VI: The Undiscovered Country, 24, 28, 30, 50, 73, 76, 77–78, 84, 85, 155, 156;
Sarek* and Grayson, Amanda* appear in, 56;
Klingon Battle Cruisers used during, 61
Star Trek television series;
Star Trek, original series, "Turnabout Intruder"* was last episode of, 68, 73;
Star Trek: Deep Space Nine, 151 Cardassians* to appear in, 130;
Star Trek II proposed television series, never produced, 71;
"The Child"* originally written for, 106;
"Devil's Due"* originally written for, 130–31;
Star Trek: The Next Generation, 56, 151, 152;
Barrett, Majel*'s roles in, 44;
Sarek* makes two appearances in, 56;
references to Tholians* in, 62;
discussion of Bird of Prey in, 77;
Cardassians* as recurring villains in, 130;
Klingon Battle Cruiser used in, 61;
stardates in, 162
Station Nigala IV, 117
Station Salem One; attacked, 157
Stiles family; members are killed in Earth/Romulan Wars, 23
Stocker, Commodore; orders *Enterprise** into the Neutral Zone, 55
Stone, Commodore; presides over Kirk*'s court-martial, 46
Stonn; marries T'pring*, 53
Stratos; cloud city on Ardana*, 9, 66, 151
Strnad Star System, 97–98
Stubbs, Dr. Paul; does research on Kavis Alpha neutron star*, 26;
begins work on decay of neutronium, 87;
does research on *Enterprise*-D*, 113
subspace radio; invention of, 156
Sulu, Hikaru, 152;
born in San Francisco, 30, 152;
serves as physicist on *Enterprise**, 30;
tranferred to helm officer, 40;
promoted to captain; takes command of *Excelsior**, 76;
helps save Khitomer* peace conference, 77;
says the "May the Great Bird..."* blessing, 42;
first name established, 78;
Sunad, Capt.; of Zalkonian* vessel, 123
Supra, Patterson; wins *Enterprise*-D* science fair, 140

*Items marked with an asterisk are also listed elsewhere as main entries. Individual **episodes** can be found alphabetically under "episodes." Look for **aliens**, **ships**, and **planets**, grouped alphabetically under those general headings.

Surak; leads Vulcans on the path to logic, 7–8;
    being calling itself is found on Excalbia*, 67
Surplus depot Zed-15; at Qualor II*, the T'pau* is sent to , 97
Sutter, Clara; is befriended by an alien, 148
Sybok; Spock*'s elder half brother;
    mother is a Vulcan princess*; father is Sarek*, 28, 153;
    born, 28, 153;
    seizes diplomats, 75;
    killed by entity on Sha-Ka-Ree*, 75
symbiotic parasite; Odan* is really a, 135
System C-111; location of Landru*'s planet, 5, 25;
    J-25; conditions on Jouret IV* are identical to those found at, 124;
    L-370; seven planets are in, 44 found destroyed, 53;
    L-374; widespread destruction found in and near, 4, 53;

Taar, DaiMon; Ferengi* leader; agrees to return T-9 Energy Converter*, 97
Talarian
    forces, attack Galen IV*, 92, 90;
    freighter, the Batris* is a, 101;
    observation craft, 126
Talosian war; nearly wipes out civilization on Talos IV*, 3
Talos Star Group, Enterprise* visits, 35, 46
Tarbolde; poet of Canopius*, writes "Nightingale Woman", 17
Tarellian
    ship, on course for Haven*, 96;
    spacecraft, is destroyed by the Alcyones*, 91;
    war, 157
Tarses, Simon, 118;
    implicated in espionage, 134;
    grandfather is a Romulan, 134
Taylor, Dr. Gillian; cetacean biologist of 20th century;
    discusses Kirk*'s birthplace , 29;
    disappears, 158;
    travels to 23rd century, 15;
    is assigned to science vessel, 75
Telaka, Iso; Capt. of the Lantree*, 107
telepathic rape, committed by Jev*, 143
television; stops as a form of entertainment!, 20
Tellun System; location of Troyius, 60
temporal causality loop; catches the Bozeman*, 72;
    and the Enterprise-D* 146, 147
temporal distortion,102, 109
temporal rift, one is discovered, 118, 159;
    opened by Enterprise-C* firing a photon torpedo volley, 158;
    as method of time travel, 159
Ten Forward lounge; Guinan* recruited to serve as hostess for the, 105, 154
Terkim, Guinan*'s uncle, 154
Terrell, Capt. Clark; Chekov* serves under, 31;
    killed, 73
Thalassa; Sargon's beloved; departs into oblivion, 58
Thelusian Flu; First Officer of the Lantree* is treated for, 107
Theoretical Propulsion Group; Brahms, Leah* is design engineer for the, 132
thermonuclear weapon, Enterprise* is attacked with a, 58
Theta 116 System; Charybdis* arrives in

the, 20;
Klingon cruiser reports wreckage in the, 109;
Richey* dies on the eighth planet of the, 21
Tholian
    Assembly, 62–63, 157;
    Loskene* is from, 62;
    attack, Riker, Kyle* is sole survivor of, 89;
    border, Defiant* disappears near, 62;
    wars, 157
Tholl, Kova; is abducted, 119, 120
Thralls; slaves on Triskelion, 57
Tiberius; Kirk, James T.*'s middle name, 40, 78
time line chart, 160-61
time loop; 109
time portal; found by Enterprise*, 51
Timicin; scientist
    born on Kaelon II*, 79;
    inventor of the helium fusion ignition process*, 134;
    discusses the Resolution*, 8
Timothy; only survivor of the Vico*, 144
T'Jon; assumes command of the Sanction*, 92
Tkon Empire; empire becomes extinct because it had too many ages, 2
    is discovered, 97
T'Lar; Vulcan high priestess, 74
T-9 Energy Converter; stolen by Ferengi*, 97
Tog, DaiMon; Ferengi*; attends banquet on Enterprise-D*, 122
Tomalak; Romulan Warbird commander, 115
Tomed Incident, The; last Federation* contact with Romulans prior to 2364, 80, 104, 157
Tomlinson, Robert; killed, 43
Tomlinson wedding; O'Brien wedding an homage to the, 129
Toral; son of Duras*, 136;
    is convicted of treason by the Klingon High Council*, 138
Tox Uthat; invented, 150;
    Estragon* is searching for the, 9;
    Vash* and Picard,* search for, 120;
    Vorgons* travel in time to find, 150, 159
T'Pau; Vulcan dignitary, 7
T'Pel; Vulcan ambassador; Romulan spy, 129
T'Pring, 53;
    born, 29;
    telepathically bonded to Spock*, 30;
    marries Stonn, 53
Tracey, Capt. Ronald; found on Omega IV*, 59
Tractor beam; attempted use of to fix orbit of the Bre'el moon*, 117;
    used to move a stellar core fragment*, 144;
Trade Agreements Conference; on Betazed*, 122
Tralesta Clan; and feud with Lornack Clan*, 21;
    massacred by Lornack Clan*, 21, 75;
    Mull, Penthor* is accused of raiding, 80;
    Yuta* is a member of the, 116
transporter; 48, 54–55, 149, 156
Transwarp Development Project; Excelsior* used for, 73;
    deemed unsuccessful, 75–76

transwarp drive, 76
Traveler, the; responsible for warp efficiency gains, 96–97;
    helps Crusher, Wesley* rescue Crusher, Beverly*, 127
Travers, Commodore; at Cestus III, 47
Treaty of Algernon; Earth/Romulan peace treaty, 23
Treaty of Armens; cedes Tau Cygna V* to the Sheliak Corporate*, 36, 71, 114
Trelane; entity found on Gothos*, 47
tribbles; killed by poisoned quadrotriticale*, 55–56
tricyanate contamination; threatens water supply on Beta Agni II*, 121, 122
Troi, Deanna; Betazoid*/human counselor on Enterprise-D*, 153;
    born, 83, 153;
    at University of Betazed*, 121, 153;
    taken over by alien entity, 11, 145–46;
    must fulfill childhood wedding vow, 96, 153–54;
    visits Betazed*, 98, 122;
    impregnated by alien life form, 105–6;
    suffers temporary loss of telepathic powers, 128;
    commands Enterprise-D*, 140
Troi, Ian Andrew; Troi, Deanna*'s father, 83, 153, 154;
    dies, 154
Troi, Lwaxana; Troi, Deanna*'s mother, 83, 153;
    and Troi, Deanna*'s wedding, 96;
    and Timicin*'s Resolution*, 134;
    to wed Campio*, 147;
    played by Barrett, Majel*, 44;
Trose, Kalin; quells an assassination plot, 83
T-Tauri type star; discovered, 131
two-dimensional life forms; cause warp drive malfunction, 128
Tyken's Rift; Brattain* is caught in a, 131;
    Enterprise-D* is trapped in a, 132
Tyler, José; discusses warp drive, 35
Typhon Expanse; Bozeman* is caught in the, 72, 146
Tyree; Kirk* meets, 36

Uhura, 42, 152;
    born, 30, 152;
    chairs seminar at Starfleet Academy*, 77
UESPA (United Earth Space Probe Agency), early name for Starfleet*, 24, 49
United Federation of Planets
    incorporated, 23, 157;
    Council of, 23–24;
    President of, 24;
    Constitution of, 24;
    territorial dispute with Klingons, 21;
    relations with Klingons degenerate, 28;
    Spock* negotiates peace between Klingons and, 29;
    fights battle of Donatu V* with Klingons, 30;
    last contact with the Sheliak Corporate* prior to 2366, 36;
    first contact with the Gorn*, 47;
    first contact with the Metrons*, 47;
    dispute between Klingons and the, 50;
    settles Nimbus III* in joint venture with Romulans and Klingons, 57;
    the Melkot* agree to diplomatic relations with, 60;

and the Tholians*, 62–63;
first encounter with the Tamarians*, 65–66;
Genesis Project* presented to the, 72;
diplomatic representative of is seized by Sybok*, 75;
peace between Klingons and the, 76;
and the Tomed incident, 80;
outposts at Delta Zero Five and Tarod IX are destroyed, 103;
first contact with the Romulans since 2311, 104;
has peace treaty with Cardassia*, 117, 129–30;
embroiled in war with Klingons in alternate time line, 118, 159;
first use of term, 24;
United Nations, the; is chartered, 13
United Nations, New; rules, 19
United States Air Force; Enterprise* avoids detection by the, 158
University of Betazed; Troi, Deanna* is at the, 121, 153
Utopia Planitia Fleet Yards; Enterprise-D* constructed at, 92;
Enterprise-D* launched from, 94;
Brahms, Leah* serves on Enterprise-D* design team at, 132
Uxbridge, Kevin; a Douwd* takes the form of, 80;
arrives at Delta Rana IV*, 92;
destroys all the Husnok*, 92–93;
survivors found on Delta Rana IV*, 114
Uxbridge, Rishon; meets Uxbridge, Kevin*, 80;
arrives at Delta Rana IV*, 92;
survivors found on Delta Rana IV*, 114
Ux-Mal Star System, 11, 146

Vaal; machine god, 5, 54
Vagh, Governor; Klingon; head of Kriosian Colonies*, 135
Valdez, Alaska, Earth; birthplace of Riker, William T.*, 82;
Riker, William T.* and Riker, Kyle* go fishing near, 86
Valo star system; Enterprise-D* goes to, 139
vampire cloud, 36, 57
Vana; miner from Ardana*, 9
Vanderberg; head of mining on Janus VI*, 48, 50
Van Gelder, Dr. Simon; assigned to Tantalus V* penal colony, 40, 44
Varley, Capt. Donald; interprets archeological evidence from Denius III*, 4;
captain of the Yamato*, 108
Varria; associate of Fajo*, 89, 122
Vash; archaeologist, 93, 120, 134
Vega Colony; 35
Vina; last survivor of Columbia*, 29;
discusses Talosians* with Pike, 3
viral parasite; life on Tarchannan III* reproduces by means of a, 133
virus, alien, 43
VISOR; La Forge*'s, 84
vrietalyn. See ryetalyn
Vulcan, 42, 53, 155;
suffers terrible wars, 7;
pre-history related to exploration by Sargon's people, 2;

schism with the Romulans, 8, 156;
moons of, 42;
reformation, 156;
Spock* undergoes retraining on, 69, 74;
ship T'pau* is stolen as part of plot to rule, 97;
Spock* disappears from, 140;
reunification with Romulans; Spock* attempts to negotiate, 29, 142, 152
Vulcan nerve pinch; first use of, 42
Vulcan princess; is Sybok*'s mother, 28, 153
Vulcans; entire crew of Intrepid* are, 58;
Riker*'s supervisor at Starfleet Academy* is one of the, 90;
dissidents depart planet, 8;
interstellar flight capabilities, 8;
mind melding ability of, 44
Vulcan Science Academy, 32

Wallace, Janet; Kirk* has romantic liaison with, 38
Wallace, Theodore, 38, 151
warp drive, 36, 96–97, 140
warp factors; discussed, 47–48
warp field; low level, used in attempt to fix the orbit of the Bre'el IV* moon, 117
Wesley, Commodore Bob; task force commander, 59;
named for Roddenberry, Gene*'s pseudonym, 59
Winter, Capt. James, early draft Captain, 31
Worf, 154;
born on Qo'noS*, 84, 154;
brother Kurn* is born, 86, 154;
goes to Khitomer* with his parents, 86;
is rescued by Rozhenko, Sergey*, 87;
moves to Earth, 89;
reaches Age of Ascension*, 91;
beats up some teenage boys, 87;
bonds with Aster, Jeremy* in R'uustai ceremony*, 115;
enters Starfleet Academy*, 91;
has unresolved relationship with K'Ehleyr*, 92;
assigned as Security Chief, 102, 105;
poses as Captain of the Enterprise-D*, 111;
resumes relationship with K'Ehleyr*; conceives a child, 111;
promoted to full Lieutenant, 113;
discovers he has a brother, 119;
visited by foster parents, 126;
kills Duras*, 127;
resigns Starfleet* commission; joins Klingon defense forces, 136;
honor is restored to family of by Gowron*, 136;
is reinstated into Starfleet*, 138;
assists with O'Brien, Molly*'s birth, 140;
takes custody of son Rozhenko, Alexander*, 143;
is seriously injured, 146;
discusses Kahless* with Rozhenko, Alexander*, 67;
step-brother of enters Starfleet Academy*, 91, 154;
World War II, 156;

Keeler, Edith*'s work delays American entry into, 158;
Hitler* wins in alternate timeline, 12
World War III, 21, 156, 157
wormhole;
Barzan* accepts bids for control of, 115;
Enterprise-D* passes through an unstable, 131

Xanthras system, 123
Xendi Sabu star system, 98
Xendi Starbase 9; hulk of Stargazer* is towed to, 98
xeno-polycythemia; McCoy* is diagnosed with, 63
Xon; Vulcan science officer slated to appear in Star Trek II*, unproduced television series, 71

Yale, Mirasta; Malcorian science minister, 132
Yanar, and Benzan*; 101, 107
Yar, Ishara; Yar, Tasha*'s younger sister, 83, 89;
born, 84;
visits Enterprise-D, 127
Yar, Tasha (Natasha); 154, 159;
born, 83, 93, 154;
Yar, Ishara*'s older sister, 84;
orphaned, 84;
escapes from Turkana IV*, 89;
meets Picard* on Carnel*, 94;
captured by Romulans, 85;
agrees to become consort of Romulan official, 85;
gives birth to Sela*, 159;
mother of Sela*, 86, 136, 138;
killed trying to escape Romulans, 88, 159;
killed by Armus*, 102
replaced as security chief by Worf*, 105;
does not die in alternate timeline, 118, 159;
shown alive in "Symbiosis"* but is killed in "Skin of Evil"*, 102
Yuta; survives Lornack Clan* massacre;
genes altered to slow aging, 75;
kills Mull, Penthor*, 80;
attempts to murder Chorgan*, 116

Zalkonians; "Doe, John"* is one of the, 123
Zarabeth; exiled to Sarpeidon*'s past, 6
Zed Lapis sector; Troi* attends conference in the, 102
Zee-Magnees Prize; is won by Daystrom*, 28, 31
zenite, cure for botanical plague on Merak II*; 66
Zeta Gelis Cluster; 123
Zimbata, Capt.; La Forge*'s commander on the Victory*, 93;
La Forge* builds model of the sailing ship Victory* for, 106

*Items marked with an asterisk are also listed elsewhere as main entries. Individual **episodes** can be found alphabetically under "episodes." Look for **aliens**, **ships**, and **planets**, grouped alphabetically under those general headings.

ABOUT THE AUTHORS

Denise Okuda has her degree in nursing, but her true love is the film industry. Her credits include *Star Trek VI: The Undiscovered Country* and promotional work for 20th-Century Fox's *The Adventures of Buckaroo Banzai: Across the Eighth Dimension*. Taking advantage of her background in nursing, Denise has occasionally served as a medical consultant to the writing staff of *Star Trek: The Next Generation*. Her hobbies include tropical fish, frequent trips to Yosemite National Park, and she is politically active in supporting environmental causes.

Denise is currently working on the production staff of *Star Trek: Deep Space Nine*. Denise lives in Los Angeles, California, with her husband, Michael, and their dog, Molly.

Michael Okuda is the scenic art supervisor for both *Star Trek: The Next Generation* and the new *Star Trek: Deep Space Nine*. He is responsible for those shows' control panels, signage, alien written languages, computer readout animation, and other strange things. Michael's work on *Star Trek* has been recognized with three Emmy nominations for Best Visual Effects. His other credits include *Star Trek VI: The Undiscovered Country, Star Trek V: The Final Frontier, Star Trek IV: The Voyage Home, The Flash, Flight of the Intruder*, and *The Human Target*.

Along with Rick Sternbach, Michael serves as a technical consultant to the writing staff of *Star Trek* and is coauthor of the *Star Trek: The Next Generation Technical Manual*.

Photo: Robbie Robinson